The Spirit of Phantom Ridge

The Spirit of Phantom Ridge
Copyright © 2025 by Jeff B. Spires

Additional copies may be ordered from the publisher for educational,
business, promotional or premium use.
For information, contact ALIVE Book Publishing at:
alivebookpublishing.com

Book design by Alex P. Johnson

ISBN 13
978-1-63132-252-5
Library of Congress Control Number: 2025902361

Library of Congress Cataloging-in-Publication Data
is available upon request.

First Edition

Published in the United States of America by ALIVE Book Publishing
an imprint of Advanced Publishing LLC
3200 A Danville Blvd., Suite 204, Alamo, California 94507
alivebookpublishing.com

PRINTED IN THE UNITED STATES OF AMERICA

10 9 8 7 6 5 4 3 2 1

The Spirit of Phantom Ridge

Jeff B. Spires

ABOOKS

Alive Book Publishing

Acknowledgments

To my wife Tricia, whose encouragement, suggestions, and hours of review made this book possible. I am truly blessed to have you in my life.

Also, with appreciation to Mary Webb, teacher and founder of the Rossmoor Writers' Group, which continues her benevolent support of the fragile creative process.

May she rest in peace.

PART I

THE BEAST

1899–1986

Chapter 1

Captive

Signposts marking train stops crawl past slower than a funeral procession: Carondelet, Barracks, White House. Each sign is inscribed in faded, black letters on a white, weathered board atop a wooden post. Though Peter cannot read, they remind him of grave markers.

He stares through the train's passenger window at the rolling countryside. Grasslands and distant forests in retreat from man's lust pass in slow progression as the St. Louis Iron Mountain & Southern Railway steams southward through Missouri. Two Black children run alongside, laughing as they wave their arms at the passing travelers. They remind Peter of his childhood, playing near these same tracks beside his younger brother, Frank. One time, they placed a penny on the rail in the path of an ore train. It flattened the coin like a blacksmith's hammer into a paper-thin wafer.

Twenty years have passed. Frank still carries that coin, a good luck charm, on a necklace. Peter wishes *he* had a charm like his brother's because he could use some good luck. Incidents like that were Peter's only encounters with trains. He never rode one until yesterday. He would like to wave back at the kids, but he cannot raise his shackled hands.

On a seat lounges a copy of yesterday's newspaper, the Friday, July 21, 1899 edition of the *St. Louis Post-Dispatch*. A front-page story tells about a Black man being escorted from Kansas City, Kansas, to the Washington County Jail in Potosi by a ten-man posse. Sent by County Sheriff James Whitehead under the leadership of Deputy Louis Monroe, the armed body will arrive in Potosi tomorrow. The prisoner will be removed, and then incarcerated while awaiting trial for the murder of a white man, James Thornton.

Worry consumes Peter, the same worry gnawing at his gut since Kansas City. Why they takin me back home? They knowed I ain't gittin no fair trial. No colored around here never did for hurtin the white folks. It don't matter none that he came at me swingin a knife. That's why I took to runnin to Frank's place all the way up to Kansas. But then they wouldn't let me stay there for no trial like that lawyer fella asked. He say they done hate us coloreds too much back home to git me a fair trial. I sure wish my friends could help me now like they done when I was hidin. But they cain't help me none with this. Bad thing is bout runnin though, I was worryin bout my Momma, how she was goin to eat and all cause she gittin old. I sure hope she gits to visit me in jail . . . if I gits to jail . . .

The posse, including Peter, had switched trains at St. Louis. They boarded a passenger car reserved exclusively for Monroe, the fugitive Peter, plus the nine temporarily deputized Potosi townsmen. Monroe, sitting beside Peter, occupies a bench seat in the rear of the wood-paneled car overlooking the row of seats to their front. Two of the temporary deputies, Mr. MacGregor (Mac) and Mr. Walton, trusted friends of Monroe, occupy a seat facing Monroe. Rumors persisted that a vigilante mob planned to forcibly remove the prisoner from Monroe's custody at the Mineral Point Depot, two miles before reaching Potosi. The Missouri governor, at the request of the Kansas governor, demanded all measures be taken to protect the Negro prisoner. All of this resulted in the sheriff's decision for the armed escort. Peter knows of these threatening rumors.

In a sideways glance, Peter observes Deputy Monroe slumped

in the seat, apparently dozing. A woolly, brown caterpillar conceals the officer's upper chapped lip. On the bridge of his nose rests a wide-brimmed hat, hinting of its once virgin white felt. His right-hand lies instinctively on his Colt. The rhythmically swaying car atop the monotonous steel-wheeled chatter has conspired with the morning's warmth to lull most of the deputies into a restless slumber.

In the same passenger vehicle ride a reporter plus a photographer from the *St. Louis Post-Dispatch*. The reporter busies himself interviewing the few conscious lawmen while the clattering train masks their conversations.

"Tell me, Sir, what is your opinion of these extravagant precautions to protect a Negro accused of murdering a white?" asks the reporter.

"Don't see the need for all the fuss about a colored who's gonna swing away," says the smiling deputized citizen.

Deputy Monroe, through half-closed eyes, catches Peter's fearful gaze.

"I know you're worried, but don't be. We're gettin you to Potosi safe and sound. Never had a lynchin in Washington County and I don't plan on havin none when I'm in charge," says Monroe, snapping a reassuring grin.

"From back at Kansas City, you ain't been treatin me like them other white folks do," says Peter, buoyed by the deputy's remark. "You always askin if my cuffs is too tight, an if I'm hungry. Why you been so nice to me, Mista Monroe?"

The deputy's grin swells to a smile.

"Well, when I was growin up, our family had a colored lady, a Mrs. Jackson, helpin Mom with the chores of raisin six kids. Mrs. Jackson was one of the kindest people I knew. Many times, she'd bring us her home-cooked pies. Apple was my favorite and she always made sure at least once a week I got a slice. She brought her son, Edward. We had a lot of fun together. That was until the neighbors started talkin and we had to play inside. Mrs. Jackson and Edward were like a part of the family.

"Peter, I knew that Thornton fella. He was one mean son-of-a-bitch. Many a night he spent in jail for bein drunk and disorderly, and I heard at home he beat up the misses. You ever hurt anyone like that or spend any time behind bars?"

"No, Suh . . . well not til that Mista Thornton when he done tried to hurt me."

Peter slumps forward, staring at the decaying leather remnants of his shoes. His thoughts drift back to that chilly February afternoon five months ago when he was returning home from the Potosi General Store carrying a fifty-pound sack of flour.

"It done rained," says Peter to the deputy.

Peter explains how he was walking in the middle of the road, avoiding the mushy shoulders. Ahead of him, James Thornton, beside his wife Charlotte, approached in a buggy. Peter stepped to the roadside, allowing them to pass. But Thornton yelled for Peter to get completely off the road into the mud-choked ditch. Enraged by Peter's slow response, Thornton leaped from his buggy flashing a Bowie knife, shouting to his wife, "I'm gonna teach that uppity nigra a lesson he'll never forget!"

Peter continues his story, saying a violent confrontation followed. The fight ended when Thornton lay dying in the mud from a knife wound severing his gut from groin to chest. While Charlotte watched, shrieking, Peter fled into the nearby woods. He escaped to his brother's house in Kansas City. Peter was later captured by the police, beaten, and arrested.

"Exceptin for that, I ain't never had me no run-in with the law before," says a subdued Peter.

"Didn't think so," says Monroe. "Well, I heard what Mrs. Thornton said about that altercation between you and her husband.

She said it happened just like you said, and she's willin to testify under oath that you acted in self-defense."

"Why is a white lady willin to do somethin like that for a colored?" asks Peter in disbelief. "Ain't she scared what them other white folks is gonna do?"

The deputy flashes a toothy grin through his mustache.

"She's leaving town after this is all over. I've even offered to help. Not all of us in Washington County are like Jim Thornton."

And for the first time since the incident occurred, Peter's spirits lift. *Maybe I got me a chance. If only Mista Monroe can git me to jail.*

Deputy Walton stands. Pretending to stretch his legs, he saunters to the front of the car. Keeping his gaze aimed forward while wiping sweat from his face, his attention sifts through the chatter on either side of the aisle. Passing four deputies in a pair of seats facing each other, he snags a portion of stifled conversation:

"Yeah, won't be long now."

"You sure them others here gonna help? If not, it's just us four."

"Don't worry. We got twenty vigilantes waitin at Mineral Point."

The dialogue stops upon noticing Walton, who continues strolling to the front. After returning to his seat, the whispering resumes.

"Ya think he heard?"

"What if he did? Him and that Monroe are outnumbered. By the end of the day that nigra's gonna be stretchin rope."

Walton takes his seat. He failed to hear the entire exchange, except for the "twenty vigilantes waitin at Mineral Point." Leaning forward, he motions Monroe and Mac to move closer. After a hushed discussion, Monroe takes a deep breath, then shifts to the side of his prisoner.

"We got a Judas on board," says Monroe to Peter.

Peter's feelings of relief scatter like scared quail. His shackled legs ache in dread.

"Me and the boys," says Monroe, nodding at the two deputies, "have come up with a plan. Just sit back quiet and try not to look scared."

Taking a pencil and paper from his shirt pocket, Monroe scribbles a note. At the next train stop, Mac delivers the note to the depot's telegraph office as the other deputies observe his movements.

"Keep your fingers crossed," says Mac upon returning to his seat.

The train starts. Monroe draws down his hat, feigning a nap. Again, he leans toward his prisoner.

"The other seven deputies in this car like Mac and Walton are just temporary," says Monroe to Peter in a hushed voice. "And just because they're short-term lawmen don't make em any more tolerant of coloreds than they were before bein sworn in. Besides one of em bein a possible spy, I'm afraid the rest wouldn't piss on us if we were on fire. So when we get to Cadet, you, me, Mac, and Walton are makin a run to Potosi, and we're not tellin anyone."

Monroe tells Peter that Cadet lies eight whistle-stops away. During each station's brief pause, Peter grows more anxious, his heart pounding harder than a sledgehammer. Mac's boot taps the floor. Walton's gloved hand taps his holster. Monroe stoops down, removing the prisoner's leg irons.

The train stops at Cadet, four miles north of Mineral Point. Mac, followed by Walton, sneaks off the train, trailed moments later by Monroe holding Peter by his handcuffs. An open carriage plus two saddled horses await courtesy of a Mineral Point livery's response to the telegram. Peter with Monroe take the carriage. Mac and Walton grab the horses. They gallop out of town to Potosi eight miles away while the train's seven deputies look on like brides left at the altar.

Smelling a not-to-miss story, the two correspondents from the *Post-Dispatch* leap from the train. Due to an obscene bribe of money, they borrow a buggy from a local merchant. They race after the four runaways like dogs chasing a fleeing rabbit.

* * *

Wind, dirt, plus rutted road, batter Peter as he grips the seat. His eyes squint against the wind, straining at every bend in the road, at every stand of trees, every clump of brush, searching for signs of hostile activity, wondering if he will live to see another sunrise.

Gripping the reins as though they are leather snakes, Monroe leans into the hurricane, sporadically looking back through the billowing dust, checking that no one follows.

"So far, so good!" he says to Peter.

* * *

As the entourage of captive and guards scramble toward Potosi, in the Washington County Jail, Sheriff James Whitehead nervously awaits, unaware of the change in plans. His pacing boots pound the pine floor of the one-room, one-oak desk office. On the white, plastered wall, the clock, which he has repeatedly checked all morning, reads 12:58. The train carrying the Black prisoner should have arrived two hours ago. The sheriff paces, ears straining for the short blast of the train's whistle announcing its approach.

On the sheriff's oak desk scattered among the desk's wreckage of wanted posters and empty cigar boxes lie two telegrams. One is from the Governor containing his demand that the prisoner must arrive safely. The second is the sheriff's affirmative reply.

Also on the desk lies a copy of yesterday's *Post-Dispatch*.

In a news article that described the extradition of Peter, included were details of how, with whom, and when the prisoner would be arriving at Potosi. The sheriff could not believe what his spectacles told him. This was privileged information.

"Shit," he shouted as he hurled his inkwell against the wall.

The blue blemish on the plaster would remain an ominous stain of today's events for years.

* * *

Fifteen minutes have blazed past since the stop at Cadet. As previously agreed, instead of the routine stop at Mineral Point, the train is to proceed directly to Potosi. However, a boiling mob of nineteen heavily armed men mounted on horseback blocks the tracks. The train rumbles to a standstill. The mob separates, riding along either side of the passenger cars, looking inside for the Black prisoner. A one-seat spring wagon with a shotgun-toting driver, the twentieth mob member, waits at the nearby depot for its Black cargo.

The deputy who was interviewed by the *Post-Dispatch* reporter leaps off the train. Removing his badge, he charges through the horse-mounted mob searching for a man known as The Accuser. As intended, The Accuser wears a white straw hat wrapped in a bright red headband which the deputy easily spots. The Accuser, a lean, sun-hardened fellow whose angular face sprouts a silver beard, coarse as a wire brush, dismounts. Streaks of brown stain his gray hair.

"They went by carriage to Potosi!" says the ex-deputy. "They only got three deputies. Two reporters are chasin em. If ya ride hard up Mineral Point Road, you might cut em off at the cross-road."

The Accuser shouts an order. Trailed by the wagon, the mob

thunders off, ascending the hilly trail until arriving at the roadway intersection. They stop a rider approaching from Potosi.

"You seen a buggy with a handcuffed colored in it?" demands a voice from the mob.

"No," answers the frightened man on horseback who is ordered to turn back.

"They haven't been here yet," shouts The Accuser. "Break up and take cover in the trees. Wait for my signal. And remember, no shootin. We want that damn nigra *alive*!"

Minutes later, a carriage followed by two men on horseback rounds a bend running towards the mob, which lies hidden in the forest on either side of the road. The carriage lost a precious fifteen minutes due to being carried over a fallen tree on the road. Peter's sharp eye catches some movement behind the trees but before he can warn Monroe, a chaos of stampeding horses shatters the remote stillness. Firing warning shots, the horde surrounds the four men leveling their guns at the captives.

"Halt!" says The Accuser.

"Oh, my Lawd," moans Peter.

"Shit!" says Deputy Monroe, reining the carriage to a stop as he reaches for his gun.

"I wouldn't do that," warns The Accuser.

All is briefly quiet except for the heavy breathing of exhausted horses. The mob, drooling in hate, stares at the captured prey.

"Throw down your guns," says The Accuser.

Three dust billows mark the weapons' impact. A dismounted vigilante collects the guns. Fear bleaches Peter's face.

"What us gonna do?" asks Peter, turning to Monroe.

Deputy Monroe shifts his eyes to the mounted mob.

"I *know* you boys," he says in a confident declaration. "Jeremiah, Hank . . . what are you doin out here on this beautiful Saturday afternoon? Lookin forward to dinner with the family after a hard day of murderin? And Tom, I thought you and the misses were goin to that church social today. I wonder what kind of blessing your priest's got for a lynchin."

The Accuser scowls as the three men lower their heads, plus weapons.

"My friends, consider what you're doing. You're breakin the law. You all could go to jail. Now, if you'll just move aside and let us pass, we can all forget this ever happened. Let the law determine this Negro's fate, not the rule of a mob."

A soulful silence settles over the crowd. One by one, pistols, rifles, and shotguns lower their deadly intent. Monroe cautiously places his hand on Peter who, in a lifted spirit, watches in awe. The two mounted deputies settle into their saddles trading sighs of relief.

A gunshot's blast pierces the silence. All turn to The Accuser's smoking pistol pointed skyward. He lowers the gun, not at the four captives, but at his men.

"What the hell's the matter with you, listenin to this sweet talkin deputy? Remember what that nigra done? He stabbed Thornton in the gut with a Bowie knife like he was guttin a pig. Made a grievin widow outta that poor Mrs. Thornton."

The Accuser takes his time riding through the crowd, looking each of his accomplices in the eye, then stops beside the Black prisoner.

"Mighty fancy words that deputy spoke," says The Accuser. "Almost make ya forget the sight of Thornton lying in that ditch ripped open from his balls to his ribs. They say ya could see his backbone through the slice. I wonder what Mrs. Thornton was thinkin, havin to watch it all. I wonder what *your* women folk gonna think if this nigra gets off and does it again—to one of you! And that damn nigra runnin like a scared dog to Kansas, thinkin he was gonna get away with it. Well, he's not, is he?"

The venomous words fan the mob's embers of hate into a frenzied brush fire.

"Grab the nigra," they shout.

"Damnit, I'm sorry," says Monroe to Peter. "But there's still hope. I'm ridin to town to get another posse. Please, have heart."

Peter's shackled hands strain towards Monroe as three men yank the prisoner to the ground.

"Lawd, please don't let em take me!"

The three drag Peter to the spring wagon, throwing him in as though he were a bag of trash.

"Don't do nothin stupid and follow us. Don't want any dead lawmen on my conscience," says The Accuser, waving his pistol skyward.

Gunfire punctuates his statement. The deputies' horses rear up in protest of the hellish deed.

Just then, a buggy containing two men flies upon the scene, skidding to a stop in a landslide of dust. As the cloud settles, a camera on the buggy's floor becomes visible.

"You two them reporters?" asks The Accuser.

"Y . . . Y . . . Yes," one of them replies, still catching his breath from dragging their carriage over the tree. "We're from the *St. Louis Post-Dispatch*."

"*Post-Dispatch*, huh? One of you been writin those stories about that nigra killer?"

The reporter nods his head.

"Well, glad to meet ya! You're welcome to come along if you want," says The Accuser, pointing to the departing mob, "but ya gotta promise—no names."

The deputies scowl as the reporters agree. The newsmen pass by, slow as circling buzzards, fixing their eyes in a hungry gaze at the departing mob. It trudges downhill back to Mineral Point, victim in tow.

Monroe, leaping from the buggy, grabs a deputy's horse.

"Meet me in town!" he shouts as he roars away in a desperate four-mile sprint to the sheriff's office.

Chapter 2

Scene of the Crime

Peter sits on the jostling wagon floor hunched against his knees. Feeling the savage stares of his abductors, he closes his eyes, then prays. His worst fear, the nightmare that has haunted him every night since he fled months ago to his brother's home, has come to fruition. There shall be no waking up. Never again will a loved one's gentle touch drive the demons from his tormented soul.

Under July's hot sun, Peter shivers with the chilling reality of death. *I done hope it not come to this. Dear Lawd, don't let em hurt me much. Take me quick.*

In agonizing patience, the wagon leads the twenty vigilantes down the dirt road to the village of Mineral Point. There, in horror, Peter opens his eyes to a crowd numbering in the hundreds. Immediately, a hail of stones pummels him.

"Dirty nigra," Bastard negro," "Burn the son-of-a-bitch!" bellows the beastly hoard in an oral stench.

While the multitude proceeds south on the road to Potosi, a journalist and photographer from the *Potosi Journal*, in addition to the two from the *St. Louis Post-Dispatch*, join them. The procession attracts swarms of spectators like a corpse draws flies.

After traveling a mile, the throng stops at the precise location where James Thornton's "murder" at the hands of the prisoner took place. In the day's heat, the horde has bloated to a thousand people spewed across a broad, grassy field.

Having stalked the wagon from Mineral Point, two muscular men draw near. Carriage whips twist in their hands. They stand beside The Accuser who commands Peter to stand up in the wagon.

"You gonna confess your murderous crime you colored bastard, or do we have to whip it out of ya?" asks The Accuser.

In silence, Peter closes his eyes while his ears blister from The Accuser's flaming words. The brawny duo lay down their whips. From the wagon, they drag Peter out, rip all the clothing from his stout frame, then turn him facing the rear wheel, tying his hands to the rim. Retrieving their whips, they face the gathering, assuming the stance of palace guards. Arms folded, they stand on either side of the unclothed prisoner while the throng watches in audible, morbid delight.

"Don't wanna hang no innocent man," shouts The Accuser. "For the last time, nigra, confess."

Unable to clasp his hands in prayer, horror quivers Peter's nude body.

"Lawd, have mercy on me!" he says, looking skyward.

The event's ruckus shrinks into silence as the crowd becomes aware of an approaching diminutive figure, the wife of James Thornton, Charlotte. The assembly parts to allow her, the only woman present, an unobstructed path. Two burly vigilantes, one wearing a faded bandanna around his neck, clutch her arms, pushing her towards the wagon. After each step, the straggly, brown hair drooping from under her bonnet bobs. A yellow calico dress, limp as an empty flour sack, sags from her shoulders. She stumbles between her abductors—two vigilantes sent by The Accuser to "request" her testimony at the "summary trial" of her husband's killer. Led to the wagon, she gazes upon the prisoner, her face melting in sorrow at the sight of the trembling, naked man.

"Mrs. Thornton, is this the colored that killed your husband?" asks the Accuser.

A muted, distressed Charlotte closes her eyes and turns away.

"Speak up, Ma'am. We all want to hear," he says, raising his arms while surveying the audience.

In the woman's presence and shamed by his nakedness, Peter drops his head. He remembers Deputy Monroe on the train saying Mrs. Thornton would testify under oath that the killing was in self-defense. *But ain't no way she gonna say that in fronta all these white folks, specially the way I'm lookin now.*

Certain of the accusation, Peter cringes, pressing his eyes closed as if to block the condemning words. But to everyone's astonishment, Charlotte speaks otherwise.

"Ya'll know he's no murderer. Jim came at im swingin a knife an . . ."

"See that, boys?" interrupts The Accuser. "She's so scared of the brute, she's gone insane."

He faces the two escorts.

"Take this poor widow home where her sensibilities are no longer offended by this butcher."

Unnoticed by The Accuser, another unanticipated reaction follows. The man in the bandanna lowers his head, glaring at his boots, his forehead wrinkled as though lost in thought. Moments pass. He looks up, dropping his scowl as he releases Charlotte's arm. Bending down, he whispers in her ear. Bewildered, Charlotte's eyes lock with his. She pauses, twists free of the other's grip, and faces the assembly.

"He did it in self-defense," she yells.

Using her bonnet to wipe her face, Charlotte plows into the dagger-eyed field of hatred as the two guards scramble behind. Someone spits on her dress. To everyone's surprise, immediately the bandanna escort pushes forward, throwing the saliva-assaulting offender to the ground.

"Ya ought not treat a lady like that!" says the escort, hovering over the prostrate man.

Charlotte proceeds unmolested.

* * *

The three approach the crowd's perimeter, but instead of continuing to the safety of her home, Charlotte stops.

"Ya'll grant a grievin widow one request? Let me stay?" she asks her chaperones.

The two men tower over her like mountains with hats. Trading inquisitive glances, they strain for a sight of The Accuser in the distance, then nod in agreement.

"Can't see no harm," says the bandanna guy pointing at the wagon. "But ya gotta promise ya ain't gonna tell nobody down there what we done."

Charlotte rises on shoe tip and kisses his cheek.

Though she stands at the base of a nearby knoll, her demure stature impedes her view. Noticing her straining to see over the ocean of hats, the chaperones shove forward, throwing people aside as though they were sheaves of wheat, clearing a path of sight.

Today's events have resurrected a cascade of troubling images in Charlotte's mind: Her husband's hand slamming her against the wall after a binge at the Trail's End Saloon. His soiled, white, hooded robe draped over the kitchen chair following another night of persecution. A blood-encrusted Bowie knife on the dining table engraved with "Ain't nonea your damn business!" Plus, the unspeakable imaginings of James' death.

Adding to her distress, she watches The Accuser parading about, aiming his arms and face skyward, a high priest inciting his congregation into hysteria. He stops. Flicking his head, he motions the whips to unleash their torment.

Unlike the crowd, Charlotte's desire to observe the torture lies not in the refuse of blood lust. Vision blurred with tears, she watches the spectacle as one who will one day bear witness to this horrific exhibition.

"May God have mercy on that poor man's soul," she whispers, knowing that when she stands before her Maker, she can righteously proclaim at least one pair of sympathetic eyes were cast upon the Black man.

* * *

Others at the fringe also strain to see the source of the unmistakable slap of leather upon flesh. One observer is an older fellow with an upper lip concealed behind a bush of gray hair.

"What's goin on down there?" he asks a man beside him.

"They got that boy who killed that Thornton fella. They're convincin im to confess."

"But wasn't he on his way to jail to be tried for the crime?"

"Yeah, but don't look like he made it, does it?"

An uneasy stillness replies.

"I said, does it?"

Others standing nearby turn their narrowed eyes toward the conversation.

"Well, no, I suppose he didn't," says the old man.

The elderly gentleman walks away, his head shaking with shame as the strike of the lash pierces the crowd's roar louder than the clap of Satan's hands.

But before the whip's first bite, and though it was a mere whisper in a riot of rage, Peter's cry of, "Lawd, have mercy on me!" was heard.

"Be still, my son. I am here beside you . . . "

Chapter 3

The Final Transition

A firm hand clasps Peter's shoulder. Eyes oval in surprise, he stares at a Black stranger next to him, a man dressed in a plain, white shirt stuffed into dark trousers, all crowned by a thatch of neatly trimmed, silver-gray hair. His reassuring smile is a lamp in the howling darkness of hate.

A great lethargy of time descends. A watch's tick lasts hours. A bee's wing moves slower than growing grass. Peter, freed of chains, untied from the wheel, and dressed in his old clothes, stands beside the stranger whose hand still grasps Peter's shoulder. In a somber calm perched on a nearby knoll, they observe the ruckus hundreds of feet below.

In awe, Peter stares at the still-life horror, a picture only Satan could paint. Awash in a sea of surreal uncertainty, he staggers, bracing himself against the stranger. To Peter's surprise, the piercing clamor of the crowd softens to the gentle babble of a brook. In these calm waters, Peter's fears drift away. A sense of detached sorrow for the figure lashed to the wheel writhing in agony, replaces his anguish. Rigid as an October corn stalk, Peter watches.

A prolonged hush intercedes . . .

"You *are* allowed to speak," says the stranger. "You *must* have something to say."

Peter's attention veers to the intruder.

"What in heaven's name is goin on? How come I'm way up here seein my own self way down there? And why ain't nothin movin?" he asks after observing the deathlike stillness. "You done stop time?"

"Time stops for no one. I slowed its rush to eternity so we can have a moment . . . to talk."

Peter stares at the gathering consumed in the wide-eyed bewilderment of a child attracted to an irresistible temptation.

"I don't feel like talkin. I just want you to answer me what I asked."

"In good time. All of this is the conclusion of your life, the closing procession to your final transition."

"What is you tryin to say?"

"I am talking about your passing . . . your demise."

Peter has a thousand questions about his impending "demise," but words stick in his mouth like porcupine quills.

"That figure you see tied to the wagon, your mortal form, will soon cease to exist. But your spirit, your soul, will live on. That is what you are *now*—a spirit," says the stranger, pointing to the prisoner below. "I have released you from that prison of blood and bone. You are free. You now exist in the eternity of your forefathers; immortal, released from the suffering of the flesh."

"Free and all? Them just white folk's words! Ain't no colored been free in they whole life, and you otta know that cause so is you!"

Peter's eyes flash at the tortured prisoner, then back to the stranger.

"You sayin I'm some kinda spirit, huh? That mean you is one too?"

The stranger nods yes.

"You one of them angels them preachers talk bout that come down from *heaven*?" asks Peter.

"Not exactly. Angels avoid anything that might get their wings dirty. I am here in answer to your cries for mercy."

"If that so, then why you ain't doin nothin to stop em? They gonna hang him and . . . " says Peter, stopping in mid-sentence as he realizes he is referring to his mortal container as "him."

"I am not allowed to interfere with the deeds of man. I can only take the essence of your being under my care and spare you the agony of death. We can leave now; no need for you to watch."

"Maybe that deputy, he make it into town and comin with that sheriff right now."

Peter's eyes rake the dirt road for fragments of a rescue party.

"I am sorry, but no one will arrive in time."

"Then," says Peter, quivering as though ice fills his bones, "he, I mean me, really gonna die?"

Questions rattle his mind. *What he mean he not allowed to interfere? How it gonna hurt anythin to save one ol colored? Sound like he bein told what to do just like any colored man. Like I say, we ain't never been free and it don't sound like heaven gon make nothin different. Always knowed Saint Peter is takin me one day fore my time, but I prayed it ain't gonna be no lynchin. An if this is the way they done answer my prayer, I wonder what hell like?*

"I know all this seems unfair."

"You readin my mind?"

"Yes, when I touch you I can hear your thoughts."

To sever this intrusion of privacy, Peter grabs the hand on his shoulder.

"Stop!" says the stranger. "If I lose contact before your mortal vessel dies, your spirit returns to your body. You shall feel *everything*."

Peter agonizes in despair. *It ain't fair what happenin down there and me up here watchin. But I guess I ain't me got no choice.*

"Yeah, I'm gonna do what you say. But I got to stay here an see it done. It kinda hard to explain, but I owe it to my ol self cause if I ain't there then ain't nobody goin be here that love him."

Thunder rumbles from the cloudless sky.

"What that?" asks Peter.

"Time demands the race resume."

"Cain't we just stay like this? Maybe talk some more?"

"Sorry, destiny is an impatient taskmaster. I have told you enough for now; we must move on. But I warn you, though I have removed your fear, the coming events will be *most* unpleasant. Are you sure you want to stay?"

"Yeah, I'm sure."

"You are one of the few that does. And fewer still," says the stranger, winking, "who express it in terms of love. Any more questions before proceeding?"

"Yeah, lots of em!"

"We just have time for one."

"You got some sorta name?"

"Yes, my son, they call me Scott."

* * *

Thunder rumbles again . . . creation rushes forward . . . the torture begins.

The two men clutching whips who had followed the wagon from Mineral Point, take their positions on opposite sides of their victim. His legs spread apart, the prisoner braces for the lashing. The Accuser shouts the command. Each man takes a turn while his leather snake uncoils, snapping a bite of the Black man's flesh.

On the knoll, Peter cries as tears rise from the well of his emotions, spilling down his cheeks in a shower of sorrow.

Worry crushing his face, he stumbles back in repulsion. *Lawd it hurt watchin. Why they doin them terrible things? His hands is tied and them tearin at him like he some kinda catfish gittin skinned. Don't mean nothin that a white folk like Missus Thornton say I killed Mista Thornton in my own self-defense. Anytime a colored hurt white folks he gonna git lynched or burned, that* for sure. So why they whippin him? Why don't they just hang him and do what they gotta do?

"You sure I don't haveta go back to my ol self, feelin them lashes," says Peter, turning to Scott. "Ain't I suffered enough for my sins?"

Scott's hold on Peter tightens.

"Have no fear, you are not going back."

But hopeless as a rose in a hailstorm, these words of comfort vanish under the ninety-nine lashes of leather tearing the naked body, a body though streaked in blood refuses the slightest vestige of pain. Finally, the condemned prisoner makes a request. The exhausted torturers rest.

"If you don't whip me no more and promise you won't burn me, then I say I done it."

Accepting the condemned's "confession," the torture stops.

"I'm damn prouda ya," proclaims Peter to his bleeding, mortal appendage. "You wore them whips out, and ya done it like a man!"

* * *

A grin stretches the sweat-stained faces of the two tormentors. They clean and coil their leather serpents, untie the prisoner, and then force him up onto the wagon's bed. Naked, handcuffed, and condemned to die, the prisoner stands erect in stern-faced silence, an actor on a macabre stage displayed before the howling audience.

The *Journal* and the *Post-Dispatch* photographers scramble for positions, aching to record the scene. The prisoner, like a lump of black clay, is molded into multiple poses by the two employees. Though their newspapers cannot yet print photographs, those deemed appropriate for women and children will be placed on public display for viewing. They hurry to complete their efforts before the escaping day takes the light from the final act.

The Accuser folds his hands on the wagon wheel—the proud hunter posing beside the trophy of his kill.

"Make sure I'm in the photograph, boys," he says, smiling.

"Mamma she never had no picture of me, and please tells her and my brother that I love em and that I'm awful sorry that I haveta leave em," says the prisoner, and asks if they'll send a "good" picture of him to her.

In the distance, Peter sobs. *Look at what they gone done. His . . . my backside look like bleedin bark. I ain't never gonna hold Momma in my arms no more, say how much I loves her, and ain't never gon say goodbye to my kinfolk. And them newspaper fellas takin my picture just like I'm some kinda freak in one of them circus shows, stripped naked as the day I was born. Dear Lawd, I ain't no freak, I ain't no animal, I'm a man, and just cause I'm colored, it don't give em no cause to beat me like that. And this colored stranger just standin here with me watchin. Don't he got no feelins? Don't he git real sad and mad, like me, at what he been seein? I don't understand, dear Lawd. I just don't understand nothin. Maybe it's best I'm leavin this world. It got too much damn hate.*

Peter reels around, facing the stranger, who says not a word.

* * *

"Did ya hear that colored son-a-bitch? He said he murdered a white man, but he ain't sorry." "That ain't no confession!" ricochets through the watching horde, intense as scattered gunfire. "Burn im!"

A group of axe-wielding men splits from the assembly, running up the knoll into the woods. A chorus of ringing metal echoes from the grove in preparation for the burnt offering to bigotry.

Hands clasped over her lips as though in prayer, Charlotte

watches the chaos as she stands between her two abductors-turned-protectors. She turns to her chaperones.

"Could ya'll gentlemen clear a path for me to the wagon?"

The men comply, plowing through the mass of spectators ahead of Charlotte. Defiant, she approaches in full view of The Accuser whose hands choke the wheel rim, bleaching his fingers white with rage. Reaching the wagon, the two escorts lift Charlotte onto the bed, turn, then stand guard. She approaches the prisoner, her bonnet the height of his shoulder. One guard removes his shirt, giving it to Charlotte, who ties it around the prisoner's waist, concealing his manhood.

"Thank ya, Ma'am," whispers the prisoner.

Charlotte and the prisoner's eyes meet. Hers release a melt of emotions. His fog behind a shroud of fear. The rabble of the crowd withers into an awkward calm stung by scattered sobs. The Accuser's face slouches in a scowl.

"If the good Lord can't change your evil hearts," says Charlotte, shunning The Accuser, "neither can I. Hang im if ya must, an ya'll can go to hell! But don't ya *dare* burn im!"

She glares down at The Accuser, who turns motioning one of his horse-mounted henchmen forward. Obeying the command, a vigilante jumps from his saddle, storming toward the wagon. But Charlotte's guards, shoulder to shoulder, block his approach. Ripe with anger, The Accuser flings his arm, rallying his gang. But they sit slumped in saddles, eyes shifting from the demon-eyed leader to the calico-dressed crusader.

In disbelief, the crowd looks on.

"Why they all just standin there and not doin nothin?" asks Peter.

"Paying respect to a brave little lady," says Scott.

"But why is she doin all them things to help me considerin what I done to Mista Thornton? Don't she know white folks turn on they own kind quicker than a pack of starvin wolves?"

"No need to worry about her. After this courageous display and protected by her escorts, she will be fine. She will even deliver the photograph you requested to your mother and then leave the county."

"How you knowin she gon do that?"

"I just do."

Aided by her protectors, Charlotte exits the wagon. The throng parts one last time. Following her escorts, she trods through the assemblage which removes their hats in respect.

The Accuser marches into his gang, glaring up at the nineteen mounted mutineers. Their faces regress to the compulsory frown. He summons a weathered mummy-skinned man, Moses, from whose saddle horn dangles a rope coiled into a noose. Rope in hand, Moses dismounts. After the two finish a hushed conversation, The Accuser remounts, leading the vigilantes up the knoll into the woods which still ring from the assault of sharpened steel upon timber. One eye lowered in an ominous squint, Moses grabs the reins of the horse pulling the wagon. He follows the vigilantes while the horde stalks from behind.

"Why ain't we lookin for a place to hide? They gon see us!" says Peter.

"Nobody can see us. We are spirits. Invisible as air."

The prisoner squats in the jostling open-air hearse lead by Moses. While the spectacle passes, the prisoner's gaze seizes Peter with the hollow gape of a deceased being. The horrifying stare holds Peter captive until the funeral march disappears in the woods. Despair's icy grasp seizes Peter, a grasp Scott fights to thaw with a tightening of his grip.

"It is difficult, but resist the dread from that doomed figure. When you left that mortal form, you took all that made the being alive and self-aware. *It*, not *he*, is the existence of a sleepwalker seemingly alive, but numb to its surroundings and deeds. Never will it awake. It is simply a decoy for the amusement of the crowd until your transition ends."

"That ain't no *figure* in that wagon, that *me*," says Peter, a trail of tears seeping down his cheek. "Maybe he seen me, maybe he don't, but he knows I'm here. My bones knows it cause they feelin that same ol cold that I know he done feelin, that kinda cold that don't never go away—cold that *sucks* the life outta ya like winter suck the heat outta an ol shack. You sure he gonna feel nothin?"

"He will feel no pain."

"Stand up, nigra!" shouts The Accuser as the procession stops under a large elm.

First The Accuser, then another vigilante, dismounts. Assuming the role of executioners, they climb into the wagon. Moses steadies the horse. Reminiscent of an exorcised ghost, the weakened prisoner rises. The executioners slide a noose over the prisoner's head, replacing the shirt around his waist with a tarp.

A rumble stirs through the ranks of onlookers. The sound grows louder, fouling the air with obscenities. Feeding upon itself it swirls, howling until reaching a tornado's scream.

"Whoa, boy, not yet," says Moses, clutching the reins as the horse rears from the commotion.

Terror contorts the condemned man's face. No courtesy of a blindfold shall be offered lest the distortion of death's anguish be obscured.

Overhead on a limb clings a red-capped boy in blue overalls. Resembling a denim caterpillar, he inches forward. Someone throws up a rope. Over the branch, he loops the rope which he drops to a man who ties it around the trunk.

"Silence!" says The Accuser, raising his arms.

The faithful obey.

"Any last words before ya meet your maker?" he asks the condemned.

The noosed man raises his head from prayer.

"Good Lawd," cries Peter to Scott. "Ain't you gonna do nothin to stop it?"

"If I did, I would have to resort to force. And that, I am also not allowed."

"If he was white, I'm bettin you would!"

"I am so sorry," says Scott.

"I'm so sorry," says the prisoner. "But that white man he done had a knife . . . "

"Enough!" cries The Accuser.

"I can't watch!" cries Peter, turning away.

The executioners jump from the wagon.

"Heyah!" shouts Moses, slapping the horse.

The wagon leaps forward. The condemned man drops. The rope snaps taught . . .

Chapter 4

The Three Choices

Wrapped in Scott's arms, Peter covers his eyes. The pair stands on the shallow knoll a short distance from the death scene. Protected from the lynching's unbearable emotions by Scott's embrace, a hesitant Peter raises his head, staring up the hill at the black cadaver, a macabre pendulum swinging from the elm.

"I gottta go up there," says Peter.

"Are you certain you want to do that?"

"Yeah, I gotta pay my last respects to my ol self," says Peter, his nervous gaze sweeping the scene. "You still sure we ain't gonna be seen?"

"Trust me. We are blind to mortal eyes."

Laughter and cheering drift from the crowd mixing with the deadly attraction in an unholy contradiction. While Scott's comforting hand holds Peter, they trudge uphill, stopping at the deceased tortured form. Tilting his head, Peter stares at the hideous figure. Streams of sorrow trickle down his face.

The rope has torn back the head of the dead man. His gaping eyes fix on the red-capped boy clutching the limb from which the body hangs. The lad stares downward in a speechless, unblinking gaze at the twisted face which holds the youngster captive tight as the cadaver's noose. The boy's bleached expression screams his shock at the irreversible cruelty. For a moment, the eyes of the boy and the corpse lock.

The Accuser gathers his men. Smiling, they brandish firearms, posing for a picture around the body. The flash of two tripod-mounted cameras burns the vigilantes and the neck-stretched body, still twitching in death's spasm, into posterity.

"Don't ya'll forget my boy!" says the father, pointing upward from the crowd.

"Sure won't!"

The photographers refocus while waiting for the boy's pose. But the youngster clings to the limb, his eyes embedded in the corpse.

"Bart!"

No response.

"Bart! Damnit, look at the camera! Wave your hat!"

The boy complies, triggering two more flashes. The red cap, which he once swung in pride, slips from his hand, spiraling to the ground.

"The father will frame and display the boy's photograph on the dresser beside the son's bed," says Scott, rendering a prediction. "Fearing his father's anger should he remove it, every night until Bart leaves home at age sixteen, he will lay the picture face down. Today's events will torment the boy for the rest of his life."

"That's damn good. I hope it's gonna drive im mad. And what bout them other folks, them vigilantes? When they gonna git what they got comin?"

Scott's answer hides behind his tongue.

"When they gonna get what they got comin?" repeats Peter.

"No one in this mob of twenty will feel the sting of the law."

"What you mean? They got them folks in that photo picture plain as day. Anyone can see who *they* is!"

"True, but prejudice is blind to justice. An inquest by the coroner will report 'the Negro met his death at the hands of persons unknown.'"

"You meanin to say ain't nobody gonna do *nothing*?" says Peter, dropping in disbelief. "Not even that Mista Monroe? He seem different from them other white folks."

"Peter, both Monroe and the sheriff will act in the cause of justice, and each will pay a price. The actions by the sheriff will eventually cost him his job."

"And what bout Mista Monroe?"

Silence again answers.

"What done happen to im?"

"The fate of Deputy Monroe is worse."

After hearing Scott's prediction of Monroe's future, gloom casts a shroud over Peter.

"That poor ol Mista Monroe. I sure liked him and he ain't to blame for nothin that happen."

"You say that now, but with time, you will not be so forgiving, and rightfully so."

Scott's statement unnerves Peter, but he has more pressing concerns.

"So, you mean them bastards that done killed me ain't gonna suffer for it?"

"Oh, there will come a judgment, but not by mortal hands."

"You meaning after they dead?"

"No, but in their final moments of life," says Scott.

"How long that gonna take?"

"In the case of the boy, eighty-seven years."

Peter's face explodes in anger.

"I ain't waitin no eighty-seven years for one of em to gits what they got comin!"

Speechless, he yanks Scott's hand from his shoulder, wheels around, then races into the vigilantes. He tries to grab someone, anyone, but his hands pass through sinew, blood, and bone as though they are fog. He reaches for a woodcutter's axe. It too ignores his attempts. With each cheer of the lynched man's fate, the self-glorifying mob seems to mock Peter's futile efforts.

"I can't watch him hangin like that," says Peter. "I gotta let im down!"

He runs to the rope tied around the trunk. Like a cat pawing air, he flails at the knot, but his hands are useless as swirling smoke. In a furnace of emotion, he lunges at his deceased, mortal form, failing to lift it.

"Good Lawd," he shouts to Scott, "you just gonna stand there and watch?"

Scott approaches. He takes Peter by the shoulders.

"*Now* do you see?" says Scott. "You are a spirit—void of body with less effect on mortal reality than a dead man's thoughts."

Peter wrenches. Less effect . . . than a dead man's thoughts? Dear Lawd, maybe I ain't nothin but my ol dyin self's thinkin. Maybe this is just a dream, an if that the way it is, what happenin when the dream done stop?

Peter stands helpless, an apparition trapped between mortal and spiritual mayhem.

Through his hands, Scott hears Peter's desperation.

"Have no fear, this is not the nightmare of a dying man. You have been transformed into a new existence, a spiritual being. As I have said, you have now joined the realm of your forefathers. You have become *immortal*."

Removing one hand, Scott guides Peter away from the crowd.

"Mista Scott, who is you?"

"I am a benefactor, master classification."

Smiling, he explains benefactors are voluntary earthbound spirits blessed with supernatural powers and abilities who offer aid and comfort to mortals and even other spirits.

"Ain't never hearda no benefactor in the "Good Book." Just angels and they ain't colored like you," says Peter as a question tilts his head. "You from that *other place*?"

"I assure you I am no angel, though we both work under the same boss. If you wish, I *could* summon something from the *other place*, but it would be rather . . . unpleasant."

Peter shakes his head no.

"And how come you talk like white folks? You uppity about talkin like us colored?"

"I have my reasons and they are *not* out of pride. But if my speech offends you, I can change it, as well as my Black appearance; just ask."

Peter eyes this benefactor. I cain't remember no time when someone ask me what I liked exceptin my mamma or kinfolk. Kinda nice to be asked, but there's somethin strange bout this, Mista Scott.

"Naw, you okay just the way you is. But tell me, I know you can tell time to go real slow and walk through things and change how you look and talk and all. But how you know what gonna happen to that sheriff and Mista Monroe?"

"Well, I can foresee the future of all my clients," says Scott.

"What you mean *clients*?"

"Clients are mortals or spirits I and other benefactors are assigned to help. There is a chain of command beginning with the highest-class benefactor down to apprentice benefactors. Mister Monroe is one of my many clients, as are you, Peter."

"So, you can see them bad things that gonna happen to Mista Monroe?"

"Yes, bad and good, but at times, Peter, I almost wish I could not."

"Mista Scott, what gonna happen to me?"

The benefactor's eyes wander while his lips press in rigid silence. Peter feels Scott's grip tighten.

"It that bad?"

"I am not allowed to tell you," says Scott. "If I did, you would act differently and change fate. The purpose of your new existence is to grow spiritually, but this growth only comes through the healing of past wounds; such is the way of transformation. But be not afraid, for I will always be near. Remember, you are an immortal spirit, you will never again die. So enjoy the show. The price of admission has been paid."

"So what does I do seein I'm some kinda spirit that ain't never gonna die?"

"Son," says Scott, his lips lifting in joy. "I have been waiting for that question. I offer you three choices, and with each I can grant you the power to achieve it."

"What kinda choices?" asks Peter, his expression pulled with impatience.

"You could be a benefactor like me; be part of something larger than yourself. Answer those prayers to alleviate the pain and terror of death's final transition, as I did with you. Work through mortals to achieve a more just world; little things like that. You would be an apprentice under my care, learning the trade until graduating as a journeyman. Then you would have clients of your own."

"Hmm, you said a more just world?" asks Peter, and then nods at the vigilantes. "Them your clients, too?"

"Yes, everyone has a benefactor, though most are unaware of it."

"Well, don't take this in no bad way, but from what I seen round here you benefactors ain't keepin the fox outta the hen house. What else you got to offer to an ol dead colored?"

"For your second option, I can take you to a place of eternal peace called Sanctuary."

Peter's eyes roll in disdain. It sure be nice to have that peaceful feelin, but . . .

"Ain't no way I'm gonna feel peaceful til I see them *bastards* that kill me pay for what they done! I'd go to hell first!"

"Peter, that is *exactly* what your third choice is—hell."

"What you gittin at?" asks Peter, the back of his neck tingling.

"You can stay *here* and avenge your death."

Peter almost laughs. Vengeance! Now that the first thing he say makin sense.

"But beware, when you pursue vengeance, you chase the dust of hate, dust you can never grasp. And the harder you try, the more dust you create, eventually suffocating in its deadly cloud, a victim of your own retribution. I know, I speak from experience."

But Peter shuns the warning. To him, punishing the mob for what happened *is* the peace he is seeking, the restitution that is owed him plus his Black brothers and sisters for all the suffering inflicted by white folks. He sees himself as a crusader. Vengeance is *not* evil. Vengeance is an obligation, a moral necessity. It is taking back the dignity gutted from his soul.

"If revenge ain't so good," says Peter, cocking his head, "why you willin to gimme them powers to do it? An if so, what *is* them powers?"

"This is all I am prepared to discuss. So make your choice. Here with us, heaven . . . or hell."

Peter casts his eyes on the mob and his mortal's self remains stretching the rope. Warnings of hell concern him, but what could be more hellish than this? His existence as a spirit, not seen, felt, or heard, is not much different than Peter's life as a Black man. As long as he dared not touch or upset anyone white, neglect and contempt were his reward.

He twists free of the benefactor's hand. Seems like things ain't no different bein dead than they was from when I was alive. Ain't never gittin away from them white folks.

"If you and them white folks lets things like that happen," Peter says, pointing to the scene of death, "I don't want nothin to do with you or your damn heaven! I takes hell!"

Chapter 5

Deputy Monroe Rides

Four hours before the lynching, with each strike of the horse's hoof, dust splashes as a desperate Deputy Louis Monroe gallops toward Potosi and the office of Sheriff James Whitehead. Trees scurry past unnoticed by the deputy, his thoughts consumed by the image of his prisoner sitting in a wagon awaiting death at the lynch mob's hand. The boiling afternoon air burns hotter than a Hades' gale as he leans into the wind. *Just two more miles and I'll be at Jim's office. Christ, I hope I'm not too late.*

Monroe rounds a bend. Blocking the road ahead, a gang of five men stands shoulder to shoulder armed with rifles. This detachment was sent to the outskirts of Potosi by The Accuser to capture the Black fugitive if the vigilante mob failed. The five are unaware the prisoner has been captured.

"Hold up there, deputy!" says the blockade's leader. "Where ya'll headin in such a hurry?"

"I've got urgent business with the sheriff. I'd appreciate you boys lettin me pass," says Monroe, his eyes darting from one man to the other.

The five trade sinister grins.

"Urgent business? That got anythin to do with that nigra on the Iron Mountain?" asks the leader to a backdrop of chuckling.

Monroe's hand slides to his holster.

"Gentleman, you're obstructin a peace officer's official duties. Step aside."

"We got our own official duties, and they outnumber yours," says the leader as five rifles rise with deadly intent at the deputy.

"Get off your damn horse and gimme your gun."

"You know you boys can go to jail for this," says Monroe as he dismounts, surrendering his weapon. *I don't like this; don't recognize any of em. I wonder just how many are mixed up with this lynchin.*

"Ain't nobody goin to jail, deputy. We're takin you under 'protective custody'. Keepin ya from encounterin an armed mob and gettin yourself killed. Now, go over there in the shade, boy, and rest til we say it's safe for ya'll to go."

One man takes Monroe's horse while another, jabbing his rifle, prods the deputy to a decaying log in the shadow of an oak. Monroe's watch counts the minutes.

The two deputies who accompanied Monroe on the train arrive. Mac rides in the buggy. Walton on horseback, holds the reins of Mac's horse. Greeted at gunpoint, they are taken to Monroe, who grunts an acknowledgment at them.

"You all right, Lou?"

Answering Mac through a flip of his eyes, Monroe huddles forward. As though in anxious prayer, he presses his hands together then yanks out his watch—1:07 p.m.

"Damn," grumbles Monroe.

Into a pit of shame, he sinks—shame for failing in his sworn duty to bring the prisoner safely to the Washington County Jail in Potosi, a vow he made during his meeting with Sheriff James Whitehead. Maybe he should have hidden in the woods and sent for the sheriff, taken a longer route, or just stayed on the train.

Though only ten days have passed since that meeting, it has been an eternity of events. His attention fixed on the watch's dial, Monroe's thoughts drift back to that meeting.

* * *

Hitching his horse, Monroe crosses the porch, pausing at the sheriff's door. Feeling a knot in his stomach, he checks his time-piece—1:07 p.m. "Hell, I'm late," he mumbles. "Jim's prickly as a porcupine for punctuality."

Monroe sets his watch back to 12:58. Grinning, he strolls into the office. Drifting in the air, a Milky Way of dust sparkles in the sunlight from the room's two curtainless windows. The six-year-old building's white plastered walls have yet to be yellowed from tobacco smoke.

Reclining with crossed arms in a swivel chair behind an oak desk, the sheriff glances at the wall clock.

"You're late!"

"Hi, Jim," says Monroe, flopping in a seat.

Monroe tosses his sweat-stained hat on the table. Using the weathered bandana coiled around his neck, he mops his head. His spindly chair creaks in annoyance as he props his feet on the desk.

"Your damn clock's fast, Jim," says Monroe, offering his watch's lying 1:00 p.m. as proof.

Glaring at Monroe through bleached, blue eyes sunk in a face chiseled by thirty-nine years of hammering sun, the sheriff flicks over a telegram.

"This is the reason you're here," he says to Monroe.

Missouri Governor Lawrence Stephens sent the telegram. The document declares, among other things, that the State of Kansas:

". . . has agreed to the extradition of the Negro accused of mur-dering James Thornton . . . All precautions necessary to ensure the safe arrival of the prisoner must be implemented."

Monroe lifts his attention to the sheriff's lowered brow. Shit, here it comes.

"Lou, I'm gonna give the governor my *word* that that colored fella will arrive here safe and unharmed. And you know how important my *word* is, and you know I can't leave my duties here."

"You're wantin me to get im, aren't ya?"

"Yeah, Lou. I want you to lead a posse of ten men countin yourself and escort the prisoner here," says the sheriff, nodding at the July wall calendar. "The prisoner'll be here on the Iron Mountain in ten days, the morning of the 22nd, a Saturday."

The sheriff points to one of two cells on his right.

"I'm lockin im in the woman's cell, not one of those upstairs, so I can keep an eye on im down here til the trial starts Monday mornin. And I want *you* here with me."

The sheriff hands Monroe a list of ten handwritten names arranged in a column. It starts with the trustworthy and most experienced at the top, descending to first-time volunteers. Deputy Louis Monroe crowns the tally.

Monroe inspects the names. Seems like a good group of men, exceptin I don't know the last three. There's five Masons on it which reminds me I haven't been to the lodge in months. Thornton wasn't the most likable guy in the county, but he was white. Damn! Bringin that Negro back so he can stand trial won't be taken kindly by a lot of folks. Scared what might happen if they get wind of it. And the way Thornton was gut-cut . . . Don't know if I wanna get involved with this.

"So, why me, Jim?"

"Cause if there's trouble, and we both know there's a good chance, I want a man who's willin to do *whatever* it takes to get that prisoner here—alive—even if it means usin force against his own neighbors and *even* against those in his own posse."

Monroe's shoulders contract like a cold vice.

"So, before I answer this telegram, I wanna know, Lou, are you that man? You willin to give your word to do anything necessary?"

The sheriff and Monroe duel in an unflinching stare until Monroe surrenders by blinking first. Sliding his boots off the table, Monroe rises in defeat. Eyes cast down and creased in thought, he paces the floor, the office resonating with the rhythmic thud of his boots. He stops, shaking the list at the sheriff.

"What about the two guys under me, Walton and MacGregor? They could lead the posse."

"Yeah, but seein how you're my only permanent deputy, you've got more experience *and* a greater responsibility to uphold the law. Besides, they're both married and got kids. I'm afraid that could complicate things."

"Yeah, funeral arrangements for a bachelor take no time at all."

Monroe folds into the rickety seat, its creak extending to a lengthy moan.

"Jim, when you gettin some decent chairs? I'm scared this one's gonna shove a leg up my ass."

"Lou, you lead this posse for me, I'll get ya a goddamn leather couch!"

"That, means I'd be spendin a lot more time here. Have to think about it."

Monroe's gaze drifts to the Milky Way in the sultry air. He remembers as a child staring into the night sky wishing one day to be a lawman. Remembering his oath to serve justice, he shifts his attention to the sheriff.

"But givin my word to use force if need be against my own men, possibly even my friends; I don't rightly know if I can."

"I know I'm askin a lot, Lou. But remember, every man has the right to a fair trial. So, if me and you don't see justice is served, who the hell will?"

"Fair trial, huh? Exceptin of course if you're colored."

Monroe remembers as a child playing alongside Edward, the son of his family's Black housekeeper, Mrs. Jackson. All those names the kids called him, names I'd never say. Damn, I should've done something. Stood up for Edward. He was my best friend.

"I want you to meet someone," says the sheriff, standing and waving his hand.

From behind a partition hiding the room's bed, a woman in a yellow calico dress approaches.

"Deputy Monroe, I'd like you to meet Mrs. Charlotte Thornton."

"Pleased to make your acquaintance, Ma'am," says the startled deputy, rising to offer his chair. "Sit real careful. This thing's temperamental."

Seating herself, Mrs. Thornton folds her nervous hands in her lap. Monroe sits on a desk corner, trading eye contact between her and the sheriff.

"Alright, what's up, Jim?" asks Monroe.

"Mrs. Thornton has something she wants to tell ya."

"Please, sheriff, call me Charlotte."

"Lou, Charlotte has something she wants to tell ya."

Monroe rubs his knee. I know what she wants—blood.

"I wanna tell ya how it really happened," says Charlotte. "Me and James were comin back from Mineral Point in our buggy. Ya'll remember how cold and wet February was. It was a Monday mornin goin on noon."

Charlotte describes how they came upon a colored man carrying a heavy sack of flour. He stepped aside, allowing them to pass, but refused James' demand to get off the road into the muddy ditch. James jumped off the buggy—not yanked off by the colored man as everyone in town is saying.

"My husband hated colored folks. James said he was gonna teach that uppity nigra a lesson he'd *never* forget!"

She describes how her husband pulled a knife and flipped it across the man's face, gashing his chin. Seizing the weapon, the man stabbed James. What surprises Monroe the most is the impassive way Charlotte tells it. Though she closed her eyes while shrieking during the gruesome event, she now shows less emotion in her recounting than in describing a steer being butchered. She then utters the most surprising remark of all.

"And I'd be willin to swear under oath that colored killed James in his own self-defense."

Monroe sits still as a corpse. Doesn't she know what could happen? If she says this at the trial, God only knows what some crackpot might do.

At that instant, Monroe makes up his mind. He turns to the sheriff.

"Jim, if this little lady's got the kinda guts to say that, I suppose I got no choice but to lead that posse. And I swear I'll do *whatever* it takes to get that prisoner here safe."

These words will echo in a black abyss of guilt haunting Monroe for the rest of his life.

* * *

A blockader's boot step snaps a twig, yanking Monroe back to the present. He glances at his two deputies. They rest in fitful slumber, propped against the log. Even the threat of pacing, armed guards is no match for the debilitating heat of the Missouri afternoon. Monroe checks his watch—5:58 p.m. Nearly five hours have passed since he with the deputies were seized, five hours dragging by slower than the lengthening shadows of woodland trees.

A galloping horse breaks the muggy monotony.

Monroe leans over shaking Mac and Walton. They watch as a lone rider approaches from Potosi. He dismounts. The blockade gathers around him. In low guttural voices while nodding back at the lawmen, the six men converse. Their loud, sinister laughter sends a chill through Monroe. After a back slap by the blockade leader, the rider remounts, heading back to Potosi in a slow trot. The leader saunters over to Monroe.

"That was one of *our* boys," says the leader, removing his plantation hat while wiping his forehead. "Ya'll can leave now. He done say it's safe."

Retrieving their weapons, horses, plus the wagon, the deputies strike southward with the urgency of lightning. They pass the rider whom Monroe would love to arrest, but he has more urgent concerns.

Entering Potosi, the three race pass the Washington County Courthouse. Monroe glances at the brick building from the corners of his windburned eyes. I got a feelin there won't be no trial there Monday.

They stop at High Street.

"You two head down to the depot," Monroe orders. "See if ya can find the rest of our men."

"Lou," says Mac, "you know goddamn good as me they ain't there."

"Damnit, Mac, take the buggy and just do it. Wait for me at the depot."

Monroe then gallops to the sheriff's office. Damn, I'd give anything not ta have to tell Jim what happened. Suppose I didn't do "whatever it takes" cause I'm not dead. I can still hear those bastards at the blockade laughing like the law is some kinda joke. And that poor Negro. Glad I don't believe in an Almighty but understand why those that do call themselves 'God fearin.' Only a fool wouldn't be scared to death of a God that lets this shit happen!

The door's hinges near to breaking, Monroe blasts into the sheriff's office.

"Jim, you here?"

"Up here, darlin," yells a prisoner from a second-floor cell, followed by stomping from the other giggling inmates.

The deserted office is just another piece of Monroe's puzzle of fear.

Monroe scrawls a note:

Jim: Saturday, 6:15 pm

Took prisoner with two deputies off train at Cadet because of vigilante mob waiting at Mineral Point. Tried riding here but stopped by mob that took prisoner. Me and deputies held by armed men for five hours, then released. Deputies waiting at depot. I'm headed there now.   Monroe

He leaves it on the desk next to the governor's telegram. Boot heels denting the floor, Monroe runs out of the office, across the porch, then swings into his saddle. Yanking the reins, he dashes towards the depot. Billows of dirt boil behind him. Empty buildings, one and two-story gabled roof structures of sunburned wood, painted clapboard, and rust-red brick, stream past silent as ghosts, adding to his premonition of doom.

Approaching Depot Street, he sees a scattered crowd of people advancing; some mounted, most on foot. He pulls back the reins. The horse skids to a stiff-legged stop. Its labored breath mixes with the murmur of the crowd. That crowd don't look good. Deputies'll just have to wait.

Monroe's chest clenches. Worry crumples his face. Kicking his horse, he heads into the approaching throng, his questioning eyes answered by coldhearted glares. But further back in the gathering, a few trudge forward, their heavy heads staring at the ground. Some bear fresh tracks of tears on soil-tainted cheeks. Monroe refrains from asking the source of their sorrow.

"Where was ya an hour ago!" yells one of the stragglers, seeing the deputy's badge.

"Damnit!"

Leaning forward while slapping the horse's hindquarters, Monroe careens through the remaining laggards who scatter with the commotion of straw in a tornado.

A haze of dust leads him to a deserted location on the road outside of town. An expanse of trampled grass bears witness to a previous, sizable gathering. It surrounds the spot where Thornton died months earlier. Monroe's mouth turns dry as a grave's shriveled rose.

Dismounting, he appraises the deserted terrain for evidence of wrongdoing. He notices a set of wagon tracks. They head down from a wooded hill turning onto the road to Mineral Point. Due to the sharp, undisturbed depressions, he surmises the wagon was the last to leave.

Monroe remounts. He surveys the road and woods. Sure wish Jim or my deputies were here. Don't really want to go up there by myself. Funny, but I otta be able to see somethin from here. It's not that far. Hmm, could be he's still alive. Maybe that's why those fellas were lookin so glum cause someone changed the mob's mind and they didn't hang im. Someone like Mrs. Thornton. Knowin her, she was most likely here. She coulda done it. Maybe he got beat up some, and maybe that's why that fella asked, "Where was ya?" And those wagon tracks, maybe they were takin im back to Mineral Point to leave im there for the sheriff. Good ol Charlotte!

Spurred by a new sense of hope, Deputy Monroe retraces the tracks uphill to the wood's edge where stands a multi-armed god, the giant elm. He dismounts, hesitating at the sight of scattered branches surrounding its trunk. The back of his head constricts in worry. Reins in hand, the deputy sneaks around the tree, eyes straining as each branch and twig bends into view. A breeze whispers through the limbs with a mournful sigh. Suddenly, the horse panics, rears up, then breaks free, galloping downhill through the heavy, evening air. Crossing the grassy expanse, it stampedes back to the road chased by a piercing yell.

"Dear God, I'm too late! Look what those bastards done!"

Chapter 6

The Four Powers

One hour after the lynching, before Deputy Monroe discovers the noosed corpse, Peter and Scott watch the evil spectacle's finale. The crowd plus the twenty-man lynch mob—their orgasm of hate sated—depart, casting the death scene into an eerie silence. Last to leave is Moses, the "mummy-skinned man", who had led the wagon containing Peter's mortal form to the execution. In a final backward glance, Moses lingers, grinning at the macabre scene. He then leads the horse and wagon to the road. As the vision of the jostling wagon weakens in the afternoon's late haze, he returns to Mineral Point.

"What gonna happen to me now?" asks Peter, awash in a tormented sea of emotion.

"Be patient my son, and watch."

An hour staggers past, dragging with it Deputy Monroe and his horrific discovery of Peter's lynched body. Monroe kneels before the corpse, cursing himself and the murderers of the prisoner, the prisoner he had sworn to protect. Head slumped in despair, he trudges down the hill as tears leave tracks on his dust-caked face.

Peter sobs, shedding his final tears for many years.

Evening obediently surrenders to the night.

* * *

In the young darkness swing six luminous pendulums, kerosene lamps lighting the path of a horse-drawn wagon leading an entourage of seven Black men uphill to the elm. Their hands held in silent prayer, the group stops, encircling the hanging body.

Two men lift the corpse by its legs. A third cuts the rope. The body slumps forward into cradled arms. While another steadies the horse, they lower the lifeless form onto the wagon's dirt-caked bed. They drape the remains in a white sheet followed by another prayerful silence. Swaying lights escort the wagon downhill, disappearing behind the black curtain of night.

Unknown to the seven-man escort, three members of the vigilante mob follow the wagon. Unknown to the three vigilantes, Deputy Monroe observes and follows them.

* * *

Scott and Peter watch the seven men from the base of the elm.

"What they doin that for?" asks Peter.

"They have come from a colored Baptist Church in Potosi. They are taking your remains for a proper burial. Would you care to follow?"

In a prolonged silence, Peter stares at the spears of yellow light piercing the darkness.

"Nawh, I already done paid my last respects to my ol self. Ain't nothin more I need to do," he says, sighing. "You know, I sure feelin kinda tired. Do spirits supposed to feel this way?"

"We shall discuss this later. But for now, lie down and get some rest."

"You gonna stay here with me?"

"Have no fear. I will not leave your side until I think you are ready."

Peter flinches at Scott's vague qualification. Though only in Scott's presence for a few hours, Peter has grown dependent on this stranger.

Chaos has reigned since the boarding of the Iron Mountain this morning. But sleep's misty veil shields Peter's thoughts from worry. His eyes close, descending into a deep slumber.

A woodpecker's knock awakens him. His first sense is the morning's chill prickle, a youthful coolness which will age to the heat of another summer's day. Peter's stiffness earned from a night spent propped against a tree surprises him. If he is void of mortal flesh like Scott said, what is left to ache?

Peter twists around. Reassured, he finds Scott resting nearby. Peter's attention then shifts to the surrounding woodland. In the meadow below, the boot-tall grass part and folds back, betraying a rabbit's stealth in a sea of green. Overhead in the branched canopy, birds drift from limb to limb in an avian chorus, blessing another day. Then soft as the morning's light, four deer on slender, silken legs tiptoe through the carpet of leaves. Their heads flick cautiously side to side. With ears forward, one dear approaches Peter, its nose flaring with each inquisitive taste of the air as though sensing something strange lies nearby. The creature stops so close that Peter feels its warm, moist breath.

Afraid to flick a hair lest he startle the creatures, Peter sits motionless. *why ain't they scareda me? They act like they don't see me.*

In a cold tremor, Peter remembers why the deer are unafraid. They never see, feel, or smell him; he is the transparent spirit of a dead man. The snap of a tree's dead limb scatters the deer. With them flee the woodlands' serenity which momentarily distracted Peter.

Leaping to his feet, he paces, recalling yesterday's decision. Of the three options Scott offered as a future in the spiritual realm: aid others persecuted like Peter, spend eternity in bliss in Sanctuary, or punish the vigilante mob, Peter chose the latter. The sole purpose of Peter's sojourn in this earthly realm will be to avenge his murder.

Rage burns in Peter. *Them powers Scott said he's givin me. Them ones I can use on the bastards that killed me. He never* done tell me what they is, but I want em and I want em now! Time's a wastin.

Kneeling beside Scott, Peter glares at him intently as a bird eyeing a worm. Observing an eyelid twitch, Peter lunges at his prey.

"You up?" he asks.

Scott's eyes pry open.

"You awake?"

"Yes, son, I have . . . "

"Mista Scott, you keep on callin me son. I ain't got me no dad. He done ran off when I was little."

"I apologize if that greeting offends you, Peter. I can simply call you by your name if you wish."

Peter rolls his eyes. We had a minister up at the Baptist Church that used to come see us. He done call me son and it felt kinda good.

"Nawh, I guess it alright. Sorry if I been uppity."

"Not a problem. You have been through a terrible ordeal, and it is only natural to feel stressed. Now, as I was saying, yes I have been awake all night," says Scott.

"Then you must be pretty tired."

"No, I am not. We spirits have no need for sleep. In time, you shall experience this. Unpleasant sensations such as hunger and pain will also vanish."

"Do I git to keep some'a them other 'sensations' like lovin a woman and the feelin of makin water?" a worried Peter asks.

"Yes, though hopefully not at the same time. Our physical sensations and emotions all get tangled together. I *can* say you will retain feelings such as fear, joy, and as you have already discovered, anger. Try not to figure it out; just accept it. More will be revealed as you experience this mystical domain."

"I kinda felt there is no easy answer. But, Mista Scott," says

Peter, his shoulders hunched to his ears emphasizing the urgency, "we *gotta* talk about them powers."

"Of course, but will it wait until after I have had my coffee?"

"Coffee? You got coffee?"

Scott's fingers snap. A campfire materializes. On the ring of stones circling the blaze sits a blackened metal pitcher. Steam swirls from the spout. Two tin mugs wait nearby.

"How you do that?"

"Oh, just one of my little privileges. In time you will be allowed to conjure up material objects, but not yet," says Scott while Peter boils in his juices of anticipation. "Well, are you going to pour us a cup or not?"

Peter runs to the fire, desiccated leaves crying underfoot. About to grab the handle, he hesitates.

"Go ahead," says Scott, "it will not burn. Remember, you are *nothing* so there is *nothing* for the heat to scorch. That goes for freezing cold or anything that might harm a mortal."

Emboldened, Peter grabs the handle, filling the cups.

"How come I'm pourin this coffee, but yesterday I couldn't even hold no rope. What happenin?"

"Enjoy your drink. We will discuss that later."

They sit with crossed legs sipping the hot brew. Propped against the elm, they survey the rolling hills, green meadows, and woodlands. For the second time this morning, Peter forgets his mission of hate.

"What you grinnin bout?" he asks a smiling Scott.

"Funny, I had to die before I saw the living beauty of this world."

An hour passes when a disturbance climbs from below.

* * *

Two men in conversation on horseback approach side by side. As their voices grow louder, so does Peter's concern.

"Right there. On that big ol limb the other side of the tree. That's where we hung the nigra," says the man whose belly spills over the saddle horn like a gunnysack of lard.

"What'd ya do with the body, Luman?" asks his willow-limb skinny partner.

"Left it hanging for the buzzards."

"So, what happened to it?"

"Some of them darkies from that Baptist Church came out last night and cut im down. They was gonna bury im," says Luman.

"Why didn't ya stop em?"

"A bunch of us was goin to, Slim, but that damn deputy was waitin for us. Drew a gun and said he'd shoot any bastard that tried to stop em."

"Deputy? You mean that Monroe fella?"

"Yeah," sneers Luman, leaning to Slim. "But he ain't gonna be no trouble cause I heard he's leavin town. Only place he gonna find work is where they don't talk American."

Slumping in their saddles, the pair trot downhill.

* * *

Anger cramping his gut, Peter scowls at his benefactor.

"Mista Scott, like I say, them powers you was gonna give me," says Peter, watching the two ride away.

Scott answers with a taciturn stare.

"Mista Scott, it done time!"

"I have already," says Scott, "bestowed your first gift. You picked up the coffee pot. Leaves crackled as you walked. You can now act upon earthly objects."

Peter grabs a weathered limb. Swinging the branch against the elm, it breaks in a sharp snap.

"Yes Suh, I sure can! What other kinda powers you gonna gimme?"

"Give me your hand."

Peter complies. A yowling wind unleashes as tree limbs resembling ghoulish arms flail about in an unholy blessing. The gale subsides, returning the morning's calm.

"What was that?" asks Peter. "I don't feel any different. You sure you gave me those powers?"

"Oh, quite sure."

"Well, what are they?"

"Have you," says Scott, "noticed any difference in your speech?"

"Now that you mention it, yeah," says Peter, his face dropping with the weight of surprise. "I'm talking just like white folks!"

"Yes, but I liked your old dialect. It had a rhythm, a resonance soft on the ear. But since you wanted so desperately to talk like those whom you will victimize, I have granted you that wish."

Peter's eyes narrow. *He's been reading my mind again.*

"You can now speak in all dialects plus every language."

"How's that supposed to help?"

"There are those in the mob whose native tongue is not English. Conversing with them in their language of birth will be much more intimidating for the purposes *you* desire," says Scott.

Like serpents, Peter's lips slither in a grin.

"I have also granted a third capability, a sixth sense that will alert you to the impending death of each vigilante."

"Why do I need that?"

"You shall discover its purpose later. Now for the fourth gift, and I have saved the best for last. You can transform your appearance into whatever living manifestation you wish, from Jesus Christ to a scorpion. These are the four powers—your supernatural abilities. Use them wisely."

Peter's face contracts in sinister contemplation.

"However, there *are* limits to their uses, my son."

"I knew there was a catch."

"Well, we benefactors also have these abilities, gifts, plus more, but even we must restrict their usage. Your use of them, which I presume excludes Santa Claus impersonations, will be limited strictly to the twenty mortals in the mob. You will be permitted only one encounter per mortal, or more appropriately 'victim', and only during this encounter can you use these abilities on them."

"Why all the conditions?" asks Peter, dangling a frown.

"We do not want you rampaging the countryside on some sort of ghoulish joy ride, disturbing the peace and tranquility of the community."

"It's not *rampaging*. I'm seeking justice!"

"Whatever. If these conditions are unacceptable, I can always take back your gifts."

"No, no . . . that's alright."

"The rest of the time, you shall remain in solitude, here, under this elm without the support of family, friends, or spiritual guidance by yours truly. And we shall impose certain movement restrictions to ensure compliance.

"You agreeable to all this?" asks Scott, flashing an interrogating eye.

Though the situation sounds similar to incarceration, Peter doesn't ask about the restrictions. To do so would expose his intentions of non-compliance. So he nods a cautious yes.

"But why are you giving me these 'gifts'? I know you won't like how they're used."

"As your benefactor, I am required to guide you on your spiritual quest. Yes, I know how you shall use them, but I will not judge or force you to take any action. Since you have refused my offers of service, eternal peace, and rebuffed my warnings of retribution, I have granted you the means to pursue your chosen path of reparation. We shall see if the trip pleases you. And keep one thought—not the destination, but the journey is the measure of one's being. I await at journey's end."

Snapping his fingers, Scott disappears.

"Scott? Scott! Don't leave! Not yet!"

Another burst of wind howling through the elm answers Peter's plea.

The day retreats to its black chamber.

Chapter 7

An Inconvenient Request

Night fades into morning's pink bloom.

It was a restless night for Peter in the dark solitude under the elm's hovering arms. As foretold, Peter's need for sleep has vanished. Stirring from his leafy bed, he surveys the surroundings on this second day of his spiritual reality. Gone is the beauty of the woodland scenes touching his eyes, replaced by the myopic obsession of vengeance.

His face warped in a wicked smile, Peter reclines against the trunk. In the senses-numbing night, he focused on one task—recreating the figure, face, and voice of each perpetrator in the twenty-man mob, then burned these memories into his mind.

Hungered by the night's ordeal, Peter seeks retribution's nourishment. In the heightened senses of a beast seeking prey, he scans the road below, the road which delivered him with his tormentors to this place of deathly gloom. Peter hopes that within the dusty thoroughfare from Mineral Point to Potosi, upon which travels family-crammed carriages, buckboards lumbering under heavy loads, lone horsemen, and plodding pedestrians, he will discover *one* of the twenty.

Hours of sharp-eyed patience reward him. A buckboard draped with white canvas approaches from Potosi. In faded red letters, the sideboard advertises BUST MILLING Co. Riding in front, a portly figure spills over the bench seat like an over-filled saucer of custard. Beside him, a twig of a man fights to remain upright, holding the bucking wagon's reins.

"That's them," says Peter aloud, "the two bastards who rode up here last evening." *Yeah, I know just that fat guy joined in the lynching, but to hell with Scott's warning to act only on the twenty. I'm gonna scare the hell out of both of em!*

Ten strides carry Peter through the elm's shadow. The eleventh pushes him beyond the shade. While one arm and then its opposing leg swing into the sunlight, horrified, he watches the appendages shrivel into decaying flesh exposing sinew and bone. He stumbles forward, exposing himself entirely to the hellish luminescence while glaring at the leaf-scattered ground through voids of putrid flesh. The stench of rot strikes his nostrils like sewage shoveled from a sewer. A burning constriction grips his neck. Panic suffocates him. Terrified, his skeletal remains crawl back to the sanctuary of darkness. Peter's accustomed appearance regenerates while the stinking choke of death dissipates.

He backs against the elm, sliding to the ground. A solitude hostage of darkness, Peter rubs his face, trying to drag the images of decay from his mind. *Yeah, Scott said there'd be limits to my movements, but that damn light. He should've told me about the damn light. I wonder what else he "forgot" to say.*

And what *good* are his supernatural abilities if Peter never escapes this prison of leaf and limb? Then he remembers Scott mentioning a sixth sense which would alert Peter to a vigilante's impending demise, allowing Peter to seek his revenge. *Is my "parole" limited to those pending deaths? Okay, but how will I get there? Certainly not through the damned light. And how will I know where?*

The isolation, the lynching's hellish visions, and the decay beyond the elm haunt Peter. And without Scott's soothing hand, Peter's tormented mind has no diversion. A war rages in his soul—loneliness, anger, sorrow. Each fight for control and no prisoners will be taken. They battle under the watchful eye of the supreme commander, fear. Maybe Scott was right. Maybe I was hasty in my thirst for retaliation. Rising from his cushion of bark, slumped in thought, Peter wanders from edge to edge of shadow, desperate as a caged leopard. With a shiver cold as the grave, he stops. What if all of this was just a ruse to punish me?

Peter slides against the trunk. Wrapping his arms around his knees, he pulls them tight against his chest, rocking like an orphaned child. But Peter's self-pity is distracted by the clatter of an approaching wagon, the one with the white canvas. The buckboard climbs the hill, stopping beside him. Flinging off the wagon's canvas, the two riders tug on the cargo in the bed. Their grunts depict a heavy load. Peter strains to see inside, but the horse blocks his view. From the back, something drops, striking the ground, startling the horse. It leaps ahead, yanking the wagon forward, exposing the fallen payload—Peter's corpse.

"Sure don't like none'a this," says Slim. His eyes twist to his partner. "I still can't see no harm in lettin them church folks bury im, Luman. Ya shoulda told me yesterday what ya needed Pa's mill wagon for."

"Like I told ya, if that nigra got buried in a cemetery, they'd give im a service and somethin markin his restin place. That son-a-bitch don't deserve nonna that. That's why me and some'a the boys followed the wagon after they cut im down."

"Is that when the deputy stopped ya sayin he'd shoot ya if ya'll interfered?"

"Yeah," says Lumen followed by a chuckle, "but we just hid outta sight, waitin. We was gonna dig im back up but got lucky when they put im in the barn. We heard they was gonna bury im next mornin so his *mamma* could watch. Hell! That ol deputy stood guard so we just took turns watchin *him*. And sure nough, he went asleep. Hah! I'd give anythin to've seen that nigra lover's face when he found the wagon empty in the mornin!"

"If Pa finds out I took the wagon, he's gonna beat the hell outta me!"

"Don't worry your skinny ass! I didn't tell ya none of this cause I knew ya wouldn't keep ya mouth shut."

Luman yanks a soiled white bandana from his trousers and coils the cloth around his head. He grabs two shovels from the wagon. Throwing one to his partner, he waddles to a location on the other side of the elm, stabs his shovel in the ground, and gouges out a slice of earthly flesh.

"We're gonna bury the bastard right here where we hung im," says Luman, glaring at Slim. "Well?"

Resembling dogs digging for a bone, both men fling dirt aside until the grave is two feet deep.

Watching the pair labor, Peter drops to his knees beside a decaying pile of limbs and lowers his head, retching dry vomit. *Scott didn't warn me about this anymore than he did the damn sunlight! Leaving me here, all alone, watching these bastards. It's more than I can bear. Friend? Benefactor? Hell! Wait til I see him again! He's no better than those two damn grave diggers!*

Other than the tarp they wrapped to conceal the corpse's manhood, Luman and Slim would have treated a skunk's carcass with more reverence. They drag and kick the body into the hole, gloating at the half-naked cadaver face down in the pit.

"Next time we'll have em dig their own," says Luman, wiping his face with the bandana, then flips open his watch. "Right on time. Takin the missus to that church social this afternoon."

"Dogs gonna dig im up. Shoulda dug it deeper," says Slim, backfilling the grave.

"Don't matter. Ain't like he's white."

"Folks gonna smell im."

"They ain't gonna come way up here lookin," says Luman. "They'll figure its justa another dead animal, and rightly so."

Grinning with satisfaction, the burial party leaves.

The horror tears Peter's soul, but in a way, he is glad the spectacle happened. The doubt and self-pity that has held him captive flees faster than deer scattered by a thunder's roar. Rather than a mound of sacrilege, the grave, with the decaying flesh and bone, shall be a monument to his vengeance.

In the pile of branches next to Peter, something dark and shiny crawls, trapping his attention. He leans closer inspecting a webbed maze of sinewy white. In the fibrous cloud wriggles the eight-legged form of a black widow spider crouching still as death, protecting a silky nest of eggs. Snagged in the web hangs a comatose mummy, the twisting, white-crusted casket of a recent prey. Peter stares at the spider, fascinated by the sight, and swears an oath: *I will endure this fate, nurturing my revenge with the same patience of this spider. From this elm's shadowy hell, I swear to punish my prey—all twenty in that murderous gang. I will stalk them, shroud them in a nightmare of unspeakable torment, and watch with glee as they writhe in horror in their final moments of death. I don't know how, I don't know when, but it shall come to pass.*

Thus begins Peter's exile.

* * *

Time ebbs slow as the elm's limbs lengthen with age. Through empty winter nights and then heavy summer afternoons, Peter crouches in solitude. He dares not leave the elm's protection even in darkness for fear of what retribution awaits. However, certain the web of time will eventually ensnare his victims, he bids his time, ready to snare his prey, then suck retribution's nourishment.

Cloaked in darkness by a malevolent force rejecting the light of day, Peter's dwelling assumes the appearance of a spider's den.

It consists of a burrow scratched out of the earth by a single claw, leaving a sunken, plowed hollow. A sticky, white web lines the depression to which clings a carpet of dead leaves, grasses, and debris. Overhead, shielding winter's sun or errant rays of summer light, hangs a silken cocoon heaped with detritus. Something unclean and demonic dwells herein. Through Peter's fourth power, the ability to alter his appearance, a metamorphosis driven by his hostile subconscious has transformed him. He has reshaped himself into the fanged, eight-legged horror of a black widow spider. Large as a grizzly when reared on hind legs, the hardened black form crouches in the eternal darkness. On its abdomen, the mark of a red hourglass throbs with hate.

The Beast is born!

* * *

1918

Never missing a day, The Beast spies through four pairs of eyes upon the parade of travelers on the road. The procession includes a scattering of the former twenty vigilantes. As nearly two decades pass, The Beast notices a change. Unlike the girth of their waist, the frequency of the vigilante transits diminishes. The prance of their passage decays to a shuffle, except for those in black, horseless carriages. But on this cold, November morning, the traffic, busier than usual, heads to Potosi to celebrate the end of the Great War.

Then he feels something, a pulsing awareness in his consciousness followed by a vibration throughout The Beast's bony hide. The web of time has ensnared a victim, someone from the mob is near death, the first one! By some transfiguration of time and distance, the demonic, stick-legged phantom discovers itself standing in a dim, foul-smelling lane between two brick buildings. Dancing with ecstasy, The Beast scurries about, rejoicing in the freedom. The creature does not understand what authority released it, how it avoided the light's decay, or how long this liberation will last, but the black apparition is here, intending to act quickly. Crouched against one wall, the creature feels the pulsating sensation again. Eyes cast to a second-story window, the black-hulled beast shudders with joy. *He's up there!*

From the alley, the spider crawls to the window, peering inside a dingy, one-room apartment. An old man sleeps in a disordered bed. The eight-eyed nightmare lifts the window's sash, crawls inside, and to the pecking of claws upon the wooden floor, sneaks towards the bed. Reaching the prey, the spider rises on its hind legs exposing its underbelly's red mark of scorn. Then shrinking, it curls into a protective black ball crouching on the floor. From this coiled mass, the figure of a man arises—Peter reincarnated in human form clothed in the ankle-length, black gown of a priest wrapped by a scarlet waistband.

In the pale green room above a cold, ash-piled fireplace, hangs a soot-stained wooden mantel over which a pendulum wall clock strikes 7:00 p.m. Wilting on the mantel, five faded, yellow carnations sag in a waterless glass jar. Next to the floral blemish, stands a greeting card:

Happy Birthday Great Grandad!
Your loving great-granddaughter, Brenda

Against the wall, next to the card, leans an unopened envelope marked:

To Marvin—Happy 83rd

Peter surveys the setting. *What a pleasant death scene. Sure beats the hell out of mine.*

Stooping, he studies the dying man whose rutted face age has sucked into an ashen prune. Slowly, Peter's eyes widen in recognition, hardly believing in his good fortune. The expiring form lying before him is the eldest member and leader of the lynch mob, the one whom Peter has hated with hell's fury: Marvin Boyers— The Accuser!

My years of isolation and deprivation have at last rewarded me!

Then, in the void of the room, a voice can be heard.

"Peter . . . "

Staring in the summons' direction, Peter finds nothing.

"Peter . . . " again calls the phantom voice, reverberating with a strange familiarity.

"Who's there?"

At the foot of the bed, a human-shaped form materializes. Silence holds its breath as Peter scowls at a long-absent apparition, the benefactor named Scott.

"After all this time, what the hell do *you* want?" asks Peter, flaming with rejection from years of unanswered prayers for his benefactor's return.

"I do not fault your displeasure of seeing me, but I . . . "

Peter refuses to let this intruder cajole him.

"Checking up on me?" he asks. "Making sure I follow the rules of engagement? Or are you here hoping to change my mind, spare this mortal from his appointment with hell? Well, my friend, forget it! I've waited *nineteen years* for this, and I'm damned well gonna administer *my* kind of last rites to this son-of-a-bitch!"

"My, my, a devil in priest's clothing. Proud of your reverent deception? Not very original, but I am certain your deceit will have its intended results."

A pang of conscience only briefly stiffens Peter's tongue.

"Damnit! *This* was the deal, payback, Scott. Remember, *you* gave me the means to do it!"

"Relax, *Father*, I am not here to interfere with your blessed sacraments. But I must admit, your priestly appearance is quite a transformation from that which crawled through the window."

So, he's been here waiting all along, but if Scott expects an apology for my actions, forget it.

"And speaking of 'transformation', why the hell," asks Peter, "didn't you tell me about that damned sunlight?"

"Oh, yes, that. Well, I did warn you not to venture from the elm."

"You would've made a great snake in the Garden of Eden."

"You poor soul," says Scott. "All this fret and worry. But I *did* keep my word. Here you are wreaking torment on your first victim."

"It's *not* tormenting! I'm seeking justice!"

"Oh yes, I forgot. And how is this 'justice' thing going? Is it bringing you great joy?"

Peter does not answer. His eyes wander about the room, settling on the wall clock. Its pendulum hangs motionless at the far end of a swing.

"I see you're still up to your old tricks of slowing time."

"Yes, old habits are hard to break. But I needed to calm things down, so we could talk. I bring bad news, my son."

"So do *I*," says Peter, eyeing the dying man.

Scott sighs…

"You remember years ago when I told you Deputy Monroe would suffer an early death?"

An old image flashes in Peter's mind, the image of Deputy Monroe on bent knees, sobbing before Peter's hanging body. But I remember something else Scott said years ago about the deputy's deeds, ". . . with time, you will not be so forgiving . . . "

"Yeah, so what about im?" asks Peter.

"Well, he lies dying in an old shack, crying out your name. I have come to take you to him."

"What can *I* do?"

"You can help him. Remember how you cried out near your own death, and I helped you?"

"*That* remains to be seen," says Peter, turning to stare out the window. "What happened to Monroe?"

"Nineteen years of unrelenting guilt. He wants your forgiveness."

"Forgiveness?"

"Yes. Forgiveness for his failure to protect you from the mob."

Peter's gaze through the glass panes continues.

"He," says Scott, "was a pawn in the eternal contest of duty. Duty that subrogates conscience for obedience. Duty that makes boys run into the valley of death, bullied by flags demanding their blood. When Monroe left the train with you, he should have taken you to safety somewhere far away and set you free. He knew you would never receive a fair trial and rues his actions. He has had to live with this for nineteen years, buried under a mountain of guilt, drowning in a river of whiskey."

"So, what am *I* supposed to do?" Peter asks.

"Honor the robe you wear and go to him. Let Monroe die in peace. Show *him* the same compassion and love he showed to *you*, weeping beside your body."

The pendulum resumes its swing, announcing time's impatient return.

"We must hurry!" says Scott, extending his hand. "His end nears."

"But what about *him*? I only get one visit," says Peter, nodding at the old man.

"This one time, you can return."

"But what if he dies before I return?"

Peter steps back, his face contorted in indecision. He looks down at The Accuser, then up at the beckoning hand . . .

Chapter 8

The Shack

1918

Within the ramshackle, Black community of Pig Nose, there live maids, laborers, and aging former slaves. The residents know well of the gray-haired white man dwelling in the sunbaked shack on the town's outskirts, a former deputy sheriff, Louis Monroe. The Black citizens sheltered him one night a month ago when he staggered drunk into town after being outcasted from a nearby settlement. But unlike neighboring white laborers celebrating the end of another week in the mines, his intoxication was birthed from regret. Pig Nose was just another lull in his Missouri wanderings. Cleaning latrines, sweeping bars, or worse, Monroe has performed any demeaning labor that would buy the next drink to oblivion.

To white society, Monroe's notoriety of befriending the Black murderer of a white man preceded him like the stench of a corpse. But to Pig Nose, he bore the fragrance of honeysuckle. Patiently with love, the residents have sheltered him in the shack as an honored family member. Four men have taken turns watching him. During the past month, day and night, someone has been by his side—his first friendly companionship in years. Warm as a robin under a spring sun, he has basked in the glow of their fellowship. They have bathed, fed, and clothed him. As they have tended to his exile from privileged civilization, they have watched the blossom of his life wither until today when they have sent for a doctor. But Monroe's stained reputation, the November storm, plus today's drunken celebrations of the Great War's end, have conspired against the arrival of medical aid. So they summoned a man of the cloth as they prayed for the clergy's appearance.

Shaking from the barrage of gale and thunder, the spindly shack moans under the elements' siege. The odor of damp earth rises from its dirt floor. In a corner opposite the one-room dwelling's single window, the four caretakers huddle around a pot-belly stove. Its stubborn flames assault the cold while blistering the wall. In the opposite corner, a straw bed cradles the dying deputy. Unaware to those inside, a figure stands in the storm peeking through the window.

* * *

Monroe, shaking and wrapped in a patchwork quilt stitched from tattered clothing, talks to a vacant bedside chair. For an hour, the feverous man's babbling competes with the wind whistling through the weather-bent siding.

Huddled around the stove, the caretakers converse about Monroe:

"That poor son-a-bitch. I know he cain't help that gabberin, but Lawd, he spookin me. He got me ta feelin like a hen in the chicken hut knowin the fox's outside."

"Yeah, I'm feelin fidgety too. All his askin bout when that Peter fella gonna git here."

"Peter? Ain't he that colored they hung? The one Mista Monroe done tried ta help?"

The others nod yes as their ward's delusion mumbles on.

"An the way he talkin ta that chair like some damn ghost sittin in it. I hope they gonna find that preacher and get im here quick."

Hours pass and as daylight fades, so does hope for a parson's appearance. Exhausted by delirium, Monroe falls into a deep slumber.

The caretakers decide that two of them, Abner and Theodore, should spend the night watching Monroe. After the others leave, the two drag stools to the stove, then sweat in the fever of its iron-encased flames.

"I sure hope he ain't gonna be fussin all night," says Abner, yawning. "We all need ta git some sleep."

Limp as candles in summer's heat, the pair slump forward in slumber. An hour passes when a coherent voice awakens them, yanking their attention to the bed. In it, they see Monroe upright and engaged in lucid chatter with the empty seat.

Noticing the pair's wide-eyed surveillance, Monroe stops his one-sided dialogue.

"Good evening, gentlemen," he says.

Jaws sagging in astonishment, the two stare at the resurrected man.

"Excuse my manners, but I haven't introduced you to my friend. Abner, Theo, this is Scott," says Monroe nodding at the empty chair. He then leans close to it. "These are two of the colored gentlemen I told you about, the ones who've been takin care of me."

Outside, the figure at the window chuckles.

With owls' eyes, the caretakers gape at each other, then at the vacant seat.

"Pleased to meet ya, Mista Scott," says Theodore, flashing a dishonest grin. "Any frienda Mista Monroe is a friend of us."

Theodore leans close to Abner.

"Least we know that there ghost's got a name. Ya know, Abner, I seen this kinda thing before in dyin folk. All the sudden, they'll git ta like ain't nothin the matter with em and git ta seein spirits of dead folk. I wonder if this Scott fella is some kinda relation? Why I remember once when one'a my . . .

"Hush, Theo! Ya want im to hear?"

"Yessuh, Mista Monroe, you sure lookin good," says Theodore, shuffling to the bed.

Monroe points to the chair.

"Yeah, Theo," says Monroe, a smile rising on his face, "with Scott touching my shoulder, I'm feeling much better. An he says company's comin."

"What kinda company?"

"Someone I've been thinkin about for a long time. Someone I've gotta talk to."

"That real nice ya got company callin," says Theodore, rolling his eyes at Abner.

Patronizing their ward, Theodore lights two kerosene lamps. Abner stokes the stove.

Monroe props himself higher. Through his scattered-hay hair, he runs his fingers, pulling the quilt taut. Trusting as a child expecting Santa, his eyes dance about the room, stop at the door, and then wait.

* * *

Though the determined storm howls, the figure at the window has heard every word. *Am I gonna have some fun with this!*

Creeping to the door, the stranger announces his arrival with a battering knock. To those inside, the commotion is due to the weather's assault. The door bursts open exposing a robed man standing outside and surrendering the folks inside to nature's fury. Abruptly, the storm's intrusion halts. In the lamps' yellow glow, all eyes strain at the stranger—a priest, but not *any* priest—a *Black* priest wrapped in a scarlet waistband.

"Someone call?" asks the priest.

With the hush of scared rabbits, the caretakers gawk at the visitor who, though standing in the rain, is dry as the stove's empty teakettle.

"Where'd the hell *he* come from?" says Abner, inching closer to Theodore.

"Damned if I know. I was expectin one'a our own reverends, not one'a them priests. An he's *colored*! Ain't never seen me no *colored* priest before."

The robed man grabs the scene with a hungry gaze.

"By the looks of that gentleman in bed, I've arrived at the right place. May I enter?"

"Beg ya pardon, Father. Please come on in," says Abner.

The priest steps inside. As the wind resumes its intrusion he turns, leans against the door, and slams it against the howling phantom. Straightening his robe while brushing his hair, he walks over to the bed, staring at Monroe through eyes of burning coal.

"How come you ain't all wet?" asks Abner, inspecting the reverent from the hem of his ankle-length gown to the white collar pinching his neck.

"I have the Lord for an umbrella, my child."

"Somethin ain't right about this guy," whispers Abner to Theodore.

With the demeanor of an undertaker inspecting a corpse, the priest hovers over the quilt-covered man.

Monroe's face expands in bewilderment. His straw mattress rustles like windblown leaves as he shoves himself from the intruder's prying eyes.

"Hello, Louis. I see you're in good hands," says the priest, and nodding at the bedside chair he adds, "Hi Scott."

Abner nods at the exit. Theodore nods at Abner. Both shuffle sideways to the door.

"How come you know my name?" asks Monroe.

"We've met before, a long time ago."

The caretakers' shuffle hastens.

"Now that you mention it, yeah, you *do* look familiar."

"It was on a train," says the priest.

Monroe's face drops in opened-mouth astonishment.

"I remember. Y . . . You're . . . "

"That's right deputy, I'm Peter!"

With synchronized cries, the caretakers tumble over each other in an avalanche of terror. They careen into the night, arms flailing with the chaos of tattered canvas in a gale.

"Must've been something I said," chuckles Peter.

Pleased by events even at the expense of his Black brothers' sanity, Peter shuts the door. But seeing tears in Monroe's eyes, he restrains his humor.

"You all right, Louis?" asks Scott, breaking his silence.

"Yeah," says Monroe, wiping away tears. "Peter, I can't believe it's you! I've waited *so* long. You've come to hear my confession and as a priest. I knew Scott would find you!"

Scott's grip on Monroe tightens.

"Must admit though," says Monroe, "haven't seen your likes before. Every priest I've seen's been white."

"Prejudice doesn't stop at the sanctuary door. But I must caution you, Louis, I'm *not* what I appear to be."

"So, you went and got religion, a man of the cloth. Must say I'm proud you've done somethin with *your* life," says Monroe, his voice trailing off. "I haven't . . . "

"I've done *nothing* with my *life*, Louis. Remember? The mob, hanging in the tree . . . I'm dead!"

"Bless me, Father, for I have sinned. It's been nineteen years since my last confession."

"Louis, you're not listening. I *can't* hear your confession."

"Why not?"

"Because I'm not a real priest!"

"Then why the robe, the white collar?"

"The man," says Scott, "*has* a valid question, Peter. You could have appeared tonight as anyone—beggar man, doctor, Indian chief. Why a priest?"

Silence answers as Peter stares out the window at the storm. *Why the hell did I agree to come here? I could be, should be, back in the apartment with The Accuser completing my act of justice.*

"Damnit, I *really* thought you'd hear my confession. I must've been a fool," says Monroe.

He pushes Scott's hand away. Without the healing touch, Monroe crumples on the bed.

"At least let me die in peace!"

Peter and Scott lock eyes in guilty stares.

Outside, the storm heaves a jagged spear of light which drags a barrage of thunder behind. The hut shudders. Dust sifts from the rafters.

"Peter," says Scott. "I think we owe this man an apology."

Grabbing a stool, Peter sits by the bed.

"Why *are* you really here?" asks Monroe with a voice barely above a breath.

"Good question," says Peter, drawing a deep breath. "Let's start over. Scott said you wanted to confess something. So do I. Louis, I didn't want to come here, but Scott insisted. You're not an evil man. I believe the things you did that day on the train were not done out of hatred for me. But standing out there in the storm, I came to realize I held a deep resentment against you. Though I'm not proud of it, I wanted revenge. I knew a confession to the illusion of a priest would soften your pain. But I wanted you to *feel* the pain, the same *pain* I've suffered at your hands. So that's why I entered disguised as a priest. That's why I refused to hear your confession."

Remorse twists Monroe's face. Scott extends his hand. Monroe eagerly accepts. Immediately he gains strength as death allows one last burst of flame.

"I regret," says Monroe, "not doing more to protect you. That's what I wanted to confess and to ask your forgiveness. Dear God, I wish I could've gotten you to jail safe!"

"Yeah, you say that's what bothering you, but *protecting* me *wasn't* the problem. I was 'guilty' of *defending* myself, not murder. On the train you even admitted it."

"Yeah, but I had my duty to bring you to jail and stand trial. I thought I treated you fair, no different than if you were a white man."

"*That's* the problem. You *thought* of me as a white man!"

"So?"

"I'm colored, damnit! I was born into slavery. My people have been persecuted all their lives. We've been lynched, remember? And good-intentioned white folks like you think you're doin us a favor by acting like we're white. But that 'white' thinking is just a delusion to escape the reality of injustice, so you can do your 'duty' with a clear conscience. Because I *was* colored, it wouldn't have made a damn if an *army* was protecting me. They would've simply been escorting a corpse-in-waiting. Jail, trial, innocent or not, I was doomed. Your color blindness lynched me as surely as that mob!"

Monroe's torrent of tears reveals his anguish.

"Go ahead, Louis," says Scott, tightening his grip, "you have come this far . . . admit it. You will not die in peace until you do."

"God help me, my duty," says Monroe as though the words were profane. "You're right! All I was concerned about was gettin you to jail, safe. Deep down I *knew* you wouldn't get a fair trial. You'd be dead in a week, all legal of course. But I couldn't admit my part in this evil, how could I? I was a deputy, sworn to uphold the *law*—the *law*, justice, that was my *life*. I should've never put you on the train. *No!* I should've helped you *escape!* I, Louis Monroe, could have saved an innocent man! Better to've broken the law than damn my soul. Peter, *that's* why I drank; that's how I've come to *this*."

Exhausted, Monroe collapses in his bed.

"But you know, I am grateful for somethin," says Monroe, taking Peter's hand.

"What's that?"

"For these kind people who took me in. I'm sure some of *them* felt I was just a willin part of the injustice that killed you. But look what they did. I'm goin to die in this warm bed surrounded by carin folks. Without them, I'd be lyin in some ditch, dead and alone, outcast by my own kind. Strange, I had to stumble like a blind man through the fires of hell to find these blessings. And Peter, thank *you*."

"Thank me?"

"Yeah, for comin here and tellin me the truth I didn't want to hear. Someday I hope you'll forgive me, if not for my sake, for yours. I'll pray that you'll find peace and forgive yourself. Maybe you can pray the same for me."

Exhausted from its blowing rage, the midnight storm exhales a timid breath. Monroe's eyes close as he descends into eternal slumber . . . the final transition.

Chapter 9

Black Shell of Armor

Peter has just returned from the shack. Standing in a corner of The Accuser's apartment, he leans against a wall. The clock on the mantel chimes 4:00 a.m. as his hand twists the crimson waistband around his cassock. Peter has returned alone to complete his "visit" with the dying man. A grunt from the apartment's bed reassures Peter that his victim has not expired in his absence.

Memories of the past eight hours echo in Peter's mind. His confrontation with Monroe about the deputy's false sense of duty to the law rather than to justice reassured Peter. But feelings of remorse, plus doubt more corrosive than the daylight that rots his flesh, plague his thoughts.

It's not my fault Monroe committed a slow suicide by drinking and was outcasted and despised by his own white folks. White folk, huh? They're crazy. They hate us colored so much that they'll hurt themselves to keep us in our place. Take Thornton. Did he really think I was going to just stand there and let him carve me up like a Sunday roast? Did Monroe really think I'd forgive him after everything I'd been through? Hiding behind his badge, pursuing his precious duty, and asking God's blessing that I forgive myself. Forgive myself for what, my crusade for justice? Then the gall to ask me to pray for him. Don't need any damn blessing, prayers, and sure as hell don't need God!

Hours pass. As the horizon glows red announcing the sunrise, Peter closes the drapes on the room's one window. He wants no errant ray of light to disturb his long-awaited encounter.

Breaking the morning's deadlock of silence, the mantel clock chimes 9:00 a.m. Footsteps in the apartment building's hallway announce the approach of The Accuser's great-granddaughter, Brenda, alongside her husband. The steps grow louder, ceasing when knocks rattle the door.

"Marvin, can we come in?" asks Brenda.

Staring at the entry, Peter's expression tightens in expectation. *Looks like things are getting interesting.*

The doorknob rattles. More pounding.

"Marvin, it's me, Brenda. Please unlock the door."

"Honey, I think he's too weak to get up. I'll go down and get the keys," says the husband. Fading footsteps echo behind the door.

Sliding a chair beside The Accuser, Peter sits. He glances at the door through eyes twinkling in menacing delight. *How sweet to have family in one's final moments.*

"Marvin . . . Marvin . . . Time to wake up," he says gently, shaking the bed.

"Someone in there with you?" asks Brenda.

Weathered as the room's sun-bleached curtains, The Accuser's eyelids rise, revealing the twilight of his fading moments. Curious, he squints at the smiling, Black priest.

"Marvin, please tell your friend to open the door."

"I'll be right there," says Peter.

Opening the door, he shakes Brenda's hand. Peter introduces himself as Father Johnson, explaining Marvin is a parishioner in his congregation.

In a wordless stare, Brenda greets the priest.

"If you'd be so kind as to give your beloved and me a few more moments," says Peter, slamming, then relocking the door before Brenda can respond.

"Thank . . . thank you for coming, Father," she shouts through the wooden barrier. "Will you be much longer?"

"Patience, my child," says Peter, then sits with the leisure that nineteen years of waiting deserve.

Deaf to the conversations, the old man continues to inspect the black-robed stranger.

"Who are you?" he asks.

"I'm Father Johnson."

The Accuser's eyes blink in increasing alertness.

"Father, you about finished with Marvin?" asks Brenda.

"Someone at the door?" asks The Accuser.

"Just some folks passing by."

The Accuser asks for his glasses. From a bed stand, upon which also rests a Bible beside a hand mirror, Peter retrieves the spectacles. His vision focused, surprise bloats The Accuser's face.

"Jesus, You're colored!"

Grabbing the hand mirror, Peter looks at himself.

"Son-of-a-bitch . . . you're right!"

"What the hell you doin here!"

"I've come to give you the Last Rites."

"Couldn't find the keys, Honey," says the husband, followed by a rattle of indistinguishable words. "You gotta be kidding. A *colored* priest in there with *him*?"

"Get your colored ass outta here! No nigra priest gonna give me Last Rites!"

A man's thundering slams shake the door.

"Open up!"

"No final blessing? Okay, Marvin, have it *your* way," says Peter, leaning forward, his face transforming into the grotesque, twisted image of a lynched man's face. "Remember me?"

Fear bleaching his face, The Accuser slowly recognizes the horror before him—the Black man he had lynched years earlier.

Smiling, Peter inches back, his body morphing into The Beast. It rears back on two hind legs, exposing the abdomen's red hourglass, previously the priest's crimson sash. Six other legs fail about. The top pair gouge shards of wood from the planked ceiling. Splinters rain to the floor. The Accuser's mouth stretches to shriek, but death grips him by the throat. From the dark void between weathered lips, not a sound escapes. Eyes dimming, he gapes at the ghastly apparition. The Beast leans down to the bed.

"You gonna burn in the fires of hell," it says softly into the dying man's ear.

Gleaming, The Beast watches The Accuser writhe in terror, fading into gray as though some dark force is sucking life's fluid from the old man's veins. Then . . . all is still.

The door bursts into fragments. The husband falls through. Jumping to his feet, he races to the bed, wooden scraps from the door and ceiling crunching under his boots.

"No priest in here!" he says to his wife in the hallway.

Brenda hesitates, then enters the silence, viewing the hideous form of Marvin. His dead eyes glare into eternity from a face twisted by terror's hand. From his gaping mouth protrudes a gray, swollen tongue. Wailing in despair, Brenda throws herself over the body. A final groan rattles from the dead man's lungs. Raising her head, she strokes the dead man's hair.

"I don't know what kinda priest would do such a thing. They're supposed to comfort the dying," she says, closing Marvin's eyes and kissing his cheek. "He wasn't perfect. But without his help, after my father died, I would've gone to an orphanage. Goodbye, my beloved great-grandfather."

Invisibly curled in a black ball in a room's corner, the eight-legged specter watches, its ecstasy of revenge tempered by Brenda's love. The next instant, The Beast stands in the shade of the elm.

* * *

Pleased by the late morning's cool breeze, the elm rustles with delight at Peter's return. In the form of The Beast, he scratches about the den, then curls his eight legs into a protective sphere. His thoughts twitch like a dying cockroach, disturbed by recent unexplainable acts of kindness: the care of Deputy Monroe by the Black citizens of Pig Nose; Monroe's blessing that he, Peter, find peace, and Brenda's display of affection for her murdering great grandad, The Accuser.

Are deeds of tolerance, of love, threatening The Beast's vengeance? Panicked, it scurries to the nearby crude cross of limbs marking its mortal remains. Still haunted by the laughter of the two men digging the shallow pit, The Beast's head pounds with their joyous scorn like a blacksmith's hammer on flaming iron. The creature looks back at the elm where Peter was lynched while a mortal, cheered on by hundreds of spectators. No love, no acts of kindness there.

The Beast *must* steel its determination and cast off all doubt, just as a priest exorcises an evil spirit. Retribution must remain inflexible as my black shell of armor until every vigilante in the mob pays for their sin!

* * *

1986

Years creep past. The Beast watches the changing world from its silken sanctuary atop the knoll. Every day, it spies on the road below used eighty-seven years ago by the lynch mob. No longer announcing the passage of patrons with a dusty explanation, the thoroughfare now wears a black carpet of asphalt. Gone are buggies and horse-backed men, all replaced with sleek, gleaming carriages galloping faster than any horse.

An occasional newspaper, which Peter long ago discovered he could read, entangles itself in the den. These chance connections with events beyond his webbed confinement speak of turbulent times. Mankind, enamored with the First World War, decides to have another. Lynchings slowly subside, replaced by the Holocaust. Race riots, assassinations, and global warming take their sequential places in the news. The Beast finds the monotony of the burrow preferable to such diversions. But through the mortal turmoil, there remains one constant, a compass leading The Beast's journey, the true north of vengeance. One by one, the men of the vigilante mob suffer their final transition. Each time, that unmistakable vibration arouses The Beast. Each time, the summons is answered. Each time, the specter appears before the dying, oozing an odor of rotting flesh while entangling them in a web of torment. Some feign remorse, begging for forgiveness, but forgiveness The Beast shall *never* give. To its delight, others curse The Beast's manipulation of their psyche so that even the most hateful feel the full slash of this Grim Reaper's sickle. Through each act of terror, The Beast's specter grows more hideous, reeking with the stench of accumulated hate.

Finally, that special day arrives. Sixty-eight years have passed since its revenge upon The Accuser. This morning, The Beast feels the familiar tingle announcing another's death. Although all twenty of the vigilante mob have died, one more still awaits judgment— the boy in the tree.

The boy, now ninety-four, has twenty-five grandchildren and fifteen great-grandchildren. While serving as a Missouri U.S. Congressional Senator, he was regarded as a champion of the oppressed. His bronze statue dominates Barkersville City Park, bragging of years in public service. Some say the senator was *too* good, like one obsessed with restitution for a secret sin. But what about that photograph of the cap-waving boy on a limb over a lynched Black man, the photograph so treasured by the young-ster's father?

Long ago, after the boy left home and the father died, the pic-ture was demoted from the place of honor on the boy's bedroom dresser and exiled to a steamer chest lost in the parents' attic. The senator's name is Bartholomew Cummings; Bart to his friends. In the senator's living room, seventeen family members wait. Some have traveled far to be near his side. Four at a time, they sit in the bedroom beside Bart. He awaits his passing in a four-poster, ma-hogany bed which he shared beside his wife for fifty-seven years. The family minister keeps vigil in a corner of the room, certain Bart will never see midnight.

Shoeless visitors come and leave Bart's side. Older than the dying man it supports, the floor moans under the heavy load of caring relatives. The noise visits the floral wallpaper soaring high to the white-planked ceiling, then descends to the floor, beginning the journey again. The cranky boards announce all visitors.

"I heard that," says Bart, smiling with his eyes closed.

"Sorry if we woke you, Greatpa," answers a youngster on tip-toes.

Through a window, manicured roses and hedges surrender their conceited display in the evening's twilight. Into this scene, mate-rializes The Beast. It stands invisible at the foot of the bed, the floor groaning under the specter's weight. The Beast has practiced this maneuver countless times; the scheme works best when the dying are resting peacefully.

"Darling . . . Darling," says the black spirit in the soft, reassur-ing voice of Bart's deceased wife.

Slowly Bart opens his eyes, perplexed by the voice he has not heard in fourteen years. As The Beast hovers near, Bart stares into the eight, yellow eyes. The stench of death overpowers the old man. His bed shakes in dread.

"Remember me?" says the feminine voice decaying into an unearthly moan. "I'm that colored man you watched kicking at the end of the rope."

Fear bleaches Bart's complexion to an ashen gray as he watches The Beast transform into the tortured image of a noosed man suffocating to death. But, to The Beast's amazement, Bart fails to react like others in the mob. For years, Bart has heard rumors swirl among friends and families of deceased vigilantes, vigilantes who near death, experienced hallucinations concerning a ghost they called Peter. The color of Bart's terror changes to a flush of curiosity.

"Peter?" Bart asks the apparition.

Knowing the end is near, relatives surround the bed, deaf and blind to the phantom.

"Dad, who's Peter?" asks one daughter.

"I've been expecting you," Bart says to The Beast. "I have a confession for you and all in this room to hear."

Listening in disbelief to their loved one's declaration, those present gasp, as does The Beast.

"Never," says Bart, "has a day in my life passed that I haven't thought of that terrible day of your lynching. I'm sorry for my part in it. Please forgive me and all of us in the mob for the pain and suffering we inflicted. I've spent my life making amends, but I can't take back the injustice you've suffered. Thank you for coming so I can tell you in person. Since I am the last of the mob to die, I hope you may finally find peace. May God have mercy on us both."

The Beast stands dumbfounded, shaking with unsatiated expectation.

"Who's that behind you?" asks Bart.

Feeling a hand touch its bony hide, The Beast yanks around, seeing Scott.

"Peter," says Scott, "you can leave now. I shall take Mr. Cummings from here, and thank you for allowing him to exit this world, finally at peace."

Having wreaked the final revenge, The Beast again finds itself in the solitude of the elm. But something is amiss. That euphoria I should feel after nearly nine decades of pursuing justice has vanished like hope at the gallows. In circles, it scurries about the den, until dizzy with defiance, doubt, and discontent, the spider collapses into a protective black ball.

Chapter 10

Intruders

In accustomed isolation, The Beast crouches under the elm. Overhead, the sun hovers midway in its daily arc. Almost four days have passed since The Beast visited the dying senator, Bartholomew Cummings. During this time, a cancerous contradiction has consumed The Beast's thoughts. *Instead of tormenting Bart, my appearance eased the dying man's suffering and filled him with a sense of closure and peace. But aren't I supposed to feel that sense of bliss? After all, Bart was the last to be tormented, the conclusion of my eighty-seven-year pilgrimage of reprisal. So why is my hate as intense now as the first day in my journey of retribution?*

The Beast, to its surprise, tingles with a subtle fear of hate's formidable potential. Hate had consumed every thought, every emotion. Hate kept him prisoner under this tree. Hate turned Peter into The Beast. Absent a mob to stalk, whom or what will now be the victim of hate's unleashed fury?

A distant twig's snap announces an intruder. The Beast skitters to the edge of the shade. Rearing on its hind legs, the black apparition peers down the knoll. Three people approach—a Black couple in their mid-twenties, holding a picnic basket between them, and an adolescent boy ahead, flinging rocks into the surrounding trees at curious onlooking birds.

For years, The Beast has detoured intruders with flashes of its silhouette sneaking along the ridge followed by utterances of bizarre shrills. Rumors of these odd occurrences crept through the community. The knoll came to be known as Phantom Ridge. And though the year is 1986, the title still lingers, leaving most intrusions to happenstance and juvenile rites of passage. Time has not dulled The Beast's zealous defense of this isolation, but something about this trio is intriguing. The Beast, fading into transparency, climbs the elm and huddling in a tangled mass of limbs, waits and watches.

* * *

"Jerome, you sure we otta be goin way up there?" asks the slender woman. "They say somethin spooky livin up there."

Beads of perspiration seep from her braided hair as they trudge uphill. Releasing the basket, she grabs Jerome's arm, gazing up into her lover's angular face of delicately chiseled coal.

"They's nothin to be worryin about, Alice," says Jerome, patting her hand. "Ya know that I'm not gonna take you and the boy up there if it ain't safe."

"Yeah, I ain't afraid of no spook," shouts the boy charging up the hill, thrusting a stick before him like a saber.

"Nathan! You stop *right* there and wait for us," says Alice.

Nathan obeys, flailing his wooden blade at the ground as leaves and rocks scatter in fear.

The three of them crest the ridge. Alice and Nathan gape at the strange vision before them. Sheltered in the shade of a majestic elm lies a sterile clearing of packed earth. Suspended over this empty area and attached to the adjoining trees, a silken webbed canopy, oddly void of any litter, casts a shadow. Clawed out of the dirt at one corner of the grounds lies a shallow, circular pit hemmed by a U-shaped hedge of brush. Stretched across this hedge hangs another webbed canopy. This one sags from years of accumulated detritus, thick as a standing man. This spindly awning seems incapable of sustaining such a load. The depression, brush, and debris-lined roof create a cave-like confine, which with its stringy white lining resembles a spider's den the size of a walk-in closet. At the clearing's opposite end, a primitive cross of tied branches marks a patch of swelled earth.

Approaching the tree, Jerome inspects the bizarre scene. He releases the basket, leans back, and looks up as though searching.

Jerome's casual response to the surreal setting catches Alice's attention and apprehension.

Nathan exhibits an excited bewilderment. In awe, he steps back, bumping his mother. Alice grabs him in a protective embrace.

"This your idea of a romantic place for a picnic?" she says to Jerome. "I'd rather be eatin cold cuts in a graveyard! I wanna go home—*now!*"

Before Jerome can offer any reassurance, Nathan wiggles free. Branched saber aimed before him, the adolescent "Don Quixote" attacks the silken cave which regurgitates the clamor of imagined battle.

Tree branches crackle as something invisible, large, and heavy thrashes through the canopy. Bark, leaves, and wooden shards rain down. Alice leans back, staring upward.

"Jerome! You hear *that?*" she says, blushing in distress.

"They's just the wind," he says without raising an eyelash.

But excluding the falling debris, not a leaf beyond the clearing flickers. Alice twinges with doubt at her partner's observation.

"Like I say, they's *nothin* to be worryin about," says Jerome. "You an Nathan come over here."

Nathan emerges from the cave's darkness draped in cobwebs, sword in hand. After Alice combs the debris from his hair, they join Jerome.

"I brought both of ya up here this mornin cause they's somethin I gotta say. So, get yourself to sittin cause this gonna take a while."

The two sit on a fallen limb. Opening the basket, Jerome

removes a glass vase holding a bouquet of yellow flowers. Filling it with water from a jar, he surveys the surroundings.

"What ya lookin for, Dad?"

His finger pointed into the shadows, Jerome saunters forward, stopping at the crossed-limbed tombstone.

"This!" says Jerome, setting the vase down.

He bows his head, hands clasped in respect as though in prayer. Mother and son stare at the prayerful scene, their heads cocked with curiosity. Jerome returns. He sits, wraps his arms around his knees, and stares at the burial site.

"What is it, darlin?" asks Alice.

Jerome says nothing, his eyes darting between Alice and Nathan.

"*D-a-a-d!*"

Curious, The Beast crawls lower, twigs snapping and leaves rustling. Alice and Nathan look up at the invisible breach of silence.

"Well, what I got to say I ain't never said before. But I gotta get them words off my mind," says Jerome, leaning forward. "Even though you two ain't my blood, ya the only family I ever did have. I run away from home when I was bout old as you, Nathan. I went ta live with my Auntie Helen. She ain't really my aunt but she treat me better than my own mamma."

"Now I done some things in my life that I ain't proud of," he continues, fixing his gaze on Nathan. "An if something happen to me, I want ya to take good care of your momma. Me and her ain't married, but I think of ya like you was my own son, so I want ya to promise."

"Ya know I will, Dad. But what's gonna happen to you?"

"Yeah, darlin, you know somethin we don't?" asks Alice.

Jerome rises to his feet and paces in front of the two.

"Well, what I have to say gonna seem pretty strange. Yesterday

I was walkin to the bus around noon when I saw this ol brother dressed real nice sittin all by hisself in front of the First Baptist Church. He just sittin there, but he starin at me real funny, so I stopped an asked him what he was doin."

Jerome explains that the black man, Wyatt, was waiting for Senator Bartholomew Cummings' funeral to start in four hours. Jerome asked Wyatt why he was there so early.

"Wyatt, he smile an look back to me an say the damnedest thing. 'Waitin for you, Jerome.'"

Alice and Nathan stare at each other. Jerome's expression reflects their bewilderment. The overhead rustling grows louder.

"I wanna run but my feet feel like they stuck ta the ground like I'm in some kina dream. I asked Wyatt how he came about knowin my name. That ol man he just grin like the devil an say some friend of his told im all about me."

"What friend?" asks Alice.

"I'm gettin to that. Then Wyatt, he pat on the step next to im an he ask me ta sit down. Ya know, me and him, we was the only ones there for a couple of hours. Like I say, nobody else come by which seem kina strange considerin somethin that important goin on."

"I remember readin that senator died a couple of days ago," says Alice.

"Wyatt, he get to talkin to me some more."

Jerome says Wyatt rambled for hours about serving the senator and family as their butler for almost forty years.

"Then Wyatt say when the senator he just a boy, his daddy took im ta watch a Black man gettin lynched from an ol tree by some vigilantes. The father, he made the boy climb that tree an hang the hangin rope over a limb!"

"How awful!" says Alice.

"Yeah, an Wyatt he say that lynchin happen right here in *this* tree."

He points up to a square piece of patina metal embedded in the trunk, a bronze plaque:

In memory of one who died here:
"The only thing necessary for the triumph of evil is for good
men to do nothing."
Quote attributed to Edmund Burke

"An Wyatt then say the senator, he the one that put up that plaque. He hung it the day World War I ended, cause that was a fittin time ta do it. The senator he say it was a memorial to that lynched man, somebody called Peter."

The Beast's black-armored shell quivers upon hearing these words. I'll never forget the first time I saw the plaque. I had just returned from a deathbed visitation to find it nailed to the trunk. I wept with joy. Someone had finally made a gesture in remembrance of me! I'd always assumed a relative or other sympathetic person was responsible; never would I have guessed the boy in the tree.

Wyatt told Jerome the lynching so traumatized the boy, that the child vowed to make amends by a life of service to the underprivileged. As a young man, Bartholomew became involved in social justice politics, rising to the office of U.S. senator with a reputation for helping the disfranchised, especially poor Black people.

"Yeah," says Alice, "he always passin laws for us. The Lawd musta been stuffin them ballot boxes to get im elected cause that senator sure made lots of white folks mad."

Jerome says Wyatt talked about mysterious events befalling the vigilantes. How on their deathbeds, a ghostly beast haunted them, a huge spider. The monster called itself Peter.

"An Wyatt, he *know* the senator got the same visit. Cause Wyatt say the night the senator die, Wyatt heard im through the bedroom door talkin to somebody called Peter. An that the family, they heard em too, but they didn't see *nobody*."

Another series of limbs crackle overhead. The disturbance creeps closer.

"This gettin kinda scary," says Nathan.

"Dear Lawd," says Alice, wrapping an arm around her son. "Then what they say about some awful monster is true. And I bet it up there right now listenin."

Shaking as though sitting on a block of ice, Alice looks upward. All hold their breath, waiting for another disturbance as if to answer yes. Regaining her composure, Alice takes Jerome's hand.

"Darlin, that was real nice of you to sit with the old man."

"I guess so. Anyway, after Wyatt tell me his story, I decide I'm gonna come up here an pay my respects to a brother. Thought it a good idea to bring you an Nathan along, too. But ya know, I don't believe that Peter is no kina terrible beast. It just like I say to Wyatt, I think that Peter, he one'a them avengin angels that *know* justice ain't gonna happen if just them white folks left up to doin it. Yeah, they's need some spookin, put the fear of the Lawd in em. Hell, I just wish we had somebody like that Peter helpin *us*!"

The Beast has never heard words of such encouragement. Finally, someone appreciates the justice I seek! The Beast feels an unfamiliar sensation—tears rolling from its eyes and down its bony hide.

Jerome's face lifts in a grin.

"What so funny?" asks Alice.

"If ya think what I just told ya was strange, ya gotta listen ta what happen next."

Alice, Nathan, and The Beast lean closer.

"Well, Wyatt, he tell me that in the middle of the night after the senator pass and everybody they was all asleep, he heard a knock at the front door. When Wyatt opened it, he seen a brother, a stranger, sittin in a porch chair, head up high and smilin like he king of the place. The stranger, he say he good friends with the senator."

Jerome says the two talked all night, and the stranger said he knew the apparition called Peter.

"Wyatt, he say that it good the way I feel about Peter cause the stranger say one day Peter he gonna be helpin *me*!"

In shock, Alice grabs Nathan's hand.

"Good Lawd," she says. "What is it you've done that gonna be needin the help of that ghost?"

"I done asked Wyatt that, an he don't know."

Alice squeezes Nathan's hand hard, as if wringing a wet towel.

"Mom, that hurts!" says Nathan, pulling free and slashing the air with his limbed sword. "Don't you be scared, Dad. I ain't lettin nothin hurt you."

"You gonna tell this story to anybody else?" asks Alice.

"Hell no! People gonna think I'm crazy."

"Did Wyatt ever tell you the stranger's name?"

"Yeah, he only say it once, some fella called Scott."

Chapter 11

The Confession

Jerome's statement that the midnight visitor on Senator Cummings' porch was Scott so shocks The Beast, that even with eight legs it struggles to keep itself in the tree.

Shadows drift through the woods in the late afternoon sunlight. The picnic plus Jerome's strange narrative concluded, Jerome, Alice, and Nathan plod down the hill in a somber exit. Even exuberant Nathan strolls in silence. In solitude, The Beast claws down to the base of the elm. Legs coiled around its darkened hide, the black spirit sheds its cloak of invisibility.

As The Beast ponders the day's events, a rotting branch strikes the ground, the descent an effect of Mother Earth's irresistible summons. Observing the fallen limb, The Beast realizes it too has been affected by an irresistible summons—that of Master Benefactor Scott.

Scott's arrival at my lynching was just the start. Nineteen years later, he reappeared at The Accuser's haunting. Then nothing for nearly seven decades until four days ago when he appeared at my call on Senator Cummings. With each of his visits, my confidence in the righteousness of my vengeance, my pilgrimage of justice, decayed. "I await at journey's end," was his promise when I started this pilgrimage. So where is he now that the last vigilante has passed, or does Scott's absence imply more torment awaits? Damn! He has a god's mania for manipulation. And though he fills a void in my soul, I refuse to be yanked about by any charlatan deity's whim. My years of black-armored self-will have proven that!

* * *

The next morning, a woodland ruckus grabs The Beast's attention. Crawling from the den to the hill's crest, the specter observes a lone, dark figure drawing nearby. At first, Jerome is suspected, but the stranger's slower gate and glistening, silver hair speak of someone older, whose presence The Beast has long awaited. Scurrying back to the den, the spider pretends to sleep.

Silhouetted in the pale light, the stranger nears the den.

"Peter . . . Peter . . . You awake?" he asks.

Through eyes feigning blurry consciousness, The Beast gazes upon the intruder.

"Scott!"

Claws scratch the lair's hardened earth. The Beast emerges, circling while examining the visitor through yellow eyes. Though incapable of displaying emotion, hidden deep below the impenetrable hide there flickers an ember of joy.

Scott eyes the eerie setting. His nose, wrinkled by disgust, tastes the noxious air.

"Love what you have done with the place. And I see you have decorated it with some mementos of the past," he says, pointing to the plaque on the tree, then the limbed cross at the grave. "And the motif inside, midnight morgue?"

"Nice to see you, too!" says The Beast, eyeing Scott as though checking a bug for lunch.

"Yes, old fellow, as promised, I have returned," says Scott, folding his arms. "But considering your appearance, how shall I address you? Somehow, *Peter* seems inappropriate. Hmm, I know. How about Bellua, Latin for monster? Has a ring. And congratulations."

"Congratulations?"

"On a job well done. Never *once* have you strayed from your path of hate. You have attended the demise of twenty-two mortals, and with only two exceptions, Monroe and Senator Cummings, your haunting presence has added to their horror of death. Never have I seen a client with more *monstrous* determination! With success such as this, what shall you try next? Children's nightmares? Haunted houses? A gig on *The Twilight Zone*?"

Scurrying back to the den, The Beast's spindly form drops to the floor in a display of twisted legs.

Scott follows inside.

"You have experienced the wrath of vengeance with every essence of your being. So, tell me, Bellua, was revenge worth the sacrifice?"

"Worth the sacrifice?" says The Beast, then rises, speaking the rationalization repeated to itself a thousand times. "If white folks would've had their way, that mob would've gone unpunished! *I* sought justice—made those bastards suffer for their crime!"

"You are evading the question, my black-shelled avenger."

"Avenger, huh? Well, even that Jerome guy said I was justified."

"We are *not* talking about what Jerome or anyone else says. Was revenge worth it to *you*?"

Searching the macabre setting, The Beast claws its head. Damnit, why after all these years, I still can't answer this simple question with absolute conviction.

"Funny thing," says Scott, shaking his head. "Void of compassion, justice becomes an avalanche sweeping away both perpetrator and victim. Within the rubble left behind, future generations toil for the truth. And you, my frightful friend, were a victim of that devastation."

"It's about time *you* admitted that!"

"But Bellua, you failed to *find* the truth. You did not even look; you simply contributed to the wreckage."

Scott exits the den, stopping at the bronze plaque.

The Beast crawls from the burrow. *And to think I longed for his return. Why doesn't he just leave again? He makes me feel like shit. Loneliness was better.*

"I like that," says Scott, pointing at the bronze inscription. "Did you know Edmund Burke was an eighteenth-century Irish statesman and philosopher?"

"Yeah, nice. Thanks for the history lesson."

But true feelings The Beast dare not share about the plaque. Tears of joy were shed the first time it saw the inscription. Denial is hate's loyal companion.

"Nice?" says Scott. "Those words represent more than a memorial."

"I know damn well what the plaque says about evil triumphing when good men do nothing!"

"Then do more than read it! *Feel* it through the heart of Bartholomew Cummings who dedicated his life to atoning for a childhood sin.

"Besides a memorial, those words confess the senator's remorse over your lynching. Even as a child, he grasped the brutality. That inscription was a vow to never again lie idle in the face of evil. Bartholomew felt in his soul the trilogy of atonement: remembrance, remorse, rededication. These lie at the heart of justice, a justice that changes people."

"Change . . . yeah, right," says The Beast.

"Except for becoming this hideous demon, *you've* never changed in eighty-seven years."

"Why should *I* change? *I* was the one lynched!"

"So, Bellua, are you *sinless* in all this?" asks Scott. "Pride blinds you from the truth. *You* committed the original sin—killing Thornton.

"You were twice his size, but you crushed him like a snail. You could have simply taken his knife and then hightailed to Kansas.

Your pride would have suffered. But I doubt Thornton's bruised feelings would have warranted a twenty-man posse to another state let alone a lynching. Releasing Thornton would have prevented the pain of your mother outliving her son. Releasing Thornton would have saved you almost nine decades of this hell and spared twenty souls the horror of your torments."

The Beast shakes under this weight of unbearable truth. "After all I've been through, what right have you to talk to *me* like this? And quit calling me Bellua!"

"What right? The right entrusted to me as your benefactor— love and forgiveness."

"L-Love?" stammers The Beast, staggering backward. "Anything but *that!*"

It scurries into the webbed shelter, huddling into a protective tangle of legs. Scott enters, dropping to his knees, blocking the entry. They trade ominous stares.

His defiant eyes falling in humiliation, The Breast surrenders to Scott's invasion of the past. The truth, a corpse entombed in years of guilt, must be resurrected. Its claw wiping back tears, The Beast recounts the murderous day of Thornton's death.

"It all happened when I was walking back home to Mineral Point the day after a heavy rain. I was carrying a sack of flour. Thornton rolled up in his buggy, yelling at me to get off the road. When I wouldn't get into a muddy ditch, he jumped down, swinging a knife at me. I knew I could easily take him. Years of hard work made me more than a match for his kind with their white, soft lives. In this way, folks like me were superior to whites, and they secretly feared us. Because of their fear, *any* perceived threat to them, even in self-defense, was a Black man's death sentence.

"He waved his knife in my face, shouting, 'Boy, you best get your nigra ass off the road, otherwise I'm gonna cut you like I was guttin a pig!'"

The Beast breaks eye contact with Scott. Tears wash down the creature's hardened face. Eight legs shake like reeds in the wind as though groping for words to diminish the horror. Seeking the solace of its old mortal Black slang, The Beast continues.

"I stares at that knife, and my head got to hurtin like it bein hit with a ten-pound sledge. I can feel the hate in Mista Thornton and the air blowin when he swing that Bowie at me. Then he cuts my chin, and he laughs.

"I puts my sacka flour on some rocks so it don't git wet, and I wipes my hand on my chin and looks at the blood. It ain't much, justa scratch. Mista Thornton, he ain't makin no sound; just lookin at me and holdin that Bowie and still smilin.

"l looks round. Ain't nobody round except Missus Thornton sittin in the wagon watchin like an ol scarecrow. There's a crossin over the ditch just up the road that I was gonna use to git outta the way, but that Mista Thornton ain't waitin that long. Then I turn and wipes my hand across my chin one more time, and I look at him.

"He look back to me and say he knows what I'm thinkin, that I'm gonna run. Then he tells me to git runnin cause he's tellin the sheriff that I stop him on the road, and that I was gonna rob him with this knife. 'Boy,' he say, 'you as good as dead!'

"My blood starts to boilin, and that when I makes up my mind. I grabs his hand that got the knife, and I holt it hard and feel them bones breakin. He starts to screamin, and that when I grabs his neck with my other hand, and he ain't makin no more sound. His face gettin blue. Then Missus Thornton starts to screamin. I don't never touch no white folk like that before and I'm feelin scared, but somethin in me won't let go. I hold that white man way up over my head til he ain't movin no more. He's hangin from my hand kinda like meat in a smokehouse. I grab that big ol knife . . . my hand is still round his neck, and . . . "

The Beast tries to speak the unspeakable, but the words hide in fear of their own sound. Swallowing, it summons the courage to say, "and I cut him with that Bowie like *I* was guttin a pig.

"I feel him moanin but he ain't makin no sound cause I got my hand round his neck. And then I does it with the knife again, and he stop. Blood is runnin down my arm. I look at them eyes. They is still open, but I know they ain't seeing nothin. I let im go, and he falls in the mud longside the road, limp like a sacka flour, and I stand lookin at him. Missus Thornton, she stops screamin and faints. Lawd almighty, I done killed a man, and Lawd, I'm glad I done it! But the Lawd, He ain't gonna let me git away, cause then I seen some white folks ridin down the road. I gits scared and I run into the woods, leavin the sacka flour. That's how that sheriff knowed it me. He find out I buys it from the Potosi General Store."

The Beast's eyes blaze at Scott.

"I know it was wrong killin that Mista Thornton. That when all of them bad things starts to happen. My momma was workin herself to death cause I was gone and couldn't help. That poor ol Missus Thornton, she got to move way across the state to live with her sister cause she don't got no man. Then they lynched me. It just like that preacher to our church say, 'That Devil is real good at his rithmetic. One sin always multiplyin to another.'

"Mista Scott, my ol heart havta be harder than molasses in winter."

Chapter 12

Metamorphosis

The hot August afternoon yields to twilight. Across the barren knoll stretches a gloomy shade with amorphous fingers clutching the monster's lair. Inside, having finished its confession of Thornton's demise, the guilt that had clung to The Beast tenaciously as winter ice begins to thaw. The Beast's voice regresses from the soft-toned language of Peter's mortal dialect to the Anglo tongue, hard as The Beast's black body.

"I've never," says Peter, "told this to anyone. Killing Thornton was so easy it *scared* me. I had no more remorse than if I'd killed a fly. But I had a *right* to protect myself. And . . . and . . . I paid for my sin at the end of a rope."

"Peter, everything you say is true, but do you regret your deeds?"

"Yeah, I suppose."

"Then this is between you and God."

"God! What damn good has He done me or any of *our* race? From what I've seen, he's just The Big White Father watchin over His beloved white children. How else can you explain the way we've been treated?"

"Peter, I understand your lack of faith, but . . . "

"Hell with faith! I'd rather live in this cursed place, in this cursed form, rather than glorify a deity who allows the world's injustice."

"Cursed place?" Scott steps from the lair, raising his arms at the cathedral of foliage. "This elm has sheltered and protected you all these years. Show some gratitude."

"Gratitude, for a tree?"

Back inside, Scott kneels beside The Beast.

"Your hate is so consuming that you fail to appreciate *any* blessing. One day, this elm will die. Its nurturing presence will decompose and crumble into dust. Then where will you sulk and hide?"

"I assume," says The Beast, its emotions exploding, "you mean when the blessing of this tree passes, I'll need something more sustaining than rotten limbs and bark. Perhaps the crutch of faith that God will protect me? Well, at least rot is *honest*! More than I can say about a God who lures His pilgrims through a wasteland of mortal ruin, forever driving them onward with fables of acceptance and the holiness of denial. And in the end, the hope, the peace the faithful seek is only a shimmering mirage just out of reach. Any deity that allows *this* is either self-serving or a sadist, and I reject Him or Her or whatever It is. Better to live alone in the company of decay than in all the sanctuaries, heavens, and Valhallas of a hypocrite's spiritual realm."

"Hmm. Sounds like the devil has serious competition. However, I can understand your anger, though I doubt if you really mean *all* of it."

"Haven't you ever felt like me—helpless, tormented by the white man's thorn? How can you be my benefactor if you haven't walked the same prickly path?"

Scott straightens himself. His imposing physique fills the den's opening.

"I know well this prickly path; I was a slave. I had a wife and son from whom I was separated when I was sold to another white owner. I died never seeing them again."

"I'm sorry, I didn't know," says The Beast, slumping in a tangle of shame.

"Both of us bear the scars of injustice. Shall we go outside for some fresh air? The self-pity in here is suffocating."

Both exit the webbed chamber into the muted light. The Beast eyes the spartan accommodations and then settles on the ground. Scott kneels beside the huddled figure.

"Eighty-seven years has not softened your hate, a hate which never asks for mercy, even to ease its own suffering." Then, in a sparkling tone, he says, "My son, there is one option left. You can follow the song's advice which says, 'I need somebody to love.'"

"Love," sneers The Beast.

"Well, do you?"

The Beast hesitates. What a silly question.

"Momma," it answers.

"I can give her a message if you wish," says Scott. "She rests in Sanctuary."

"Tell Momma I miss her. That I'm sorry I had to run away. Tell her I . . . I care for her."

"Care? We are not talking about a pet hamster. Come on Peter, you have not seen, thought of, or spoken to your mother for eighty-seven years. Surely, you can pry some word or phrase expressing your deep affection for her from your black frame."

"Tell her . . . I love her."

"Of all the four-letter words, why is love so hard to say? Any others on your list of loved ones?"

"Well, there's my brother, Frank," says The Beast after a twitching silence.

"Who else? What about your father?"

"That son-of-a-bitch? He ran away when I was three. Never heard from him again. You can give *him* a message: Go to Hell!"

"We only deliver four-letter memos of love. Any acquaintances, buddies?" asks Scott.

"I was too busy working the farm and helping Momma to make any."

"Your list of loved ones is shorter than a two-year-old's

attention span. And all those years as The Beast have not helped. Revenge makes for a small circle of friends."

Agitated, The Beast claws the ground. *Damnit, he's right. I do want a change, but . . .*

"Want to enlarge your circle?" asks Scott. "Join us. Become a benefactor."

"How can I with what *I've* done, and how I look? I killed a man. Hate God. That alone must disqualify me."

"If sainthood were a prerequisite, benefactors would be scarce as party favors at a funeral. Peter, most of us *have* a shadowy past. *That* is why we can be of service. We have experienced suffering's pain and have a desire to make restitution for our sins," says Scott and leans closer. "I even have the *perfect* client for you."

"Who?"

"Jerome. And if you want, his adopted family."

"I knew it!" shouts The Beast. "It was *you* who sent them yesterday. You've contrived all this!"

Scott's cheeks crinkle in a grin.

"Contrived is such a harsh word," he says. "I have *influenced* the actions of people and their situations. But since you have run out of vigilantes, you need another challenge. Jerome, Alice, and Nathen are just that challenge."

Scott spends an hour detailing the nightmare of events awaiting the out-of-wedlock family. In less than six months, Jerome will lose his job. Resorting to crime to help support them, he initiates their deadly downward spiral.

"Damn, what a mess they're making of their lives," says The Beast. "Some fool is gonna waste years trying to help those poor souls."

"I know the feeling. I have wasted eighty-seven trying to help *your* poor soul."

The Beast's prickles with the sting of truth.

"Haven't you got any *uplifting* customers, say like Abraham Lincoln? He rose above his childhood of poverty and became president."

"You are forgetting the part where he was assassinated," says Scott.

"Yeah, well you know what I mean. This Jerome thing seems so damn futile."

"Somebody already took the easy ones. Peter, with your past, you can help Jerome and his loved ones like no one else can. But I must caution you that you cannot save them from their fate."

"Then what *good* could I do?"

"The same *good I* did for you when you cried for God's help the day of your lynching. I have loved you and tried my best to guide and comfort you ever since. *That* is what a benefactor does."

Into the woods stares The Beast, its mind a battleground of opposing thoughts. Comfort them, love them, as Scott has me? But why does God have to let them suffer? What purpose will their hardship serve? What purpose has mine? Damn!

"Peter, you can ease their pain. But you must have the willingness to change. Are you . . . willing? Have you had your fill of all this?"

Standing, Scott waves his arms at the scenery of gloom.

The Beast walks about the clearing. Stopping at the grave, the monster claws the mound while the dust-caked soil boils with the impact of tears from eight yellow eyes. Motionless, the monster faces the den, then rises on its rear legs, staring up into the spires of leaf and branch. Sighing, its eyes follow the convergence of limbs down to the trunk and the bronze plaque grasped by chapped fingers of bark. The black specter cries with gratitude that someone, no less than a perpetrator in his lynching, had loved him enough to place a monument to Peter's suffering. The Beast cries for the blessing of the elm which has nurtured him, though he has refused to acknowledge the sanctity until now. It cries for the gift of love from his benefactor. Gradually, a strange sensation cloaks The Beast as the black shell softens.

The Beast collapses into a gnarled heap of legs. Seconds lengthen to hours as a metamorphosis occurs. Slowly, from The Beast's twisted remains of the black widow spider, the image of a man appears. Pushing himself into a hunched, seated position, he circles his arms about his legs. Sobbing, the figure rocks back and forth, forlorn as an abandoned child. As he rocks, light sneaks into the dreary clearing, at first a filtered glow, then slowly increasing to the brilliance of a noonday sun. Peter will no longer need to fear the light of day. The stench of despair lifts, replaced by the fragrance of hope. And though Scott's witnessed such events countless times, the beauty moves him to tears. His years of influence, sometimes not so subtle, have succeeded. The huddled ebony figure freed of his hellish bond stands. He turns, and embracing Scott, declares:

"My trusted friend, let me serve with you."

PART II

CITIZENS FOR JUSTICE

1988

Chapter 13

A Hole in the Heart

1988

*D*AD'S BIRTHDAY, handwritten in red on the wall calendar, advertises this special twelfth day of February. In the kitchen, seven candles stand at attention on a three-layer cake decorated with:

HAPPY 34th BIRTHDAY DAD!

"Timmy," says his father, "how'd you like to go to the store with me and get some ice cream for my cake?"

"Sure, Dad!"

Timmy will do anything to spend more time accompanying his father, Kevin. The two walk to the driveway and climb into Kevin's old pickup, then rattle off, stopping in front of Mother's Groceries.

"Stay here, Son. Only be a minute. I'll leave the ignition on so you can listen to the radio."

* * *

A Barkersville squad car rolls to a stop in front of the residence of Kevin and Mary Cook. For two frantic hours inside the home, Mary had paced from the kitchen to the living room, stopping to check their driveway through the front window for Kevin's pickup. Hearing a car door slam, her slim frame races to the window, her auburn hair flagging behind. She watches a police car pulling away. Kevin, stooped-shouldered, shuffles to the front porch. Mary immediately knows something has happened to their eleven-year-old son.

"Where's Timmy?" she cries, throwing open the door.

Kevin staggers into the living room. His shoes thumping the floor in the cadence of a funeral march, he collapses into a maple armchair.

The next morning, Mary regains consciousness on the living room couch. Tears still dampen the sofa's yellow floral upholstery. Strange, but she does not remember crying. She does not remember anything other than last night's unimaginable dirge of words that Timmy was shot to death during a robbery at Mother's Groceries.

* * *

Time passes without meaning or awareness. In this vacuum of cognizance, Mary's emotions careen about as unpredictably as a rebounding pinball. When not cleaning the appliances with a toothbrush, she sleeps until noon. She and Kevin argue—violent arguments which she pursues with the resolve of the Inquisition.

In the past, Kevin was the one who had the hair trigger. He seemed proud of this impulse, saying, "Why waste time with a fuse? Stick the match straight into the dynamite keg." But a consistent state of depression now entombs Kevin. Though his anger still detonates, it is rare but brief as a lightning flash. Sometimes during one of Mary's countless emotional eruptions, he will not say a word. He just walks away to do his dead man's thing in the armchair.

The couple even went to see their pastor, all initiated by Mary.

"Everything you're telling me is normal, Mary," said the minister in their latest consultation.

"But I've read there's five stages of grief: denial, anger, bargaining, depression, and acceptance," said Mary. "Why am I stuck at anger and *he's* way up to depression?"

"I've always been a quick learner," said Kevin.

But his attempted humor to defuse the situation only ignited another conflagration of words. Mary stomped out of the room returning five minutes later, unapologetic.

"Everybody processes grief differently," said the pastor. "And the death of a child is one of the most challenging tests of any marriage."

"So, what do we do?" asked Mary.

"Did you know," said the pastor, his face folded in a smile, "that before becoming a man of the cloth, I was a home repair man?"

Both clients turn to each other in a "what's that got to do with anything?" expression.

"Oil the squeaking hinges in your marriage with love and tolerance. Try allowing the other to process grief in their own way."

Kevin stopped seeing the handyman-turned-pastor. Mary found consultations pointless going alone.

* * *

Seven months grind by since Timmy's death. The day approaches when the two perpetrators of the failed store robbery will stand before Judge Charles Daring and a jury of their peers. One of the accused, a Black man, Jerome Manning, has been incarcerated the whole time. The second, a white man, Anthony Gallon, has been freed on bail.

Kevin submerges himself in their apparel business, Cook's Clothing. Mary, careening between anger, then denial, continues her cleaning obsession or any activity requiring no critical conscious concentration.

The villainy of Timmy's death has infected Barkersville's otherwise tranquil community with fear. A group of influential residents congeal, calling themselves the Citizens for Justice Committee, to ensure a speedy punishment for the wicked deed. Former mayor and self-appointed Committee Chairman Oscar Wilson has been the most outspoken of the group:

"The colored community continues its tradition of violent behavior. We of the Citizens Committee will take *all* measures necessary to see that Black man Manning who masterminded this heinous crime suffers the death penalty. His execution will serve as an example to *all of his kind* that this deviant behavior will not be tolerated!"

* * *

Mary sits in her kitchen. Her eyes flit about the oak cabinets and avocado appliances finally landing on Cynthia, who sits sipping coffee across the table. Cynthia, a member of the committee, has stopped by regularly since Timmy's death.

"They talk like that Anthony guy wasn't even there," says Mary after reading Wilson's last interview in the *Barkersville Gazette*.

"Both of em held up that store and both bastards should be gassed!" says Mary, slapping the paper down. "I'm tired of all the crap from that committee. I'm so fed up, I . . . I don't think I'll even *go* to the trial next week!"

Mary grabs her coffee, staring at her friend, the same stare she gives Cynthia during each visit. *It's too bad she's leaving for St. Louie with her husband for his new job. Damnit, Cynthia's the only one I can talk to. Kevin won't.*

"Mary, you keep saying you won't go but honestly," says Cynthia, "the trial will give you closure. Besides, if you don't go, well, you know folks will say you don't love your son enough to see his murderers die. You've got enough on your plate without *that* gossip."

"Gossip? I'd have to be dead to care less! No damn trial will fill the hole in my heart left by Timmy's death. Nothing will do that even if his two killers are sent to the gas chamber!"

Immediately, an unspeakable contradiction invades Mary's thoughts. *If their deaths won't fill the hole, what good's their executions?* Bewildered, she buries the unexpected pang of doubt under a mountain of righteous hatred.

Like a pandemic, rumors of Mary's reluctance to attend the trial contaminate Barkersville. Her threatened absence also concerns Kevin. "It could jeopardize the trial's outcome," he said, "and the store's business." Due to the urging of, plus intimidation by the committee, Kevin convinces Mary to attend a clandestine meeting with prosecuting attorney Zackery Thurman. They meet in a café, miles from town.

"Mrs. Cook," says the prosecution, twisting the sweaty ice tea glass before him, "we've never had this conversation, okay?"

Mary nods yes.

"Your presence in court is *imperative*," says Thurman, concern creasing his face. "I realize you've been through an emotional period . . . "

"Hell, Mr. Thurman. I've been through hell!"

"I stand corrected—hell," he says, taking a drink. "Think of going to the trial as something Timmy would've wanted, something the community needs. We can't take any chances the accused, especially that colored, elude the punishment they deserve."

"There it goes again," says Mary, leaning across the table. "'That colored'! I don't care if the hand that shot my Timmy was Clorox white or Black as a moonless midnight, they *both* are to blame for his death. And if both of em don't die, it's not justice!"

"All the more reason for your attendance. And whatever

emotional displays you are 'powerless' to control, will most assuredly be noticed by the jury. We've even arranged a place for you plus your husband close to the jury box."

Thurman lowers his gaze. He brushes crumbs from his pinstriped suit, allowing Mary a reprieve from his steel-blue stare.

"But do I *have* to take the witness stand? I don't think I can do that," she says.

"Don't be concerned, Mrs. Cook. You won't be testifying during the guilt portion of the trial. And in the sentencing phase which follows right after, you only need testify if you so choose."

"That's just fine. But what if they're not found guilty?"

Leaning forward, the prosecution turns his head, confirming their privacy.

"Don't you worry, Mrs. Cook. I can assure you it's *all* been arranged."

Chapter 14

A Sour Taste

On Mary Cook's kitchen counter lies today's September 2, 1988, P.M. Edition of *The Barkersville Gazette.* The following announcement commands the Friday front page:

"The Citizens for Justice Committee meets tonight at 7:00 pm in Barkersville City Hall Auditorium to discuss next week's sentencing of Jerome Manning, the 24-year-old Black man convicted today in Circuit Court of first-degree murder in the death of 11-year-old Timmy Cook. Manning shot Timmy to death during an attempted robbery in February at Mother's Groceries. This meeting is closed to the public."

Mary shuffles into the bedroom to change for this evening's City Hall meeting. Her thoughts clatter from worry, envisioning herself tonight on stage making that speech which no matter how many times she repeats, the closing still tortures her tongue. As Mary stares into the dressing table mirror, lipstick in hand, events of the trial's past three days blaze in her mind, beginning with that haunting distraction on the first day.

* * *

Escorted through the gallery by the guard at the courtroom door, Mary and Kevin sit in the front row pew next to the jury box. State Prosecutor Zackery Thurman, as he promised Mary during their private meeting last week, has made sure the couple's presence will be noticed by the ten men, two women white jury deciding Jerome Manning and Anthony Gallon's fate.

Unaware of the private meeting with the prosecution, some of Mary's so-called "friends" take credit for her appearance this morning.

"You, the mother of the murdered child, could cast the biggest stone. Sit in the front row so the jury'll see you!" said one of them.

Though Mary enters the courtroom consumed by hate for her son's murderers, something unexpected happens. Sitting in the white, marbled cavern, she cannot ignore the sobbing of someone behind her. She glances at Kevin to see his reaction. Nothing. He glares at the backs of the two murderers seated before him at the defendant's table opposite the rail separating the court well from the gallery. Mary twists back to the tearful sound. Pretending to watch people filing down the aisle, she notices a young, Black woman crying, her arm wrapped around a boy whose eyes fight to repress his tears. The child looks about the same age as Timmy.

"Mom, is Dad gonna die?" whispers the boy.

"Don't rightly know, Nathan. All we can do is pray that the good Lawd let im live." She squeezes his shoulders like an accordion.

Mary remembers from a picture in *The Gazette*, that the woman is Alice Smith, Jerome Manning's live-in girlfriend. Mary turns around, her gaze landing on the defendant, Jerome, the object of Alice's sorrow. Against her will, Mary's heart skips with an unsettling pang of sympathy. Damnit! Her muscles tense. Nothing— not the pitiful diversion behind her, not the undisciplined spasm of her emotion must be allowed to jeopardize her hatred. Those two monsters who killed my little Timmy, they've got to pay for their crime. Pay for it with their lives!

For seven months, from deep inside her brain's primitive cortex, Mary's emotions have erupted, nurtured by the hateful rhetoric from the townsfolk, newspapers, plus the Citizens Committee. The consultations with her pastor and his proclamations of forgiveness have only added a shroud of guilt over her anger. But now, witnessing the sorrow of Alice and Nathan, the Black monster seated before her morphs into a person, a person who has loved, a person whose passing will be mourned just as much as Mary mourns Timmy.

Near the point of nervous exhaustion, Mary has what she thinks is an epiphany. All this trouble with my feelings, soul searching, is actually good. It's a sign of my Christian righteousness. She hopes this religious zeal will sanctify vengeance's desire, and then mute her nagging conscience.

* * *

After three days of testimony, objections, overrules, and sustains, the trial ends in a verdict of first-degree murder for Jerome. Anthony receives a lesser charge of manslaughter. To Kevin's annoyance, Mary doesn't leap off the courtroom bench clapping and screaming with joy like him. Mary's friends also fret about her restrained response, later gossiping that her moderation must be due to grief.

As the jury foreman's words thunder in the court, other words echo in Mary's mind:

"We of the Citizens Committee will take *all* measures necessary to see that Black man Manning . . . suffers the death penalty."

"Don't you worry, Mrs. Cook, I can assure you it's *all* been arranged."

Mary sits squirming on the pew, as the gallery stands cheering. Her thoughts swirl like trash in a tornado. If both of em had been found guilty of first-degree murder, then at the next stage of the trial they would've both gotten a death sentence. Just like it should be, and justice would've been served. Her hunger for vengeance would have been sated.

Hate and its mirror image, revenge, require no discerning thought. In fact, these emotions are justifiable, respected, and even expected. Right? But this murder/manslaughter verdict churns an inner conflict Mary is at a loss to handle. Yeah, Jerome deserves to die, but why should only the Black man suffer death? His partner will probably only get twelve years. Police never found the bullet that killed Timmy, so how do they know Jerome's gun was the murder weapon and not Anthony's? Is this justice? There is a fly in the ointment of revenge. Retribution's sweet taste has been soured by prejudice.

* * *

"Excuse me, Mr. and Mrs. Cook," says Oscar Wilson as they exit the courtroom. "I have something urgent that needs discussing. Could we meet at two o'clock this afternoon in your home?"

"I assume this's got something to do with Manning's verdict?" asks Kevin.

Oscar nods yes.

The meeting is on.

Mary and Kevin finish a late lunch in the kitchen. He takes a shower. She clears the red rose Formica table, setting the dishes by the sink. Hot water fills the basin. Mist rises, fogging the window which stares across the lawn at two boys playing soccer in the street. One boy sprouting curly, blond hair reminds her of Timmy. Mary opens the window, preparing to shout a warning about cars, but catches herself in mid-breath. It's like Timmy will run through the door any minute.

The aching void left in Mary by Timmy's passing pulses

persistently as surf against an ocean cliff. Sometimes the pain laps in languid waves. Other times, the grief crashes with thundering, white foam breakers, pounding in a futile furry. Right now, Mary feels a storm brewing. She wills her attention to the dishes. Instead of using the dishwasher, she washes them by hand, occupying her thoughts with manual repetition.

Using a Brillo pad, Mary scrubs a casserole bowl as she watches a black Lincoln Continental park across the street. A short, portly man in a white shirt divided by a red-striped tie, steps out of the car. Slipping on a black dress jacket, he bows, looking into the side rearview mirror. A smiling reflection watches him adjust his tie as he combs the near-extinct strands of hair. Just then, a soccer ball skids off the car hood, striking the man's forehead. The two perpetrators initiating the assault scatter in opposite directions.

"Fucking brats!" shouts Wilson, heaving the ball at the Timmy look-alike so hard, his jacket seam splits.

A siren of profanity pierces the placid proximity. Throwing the black rag in the back seat, he reorganizes his disheveled hair. He stomps across the street to the Cook's front porch, then punches the doorbell button.

"Kevin! That's Wilson," says Mary.

The doorbell rings again. She drops the bowl in the sink, breaking a dish.

"Shit!"

Before she can dry her hands, the doorbell chimes again . . . and again, the incessant summons adding to the bumper car bedlam of her thoughts.

"I'll get it, honey," says Kevin.

The oak floor cries in pain as he hammers his way to the door.

"Hello, Mr. Wilson. Please come in."

"Hello, Mr. Cook," is the impassive reply as Wilson dabs his forehead's bubbling perspiration with a handkerchief.

They enter the maple furniture living room. Kevin offers Wilson the armchair. Checking his watch, Wilson declines to sit.

"Mr. Cook, I . . . "

"Please, Mr. Wilson, call me Kevin, and this is Mary," he says as Mary enters the room.

"Hello, Mary," is Wilson's monotone reply.

Mary grunts hello, then stands beside Kevin, taking his hand. Wilson's irrational street performance prompts a scowl in her eyes.

"Mary, Kevin . . . I hate intruding on such short notice, but like I said, this is urgent. I've called for a Citizens for Justice Committee meeting tonight at City Hall. You know the sentencing phase of Manning's trial starts Tuesday. Under *no* circumstance will the committee representing the people of Barkersville tolerate *anything* less than the death penalty," he says, nailing his gaze at Mary. "And I just wanna make sure we're all on the same page."

Mary senses her reserved response to the verdict has already stirred the waters of gossip. Her grip on Kevin's hand tightens.

"And what page is *that*? The obituary column?" she asks.

"The *page* that says we the voting public want Judge Charles Daring to heed our demand since his reelection is only two months away."

The room swirls in distrustful silence.

"So, why are you here?" asks Kevin.

"I'll get straight to the point. I want both of you to appear before tonight's committee, showing your support for the death penalty," says Wilson, stepping toward Mary. "And I want *you* to say something about that support, Mary."

Spouses trade sideways glances. They have been approached, no hounded, by the news media and civic organizations to speak on this topic. However, due to the painful memories, respectfully they have declined.

As the three stand in the mute afternoon heat, through an open window drifts the hollow thud of a ball striking sheet metal.

Children laugh. Tennis shoes slap the pavement. As Oscar stares out the living room window at the fresh dent in his Lincoln, his jaw clenches under a crimson flush.

Mary restrains a giggle. *I hope that was the blond-haired boy.*

The Cooks' prolonged silence prompts a repeat of Wilson's request.

"Mary, what'll it say if you and Kevin don't attend tonight's meeting? That you don't care what happens to that nigra who killed your son? We've gotta send a clear message to coloreds that we're tough on crime! What happens if he only gets life? You wanna be responsible for that?"

"Well, I . . . "

"Of course, you don't! That settles it. Both of you be there tonight," he says, handing Mary a note. "I've written a few words that we'd *really* like to hear in your speech. Leave the rest to me."

Mary feels rage tingling in the back of her neck. *Who's this pompous ass coming here like he's still mayor, or God? I wonder what few words I'd hear if I shoved this paper up his . . .*

"Mr. Wilson," she says, composing herself, "I . . . I'm sorry, but I just can't go. It's too painful. Can't I write something for you to read?"

For the third time this afternoon, Wilson's face boils red in emotion.

"Mary, you don't seem to realize how much I've helped you and Kevin these past months. Being a former mayor, I know a lot of people, and I've been telling all of them to patronize Cook's Clothing. Unfortunately, I don't know how much longer I can continue this if . . . "

"Thanks for your support, Mr. Wilson," says Kevin, dropping Mary's hand. "We'll be there!"

A few hours later, Mary sits at her dressing table completing her facial decoration. After this afternoon's meeting with Mr. Wilson, her head aches with thoughts of the trial. She slams the lipstick down, the mirror reflecting her flushed anger at Kevin's capitulation to Wilson. Though no argument ensued after Wilson's departure, their silence could have broken glass.

* * *

On the Cook's drive to City Hall in Kevin's BMW, squeaking wiper blades and pounding rain from a sudden thunderstorm fill the wordless interior. The occupant's mute displeasure makes the twenty-minute trip seem like twenty hours. At the auditorium, a uniformed police officer stands guard at the double brass door entrance.

"Are you the Cooks?" he says.

Kevin nods yes, shaking his umbrella.

"Please follow the gentleman inside."

All eyes fix on the couple who follow the escort to their assigned front-row seating. On Mary's left sits her friend, Cynthia.

Grabbing Cynthia's hand for moral support, Mary surveys the intimidating audience behind her, intimidating because of insults such as: "Any mother who truly loves her son wouldn't hesitate in condemning that colored who killed her boy."

Kevin has also expressed concern over Mary's silence.

"Honey, for our financial well-being, you need to speak up, say something about the pain that Black bastard's caused. Customers are staying away."

Instead of an accelerant for another fire of words, Kevin's criticisms have pushed Mary into the ash heap of depression. *At least I'm making progress on the five stages of grief.*

As Mary's attention concentrates on the rear of the auditorium, the murmuring of the audience explodes into cheers. Oscar Wilson has just entered the building.

Chapter 15

Chairman of The Committee

Two hours ago, Oscar returned from his meeting with the Cooks to his business, Wilson's Jewelry. Alone, he sits in a secluded room. Stretched out before him on a counter-high oak worktable lies today's *Gazette* with its notice of tonight's Citizens for Justice Committee meeting.

Oscar eyes his windowless, bleak surroundings, formally the embalming room of the mortuary he had purchased over twenty years ago, then converted into his business. Late at night, he swears he smells the formaldehyde embalming fluid which had seeped into the cracked concrete floor during the mortuary's half-century of business. The viewing room of the dearly departed he remodeled into a showroom.

Jealous competitors refer to the establishment as DMD, short for Dead Man's Diamonds. They have good reason to be jealous. Wilson's Jewelry is one of the most profitable ventures in Barkersville. However, the foundation of this financial success lies not in Oscar's astute business sense, but in the fencing of stolen jewelry conducted within this confine, his Buying Room. This nefarious sideline, his "appraisal service," he offers to an elite cadre of "suppliers."

To facilitate this secret endeavor, Oscar bricked the room's window, then soundproofed and mahogany paneled the walls. Though the spartan interior is reminiscent of an abandoned mine shaft, he feels safe within the wood-lined vault. He upgraded security by replacing the two wooden entries with thick, steel-clad doors and added peepholes. The contractor, whom Oscar paid an obscene bonus to keep the improvements secret, said, "Ya could castrate a grizzly in here and wouldn't nobody hear it."

One door leads to Oscar's private office. The other exits to the rear alley which the suppliers use. Both are always locked. The room's interior includes three pieces of furniture in the center: the counter-high, oak worktable between two stools. On the desk stand three photographs of his beloved grandson, Michael. An enlarged, framed photo of Oscar with Michael hangs on a wall. Behind the picture hides the wall safe with treasures including several thousand dollars in cash, and the wedding ring of his deceased wife, Sherise. Absent are pictures of Sherise, and his son, Sherman.

Contrary to "everything's coming up roses," as goes the refrain of Sherise's favorite song, Michael suffers from cystic fibrosis. Upon the first diagnosis of this fatal disease, Oscar started the appraisal service. In his two terms as mayor, he had interceded in criminal investigations of two prominent constituents having rumored ties to crime syndicates. Before having their charges dropped, Oscar extracted an agreement.

"Today, I'm calling in some markers to save your ass. Tomorrow, I'll be calling on you to do a favor for me."

When tomorrow came, the pair rejoined, granting Oscar a monopoly on fencing jewelry, a monopoly enforced by the pair's lethal rigor.

The appraisal service's proceeds pay for Michael's extensive treatments, including sizable Cystic Fibrosis Foundation contributions. Such use of his ill-gotten gains smooths the edges of his conscience. However, Oscar is willing to go to *any* extreme to protect his illegal sideline. He dwells in a fantasy of denial that as long as the money is there, Michael will be fine. Few compromised by this disease will see their twentieth birthday.

Glancing at the *Gazette* article, Oscar's thoughts drift back to events occurring in this room months ago.

* * *

Jerome Manning sits in the Buying Room on the opposite side of the oak table.

"Suh, this here's a fine ring. I done found it in the trash yesterday," he says.

Oscar hunches over the table. Through his jeweler's loupe, he inspects the ring's diamond centerpiece set in a band of white gold. The ornamentation is indeed a fine specimen. The diamond, a round brilliant cut with no inclusions and minimal blemishes, weighs two carats. Embossed in the gold are two crosses on either side of the diamond.

Oscar knows this is stolen property. Found it in the trash my ass! Probably came from that Greenville home burglary I read about.

"I'll give ya two hundred bucks for it," he says, knowing he will sell the ring for over five thousand.

"Two hundred dollars!"

"Don't raise your damn voice," warns Oscar, removing his loupe. Rather than a fear of being overheard, the warning is a demand for respect.

The intercom rings, announcing Wilson's noon appointment has just arrived.

"I'll be right there," he says, muting the intercom as he glares at Jerome. "Take it or leave it."

Hostile silence fills the room.

Oscar throws the ring across the table. He shoves his chair aside, stomps to the alley entrance, and grabs the doorknob.

"If you don't fucking like it, maybe one of your Black friends'll do better."

Though insulted, Jerome knows this is the only game in town.

"Ok, I'm gonna take the money, Suh."

Oscar returns to the desk, yanking open a drawer. Sliding the golden bargain into a divided compartment, he slams it closed. The Colt .45 revolver inside crashes against the drawer's back reverberating through the desk. Ordering Jerome to wait outside, Oscar retrieves two hundred dollars from the wall safe. He yanks the alley door open, shaking ten twenty-dollar bills in Jerome's face.

"Take this and get the hell outta here before somebody sees you."

Jerome stuffs the wadded cash into his trousers.

Flicking his head, Oscar checks the alley. All clear. He slams the door. Disappearing into the showroom, he attends to his waiting customer.

"We just got this beauty several days ago," says Wilson, pointing to an engagement ring purchased from another supplier. "It's one of a kind—a steal at only $6,999."

The customer leaves with the engagement ring. Wilson gloats over another nice return on an investment, fantasizing about the white gold acquisition in his desk drawer.

* * *

That night, Oscar returns to the Buying Room. He retrieves the ring, then after meticulously fondling it, makes a decision. This little gem will be the perfect sixteenth birthday gift for Michael. But to Michael's family, any additional time they have with Michael is the most treasured gift they could receive.

"Gift?" Oscar would snarl. "How can you say anything about this fucking disease is a gift? The only *gift* is the money I give you for his treatments!"

Placing the ring in the drawer, Oscar reaches back for the .45

which ensures his security in case another supplier is not so easily persuaded. However, no cold steel greets his twitching fingers. *What the hell?*

Kneeling, he squints inside, confirming the weapon with the duct-tape-wrapped handle is missing. His attention jerks to the slightly ajar alley door. *Damnit, someone's been here!* In his rush to the buyer's appointment, Oscar didn't check the door. *Musta been Jerome. Bet he heard the gun bang when I slammed the drawer.*

The theft is never reported. A Lugar will replace the missing Colt and will be secured in the wall safe. The lock security of both doors will be upgraded using deadbolts plus hinged steel bars.

* * *

Oscar forces his attention to the *Gazette's* article. In addition to details about tonight's Citizens Committee meeting, the report mentions that the child, Timmy, killed by Jerome Manning ". . . was the son of Kevin and Mary Cook."

Reading "son," thoughts of his son, Sherman, Michael's father, soil Oscar's memory. With a guillotine's empathy, Oscar's memory berates his offspring. *Pussy! Weak as a girl. Lord knows I tried to beat it out of im, make the little wimp a man!*

By the age of fourteen, Sherman had resorted to chemical warfare—alcohol—to combat the civil war incited by his father. As Sherman advanced to adulthood, married, dealt with Michael's illness and Oscar's escalating assaults, to this chemical arsenal he added drugs, then prescription pills. Inevitably, these overwhelming forces resulted in the loss of Sherman's job which provided insurance that covered a portion of Michael's treatments. By the time Michael was three years old, Sherman, shamed and bankrupted, had abandoned his family. They nor their friends ever heard from him again.

How that loser of a son could come from my loins, I'll never know!

Other insults about his son ricochet in Oscar's head. So what if Sherman's son got sick? Like I always said, overcoming a little adversity's good for ya . . . makes you a man. I suffered adversity. Came from poverty, worked hard, made something of myself. Anyone who can't rise above his misfortune deserves what they get like Sherman and his fucking addictions. Like Manning and his murder conviction. Manning . . . the shiftless bastard isn't any better than all those other degenerate nigras.

The shotgun of Oscar's thoughts now aims at his wife, Sherise. So what if I worked long hours at the office? Yeah, I was strict, frugal, and expected the same from Sherman. But when he didn't measure up a little corporal punishment was good for the boy. Look what it did for me. She said I was too hard on im. But what example did she set, "to escape the constant domestic turmoil," which she blamed on me? It was her bad genes that made im drink.

However, the one thought, the one image Oscar seldom allows himself to revisit, is the day he found Sherise in the master bathroom thirteen years ago. There, beside an empty bottle of gin, amongst scattered pills, he saw her on the floor with the pistol still clutched in her hand. By the body lay a blood-spattered picture of Sherman cradling one-day-old Michael in his arms.

Oscar's eyes wander from the newspaper to his watch which reads 6:45 p.m.

"Shit, I'm late!"

After securing the room, he thunders in his black Lincoln Continental to City Hall. Fortunately, the building lies only five blocks away. He parks in a stall marked *RESERVED—CHAIRMAN*. Exiting his rolling fortress, Oscar marches through the rain holding an umbrella. He crosses the sidewalk, then up the building's granite stairs.

"Good evening, Mr. Wilson," greets the blue-uniformed police officer guarding the main entry.

The brass-framed double doors open.

Handing his umbrella to the usher inside, Oscar enters the auditorium which boasts a fifteen-foot-high ceiling atop polished marble walls. The membership cheers. All eyes shift to him as he saunters down the aisle, up the stage stairs, and stands at attention behind the podium.

Chapter 16

Friday Night at the Movies

The summer's storm fails to dampen the concerned committee's spirits as the last of the attendees enter the auditorium. They see Oscar onstage. The police officer checks members' IDs. After all have arrived, the officer returns outside guarding the door.

Surveying the audience, Mr. Wilson waits patiently for silence. Hands clasped, he waits a full minute before welcoming the crowd. Sweat rolls off the top of his head down into his crescent moon sponge of black hair.

"Thank you all for coming this Friday evening," says the short, overweight, middle-aged man.

Eyes cast down, he leaves the podium and strolls to the front of the stage, staring into a churning sea of white faces—nineteen committee members accompanied by spouses and friends plus the guests of honor, the Cooks.

"In Circuit Court this afternoon, a jury of twelve highly respected members of our community convicted Jerome Manning, that Black man who killed little Timmy Cook, of first-degree murder!"

Applause erupts.

"On behalf of all of those here tonight," he says, glaring at Mary Cook who sits directly below him, "I extend my heartfelt condolences for what you and your husband have been through. Why the trial dragged on for three days we'll never know, but at least they found that son-of-a-bitch guilty!"

More clapping.

"There's nothing they can do to that Black scum to punish him enough for the sin he's committed! May his soul rot in hell!"

Cheering mixed with thunderous applause reverberates throughout the auditorium.

"The sentencing portion of the trial begins this Tuesday. We, the voting citizens of Barkersville, want Judge Charles Daring to know that under no circumstance will we tolerate anything less than the Death Penalty. Judge Daring should be mindful of this demand considering his re-election is only two months away!"

The audience roars their approval.

"We now open the meeting to all who'd like to speak starting with Timmy's mother, Mary Cook."

Mary trembles during the introduction – her dreaded public engagement begins.

"I'm having second thoughts," she whispers to Kevin. "Do I really have to make this speech?"

Kevin's eyes lift from his lap to Mary in silence.

Taking a deep breath, Mary rises. Looking at Kevin, she waits for his escort.

"Honey, I'm sorry, but I can't," he says, cowering in his seat low as a submerged frog. "You'll just have to go up there without me."

Summoning all her strength, Mary composes herself. She takes his hand.

"It's alright darling, I understand."

Cynthia reaches to her side and pats Mary's hand with encouragement.

Mary steps forward, her shoulders thrust back atop a posture straight as a marble column. But trembling, she stops grabbing an armrest. Immediately Cynthia stands extending her forearm for support. The audience assumes a respectful silence while the pair plod to the stage.

Wilson steps aside. Mary who towers over him, positions herself at the podium.

"Now, don't let us down," says Wilson, looking up to her frightened eyes.

Mary brushes aside her long, auburn hair revealing a once flawless complexion eroded by the storm of recent events. Slight of frame by nature, she has lost weight since Timmy's death, a fact advertised by the white blouse hanging from her shoulders like an old curtain. She stands expressionless at the podium seemingly unaware of the audience, her molasses brown eyes weighing on Kevin.

He returns her gaze.

A prolonged silence follows—an eternity—interrupted by an occasional nervous cough.

Gazing at Kevin, Mary considers how the tornado of Timmy's death struck without warning leaving their lives scarred and barren. Cynthia steps forward whispering in Mary's ear. Lifting her eyes, Mary stares into the assemblage as if awakened from a trance. She begins her story by saying how on a Friday night this year in February, Kevin's birthday, Kevin took Timmy to Mother's Groceries to buy ice cream. After several hours, a police sedan stopped in front of their home:

"Kevin got out of the car, alone. He staggered inside. His face was gray as ash. I immediately knew something had happened to our son. 'Where's Timmy?' I cried. He said, 'Honey, Timmy's been shot during a robbery at Mother's Groceries . . . he's, he's . . . '

"The next thing I remember was regaining consciousness on the couch the next morning. Kevin was sitting in a chair looking like a dead man."

Thanking friends and neighbors for their help, Mary tells how their lives have changed. Instead of a celebration, Kevin's birthday is now a day of dread. She grips the crumpled note Mr. Wilson gave her at this afternoon's meeting in their home. Tensing, she ends with a phrase from that note:

"And nothing is too severe for that animal who killed my little Timmy!"

Cynthia escorts Mary back to her seat. With the force that squeezes carbon into diamonds, Mary clenches Kevin's hand while a Niagara Falls of applause thunders behind.

Thank God that's over. If I had to speak at least I was able to say thanks to the few kind people who've supported us. But that closing Wilson insisted on . . . I feel sick to my stomach.

Friends plus neighbors testify to the hell Mary and Kevin have suffered. Each testimony adds to the pressure cooker of emotions. Wilson stands at a stage corner in self-satisfied silence while the crowd's passions boils to a fever pitch.

"Gas the bastard!" spews forth from the audience in an organism of vengeance followed by a booming man's voice from the back of the room.

"Possibly I can help!" he shouts above all the rest.

The commotion ceases. All turn straining to see who made the offer. A figure emerges from the darkness—a tall man with lean angular features in his early forties. The stranger with sandy brown hair approaches the stage greeting the audience on both sides through steel-gray eyes as he flashes a gregarious smile. He carries a brown briefcase, a metal suitcase plus a four feet long black, cylindrical container. Though he moves briskly, he strains under the luggage's weight.

He proceeds to the stage podium dropping his cargo while sighing in relief. Wilson demands the stranger's name and the nature of his business, but the request is ignored.

"Hi, everyone," says the gentleman.

With his back to the audience, the man unpacks his baggage. From the metal suitcase, he removes an old movie projector setting it on the podium. From the cylindrical container, he unpacks a small movie screen and then a folding, wooden tripod stand. But the briefcase contains the most puzzling item: a two-foot square white panel centered with a large black push button similar to a round door chime button.

Minutes pass. Curious as a child watching a magic trick, the audience concentrates on the stranger's activities. Setting the white panel on the tripod, he erects the portable screen. Then, facing the audience he extends his hand palm up. Seconds pass when from nowhere a reel of film drops onto it. Muttering profanities, the stranger loads the projector fumbling with its cams and shutter. Preparations completed, he turns to the crowd.

"I've got a little movie I'd like to show you."

The people in the back complain the screen is too small. They also whine that the projector's speaker will be too tiny to hear.

"Don't worry. You'll see and hear well enough!"

Having lost control of the meeting, Wilson's face stews in resentment. Pouting, he stomps into the audience taking a rear seat in the auditorium.

"Ladies and gentlemen," proclaims the stranger with outstretched arms, "it's show-time!"

Snapping his fingers, the auditorium plunges into darkness punctuated by the ominous clack of locking doors. A coffin-like silence engulfs the room. Mary's grip on Kevin's hand tightens as, under the protection of darkness, Wilson's arrogance surrenders to fear. Moments pass slowly as a funeral procession. The movie screen illuminates. Shuttering, the old projector chatters into action.

* * *

Albert Fillmore, owner of Fillmore Motors, shines on the screen. Bent into the engine compartment of a car in his auto sales lot, he cleans something. The picture zooms in to show a grimy master brake cylinder from which dark fluid drips. The cylinder needs replacing, but the expense will wipe out Albert's profit.

"There," he mumbles, "good as new. Car looks pretty good considering it's five years old."

A sign stuck on the vehicle's windshield reads:

'83 Chevy Impala. V-6, 110 horsepower,
3-speed automatic transmission
Low mileage, Good Condition–$1,600.

The movie flashes forward, showing Albert talking to the elderly Mrs. Sally Thomas in his office.

"Yes, Mrs. Thomas, this indeed is a fine car. But as you know with all older cars, it's important that you have the service station attendant check the engine every time you get gas."

Albert clears his conscience. If I tell the old broad about the leak, she'll never buy it. Yeah, the cylinder needs replacing but all she's gotta do is follow my advice. And what's the worst that could happen except some oil stains on the driveway?

Surprisingly, the audience can hear Albert's thoughts in the movie as a background narration in a voice sounding like the stranger's. Besides thoughts, this narration also describes events, even people's feelings.

Months pass. Sarah stands in her customary self-service station struggling, as usual, to fill her gas tank. This time she spills fuel on her favorite pink dress.

Deciding to help the old lady, a service station attendant approaches. She hasn't opened the hood once since she's been comin here. Probably too weak.

"Ma'am, I'd be glad to do that and pop the hood," he says.

"No thanks," says Sally, not wanting extra costs for service.

"There's no charge."

"That's alright, sonny. I'm sure it's okay." And if it isn't, can't afford it anyway. Besides, what's the worst that could happen? Never drive fast or far. And someone always seems to stop to help if I need it.

Sally slips the nozzle back in the pump, then drives off after paying the attendant. He notices her gas cap resting on the pump, again, while fuel sloshes from her tank. Horns blare. Motorists curse. She whizzes out of sight on the highway as a jogger runs past her.

Beautiful is the summer's day. Annoyed by the odor of gasoline, Sally drives to her friend's house outside town. Dust from passing cars on the gravel road fogs her vision in the noonday sun. Already late for the tea party, she drives a bit faster than usual in eager anticipation of the latest gossip.

Five blocks away, Laura finishes her peanut butter and jelly sandwich lunch.

"Mommy, I'm going out and ride my trike," she says.

"All right, darling. But remember, don't go in the road; just stay in the driveway."

"Okay, Mommy," says Laura to the tone of the voice but not the words.

She pedals to the edge of the street enticed by the road's billowing dust, a great fluffy cloud through which her magic wheeled carpet will fly.

Car service has never cluttered Sally's thoughts. She will avoid any mention of deferred maintenance when later questioned by the police. Suddenly Sally shrieks in terror as little Laura pedals directly in front of her car. She stomps on the brake, but this time nothing happens, and "what's the worst that could happen" happens as Sally strikes the magic carpet's passenger.

Aided by a prosthesis, Laura will walk with a limp. But the

head trauma's deformity shatters all dreams of becoming a movie star "just like Marilyn Monroe."

"Mrs. Thomas' stroke was probably a result of stress from the accident," says the coroner several days later.

The projector clatters in the background . . .

* * *

The reels of time slowly unroll. On the screen burns nineteen more exposés, one for each of the twenty committee members.

* * *

The final scandalous presentation flickers onstage. Pictured is a brick storefront. Over the business's double door entry, painted in black on a white background, reads the following:

Wilson's Jewelry
Oscar Wilson, Proprietor
Est. 1959

A gentle rain washes the masonry as the scene changes to a small back room inside. A March 1987 calendar hangs on the paneled wall.

Pictured is the Buying Room where Oscar conducts his fencing operations. The audience views two men seated on opposite ends of a waist-high worktable. One is Mr. Wilson. To the audience's dismay, the other is Jerome Manning. Their negotiation for the purchase of the stolen gold ring looms large on the screen.

But while Oscar's illegal enterprise has prolonged his grandson's life, some of the investments have cost others dearly. Some suppliers have been more ruthless than Mr. Manning. Last year one of the investments, a watch, cost a young store clerk his eyesight. In another, a necklace was taken off a dead body.

Similar to the previous movies, a voice that sounded like the stranger's spoke in the background about these events.

* * *

Light floods the room. The projector rattles to a stop. Sweat pouring down his face, Oscar sits frozen in his chair. The ghostly images of his past drift through his mind. *How the fuck did this guy on stage know about everything that happened? How'd he get this movie, read my thoughts? Who is this guy and what the hell does he want?*

Anxiously he awaits the audience's condemning stares.

* * *

The stranger watches the crowd's reaction. So far, he is pleased with the meeting's progress. But one thing bothers him, a warning he received when he took this assignment: "I know you are eager for this challenge—your first solo as an apprentice benefactor. However, Peter, trust the process even if the outcome is not what you may have wished."

Chapter 17

The Black Button

Oscar sits motionless, unflinching eyes fixed forward. After an uncomfortable wait, he dares to turn his head to survey the crowd. Something is strange. The entire assembly exhibits the same immobility as though frozen in guilt. Moments pass. People glance at their neighbors, but if they make eye contact, instantly they divert their attention in shame.

Mary and Kevin also exhibit uneasiness.

"Was something wrong with the projector? I didn't see a thing. Did you, Kevin?"

"No. All I saw was a black screen for the few seconds the lights were out."

Kevin surveys the auditorium then his watch.

"Honey, something's wrong. My watch's stopped. I checked it just before everything went dark, but now it says an hour's passed."

"Mine too," says Mary, grabbing Kevin's arm.

Meantime, the storm rages outside.

The audience grows anxious about the stagnant situation. At first, a few hurry to the exits. But the doors, cold as the North Pole, will not budge. No matter how hard they push, the doors stand immovable as Mount Rushmore in winter. Fear bleaching their faces, the would-be runaways glare at the rest of the gathering.

The crowd erupts in panic. People shriek. They leap from their chairs, stampeding to the doors. Yelling while staring through glass panes, they wave their arms, hoping to catch someone's attention. But all witness the same static-in-time scene: headlights shining from motionless vehicles, tire spray frozen in mid-air, tree limbs stunned in unnatural positions from the once-howling wind. Scattered prayers whisper in the mayhem.

"Ladies and gentlemen, please . . . please be seated," says Peter. "There's no reason to be afraid. You're just suffering from mass hysteria. Why don't we take a little break? I'll order refreshments."

His soothing words have their intended effect. The shrieking subsides to murmurs, fear crumbles to anxiousness. Everyone gawks in astonishment as a buffet materializes in front of the stage after Peter snaps his fingers. The hesitant crowd approaches the table. They dine on oatmeal, Oreos, and chocolate chip cookies.

Oddly, the crowd has accepted their paranormal circumstance. Peter had hoped they would. So far, so good.

Calm restored, Peter asks them to be seated.

"Hey, fella," says a member of the crowd. "You gotta a name?"

"Yeah, just call me Peter.

"I apologize," he says, "for putting you through all this. However, it was necessary to ensure you're in the proper mood before we proceed."

Peter pauses for *the* question.

"What'd ya mean, 'proper mood'?" someone asks.

"Folks, I need to explain something about the movie you all saw."

"I certainly hope so!" demands Oscar.

Smiling, Peter ignores the interruption.

"There were scores of movies shown tonight, one for each person in the audience, and all ran concurrently. However, each of you saw only *one* movie that was about some transgression you made in life. These 'individual exposés,' as I call them, show the tragic consequences of that transgression. It could have been a one-time indiscretion or multiple wrongdoings, unintentional or deliberate. For some of you, it's not the deed you're ashamed of, but the fear of being exposed.

"Everyone has these nasty skeletons buried in their past. Pervert or priest, none are immune. Having viewed your bag of bones, search your soul asking how you feel about your misdeed. I want you painfully aware of your contribution to evil before proceeding further tonight, before you make *any* judgment of others.

"Now, I've spared the Cooks from these exhibits. They have their issues. But they've done enough soul-searching since the death of their son."

Upon hearing Peter's explanation, neighbor again speaks to neighbor, secure in the knowledge their sin is a private concern safe from public humiliation.

"How can he make such a movie?" ripples through the crowd.

Some think their behavior was not so bad.

"I'll tell you mine if you tell me yours . . . "

But the polite conversations are just whitewash on a dry-rot fence while persistent as a maggot, the buried truth, gnaws at the decay of their conscience.

Now comes *the* question about the oversized push button on the tripod stand.

"What's that round black thing you've got up there?"

"That's the Black Button," answers Peter.

"I can see *that*, but what's it *do!*"

"It's a mechanism endowed with supernatural powers. When it's pushed, someone will be punished for their sin. We'll witness that future punishment tonight, right here on this screen."

Having witnessed their wickedness on-screen, murmurs of dreaded anticipation fill the room.

"Whose sin. What punishment?" someone from the crowd asks.

"That will be determined by the person pushing the button," says Peter. "He or she simply makes a 'declaration' by stating the offender's name, the crime, and the punishment. Then with one little shove of the index finger, justice is served."

"You mean," says Kevin, breaking a prolonged inquisitive silence, "I could walk up there and say the name, Jerome Manning. Say he's guilty of murder. That I want him to pay for his crime with his life. Push the button, and it'd happen?"

"You'd have to say exactly how he would die, but yes, that's how it works."

"Jesus!" says Kevin. "That's a hell of a lot of force for a simple button, more like a kill switch. Hope that thing's kept under lock and key."

"Rest assured, security's not an issue."

"What's to keep someone from lying, then pushing it for the wrong reason?"

"Another excellent question, Kevin. Unfortunately, as in life, there's no divine administrator to guarantee it's used justly."

This response pleases Oscar, including other committee members.

"Now," says Peter, "we'll demonstrate how the button works." He holds out his left hand, palm up. Onto it materializes a roll of parchment wrapped around a silver baton. Unwinding it, Peter reads to himself, repeatedly looking into the audience as though searching for someone. Upon finishing, he rewinds the baton.

"I hold in my hand a list of names—your names—a list known as the Silver Scroll of Sin. The names are ordered in ascending severity of sin as viewed in this evening's exposés. Starting with the first name, I will state a declaration. We'll watch the resulting offense and the punishment unfold on this screen. Then I'll make a declaration for the next name, and the next until I've finished the list. Doesn't this sound like fun?" asks Peter, waving the scroll high over his head.

"Why in God's name do that?" shouts a male committee member.

"Well, since we all came here to declare Mr. Manning's

punishment, why stop there? Aren't you curious as to how your secret misdeeds stack up to his? Who knows, maybe one of yours is as heinous as his. Then what?"

Oscar's stomach churns like a clothes washer as a member of the gathering rockets to his feet.

"*If* one of us has done some questionable deed, I'm sure there must've been a good reason for it. Speaking for myself, there's no fucking way I'm gonna punish em for it, and you better not try!" says the man.

The hall explodes in roars of approving applause.

"And what makes you so high and mighty, Peter? Are you so sinless that you can cast stones?"

"No," answers Peter. "In fact, some say I'm as evil as Mr. Manning. But as you just said, I had my reasons. I paid for my sin. But if you wish, I'll show you my movie of crime and punishment, but it would be rather uncomfortable to watch."

A cemetery of silence creeps through the assembly when Oscar leaps from his chair.

"This meeting," he says, "is supposed to be about that bastard Manning getting the death sentence, not a referendum of our sins. You've said you're here to help. But since taking over, you've caused a near riot, threatened us with the supposed mystical powers of this button, and preyed upon our fears. Whatever *our* offenses, we're still no closer to seeing that nigra Manning pay for *his* crime than when I stood up there. Exactly what did you mean when you stood in the back shouting, 'Possibly I can help!'?"

With these words, the graveyard's inhabitants stir to life.

For the first time tonight, Peter stands uncharacteristically silent. The Black Button looming behind him, he strolls to the edge of the stage.

"Friends. When I said I'd possibly help, I meant I'd facilitate your quest for justice. With the movies plus my unorthodox practices, I've tried to instill in you the same consideration of understanding and forgiveness for the accused, Mr. Manning, as you've exhibited for yourselves. I've done this so that you carefully consider the decision for punishment in any declaration you make. If your decision is death, it not only carries deadly consequences for the accused but also for some of *you*.

"Are there any more questions?"

Inquiries murmur through the gathering, especially the part about deadly consequences for some of them. Who? But none dare to ask.

"Good," says Peter. "We've arrived at the moment of truth. One of you needs to make a declaration. Everyone must accept it. Then we'll push the button, and the future will be instantaneously realigned to achieve that declaration. But beware, once initiated, this future cannot be altered."

Oscar senses Peter's deadly consequences statement is undermining a condemnation of Manning. Still standing, Oscar scans the crowd, then raises his arms.

"Jerome Manning, murder, death!" he shouts with evangelistic enthusiasm.

The audience breathes a communal sigh of relief.

"Jerome Manning, murder, death!" they chant. "Jerome Manning, murder, death."

"Very well," Peter says, "but you must be specific. How will Mr. Manning die? Hanging, beheading, drawn and quartered?"

"Gas the bastard!" echoes through the auditorium.

All stand cheering, except Mary.

"Now, someone must step onstage, and then agree to push the button. No more worry if the murderer gets life, no more concern about the judge; complete, incontestable, final justice. Who dares play God and end Jerome's life? Who in this righteous assembly will come forth to perform this civic duty?" asks Peter.

Under a shroud of silence and trading awkward glances, hesitant eyes roam the auditorium.

"I will," says Oscar.

Thunder booms as a flash of lightning ignites the room.

"Well come on down!" says Peter.

Though vexed by the storm's display, Oscar remains standing. Buoyed by his righteous declaration, he struts down the aisle and up to the stage podium.

"I commend your courage, Mr. Wilson," says Peter, eyeing the crowd. "However, to fulfill my promise of facilitating your quest for justice, I present a *second* feature film. Pay close attention keeping one thought in mind: not the destination, but the journey is the measure of one's being." Then focusing on the Cooks, he says, "You'll all see the same movie."

Stomping off the stage, Oscar takes a front-row seat.

"Damn," he growls, "not another one."

Chapter 18

Jerome

After a new movie reel materializes, Peter weaves it through the projector. The auditorium again plunges into darkness as a new scene flickers on the screen.

* * *

In the mottled, soiled hallway of a two-room apartment stands a Black child. His hand raised, he taps on the door to the bedroom.

"Mama?" Knock . . . knock. "Mama, is you in there? Ma?"

"Git your ass away from that door, boy!" an agitated female voice answers.

"Mama . . . "

"Don't ya'll make me come to dat door!"

"Mama, I . . . "

But before the boy completes the sentence, the bedroom door flies open. The boy's mother grabs the source of her irritation by the T-shirt, then backhands his face, flaying the boy to the floor.

Like a frightened spider, he skitters to a corner on hands and knees.

"Don't hit me no more, Mama! Don't hit me! I gonna be good!"

"Damnit, chile, ain't I told ya don't never bother me when I'm wit my gentlemen friends? Git your ass outta here befo I hit ya again!"

Running downstairs from the second-floor apartment to the street, the child does not shed a tear. An hour later, he climbs the gnarled steps to the dry-rot porch of old Mrs. Walker's shack.

Knock . . . knock . . . knock.

"Is dat you, Jerome?"

"Yesum, Auntie Helen, it's me."

The movie's narrator, who still sounds like Peter, says Helen is not Jerome's aunt. Jerome does not know of any aunts. The narration explains how one day Jerome was walking by the weather-stained Walker residence, head hung low, aimlessly kicking pebbles on the unpaved path. Helen sat in her front porch rocker watching the child. She could tell he was troubled.

"You lookin lost as one'a them stray dogs, chile. How'd ya like to come inside? I got some cookies an lemonade."

Since Jerome was never told not to accept a stranger's invitation, he lunged at this rare, kindly opportunity. That was two years ago when Jerome's mama began receiving gentlemen callers after her welfare checks were reduced to one dependent instead of five. Jerome's been visiting the gentile, old widow at least twice a week ever since.

"Well, git in here Jerome an have some'a my just made gingerbread!"

Opening the door, Aunt Helen notices the wound over the boy's left eye.

"Lawd, chile, dat gonna be some shiner. Lemme git ya somethin."

With the aid of a cane, she shuffles to the kitchen, careful not to trip over the rags called rugs. From the icebox, she pulls out a roll of hamburger and slices off an end.

"Here, chile, put this on ya eye."

The two have an agreement. She never asks about his reoccurring injuries and he never asks about the stumbling when she clutches her chest. Aunt Helen props him on her generous lap, holding the cool flesh over his brow. For an hour they sit, Jerome pressed against her bosom.

Years pass . . .

One afternoon as Jerome approaches Aunt Helen's home, he sees a sheriff's car with a black van parked in front. Two uniformed men stand outside. He stops. Something cold grips his body.

"Is that him?" asks the coroner, pointing to the Black youth standing motionless.

"Yep, that's Jerome," says the sheriff. "He's been living here with the old woman. They say the two are . . . *were* . . . like mother and son. He got a part-time job at the feed store and was giving her all his money. This's been going on ever since the murder of his real mother."

"I remember that case," says the coroner. "It was a mess, her throat cut like that. I heard that poor son-of-a-bitch (pointing to Jerome) was the one who found her. You ever find the killer?"

"Nope, never did. Thank God the victim wasn't white. I'd still be lookin!"

Both chuckle.

"Well, suppose I'm the one to break the news."

Raising a hand over his head, the sheriff motions the boy forward. However, Jerome has never had a good experience with the police. This appears to be no exception so he turns and bolts into the woods, never to be seen by the local authorities or residents again.

* * *

Mary watches these scenes, disturbed, as are others in the audience, by the boy's violent life.

Oscar is also disturbed. I think I'm losing support. Fucking movie!

Chapter 19

A Love Affair

Clatter, clatter, clatter sounds the projector in the oppressive darkness while narration explains the next scene:

* * *

After running away from his hometown in Jeff City, Jerome wanders the countryside, finally arriving here in Barkersville. The community has social services available, but the town's cadre in City Hall makes qualifying difficult for "people of his kind." So, left with no alternatives, he finds shelter on the outskirts of town in a homeless encampment. It consists mostly of Black indigents who call the tarp-walled settlement Camp Hilton.

From his fellow residents, Jerome learns the ropes of surviving on the fringe: day jobs, panhandling at the local churches, and petty crime. But Jerome's most valuable asset is his adaptability. He soon mends his behavior to white folks' expectations of people in his social class, a survival skill shared by most Camp Hilton patrons. But unlike most patrons, he bears no animosity against white people. Aunt Helen used to say, "Don't do you no good hatin folk. Just you dat git da belly ache, them don't."

Jerome finds the folks in the nearby First Baptist Church a good excuse to continue his tolerance of white folks. He becomes friends with one person in the congregation, Betty Pinch, "Miss Lollypop," as he calls her. A short, plump, middle-aged spinster, she dressed in crimson perched atop white nylons and white high heels. She reminds him of "one'a them sweet, ol red lollypops."

Betty always gives Jerome fried chicken whenever he panhandles at the church's back door, but nothing comes free.

"Do you accept Jesus Christ as your savior?" she would ask. "You prepared to Meet your Maker on Judgment Day?"

"I sure am!" is his self-defense reply, as though interrogated by a prosecuting attorney.

But the ritual pays better than a rigged slot machine. The crispy poultry jackpot Jerome shares among Camp Hilton's aristocracy.

The church runs a daycare facility, Open Arms, which caters strictly to single mothers, mostly Black. Luckily, Miss Lollypop supervises the facility. At her urging, and since the shelter needs one, they hire Jerome as a janitor. His imposing appearance, at first, concerns the young mothers. But soon the ladies grow to trust him, plus his intimidating muscular frame helps with security.

Jerome becomes a pleasant, secret diversion for the clientele.

"That man can dirty my sheets any night!" can be heard amid muted giggling and blushing.

Besides receiving a small stipend, Jerome is allowed to sleep in the basement next to the coal-fired furnace which he keeps stoked in the winter.

At the shelter, Jerome discovers what he describes as "the Black angel from God." Jerome's reverent reference testifies to Ms. Pinch's daily Baptist indoctrination.

The angel arrives at the daycare on weekdays at 7:30 a.m. sharp. Leaving her six-year-old son, Nathan, she walks to her waitress job at Howard Johnson's. At 5:30 p.m., she returns. Jerome aches to meet this dark beauty. Fortunately, the daycare's school offers him the opportunity.

"My name's Jerome," he says to the boy at recess. "What's yours?"

"Nathan."

"That a real good name! Do ya play checkers?" asks Jerome, struggling for a topic.

Nathan's face lights up.

"I'm the best checker player here!"

"Ya know, I get ta playin myself. Maybe me an you can have some games. But ya know, ya gonna have ta let me win some of da time."

"Okay!"

So, every weekday, Nathan and Jerome, during lunch recess, battle on the checkered field of honor.

The movie documentary flickers ahead several weeks.

* * *

"Mamma, this is my friend that I play checkers with. He's Jerome."

"Pleased to meet ya, Jerome. My son told me a lot about ya bein good at checkers, almost good as him."

They chuckle.

"I'm Alice, Alice Smith."

"How ya doin, Miss Alice," says Jerome, his heart pounding so hard he is sure everyone can hear. "I like do da janitor work around here. An I kin'a watch out for them kids and you ladies."

"Yeah, I know. I'm real glad that ya watchin extra hard over my boy."

But Jerome's advances to walk her home die at the shelter doors.

A month passes absent any escort success. Frustrated, Jerome takes his predicament to three friends in Camp Hilton notorious for their "innovative" problem solutions.

"Man, she ain't lettin me walk em home. Like I said, I just wanna get ta know her and the boy better."

"Sounds like this here's a job for 'The Three Hoodlums,'" says the trio's leader.

Sniggering with schoolkid excitement, the four conjure up a staged encounter.

"Okay, Jerome, tomorra night you be at da church, an we gonna be out front an . . . "

Thorough as a Broadway production, they conceive a plot, create their roles, and then practice their lines until they are perfect.

The next evening, as Alice and Nathan are preparing to leave the daycare, three sinister conspirators block the sidewalk to Open Arms' side door entrance. Pushing the door open, Alice stops upon seeing the menacing assembly. She grabs Nathan's hand, wondering what to do next.

"Miss Alice?" asks Jerome who just "happens" to be walking by in the hallway. "Ya looks worried. Somethin wrong?"

"Jerome! Lawd, ya scared me!"

"I'm sorry. But what ya doin wit the door open?"

"Oh, I'm waitn for them to go away," she says, pointing to the threatening trio.

Pumping himself up, Jerome steps through the door, his muscles rippling like the "Hulk." He glares at the menacing group who, just as rehearsed, shuffles to a street corner. They scowl at the door, then form a circle, mumbling amongst themselves.

"It's goin pretty good. Did ya see how big them eyes got when she seen us?"

"An Jerome, he's grinnin like a kid at Christmas!"

They chuckle, complementing each other's performance.

Back at the door, Alice hears the menacing amusement. A shiver runs down her back. She cannot stand here all night.

"Miss Alice, is they anythin I can do ta help ya?" asks Jerome.

"I need to git home but them men over there."

"Mamma, I'm hungry. When we goin home?"

"Miss Alice, ya want somebody ta walk with ya?"

"I ain't one that normally imposes, but could ya walk me and the boy down the street?"

"Ain't no imposin, Miss Alice," says Jerome, hardly believing his ears.

They hurry down the steps, turn at the street, and then proceed homeward, Jerome strutting proudly as a rooster protecting his brood. Alice checks the trio of thugs following in the shadows. Her grip on Nathan tightens. Unconsciously, she grabs Jerome's arm, pulling close to her muscular protector.

After five blocks, the gang stops. After another five, Jerome prepares for his fateful line.

"Miss Alice," he says exactly as rehearsed in front of the trio, "I don't see em followin us no more. So, I guess I'll be goin now."

With his heart in his mouth, Jerome releases Alice as he turns, heading back to the church.

"Jerome, wait!" says Alice, surprised by her exclamation. "Uh, I mean it alright if ya wanna walk the rest'a the way with us."

"Miss Alice, I will if that what ya really want me to," he says. Halleluiah brothers, it done workin!

"Yeah, I really do. And Jerome, you can stop callin me Miss. Just Alice is fine."

* * *

The movie screen fades to black, reigniting in a pandemonium of still pictures representing the stampede of time. By now, the gathering has acquiesced to this surreal presentation as though observing events through a deity's eyes.

Three years later, according to the narration, Jerome has taken residence in Alice's apartment. On-screen, evening descends. Alice has just returned home from work as she, Jerome, and

Nathan inspect a pink package perched in the middle of the kitchen table.

"What's that?" asks Alice.

The foil-encased surprise gleams under the unshaded ceiling light bulb. Crinkled with ragged edges, the box tattles of the failed attempts at crisp, folded corners. Scotch tape repairs punctuate the wrapping. The package, crowned under a red and black bow resembling a squashed snail, has ascended to its location of honor after being rescued from its hiding place under a gallon of Clorox in the closet.

"Happy birthday," says Jerome and Nathan.

Alice's face ignites in surprise.

"Why bless ya heart. That's the prettiest present I ever did see!"

"Hurry up, Mamma. Open it up!"

Alice's usual care of salvaging the wrapping paper surrenders to lustful greed. She dismembers the package with a six-year-old's birthday party enthusiasm. To her amazement, she finds . . . tissue paper? She disembowels the package, discovering more of the same. Finally, in a corner, she sees the surprise, glossy white about the size of your thumb, the porcelain reproduction of a nesting dove.

"God bless ya," she says.

Alice holds the figure in her hand. A golden inscription on the bottom reads:

With love: Nathan and Jerome.

Gently grasping it as though it were alive, she cups the figurine in her hands against her chest.

The projector flashes more scenes as months pass, the happiest months the informal family will ever experience.

* * *

The spectators next witness Jerome at the daycare performing the morning ritual of swabbing the main hall. Mop in hand, he whistles "Onward Christian Soldiers," a tune never failing to stimulate the church staff. Ms. Pinch approaches, marching down the hall to the war melody's cadence. Jerome watches from the corner of his eye. He knows that march, that bearer-of-bad-tidings march. *I sure hope she ain't commin for me.*

"Jerome, can I talk to you for a minute?"

"Yes, Ma'am." Jerome's heart beats double time.

They enter an unused office.

"Please take a seat, Jerome."

Jerome sits, slouching in his chair. *I know this ain't no good news.*

Ms. Pinch draws up a chair.

"Jerome, I don't know of an easy way to say this, but we have to close the shelter. It's a shame, but after eight years, Open Arms will no longer exist."

"Ma'am, why is ya doin that?"

"We don't want to, but six months ago the City Council enacted Mayor Wilson's ultimatum about accrediting daycare facilities. We can't afford to comply with the accreditation's requirements, so we have to close."

"When . . . when's that?"

"End of this week. Friday'll be your last day."

Head in his hands, Jerome sobs.

Ms. Pinch rises, wrapping her arm around him.

"There, there, Jerome. I'm awfully sorry. We took a collection, not much, four hundred dollars. We wish you the best."

* * *

As Oscar sits in the auditorium, he remembers his daycare ultimatum when mayor.

"Let those damn leeches of society fend for themselves!" he said in private to his staff.

Though this feature highlighting the life of Jerome bores him, Oscar's concern that he might be losing audience support grows.

However, Albert Fillmore, mindful of his auto dealership sins, is not so bored. Albert was moved by the documentary picturing Jerome as a compassionate fellow though a bit of a rogue. *And just like me, Jerome's facing hardships, struggling to support a family. If it weren't for the fact that he's Black . . .*

* * *

Rattle, shake, clatter. The projector continues the presentation which moves forward several more years.

A closeup of Jerome, now in his late twenties as he sits at the table beside Alice, fills the screen. Head bent forward with downcast eyes, Jerome stares at a pile of ten twenty-dollar bills stacked before him.

On a cot in a corner of the room sits twelve-year-old Nathan. Pretending to read a *Sports Illustrated*, he tunes his ears to the conversation at the table.

"I know that it hard bringin home money and God knows we need it, but darlin where ya git them two hundred bucks?"

Alice holds Jerome's hands. Several times he has appeared carrying a substantial amount of unexplained cash. Alice fears how he got it. Listening, head still lowered and eyes leaking tears, Jerome concentrates on the feminine hands clasping his—red, chapped hands from their toil at Howard Johnson's.

"Baby," Jerome says, "ya know that I been tryin ta find another job ever since that church's daycare got closed. I see ya workin hard all day an I'm no damn help."

"Darlin, we need that money, but it ain't worth no jail."

But Jerome never forgot what Aunt Helen said: "The family, they come first. A man do what a man gotta do to take care'a em even if you gotta steal." He knows Alice will never support them by herself. Seeing her struggle tears him apart.

"Baby, I told ya that Wilson fella he ended up givin me them two hundred bucks for that ring I found in da trash. They's nothin wrong with that," says Jerome, unable to look Alice in the eye.

"Ya think I'm stupid? I seen that ring ya 'found in da trash' an it worth a hell'a lot more than them two hundred bucks. Shit! I know that it got somethin to do wit your damn friend Anthony! Don't ya be messin with him no more. He ain't no better than the rest of them white folk, he and that damn Wilson fella! They lowdown snakes an gonna git ya in trouble with the law. Then what ya gonna do? An then what gonna happen to me an the boy? Ya hear me?"

Alice glares at him, waiting for an answer.

"Ya hear me?"

"Uh-huh. But Anthony, he the only white man ever paying me any mind."

Jerome stands. Anxious as a caged bear, he crosses the room, stopping at the foot of the cot. He stares down at Nathan, "A bright, though sometimes violent child," as a social caseworker wrote. Police know the violent part. But since Jerome's lived there, Nathan's encounters with the law have ceased. Nathan learned about this ring "found in the trash" from his street buddies. They told him about this Wilson guy, a fence with ties to organized crime, saying, "Snakes even scared of im."

Alice overcomes her anger; she always does. Walking around the table, she wraps her arms around her big, Black bear.

"That boy he love ya like you was his real daddy. Don't ya, Nathan?"

Smiling, Nathan looks at the two.

Holding each of his beloved by the hand, Jerome gazes upward. *Man, it real nice bein with this wonderful family. An I just wish that ya was here with us, Auntie Helen.*

* * *

The movie pauses. Murmurs drift through the audience.

Oscar sits in his chair, contorted as a dead hornet. *I can't believe the shit this Peter guy is showin about poor ol Jerome. And those things his friends said about me and snakes. If this guy's trying to help us in our "quest for justice," he's just clouding things up. Jerome's a murderer and the only "quest" is to fucking make sure he dies for it!*

However, Oscar would be pleased by Kevin Cook's thoughts. *So, it looks like ol Oscar's been buying stolen merchandise. I'm a little surprised. But I remember Peter's words: "I want you painfully aware of your contribution to evil before proceeding further tonight, before you make any judgments of others." So, what if Oscar's got a little sideline? Suppose it isn't much worse than my switching a Macy's label with an Armani. We gotta remember why we're here, to protect us from real criminals like that nigra Manning. He's gotta pay for Timmy's murder, even if I gotta deal with the likes of Wilson or the devil himself! So, if whoever made that movie's trying to make Jerome look more pitiful at Wilson's expense, well, fella, it backfired!*

Infectious as a pandemic, Oscar and Kevin's opinions pass from one spectator to another with only a few, including Mary, showing immunity to the epidemic of hate.

Chapter 20

Mother's Groceries

A s the images of Alice, Jerome, and Nathan fade, the silver screen reignites with a scene eleven months later...

* * *

Playboy pinups adorn the once-white plaster walls of a one-room apartment. On a sofa infected with a rash of stains, reclines Anthony Gallon. His complexion, a reflection of the couch, itches from a two-day beard. In one hand, he clutches a bottle of gin and in the other, he rakes the greasy, black hair from his spider-veined eyes. Anthony continues his volley of insults at Jerome who sits slumped in a kitchen chair.

"Use an empty gun?" Anthony mocks after discussing plans for their next crime. Sucking another drink, he pushes himself upright. "You can't be fuckin serious!"

"I am too!" says Jerome. "Ya know that home me an you broke inta last year? Well, we never used no guns! So how come we need em tonight?"

Peter, in his narrator's voiceover, reminds the audience this was the burglary in which Jerome had stolen the infamous gold ring which he later sold to Oscar Wilson.

Disgusted, Anthony takes another swig from the bottle.

"Hey, man, that was different. The maid said the owners didn't own a gun and they wouldn't be home. So we didn't need any."

But the narration of Anthony's thoughts reveals the truth. *Besides, I cased the place myself. The owners were old and* crippled. If the maid was wrong and they were home and even had a gun, I could've taken care of em with my bare hands.

"Haven't I been your friend," he asks, slamming the gin bottle on the floor, "your *only* white friend? And haven't I brought you in on some real easy jobs cause I feel sorry for you? But this one's different. They got guns so you'll need a loaded one to protect yourself. What'll happen to Alice and Nathan if somethin happens to you?"

"Like I say," Jerome says after considering Anthony's statement. "I'm not gonna end up hurtin nobody. You lissen ta me. It just a grocery store. Them just seein that gun will git em doin what we tell em to. Don't need no bullets an I ain't gonna bring none!"

Twisting in his chair, Jerome pulls from his jacket the firearm he stole from Wilson's Jewelry, the one with the duct tape-wrapped handle. Glaring at the revolver, he flings it on the table.

"Can't count on it firin anyway," he says.

"What's that you said?"

No response.

"I've never seen no one so damn stubborn. Okay, you don't haveta load your gun if that makes you happy."

Exceedingly tolerant of Jerome, Anthony knows he will never find another partner so loyal, gullible, or willing to work for such a low cut of the take.

"Goddammit, Jerome, you're skittish as a squirrel in traffic!"

Anthony's wiry frame springs off the couch, landing in a chair at the table. On the table's Formica top, Anthony slams his imitation pearl-handled revolver. After loading his gun, he slips it back into his waistband. Jerome goes outside to cool off, leaving his ailing pistol behind. While Jerome paces on a sidewalk, Anthony grabs and loads the duct-taped weapon.

* * *

The scene dims, changing to Kevin Cooks' pickup parked in front of Mother's Groceries a few hours later that evening.

"Stay here, Son. Only be a minute. I'll leave the ignition on so you can listen to the radio."

Exiting the truck, he enters the store through its glass door.

Rolling down both windows, Timmy turns the radio volume up.

Grabbing a gallon of vanilla ice cream, Kevin sets it on the checkout counter. The store owner in a shirt labeled "Casey" on the pocket rings up the sale. Kevin pulls out his wallet. Just then, the glass door bangs open. Two men wearing nylon stockings over their heads burst inside. One man wears a red baseball cap, the other a gray one. Both brandish firearms, but something inconsistent clouds this scene: the thief in red shakes uncontrollably to the point one would think he is the one being robbed.

Red's anxious behavior emboldens Casey who, displaying a sinister smile, glares at the armed intruders. Unnoticed, his hands drop under the counter, grasping a pistol.

"Watch me blow these fuckers away just like the last one who tried to rob me," whispers Casey to Kevin.

Casey's calm collected demeanor unnerves the gray intruder, who sensing he is losing control of the robbery, lunges forward.

"Get your fuckin hands up where I can see em!" says gray, pointing his handgun at Casey's forehead.

To the thief in red, this is the nightmare scenario that awakens him at night. Though red holds a gun, in this all-white, redneck neighborhood, the threat of a weapon seems to frighten no one. Then, hearing a police siren's approaching howl, the robber in red panics. In suffocating fear, he tears off his stocking, exposing the face of Jerome Manning. Though the audience knows Jerome committed this crime and though they know the deadly conclusion, they still gasp. The shock of seeing the crime in its unvarnished progression adds a dimension absent in spoken or written words.

Jerome's thoughts of terror thunder throughout the auditorium. Terrorized as if fleeing a burning building, Jerome runs to the front door. Gray, whom the audience now realizes must be Anthony, freezes in horror.

"Stop, boy!" yells Casey, firing his weapon at the fleeing Black man.

The approaching siren howls over the gunshot's blast.

Jerome tumbles to the floor with a bullet in his leg. Smoke drifts from Casey's pistol. Blood gushes from Jerome's wound. Fortunately, Anthony holds his fire as the camera zooms in on the owner's "Marksmanship—First Place" trophy on the counter. Bolting for the door, Anthony slips on the blood, falling on Jerome. Both of the thieves' handguns discharge simultaneously. The two bullets shatter the door.

Numb to the burning pain in his leg, Jerome recoils in shock at the blast of his revolver. He realizes Anthony must have loaded his weapon, but Jerome didn't feel the extra weight. *Dear Lawd, please don't let nobody get hurt!*

Then, as Jerome lies in his pool of blood, the siren's wail begins to fade. *Damnit!* He realizes the siren was pursuing a different emergency.

"I've got you two bastards covered. Throw your guns forward and stay down," says Casey, and shoves a phone at Kevin. "Call 911!"

Casey walks out from behind the counter, aiming his gun at the two while he turns to Kevin.

"I otta save the state the trouble and shoot these two bastards on the spot!"

After an eternity of minutes, two squad cars arrive to the relief of the robbers. They have been frozen to the floor, too scared to move for fear the gun-toting owner will fulfill his threat.

After seizing both guns and removing Anthony's stocking, the police cuff both robbers' hands behind their backs, then drag them to separate cars. In the darkened anonymity of one police vehicle, metal batons club Jerome. The beating's slow-motion closeup delights the audience. Police drive the unconscious criminal to a hospital. Doctors treat Jerome for the bullet wound, blood loss, and injuries sustained during his "attempted escape." Anthony arrives at the police station alert with a broken nose plus a black eye, wounds incurred during his "attempted escape."

Back at the store, authorities photograph the crime scene inside and exterior. They search the street in the vicinity of the store for traces of the bullets but find none.

The movie flashes back to Kevin's 911 call. After cradling the phone, he races over the floor's two tangled bodies and sprints through the doorway. Stopping at the pickup and not seeing his son, Kevin assumes Timmy must be hiding on the floor.

"It's alright, Timmy. You can get up now. It's all over."

As he opens the pickup door, the father's wail pierces the auditorium's darkness.

Chapter 21

The Trial

The projector rattles to a pause as darkness flees before the light.

Silence betrays the storm of emotions engulfing the audience.

"If this guy Peter is tryin to make us feel sorry for Jerome, why show the robbery and Timmy's death?" says one spectator to his wife.

"If this doesn't put that nigra in a coffin, nothing will," says another, delighting in the gruesome presentation.

Mary sits immobile in cold agitation. Never has she witnessed the event of Timmy's death. *Why did Peter have to show this horror on the screen?* She grabs Kevin's hand.

Kevin feels the warm caress, but he cannot return it. The terror of finding Timmy dead still eviscerates his soul with a butcher's disregard. All emotions of tenderness or compassion have been cleaved away, leaving only the gristle of hate. He pulls his hand from Mary's grasp. *If that rerun of Timmy's death helps send that fucking murderer to hell, I'd watch it a thousand times!*

Peter, mindful of these feelings, walks to the front of the stage.

"Ladies and gentlemen, let's pause for a little intermission," he says, then sweeps his hand as snacks plus beverages again materialize below the stage.

Eavesdropping on the audience, Oscar leaves his seat on the pretense to eat.

"Did you see all that in the movie?" someone says. "Both guns shot out that glass door. Maybe Jerome's gun wasn't the murder weapon after all."

"That poor Jerome. What an awful childhood. Ya know, he don't seem like the type that'd set his mind to hurt anyone," says another to his friend.

Oscar senses the mood is changing. I can't believe it. Seeing Timmy's death should've made em scream for that nigra's blood. In his years as mayor, Oscar could manage a crowd as deftly as a captain maneuvers his ship, but right now this one looks like the *Titanic*. Taking the initiative, he marches on stage.

"Peter," he says, "we came here tonight to deal with the facts about Timmy's murder, not to watch your damn soap opera. Everyone here's had hardships like Jerome, but no one's shot anybody. All your crap's got nothin to do with his guilt or innocence. That's why none of this was brought up at the trial."

Oscar's speech ignites a blast of applause from the audience.

Joining the crowd, Kevin fans the flames, shouting his approval. However, Mary, besides a scattering of others, remains silent.

"Right you are, Mr. Wilson. *None* of this would be admissible. But these documentaries of you and Jerome, like I've said earlier," says Peter, facing the audience, "tried to instill in you the same consideration of understanding and forgiveness for the accused, as you've exhibited for yourselves."

Adding a little theatrics of his own, Oscar stands silent, waiting for the attention of all eyes on him. This Peter is convincing. I gotta use every bit of my influence to keep all hands on deck.

"We must not forget," says Oscar, "if Jerome had refused to participate in the robbery, little Timmy Cook would still be alive. We can't deny that simple fact."

More cheering from the assembly, just what they *wanted* to hear. But the stubborn, bleeding-heart minority still remains silent.

"There's something else you can't deny," says Peter. "None of you expressed any concern about Mayor Wilson's success at closing charities for the destitute. 'Let those damn leeches of society fend for themselves!' right Oscar? Well, congratulations everyone. Happy with the results?"

Silence punctuates Peter's comment.

"Oh, the many fingers that pulled the trigger," says Peter, returning to the projector. "And if 'this crap' were admissible in a trial, courtrooms couldn't hold all the defendants."

Every eye shifts to Oscar, whose boldness drains to his feet. *Damnit, I'm losing control, again. Dear God, help me.*

"Peter, in spite of everything we've seen, just tell us one thing," says a gray-haired man from the audience. "Was it Jerome's bullet that killed Timmy?"

Attentive as a cat at a gopher hole, Oscar listens.

"Yes," answers Peter with an undertaker's dispassion. "Jerome fired the fatal shot."

A pall of silence enshrouds the gathering.

Oscar cannot believe his ears. *Praise God!*

"See. I told you all he did it," says Oscar, turning to the mysterious projectionist. "And Peter, if you're supposed to facilitate our quest for justice, why didn't you tell us at the start? You would've saved us a lot of time. What else you holdin back?"

The audience waits for a response as a composed Peter surveys the gathering.

"In answer to what else I'm holding back, this meeting hasn't concluded and more information will follow. And why conceal Jerome's unintentional shooting until now? Because I wanted you to experience all the events leading up to the shooting first. Then," says Peter, pointing to the gray-haired fellow, "when you asked this question, I'd tell you, 'Jerome fired the fatal shot.'"

"You're . . . you're saying you knew this question would come up, that I'd be the one asking?"

Mute, Peter maintains his composure.

The assembly hums in a chorus of whispering voices.

"Is this Peter guy saying *he* can foretell the future?"

"What is he, one of those prophets like you hear about in the Bible?"

Like Fourth of July fireworks, questions explode from the audience.

"How long will I live?"

"Will my baby be a healthy girl?"

"Can I . . . "

"Silence!" shouts Peter. "Intermission is over!"

Encouraged, Oscar struts to a seat, this time in the front row.

As the lights dim, so does the assembly's plea for answers. Then to the projector's clatter, the trial episode of the documentary illuminates the screen. The narration says one week has passed since the store robbery.

* * *

The images of two well-dressed professionals appear. They face each other over a corner table in a coffee shop. Each man nurses a paper cup of "Calming Colombian." In front of one man, Bernard Stockmeier, Esq., lies a letter typed on the stationery of *The Honorable Charles Daring*. It states that Stockmeier has been assigned court-appointed attorney to represent Mr. Jerome Manning. Stockmeier will also be privileged to perform this service on a pro bono basis.

"The paint on your shingle's still wet and you get stuck with that Manning case," chuckles the other associate. "You need this publicity like 'Barbie' needs a breast implant," he says, tossing a five-dollar bill on the table.

"What's that for?"

"Rolaids."

"With luck, I'll have a coronary," says Stockmeier.

"A coronary you can survive. But I warn you, your career will be as dead as Hoffa if you get that colored off."

Jerome awaits the trial's commencement in jail. A twenty-thousand-dollar bail frees Anthony, a rare respite from detention due to efforts by his expensive, respected counselor, Franklin B. Hayes. His services, including Anthony's bail, were arranged and paid for by an anonymous donor.

Seven months tumble across the screen. A cascade of Hayes' contrived requests for continuances, all granted by Judge Daring, delayed the trial's commencement. Stockmeier agrees to these continuances since his client is in no rush for what seems an inevitable death sentence. Normally, a trial involving a Black man accused of murdering a white man, or worse a white child, would commence in days, not months. However, these continuances "unintentionally" benefit His Honor by postponing the trial until just weeks before his November reelection. How better to win the hearts and minds of voters than by handing them the murder conviction of an "indigent, violent Black man" as reported in the *Gazette*?

Judge Daring harvests a Mt. Everest of political hay. Thanks to the inflaming rhetoric of the Citizens Committee, everyone in Barkersville follows the proceedings, including the judge's political opponent. But publicity is a double-edged sword. Not only does the judge have to get a conviction, but again, thanks to the committee's harassment, he must get a death sentence. Accordingly, the defense attorney's motions to reduce Jerome's first-degree murder charge to manslaughter are denied.

The trial's turning point is Anthony's plea bargain: He will testify that the robbery was Jerome's mastermind, followed by a guilty plea to a reduced charge of manslaughter. The court and district attorney accept the plea.

Hayes spends hours coaching his client.

"Don't look at me, Anthony," says the attorney. "Look at the jury. Be sure you catch each juror's eye. Talk slowly."

Rehearsal follows rehearsal until the performance satisfies the director. Finally, the curtain goes up. Anthony marches onto the witness stand to deliver his soliloquy.

"From start to finish, the whole thing was Jerome's idea. You should've seen im braggin about getting another white man's notch on his gun! He threatened if I didn't go along he'd get some of his 'friends' to make a 'call' on my parents. That son-of-a-bitch! I was scared to death of hurtin someone, so I took all the bullets outta my gun. But when I wasn't lookin, he put em back in. I was so nervous that I didn't notice. When we're lyin there on the floor, after the guns went off, he tried to grab my pearl-handled gun and gimme his, the one with the grip wrapped with duct tape. He knew it was his gun that shot the boy, but I wouldn't let go. That's when he hit me with his gun and broke my nose," says Anthony, pointing to his wounded protrusion with both fingers.

He glances at his attorney, who winks reassuringly.

"Your Honor," Mr. Hayes then asks, "permission to display my client's injury before the jury?"

Request granted, Anthony parades before the jurors, exhibiting the deformity. However, this is the same wound inflicted by police in the squad car while taking him from the crime scene to jail.

"They's all lies!" says Jerome to his attorney. "I wanna say what really ended up happenin!"

Stockmeier remembers "your career will be dead as Hoffa" warning if Manning is acquitted. That warning, plus Stockmeier's oath to act in his client's best interest, wrestle in his conscience. The struggle is a tie.

"Mr. Manning, I strongly advise you not to testify," says Stockmeier. "That prosecutor will tear you apart on the witness stand."

Jerome's lack of testimony, even though the judge warns the jury otherwise before deliberations, does not sit well among jurors. However, after only a day's deliberation, the jury says they are unable to reach a unanimous verdict. Judge Daring gives them a "hammer instruction"—a statement in which he declares the importance of reaching a unanimous verdict due to court time and cost.

Judge Daring glares at the jurors. *Besides, I've got that fucking election in two months. I need that Black son-of-a-bitch found guilty!*

Justice has its motives. So, an hour after receiving the judge's instructions, the jury returns, declaring a unanimous verdict of first-degree murder.

The night's second feature ends with the blinding burst of auditorium lights. Peter waits . . .

Chapter 22

The Decree

"Well, everyone, what did you think of that?" asks Peter.

"If I'd been at the store that night, the last picture you would've been watchin would've been a funeral, not a trial!"

"That damn colored got just what he deserved!"

Other insults spew from the gathering like pus from an infected wound.

Peter waits for the gathering to spend itself when an elderly spectator speaks.

"Not all of us were at the trial, but I was. At the time, I agreed with the verdict, but after seeing these movies . . . If Anthony hadn't loaded Jerome's gun, Timmy'd still be alive. The way that hotshot lawyer coached Anthony to act before the jury and even to lie that Jerome was the mastermind. Now I know how the judge used the trial as a reelection ad. The whole thing stinks! We're the only people on earth who know 'the truth, the whole truth, and nothing but the truth.' How can I, we, in good conscience sentence Jerome to death knowing all *this*?"

Scattered nods of approval twinkle through the assembly.

In his seat, Oscar twists like a dead leaf about to fall from its winter branch. How did Peter find all this shit about the trial?

Mary felt the whole legal process was questionable. First, it was Anthony's questionable bail, then the first-degree murder conviction. After seeing this film, I'm convinced he shouldn't die. I wonder what Kevin thinks.

Kevin's scowl answers her question.

"We seem to have two very different interpretations of these movies," says Peter.

He looks down at Oscar in the front row.

"Well, Mr. Wilson, what about it? After all you've learned about Mr. Manning's life, the crime, and the trial, are you sure you still want to push this button? Upon casting the pebble of death into humanity's sea, deadly ripples travel to innocent shores. This might be an appropriate time," says Peter, scanning the audience, "to ask for divine guidance."

In silent anticipation, all consciousness focuses on Oscar.

"Before I agree to anything again, are you gonna spring any more of your 'quest for justice' movies on us?" asks Oscar.

"Rest assured, Mr. Wilson, I am finished showing movies about past events. However, there are future and even more inflammatory scenes about Jerome, his adopted family, and the legal proceedings. But to show them all we'd be here all night. So I've selected movies of what lies ahead that will enable this assembly to complete its quest."

A perturbed Oscar sighs with relief. More fucking movies, but at least we're done with those of the past. Thank God Peter's not showing that discussion I had with Daring.

Oscar is concerned about a clandestine meeting he had a month before the trial with Judge Daring in the judge's residence. A desperate, frightened Oscar had confessed his fencing operations, including his business dealings with Manning, to His Honor.

* * *

"Hmm, Oscar," says the judge, "I can see why you're worried about Manning's trial. But considering our friendship over the years, I think I can help. A contribution to my campaign fund from my county fair fundraiser later this month, if you'll kindly agree to manage it, of let's say fifteen grand, should keep the nasty little embarrassments about your illicit operation and its providers from surfacing in the courtroom.

"As a former mayor with your contacts, fifteen grand shouldn't be a problem. However, since you are such an esteemed member of the community, you should be more careful of the merchandise you buy and the company you keep. Oh, and that duct-taped gun Manning used in the store robbery? It'll be our little secret that he snatched the weapon from your office. But what about Manning? What's to keep him quiet?"

"Don't worry," says Oscar. "I use the services of a *very* persuasive associate who informed Manning what would happen to his Black girlfriend and her little boy if he opened his mouth about any dealings with me. That Black bastard won't give us any problems."

* * *

Several moments pass as everyone waits for Oscar to speak.

"Mr. Wilson," says Peter. "I repeat, are you still sure you want to push the button?"

"You're damn right I'm still sure!" says Oscar, jerking up as though startled from a nap.

"Gas the sinner!" screams someone from a back row, followed by, "God *damn* his soul! Send im to the eternal fires of hell!"

The assembly roars its approval while a sea of raised arms flails about in a revival's zeal. Overwhelmed by the spirit, the hysteria pounds the walls like waves striking the rock-faced shore of Evangelical righteousness.

Peter waits until the storm subsides to the calm of a tempest's eye.

"Are we," Peter asks, "then united, each of us as the link of a chain, joined together in this virtuous bond of death?"

"Amen brother," thunders the faithful.

However, Peter knows some have kept silent as an empty confessional. He walks to the edge of the stage raising his right hand, into which materializes the Silver Scroll of Sins for the second time tonight.

"Now what?" mumbles Oscar.

"Remember, your decision must be unanimous— everyone here, committee member or not. I will read from this list. When your name is called, declare Mr. Manning's fate by saying either life—or death."

"You getting paid by the hour?" says an exasperated Oscar. "Didn't you hear the crowd? It *is* unanimous!"

Words of support bark from the gathering.

Glaring at the all-too-eager executioner and crowd, Peter decides to cool this boiling cauldron of emotion. Swinging his hand across his face, Peter's countenance degenerates into the macabre, black-robed Angel of Death. Spectators gasp as the apparition aims a bony finger at Oscar.

"Unanimous?" it growls. "Thy guilty conscience doth protest!"

The specter then directs its appendage to the audience.

"Anonymity of the crowd shall fail you in this moment of truth. Each of you shall declare the Black man's fate for all to hear. But choose wisely lest you forge another link to your Marley's chain."

One could hear a palm sweat while the audience assumes a soul-searching silence.

"Daniel Smith, how shall you say?" asks the angel of demise. "Death!"

And so goes the responses down the list.

Albert Fillmore huddles in the crowd, trying to hide in the populace. Still unnerved by his movie exposing the finagling of the used car brakes, Albert prays his name escapes the dreaded angel's summons. Yeah, at first I wanted Manning dead, then after seeing his movie . . . But why do I have to choose in front of everyone? That's why there's courts and juries. That's why there's a blank round in the firing squad. Let others make the decision, get their hands dirty, because whether I say life or death, something's gonna die. If not Manning, it'll be my dealership. That fucking Wilson will make sure of that. If those doors weren't locked, I'd just get up and walk . . .

"Albert Fillmore, how shall you say?"

Albert's mental gymnastics were a ruse to soothe his conscience. His livelihood's demise was never an option.

"Death," he says.

The finger continues its lethal directive until it summons Mary.

Her conscience in turmoil, Mary again turns to Kevin for support, but he stares straight ahead. Mary's anxiety when she closed her public address saying, "And nothing is too severe for that animal who killed my little Timmy!" has soured into remorse. The words Oscar coerced her to utter have fanned vengeance's flame. I resent Wilson's damn intimidation, but what can I do? Avenging Timmy with another death only adds to the violence. But is she willing to pay the price of opposing the committee? Social banishment, boycotts of their clothing business, marital discord? And God only knows what other wretched wares her courage would buy. I must speak up and ask for mercy, I must . . . I . . .

Her knees shaking, she prays for strength to act her conscience. Sensing she is the last hope for Manning's life, Mary stares at the deadly finger. It demands a verdict. Turning to the audience behind her, she searches for encouragement—a nod, a friendly smile, a gesture of support. But though some feel like her, they too are afraid to express sympathy. Void of compassion, the sprout of hope withers in this desert of vengeance.

Noticing her agitation, Cynthia clasps Mary's hands.

"Get a hold of yourself, Mary. Don't betray the love these good people have shown. Support them, Kevin, and the memory of your beloved son. Say it—death!"

For the last time, Mary turns to Kevin, but her pleading stare he still rejects. The finger has yet to summon him, but Mary knows his decision. Never has she felt so alone. Never has she felt such anger with the community. Never has she felt such disappointment with herself.

"Death," she whispers.

"Louder, so all may hear!" demands the angel, shaking its bony appendage.

"Death!" she shouts, knowing its bitter taste shall never leave her mouth.

In shame, she drops her head. Kevin sits still as stone, ignoring the appeal of her extended hand. The couple shall never speak of this night again.

For the handful who felt forgiving of Jerome, Mary was their last hope. If she fails to resist, how can they? So, when the dark spirit beckons them, "death" is their response.

With no voice for life, the roll call concludes.

"*Now* we're in complete agreement!" says the apparition.

Upon its rewind, the scroll disappears for the final time in a twisting vapor.

Shedding the ghoulish disguise, Peter assumes his normal appearance.

"What are you waiting for, Mr. Wilson?" he says to a gleeful Oscar. "Step forward, push the button, then let justice be served!"

Rising from his seat, shoulders arched back in triumph, Oscar struts up to the stage. In a deafening applause, the crowd approves. Oscar stops beside the black button. Finally, after all I've suffered to protect my good name and save the business that finances Michaels' treatments, I have the ability to control fate—mine, Michael's, and Manning's!

Satisfying the instrument's protocol, Oscar declares the name of its victim, the crime, and a punishment of "execution by lethal gas." Theatrical as Caesar at the Coliseum, his finger poised to dispense judgment, Oscar awaits the mob's declaration.

"Death!"

Nodding in agreement, Oscar turns to the unholy instrument and pushes the button.

After a roll of thunder proclaims destiny's new direction, the gathering's frenzy dies in a gasp. Darkness shrouds the auditorium as the universe succumbs to the assembly's decree.

Chapter 23

The Last Walk

"Congratulations, Mr. Wilson," says Peter, his steel gray eyes aflame, "and to all of you. The movies you have seen so far tonight are reflections of past occurrences. But since you've decided to play God this evening, you will be privileged with His supreme capacity to witness the future, a future *you* have created. It will be shown in tonight's final feature film, *A Preview of Coming Attractions*. Ask not how you could have changed the unalterable events you are about to see. Ask how you can forget them. No one can leave until the end of the final scene when *I* say it's over."

A folding metal chair materializes and falls to the stage, crashing in front of the screen.

"Your throne, Mr. Wilson," Peter says, waving his arm at the chair.

A sulking Oscar sits. The clanking projector shutters as the lights go out in a flash of darkness.

* * *

The movie begins. As with previous presentations, a narration describes scenes, feelings, and even thoughts of onscreen characters. The audience is thrown ahead in time three years into a dingy hallway in front of Alice Smith's apartment.

Nathan stands in the hall, key in hand, wondering if he dares open the door. His mom spent yesterday drinking herself into unconsciousness, again. He left to spend the night among friends. Resigned, he opens the door. He sees her slumped face down, arms stretched across the kitchen table between a once-full vodka bottle and an overturned, finger-smeared glass.

"Mamma!" he says. "Git up an sleep it off in bed!"

After Jerome's death sentence three years ago, his mother started drinking. During the five days following the notification all appeals had failed, she escaped reality in alcoholic oblivion. Under Alice's arm lies yesterday's *Gazette*. It features a front-page article plus a half-page picture of the City Council's 1991 Citizen of the Year, Oscar Wilson. The newspaper states this honor was bestowed on Mr. Wilson for his efforts in ensuring Jerome Manning received the death sentence.

The Sunday, October 13th article goes on to say:

"All appeals for Mr. Manning have been exhausted. Judge Daring has set Saturday, December 14th as the execution date. The Citizen of the Year Award Ceremony, normally scheduled for the first Saturday in November, will be postponed until December 14th. The festivities will end by 7:00 p.m., allowing Mr. Wilson sufficient time to travel to the prison for the Manning 11:00 p.m. execution. This will be a day of double celebrations for both Mr. Wilson and our community."

"Mamma . . . Mamma!"

Growing more desperate, Nathan shakes her body. Then he sees it, an empty vial of sleeping pills clutched in one lifeless hand and a white ceramic dove in the other.

Nathan sits by his mother all day. Evening comes. Nathan ties a small, black bag to his belt. Into the bag he shoves his only worldly treasures: his mother's gold necklace, her two heart-shaped gold earrings, plus the white ceramic dove. Snipping out the "Citizen of the Year" article, he stuffs the clipping in the bag. Nathan rips the picture of Wilson's smiling face staring up at him from the newspaper. Cramming the torn paper into the drinking glass, he hurls it against the wall.

"I'm gonna fuckin kill that Wilson fella one day!"

A neighbor's door sneaks open, its occupant spying on the Smith residence's door.

Nathan storms down the hall and out of the building to start his new life on the street.

* * *

As Oscar sits in his chair watching the movie, Nathan's on-screen threat blows a cold breath of fear down the back of his neck. Quite a change from the movie's earlier scene when he basked in the glory of the Citizen of the Year award like a vulture sunning itself after a meal.

* * *

The movie switches scenes from the apartment to the Iron Mountain Correctional Center.

"Hey, boy," says a prison officer to Jerome the day after Alice's suicide. "There's somethin in the paper you might find interestin."

Under the cell bars, the officer slides a copy of the *Gazette* with a back-page headline:

"Black Woman Found Dead"

While Jerome sobs in the background, the screen fades to black.

* * *

An image of Mary ignites the screen as the movie rolls ahead two months to the day before Jerome's execution.

Mary waits all morning in the Iron Mountain Correctional Center (IMCC) lobby for her last visit with Jerome. Her four-hour hiatus is a deliberate ploy by the prison officers intending to make this final encounter as uncomfortable as procedures allow.

"Mary Cook!" resonates through the lobby.

Boot steps of an approaching, scowling, khaki-uniformed escort echo in the room.

"Follow me!" he says.

In his hand, the armed usher carries a brass ring which coils through a collection of keys chiming their flat, metallic tune to the rhythm of the strutting guide.

Mary trails the officer through an opened steel door into a short, shadowed hall. On one side roosts a row of metal, folding chairs. On the other, five wire-reinforced security windows glare through the concrete wall.

"Sit there!" says the officer, skidding a chair towards a window.

Mary sits, squinting through the window into an empty, black room. The officer marches to the hall's end. Throwing himself into a chair, his pistol clangs against the metal seat. Arms folded, he stares at Mary. After a half-hour wait, the empty room alights. In walks Jerome through a rear barred door. He sits at the window, forcing a smile.

"How ya doin, Miss Mary?" he asks through a circular, grilled opening.

"I'm alright, Jerome. How are *you*?"

"I'm doin fine."

Briefly, they discuss trivial concerns. Then, after an awkward silence, Mary leans to the grill.

"Jerome, I know we've talked about this before, but *please*, let me come to the viewing room tomorrow. I want you to have at least one friend there as a witness."

"Like I say before, Miss Mary, No! Ya know how them people is always talkin bout ya helpin that damn colored. So, don't ya be wastin any more time with me."

"I'm *not* wasting my time, Jerome. I know you didn't mean to hurt my Timmy. You should've only got manslaughter just like Anthony. Like *I've* said before, I blame him and that damn Wilson for my boy's death more than I do you."

Tears trickle down her cheeks.

"Most all of my friends are givin me the cold shoulder. And Kevin and me haven't talked since the divorce. But that doesn't matter. This is something I want . . . something I *have* to do!"

Seeing the officer staring from the corner, she leans so close her lips almost touch the grill.

"Why I let Wilson talk me into saying that horrible thing about you at the Citizens Meeting will haunt me the rest of my life."

"Now you just lissen ta me! Don't ya go blamin yourself! You ended up bein one of my best friends. Visitin me, tryin for a retrial, gettin them ACLU people. Considerin what I done, you a blessed miracle just like that Virgin Mary."

Mary wipes away a tear.

Silence softens the room.

Motionless, Jerome stares at his hands folded on the counter. One thing bothers him as much as his impending death—the fate of Nathan. Many a sleepless night, Jerome has lain on his cot reminiscing of the boy who was the closest thing he had to a son. Jerome prays he could see the boy one more time before

. . .

"Miss Mary, ya hear anythin bout Nathan?" he asks, raising his head.

"I've been told after he left the apartment, he went to live with some street friends. I put the word out that I want to see him. I've even gone to the homeless encampment."

"Miss Mary, you stay away from that place. Ya know that ain't nowhere for a lady ta be goin!"

Jerome gazes into her eyes. Another lengthy silence follows. He wants to savor these moments of the last friendly face he will see, wishing he could reach out, hold her hand, and then hug her.

"Miss Mary, I . . . I wanna say . . . thank ya."

Mary responds by pressing her hand against the window. Mist, like a halo, condenses around her palm. Jerome holds his hand up, opposite Mary's, pressing tight against the chill surface. Soon his beckoning palm is answered by a growing, warm radiance, a loving glow, as though the two are touching. Jerome drops his hand. The warmth succumbs to the room's isolation.

"Ya know, Miss Mary, they's right. If I'd just stayed away from the store that night, I wouldn't be havin none of these problems, nothin." Casting his eyes upward, he cries, "Oh Lawd, take this sinner ta my dear ol Auntie Helen!"

"Time's up!" says the officer.

* * *

"Did . . . did you hear *that*?" says Oscar, leaping from his onstage chair. "Even *Jerome* admits his guilt! Just . . . just . . . just like *I* said!"

"What's that quiver in your voice, Mr. Wilson? Fear?" asks Peter. "Now keep quiet and sit."

Oscar slumps into his chair.

* * *

The next scene transpires in the IMCC execution wing on the day of Jerome's execution.

"Full house!" shouts Correctional Officer James Kinsley, slapping his cards on the table.

His voice bounces from one bare concrete wall to another in the death watch room.

"Keep your voice down, Jimmy. That 'Silent' sign outside means us too," says Sergeant Branch, irritated at winning only four poker hands all evening.

"Sarge, you know he can't hear anything through these walls."

Jim steps to the window through which they have observed the condemned prisoner, Jerome Manning, who occupies the death watch cell across the hall. Jerome, dressed in an orange jumpsuit, sits on a cot. In the hall between him and the window sits a Black minister from the Baptist Church. A closeup of the prisoner's right hand reveals Jerome is wearing a large ring, white gold, with an embossed cross on either side of a large diamond.

An elbow pressed on each knee, Jerome hunches forward on the cot's edge holding a letter stretched between his hands. His eyes, wide in astonishment, stumble word by word across the handwritten document. The sitting minister blocks the officers' view of the letter.

"Sarge, he's *still* sittin on the cot. I bet he hasn't moved an inch in over an hour."

"Not surprising. They all either freeze or pace like wild animals in their final hours."

"It's 10:15," says Branch, glancing at the wall clock. "Better be gettin im ready."

Saturday's death watch comes to an end. For over twenty-three hours, two correctional officers in eight-hour shifts spied on Jerome. Jim and Branch were assigned the final watch. During the last three hours, the minister has sat beside the cell, consoling the condemned. In forty-five minutes, Timmy Cook's murderer will exhale his last breath. The establishment believes that death at the "eleventh hour" is poetic justice, plus it avoids the blasphemy of a Sabbath execution.

The officers stand. Amplified by the hallway, the squeal of the opening door startles Jerome. His face distorted in fear, Jerome watches the uniformed men march forward, one clutching handcuffs and leg shackles. Their black, leather boots step in unison as the cadence of their death walk reverberates throughout the concrete enclosure. Trembling, Jerome folds the letter. Along with the ring, he slips them into a leg pocket.

The leftovers of the fifteen-dollar last meal of well-done steak, French fries, and vanilla ice cream, wither in a plastic tray on a stool beside the cell door. On a table cantilevered from a wall, an unopened Bible beckons. On the opposite side of the concrete cell hangs a metal cot. Its brown blanket barely wrinkles under Jerome who sits on the edge.

"Mr. Manning, it's time," says Sergeant Branch.

Clank. The cell door unlocks. Its low-pitch grown announces the officer's entry. They stand at attention in front of Jerome who looks up at the somber-faced pair.

"Please stand," says Branch.

The acid taste of fear burning in his mouth, Jerome rises, shuddering.

"Jerome, you'd like me to make the walk with you?" asks the minister, standing.

"Yeah, I'd like ya ta do that."

"After our walk, I'm going to the viewing room. You rest your eyes on me, my child."

Jim kneels to shackle Jerome's ankles.

"Mr. Manning," says Branch, noticing a bulge in the prisoner's pockets. "I'm gonna have to take whatever contraband you're hiding. Nothing on your person besides your jumpsuit is permitted outside this cell."

"Yes, Sir." Removing the ring and letter, Jerome hands them to the sergeant.

"The other pocket, too."

Jerome feigns a querying stare.

"Mr. Manning, I said empty your other pocket, now!"

A wad of tissue paper drops onto the sergeant's extended hand. Branch unwinds the bundle, exposing a small, white, ceramic dove.

"Reverend, you were warned *not* to give the prisoner anything," he says, turning to the minister.

"The Lord make me do it," says the preacher. "Can Mr. Manning keep the items? It *is* the Christian thing to do."

Clenching his fist, Branch glares at the minister.

"Sarge, I know the regulations," says Jim, "but what can it hurt? I can put his stuff in my trousers. After I've strapped him in, I'll give it back to him. No one will notice. I'll be sure and take em back when he's, uh . . . *after* it's over."

The condemned watches Branch scratching his cheek in thought.

Avoiding eye contact with Manning, Branch agrees.

"But for Christ's sake, Jimmy, uh, pardon me, Reverend, *don't* tell anyone," he says, handing the items to Jim.

"Thank ya, Sir," says Jerome.

"Slide your feet together," says the sergeant as Jim locks the leg irons.

Staring into the distance, Jerome hears the ratcheting of handcuffs on his wrists as he feels their cold embrace. After securing the cuffs to his waist chain, the officers lead the weak-kneed prisoner into the hall where the chaplain awaits.

"Fear not my son . . . " hears Jerome as terror pulls his senses to the scene before him.

Half dragged by the correctional officers on either side as his heart thumps and leg irons rattle, he shuffles the fifty feet to the gas chamber. Its interior matches the description made by that nice officer in the first eight-hour shift.

"It's got six sides, green, and it's about nine feet wide. Three windows face the viewing room. They'll be covered with a curtain when you go in. A steel chair is in the middle of the chamber facing the windows. They'll strap you in it, then open the curtains. You'll see the witnesses, already seated, about twenty or so. That's about the biggest we've had for one of these."

Jerome stands frozen at the chamber's open door, resigned to his fate. From the moment he was told one of the bullets he and Anthony fired at Mother's Groceries had killed a little boy, he knew *he* was a dead man. Who fired the shot made no difference. The child was white. Anthony was white. He was Black. No one in Vegas would take those odds.

Jerome fails to notice a man seated in a metal chair to his right. The man is the executioner, a twenty-one-year veteran correctional officer who brags of nine exterminations—two whites, and seven Blacks by his hand. At the appointed time, the warden will order him to throw the lever, dropping the potassium cyanide pellets into the sulfuric acid tank.

Staring over his shoulder, the executioner concentrates on the execution clock, its white face accenting the large, black numerals which read 10:34 p.m. A red wall phone waits under the clock, a direct line to the governor's office that has never rung for a Black man's stay of execution.

Into the nearly full viewing room walks the minister. He talks to an officer who points to the first row in front of the gas chamber, the row reserved for the Cook family and their guests. The minister heads down the aisle passing friends of the family, high-ranking prison officials, reporters, committee members, and the prosecution. He stops at the front where Kevin sits.

"Excuse me, but are you Kevin Cook?" asks the minister.

As Kevin nods yes, the minister offers his condolences.

"Thank you, Reverend," Kevin says, pointing to three vacant seats beside him. "Take one. No one else from the family or friends will be here."

"Don't know what's happened to Wilson. We're still waiting. That's his seat," he says, pointing to the last one on his right.

Declining, the minister moves to the rear of the room.

Kevin leans back, glaring forward.

* * *

Like a child watching a horror movie, an increasingly alarmed Oscar squirms in his chair. First, it was Nathan's death threat. Then it's the ring I bought from Jerome. What the fuck's he doing with it? Now I'm not in the viewing room. No way would I've of missed this execution. All this adds to Oscar's weight of impending doom. He wonders if that thumping in his head is his throbbing heart or the thud of dirt on his coffin . . .

* * *

Onscreen, in the gas chamber, Mr. Manning's uncoupled chains lie on the floor. He sits in the steel chair as the two officers bend over him, fastening the leather straps.

"Mister?" asks Jerome, looking up at Sergeant Branch.

"What?"

"I gotta go pee."

"They all say that," says Branch, glancing at Jim. "Just ignore it. Be sure the straps are good and tight. Towards the end, they'll writhe and pull with superhuman strength."

He speaks as though Jerome was not there.

After Jim finishes the straps, he surveys the area, confirming no one watches. He places the gold ring on Jerome's finger. Folding the letter tightly, he slips the paper in the hand with the ring. Into the other hand, Jim places the dove.

"Thank ya," Jerome says. "You been the kindest of em all."

The straps cut deep into the condemned man's wrists and ankles. Within moments, the veins protrude, screaming for blood. Onto Jerome's chest, the officers tape a stethoscope attached to a tube extending through the chamber's wall to an earpiece outside. Through this, the doctor will listen to determine when the condemned's heart stops.

"It's working," says the doctor, giving the okay sign.

Branch, then Jim, exits the chamber. They close the airtight door which locks in a heavy thud.

All preparations completed, the warden gives the signal to open the curtains.

Jerome stares into the room before him . . .

Chapter 24

An Ember Turns Cold

Mary stares at the movie screen. She couldn't be more distressed at the events she witnessed. I wanna leave this auditorium, run away to someplace where no one knows me or I them. But since Jerome didn't want me to witness his real execution in person, I feel I have to stay and watch this morbid show. After all, I am partly to blame. Dear God, how will I ever be able to live with myself?

The auditorium lights turn on briefly while Peter makes some adjustments to the projector.

"I want to make sure everything's in sharp focus with this contraption. Don't want you to miss a single hair on the condemned man's head."

Chore completed, Peter closes the projector door with a slam as the room falls into darkness. The image of Jerome strapped to the death chair fills the screen. The narration echoes through the auditorium.

* * *

Jerome strains to see Mary in the execution viewing room. To his relief, he finds her absent.

To his surprise, he also notices Mr. Wilson is missing. Jerome then views the rest of the witnesses. Most watch through cold, somber eyes except for a shaved head, smiling man in the last row.

"Die nigra," he mouths.

Jerome focuses on the front row seats in which sits just one person, Kevin, who watches with a hateful stare.

"I'm sorry," Jerome whispers, though he knows Kevin cannot hear.

Reading Jerome's lips, the unheard apology enrages Kevin more. Before coming to tonight's execution, he read an article concerning deaths by cyanide gas. Glaring at the condemned man, Kevin prays the execution is as horrific as what he read.

"The victim," says the movie's narrator, reciting the article to the assembly, "is told to avoid needless suffering by taking deep breaths which speeds unconsciousness, but few seldom do. They show unmistakable signs of extreme horror and pain, looking as though they're strangling as they gasp for air, drooling profusely. Sometimes it can take over ten minutes for the condemned man to die. During this time, the victim can be heard moaning. In one ghoulish execution, the victim died while smashing his head against the steel pole next to his chair, blood pouring down his purple face with bulging eyes. Some executions are so gruesome to watch that the warden has ordered the curtains closed and the viewing room cleared."

Though despised by those present, Jerome, having made peace with himself and God, is freed of hatred. Though he fears death, he is consoled by the folded letter in his hand. At least one person cares . . .

* * *

"For God's sake, do we have to listen to this morbid garbage?" says a bearded man in the audience.

"Would you prefer real-life footage instead?" says Peter.

"And what's that damn letter say?" asks the man, ignoring Peter's question.

"Words of encouragement and love."

"Who wrote it? Alice, before she died? Nathan? Who?"

"You wouldn't believe it even if I told you. Some things are best left to our imagination."

* * *

But Jerome's sentiments of peace are about to change. Through the chamber's window, he sees the viewing room clock. It shows 10:58. Only two more minutes. In a flame of panic in this, his final life's episode, he abandons all his preparations: praying, meditating, concentrating on the minister's words of forgiveness and eternal life, focusing on Mary's conversations about how she will be beside him in spirit. He yanks on the leather straps. His racing heart and labored breathing work against all efforts to calm himself. Alone and afraid, he sits in the cold, steeled chamber.

His torment pleases the vultures perched in the viewing room. Their prior dispassionate faces break into jagged displays of hatred tinged with joy as they await their feast.

"Dear Lawd," pleads Jerome in a mournful prayer, "please help me."

All seems hopeless. Then as he gasps preparing to scream, cursing fate, God, and all those present, he looks up, locking eyes with the minister at the rear of the room. Their spirits embrace. Time, then anguish, seems to stop. Jerome surrenders to a protective calm as though being smothered in his Aunt Helen's bosom. The scene of the viewing room softens, drifting into an amorphous blur, leaving only the serenity of the minister's caring eyes into which Jerome loses himself—for the rest of his life . . .

The warden reads the death sentence.

"Are there any last words before the sentence is imposed, Mr. Manning?"

Jerome's eyes are still locked on the reverend.

"The Lawd," says Jerome, "he know I never want ta hurt that

child an I knew what we was doin is wrong, robbin the store an all. But Auntie Helen she tells me ya gotta take care'a ya family even if ya gotta steal. I brought a gun that wasn't supposed ta be loaded just ta scare people, but Anthony he put them bullets in an I . . . "

A long pause follows.

"If they only done kept that shelter open, an if I done never met Anthony . . . "

Breaking eye contact with the minister, Jerome looks up.

"Auntie Helen, I'm comin for a long visit."

As is the custom, no black hood covers the victim's head. The callous prison clock marks the eleventh hour as the executioner pulls the lever, splashing its poison into the toxic broth. Slowly the brew boils, spitting out its lethal vapor that rises, filling the chamber with the aroma of death. Jerome, wide-eyed, waits. Each labored breath echoes in the steel tomb while the bellows of his chest heave, fanning the flame that heats the ember of life.

The bellows turns silent. The ember turns cold. The screen turns black.

A dark, mute stillness pervades the auditorium.

Chapter 25

A Warning

The audience reacts to Jerome's demise in an explosion of applause, cheers, and jeers.

"Say 'hi' to your aunt!"

"Don't forget to dress cool!"

"Bravo. An Oscar-winning performance!"

* * *

Tired of being center stage throughout tonight's assembly, Peter leaves the podium and stands in the back of the room. Though submerged and unseen in the auditorium's darkness, he observes the celebration. This is not the reaction for which he had hoped. Two years have passed since Peter's metamorphosis from The Beast to a benevolent spirit. During that time, he trained as an apprentice benefactor under master benefactor Scott's tutelage. Peter had reluctantly taken this citizen's meeting assignment as his apprenticeship initiation. The outcome—bundled with emotion and laced with prejudice—was traumatic, even though he foresaw the meeting's conclusion. But unlike a veteran of the trade, Peter was desperate to alter the future of Jerome, Alice, and Nathan.

"You cannot save them from their fate," warned Scott. He often talked about the natural desire to alter mortal affairs. "But what would intervention accomplish, what would mortals learn? Wisdom and love can flower from the bitter seeds of pain. Benefactors suggest and enlighten but allow free will to wind its way through life's maze."

Though Peter never told Scott, lured by the rebelliousness of a novice he was hopeful he could alter events. *At times, it's a curse, this knowledge of the future. But with my supernatural abilities, I believe I can intercede and compel acts of love.*

* * *

"Turn on the lights!" someone shouts.

As if obeying a director's command, the auditorium illuminates. But on the stage, Peter no longer stands by the podium. All in the audience twist their heads, searching the auditorium, but he is nowhere in sight.

"Where's that Peter guy? Look, he left all his stuff."

"Might as well. None of it worked anyway. Maybe he's looking for a rabbit and a hat."

"I'll take King Kong's door chime!"

One by one, the assembly rises, slapping one another on the back as they shake hands. Congratulations are due for a job well done and a rewarding evening.

However, Oscar struggles from his chair. He trudges off the stage preoccupied by the disturbing scenes of the ring plus his absence at the execution. The audience, blind to the ring and the nonattendance's significance, is surprised at Oscar's demeanor as they offer congratulations on his future Citizen of the Year nomination.

"What's the matter, Oscar?" someone asks. "You look like you've seen a ghost."

"Yeah, Jerome's!" another replies, laughing.

The sound of merriment pains Mary's ears. While the fruit of her statement about Jerome, "that animal who killed my Timmy" ripened upon the screen, she covered her eyes. *Maybe I could've stopped this tragedy, but in my moment of truth, I chose the* hell of hate. I pray my Maker exhibits more compassion when I enter the Pearly Gates.

Others besides Mary disdain her actions tonight. Her images of comforting Jerome make Mary as welcomed as a skunk in a perfumery. Her girlfriend rises from the adjacent seat, wheels about, then storms away. Even Kevin turns his back. He remembers Mary's statement in the movie about a divorce. Based on what she's done and will do, a separation can't happen soon enough. I don't want to be within range of that splattering shit.

Alone, Mary sits. What have I gained?

The night's agenda complete, people head to the exits.

The first to reach a door, Albert Fillmore, notices a figure leaning against a wall in a nearby shadow. Stepping into the light, the figure says, "And where do you think *you're* going?"

"Peter!" says Albert. "We were sure you'd left."

"And leave all my stuff behind? You wouldn't want those contraptions to fall into the wrong hands, would you?" asks Peter, placing his hand on Albert's shoulder.

Coincidentally, returning later to confiscate the projector plus the Black Button had been considered by Albert. Surely, they'll not be missed and could be useful in my business.

"I'm sure they could," says Peter, failing to say he can hear thoughts when in physical contact.

Releasing a startled Albert, Peter faces the throng heading towards him.

"I hate to interrupt this procession," says Peter, "but we're not quite finished."

Upon hearing his familiar voice, all stop looking up to the exit.

"Peter? We thought you'd left," someone yells.

"So I've been told. But like I said before, it ain't over til *I* say it's over, and it's not. So, I must insist, return to your seats."

The sounds of celebration concede to the clatter of chairs and uneasy gossip as all return to their places. Consumed by a sense of foreboding, Oscar trudges back to his onstage seat. Peter weaves to the stage through the crowded aisle. Standing beside the podium, he waits for silence.

"What's happened to the celebrating?" asks Peter. "Was it something I said?"

"Yeah. Every time you talk to us in *that* tone, something bad happens!" a woman shouts.

The stillness of the audience confirms the statement.

"Well, that's understandable. I've confronted and pushed you outside your comfort zone. My task tonight was to assist you in justice's quest. I challenged you to look at justice from a different perspective. Unfortunately, had a more compassionate outcome occurred, its unpleasant repercussions could've been avoided."

"Unpleasant repercussions? Jerome got all the compassion he deserved!" says the woman.

"I wasn't just talking about Jerome. I was also talking about all of *you*."

A hush follows as the audience turns, looking at each other with worried faces.

"As you've all witnessed, *you* have set in motion a series of events. They will lead to Jerome's death sentence, Alice's suicide, and Nathan's life on the street."

"So what!"

"So, the street gang becomes Nathan's family. The brotherhood of violence increases its membership by one, and this violence will eventually come knocking at *your* door."

Hearing this prophecy, more uneasiness grips the audience.

After a long silence, Albert Fillmore raises his hand.

"Yes, Albert, what is it?" asks Peter.

"If we change our vote, will the future be different?" he asks in a barely audible voice.

Oscar, though still concerned by onscreen events, refuses to let Albert's question slide by.

"For Christ's sake, Albert," he says, leaping up, "act like a man! Things have to run their course, good and bad. But I don't believe any of this shit about violence knocking at our door."

"Spoken with your usual eloquence, Mr. Wilson," says Peter. He turns back to Albert. "Had a change of heart, Mr. Fillmore, or are you just afraid of the consequences?"

Though Albert's motive is a bit of each, the question offends him.

"Peter, you know we're not all like *him*," he says, pointing up to Oscar.

"Well, tell me Mr. Fillmore, why are you here tonight?" asks Peter before Oscar can respond.

"Because he threatened me!"

"Threatened you?" Peter turns to Oscar. "What have you done to this poor man?"

Glaring at Albert, Oscar says nothing.

Furious at being mocked, Albert overrules his financial instincts.

"Oscar said," Albert confesses, "if I didn't show up tonight to help 'teach that nigra a lesson,' he and his friends might start taking their business over to Barkersville Chevrolet. So you see, I'm not here for the same reasons as him. I'm not a bigot!"

The audience can almost hear Albert's gasps as he realizes what he just said.

Rubbing his chin, Oscar flashes a sinister smile. The little shit! I can already see the "For Sale" sign on his showroom window.

"So, Mr. Fillmore," says Peter, "your presence tonight is just financially driven, and for *that,* you sent Jerome to his death. I'm sure he, Alice, and Nathan will appreciate it wasn't personal."

Thankful not to be in Albert's shoes, all watch the soon-to-be-blacklisted auto dealer's face fade in fear as he takes his seat.

Peter looks upon the crowd, awaiting the attention of all anxious eyes.

"Ladies and gentlemen," he says, "I am privileged to have assisted you. It has been a difficult and emotional evening."

"You can say that again! Ain't no one gonna believe what happened here tonight," says a worried spectator.

"Right you are!" says Peter. "And because of that, once you walk through those doors, you'll all forget about me and the supernatural events that have occurred. You'll only remember unanimously agreeing to send a death petition to Judge Daring."

Looming behind the podium, Peter adds this warning:

"You shall be visited in your dreams by the haunting images of this evening's events. And each of you will suffer the consequences of your actions tonight. May you rest easy with your decision."

Peter proclaims an end to the proceedings.

Outside, the tempest phantoms thunder their approval. The auditorium's doors fling open, offering the hall's attendees as a sacrifice to the howling storm. Solemn as a wake, the gathering rises, trudging to the exits.

PART III

THE APPRENTICE

September 1988

Chapter 26

Kryptonite

Within a remote hilltop grove stands a stately elm. Trusting Mother Earth will sustain it through drought, storm, and flames, the ancient tree waits in the present, content with its stationary existence. For decades, the foliaged sentinel has observed under a branching silhouette the curious events of mortals and spirits. In horror, the elm remembers the evil committed by men at the end of a rope. In joy, the knoll's custodian watched the transformation of a tormented soul named Peter.

Rooted in the wisdom of age, the barked beauty wonders why these sapiens never seem at peace, either fretting over what might happen or resentful over that which did. Never do they appreciate the beauty of the moment. The bark-clad soul pities these restless beings, the professed pinnacles of evolution, offering them grace the only way the tree can, a place of respite under its shade. Pause, be still. Appreciate the offering.

With wrinkled fingers of bark, the elm clutches a seven-decade-old bronze plaque. Draped in an aged patina, the plaque displays its embossed inscription:

In memory of one who died here:
"The only thing necessary for the triumph of evil is for good men to do nothing."
Quote attributed to Edmund Burke

Leaves chime in the wind.

In the summer afternoon shade stands a high-backed, oak bench encrusted with dead leaves on which sits a Black man. His face, eroded by time, rests under a cap of once-black hair bleached to a silvery gray. Leaning on a worn, leather-cloaked tome, he surveys the surroundings.

Panting, Peter quickens his pace, his thoughts in harmony with his worried face. He can see his benefactor, Scott, up the path on the bench. Peter knows Scott can hear the aggregate announce each step. As Peter approaches, Scott's face shrinks to a scowl.

"You are late. I expect my apprentices to demonstrate their commitment by promptness."

"Sorry, overslept," says Peter, fidgeting with a copy of the *Barkersville Gazette* in his hand.

"Long night?" asks Scott with a softening tone.

Peter nods yes.

Scott motions him to sit.

Peter slaps down the newspaper. Leaves scatter, boiling in the air. Seated beside his benefactor, Peter mops his brow with a handkerchief.

"I see you are still wearing the disguise as a white man you used last night," says Scott.

"Yeah. If I'm gonna work with those people, I suppose I better look like em."

"So, how do you feel being white?"

"Looking like my mortal oppressor is unnerving. In a way, being white's worse than being The Beast. So, I'm wearing my disguise full-time to get used to it because, in the short time I've appeared white, I've noticed people treat me differently."

"Oh, really?" says Scott through his all-knowing smile.

"Yeah. White folks nod, smiling at me. But my brothers and sisters seem distant—avoid eye contact. I also find myself not being so concerned about what's going on around me, like a weight's been lifted. But I feel guilty enjoying it."

"The weight lifted is called fear. Welcome to the world of the privileged. Oh, speaking of the privileged, how did things go last night with the Citizens Committee?"

Avoiding Scott's stare, Peter's expression darkens.

"Well, your look says the meeting was a disaster. I assume someone pushed the button?" asks Scott.

Silence verifies the remark.

"Peter, you *are* allowed to speak."

Cramped against each other on the bench, Scott listens to Peter's mental dialogue. But Scott blocks his thoughts to Peter, whose stoic silence snaps.

"You're my benefactor. You know my past and future, so you tell *me* how it went!"

"Yes, I know what happened, but you will feel better getting all your frustration off your chest."

Peter grabs the *Gazette*, exposing the headline:

"Citizens Demand Death"

The headline's picture shows Oscar Wilson standing behind an onstage podium at City Hall.

"How can this pompous ass live with himself?" says Peter.

The headline's article states the Citizens for Justice Committee, including its guests, voted unanimously to send a petition to Judge Daring demanding the death sentence for Jerome Manning. The article concludes with:

"Former Mayor Oscar Wilson, Chairman of The Citizens Committee, declared, "We want Judge Charles Daring to know what the voting citizens of this community are thinking. We, under no circumstances, will tolerate anything less than the death penalty. Judge Daring should be mindful of this considering his reelection is only five months away."

"I'm keeping this page," says Peter, "as a reminder of last night's failure."

"My son, if you keep a scrapbook of every disaster you have as a benefactor, you will need a moving van to carry it."

Peter, his words tasting like spoiled milk, speaks of last night's fiasco. He describes the movies, and how he tried to instill sympathy for Jerome by showing scenes of Jerome's childhood, including the love he showed for his adopted family of Alice and Nathan. Peter details the rigged trial plus how he threatened to read committee members' evil deeds from a list called The Silver Scroll.

"The way you handled the meeting was ingenious. I was impressed by your formal, commanding manner of speech," says Scott. "I especially liked the scroll bit."

"Thanks. But I didn't have to read it . . . To them, the *fear* of exposure was more terrifying than the shame. I wanted them to savor their evil, to marinate the sin in their conscience until their deeds tasted as foul as rotting flesh, hoping the deed would soften someone's heart. Just *one* courageous person, only one, to defy the committee and show mercy."

"Not one person did. So, how do you feel?"

"Damned disappointed, especially that chairman, ex-mayor Oscar Wilson. I *don't* like that asshole one damn bit! Does he *have* to be one of my clients? Without him, I might've changed the committee's mind. *He* was the one who finally pushed the button," says Peter, shaking his head. "I hate them all, the bastards! Well, not so much Mary, she almost voted for Jerome's life, but she didn't have a chance considering all the pressure from the blood-thirsty mob."

"You will require more than a few movies to have them dropping to their knees in shame," Scott replies. "Speaking of mobs, you need a refresher course in hell. Remember how you tried to impose your will on the lynch mob as The Beast? Nothing good resulted for them or you. Well, son, you are doing the same thing with the Citizens Committee."

Peter squirms on the bench. Leaves crackle.

With a handkerchief, Scott wipes the sweat and concern from his face, exposing a lopsided grin. He stands, surveying the clearing around the elm.

"Things have certainly changed; not like the *ghoul* old days, is it?" he says.

Scott refers to the new Phantom Ridge Park, a public works gift funded by a trust bequeathed in the late Senator Bartholomew Cumming's will. The impetus for this park was the recently completed state prison, Iron Mountain Correctional Center. It is clearly visible below from the park's knoll via a twenty-minute walk on a gravel path starting at the prison's parking lot then rambling through the woods. Peter walked this path this morning.

For years, the senator had fought against the construction of the massive jail with its "walls of concrete, barbed wire, and sorrow." At least he could offer visitors of the penitentiary's inmates a retreat, a place of serenity, dedicated to another victim of society's inhumanity, the anonymous Black man lynched from this elm decades ago.

Gone is the debris-lined canopy including the cobwebbed lair of its former resident, The Beast. The decayed cross of limbs marking Peter's grave has been replaced with a granite tombstone upon which is chiseled *Unknown.* In addition to the one on the elm, recently added was another bronze plaque attached to a stone pedestal beside the bench. The plaque commemorates the notorious history of Phantom Ridge. This former isolated site of fear now glows in the warmth of loving attention.

Scott resumes his position between his client and the tome.

The BOOK, inscribed in silver, gothic letters adorns the massive brown, leathered volume. On the silver-gilded fore-edge are a dozen indentations sequentially inscribed in gold Roman numerals. Each tab marks a statute, a code of conduct, to which all benefactors must conform. The publication is referred to as the Benefactor's Bible.

Peter glares ahead, pretending disinterest.

"As I have said, we have little control over the free will of mortals. Humanity must be allowed to act without our interference," says Scott, slapping Peter's knee. "Just as stated in these pages."

Peter answers with a mute stare, but his attention peeks through the corner of his eye. "I know . . . I know," he says. Then he opens the tome to Statutes XI and XII:

"XI: A client's free will is supreme, therefore, benefactors shall never coerce a client, mortal or spirit, into an act regardless of the consequences, nor shall a benefactor directly intervene to alter fate. A benefactor shall influence behavior and situations solely as an appeal to the client's conscience, and all powers and devices bequeathed to a benefactor shall be used only as a means to that end. Such powers shall include prophecy, telepathy, time dilation, teleportation, shapeshifting, polyglotism, invisibility, and conjuring material commodities.

XII: Beneficiaries are children of God and as such shall at all times be treated with love. Their deeds are never wrong, for they cannot act in any other way. A client shall never be abandoned, judged, or ridiculed."

Without looking at the manuscript, Peter recites verbatim both statutes.

"Good," says Scott. "You sound like a bored Sunday school hostage. But after memorizing them, practicing them are choirs of the faithful. 'Influence behavior and situations' is not a carte blanche for action. Some clients ask for our help, like you when you cried to God for mercy before your lynching. Others never request help, especially those tormented by an obsession, like you when seeking vengeance as The Beast. However, a few of the tormented, after enough fear, pain, and remorse, *may* be willing to change. But without *willingness*, they fail. Neither you, I, nor God can fix that. For this reason, you had no success last night, except for Mary. They have yet to suffer the pain of their actions."

"I felt like an idiot saying they'd suffer for their actions. Other than Mary helping Jerome, I haven't a clue what the future holds."

"As an apprentice, you can only see fragments of your clients' fate. But this current inability is not *your* concern. They have free will. Some are unwilling to accept the gifts of suffering, gifts that only come through the pain of change."

"Yeah, unwilling," says Peter. "Like my first act of justice, The Accuser. There I was beside his deathbed. I really thought my hideous presence as The Beast would scare him into some sort of submission, an apology, but his hate . . . "

"Son," says Scott, "as a fearful mortal and then The Beast, you lived in hatred but still transformed into a benefactor. You have watched and learned from me. Last night was your initiation into our ranks. So tell me, after going through all this, what do you want as a benefactor?"

What do I want? The same thing I wanted when I became a benefactor under this elm. The same thing I wanted last night when I took control of the meeting. But in spite of everything Scott's taught me about free will and accepting clients as they are, this desire hasn't changed.

"Quite simple. What I want is to make a difference. I want to be the protector of the oppressed, fight a never-ending battle for truth, justice. Just . . . just . . . like Superman!"

"Whoa there, Man of Steel. Noble motive, but inconsistent with the benefactor's creed."

"Then why ask?"

"Because your desire has been boiling inside you for years. You needed to hear yourself express this yearning," says Scott. "Let the steam out."

Defiance shoving Peter to his feet, he paces around the bench.

"Though we assume human form," continues Scott, "and interact with mortals, we do not *make* a difference. We never *fight* anything. Those dubious luxuries belong to mortals. We exist in the spiritual realm now. Our days of forcing results died when we did. We are akin to a thought, an intuition appealing to mortal conscience, the inner light of love. Everyone has these thoughts and feelings but for some, they are but the distant glow of a firefly."

Though Peter considers this lecture esoteric jabber, curiosity overrules.

"You are as unhappy now as when you were the monster hiding under this elm. Your intentions have changed, but your self-will has not. It wants absolute control over the Citizens for Justice Committee, control you can never wield. So you are still plagued by resentment and anger.

"Superman had things easy. He could stop a speeding bullet, but we must influence thoughts to prevent the gunfire."

Convection flames in Scott's eyes.

"Assume," says Scott, "we could also bend steel, the steel of fate, thereby purging all suffering. How would our clients navigate the adversities of life on their own? In fact, what would be the *point* of life?"

"Okay, what *is* the point?" asks Peter.

"To learn from life. Plus, just as important, to *enjoy* it."

"Enjoy it? My mortal life was anything but enjoyable," says Peter.

"Because you never paid attention."

"To what?"

"To the joy," says Scott. "Like the love of a mother, children laughing, lemonade. The *point* is that you lived life clutching at thimblefuls of bliss when you could have been swimming in an ocean of delight. You never appreciated the blessings of suffering. Though painful at the time, they were gifts, opportunities for growth from which you would find more joy. In death, you must learn what you failed to discover in life. So, what have you learned since your demise?"

Silence begs for an answer as Peter shuffles, thinking.

"What have I learned? Life, mortal or spiritual, isn't fair. Though vengeance wasn't the answer, you're right, resentment and anger still fill my soul. Damn. I *want* to see the joy, but I'm blinded by the world's evil. When I see free will's harm, I can't accept the pain. I want to change their will, the harm, even if that's against the benefactor's creed. I'm sorry, but . . .

"You know, I have seen that joy," says Peter. "I saw it in Monroe and in the senator when they apologized for the harm they did to me. In Mary, when I see her in the future befriending Jerome. Mary . . . You talk about the light of love? That's her, like a new moon's glow into the darkness."

"Want some of this joy?" says Scott. "Acknowledge those amends, then make some of your own."

Peter's eyes harden.

"I know what you're up to, Scott. Accepting Monroe and the senator's apologies is one thing, but if you're insinuating *I* make amends to someone like Thornton, forget it! Even though I might wish I hadn't killed him, if I hadn't, he would've killed me!"

"You are forgetting the mob . . . "

Peter's face bloats in anger as he squeezes himself on the bench.

"And concerning Mary," says Scott. "Imagine forgiving some-one who has killed a loved one, even showing him kindness."

Yeah, I admire Mary's courage, but I can't bring myself to be as forgiving as that mortal.

Responding to Peter's thoughts, Scott slaps *The BOOK.*

"Pity, but until you make your peace with Thornton *and* the mob, you will never be an effective benefactor, or experience the joy."

"Experience the joy, huh?"

"Yes. Shed your veil of pride. Humble yourself before a Universal Authority, a Divine Power—God, Allah, Buddha—whatever. Let that spirit beyond oneself guide your actions, not your self-will. Can you, Peter? Can you humble yourself?"

"Hmm," says Peter, rubbing the back of his neck. "You know, this benefactor thing is like putting a puzzle together in the dark. Even if you get all the pieces to fit, you still don't know what the picture looks like, or even if it's the right picture."

"True, but the Divine Power knows, and that is enough."

"And there's my problem. The Divine *does* know, but still allows evil to flourish."

"Peter, what kind of Universal Authority would you like?"

"Like I've got a choice?"

"Certainly, as long as that authority is not you."

Twitching on the bench, Peter searches the heavens.

"I don't know," he says. "Something kind, compassionate. But why some *super being*? Why not a spirit, a benefactor, like you?"

Now Scott searches the heavens.

"I am not perfect. I will fail you. Remember, you serve in an unjust, mortal world. Its inequities will test you, gnaw at the foundation of your soul. If you do not have a source of strength beyond yourself or me, these assaults will beat you back into The Beast."

An overhead rustling summons Scott's attention. Flailing in a sudden gust of wind, the elm's branches beckon. Scott grabs Peter's shoulder.

"Something kind, compassionate?" Scott asks. "What about the spirit of the elm?"

Peter stirs with discontent. Gazing into the canopy, he remembers the decades of its shelter. Since his transformation from The Beast, Peter, obsessed with his concerns, has ignored this leafed protector. But the tree endures, accepting all things.

"What kind of Universal Authority would I like? One that's a compassionate spirit freed of the judgment and demands of a god. That's what I need."

"I hear you," says Scott, "and that *need* is the power of the elm. If you tap into that power, you tap into the Universal Authority. In time, you might even come to trust God.

"Doubts are normal. Being a benefactor is not. Most spirits never become one of us."

Peter is not surprised. Free will, suffering, Universal Authority. Damn. Sure would've been a lot easier if they had made me Superman. All I'd have to worry about is kryptonite.

"Know what I love about this job?" says Scott. "Those joyous moments when the night of despair fades before the dawn of hope, like your redemption from the horrors of The Beast."

Chapter 27

Got Car?

With an hour of labor remaining, the sun's daily toil ends in a joyful pink glow.

Peter, exhausted, slumps on the bench entranced by the horizon's blush.

"Enough talk about committees, statutes, and Superman," says Scott. "All work and no play. How about I treat us to some mortal decadence—hamburger, fries, plus a cold beer?"

The hollow thud of *The BOOK* slamming close rouses Peter from his daze.

"What is the problem? Worried about all the cholesterol?"

"They didn't have hamburgers or fries when I grew up," says Peter. "Momma said beer was the devil's brew, so I didn't drink. Not only that, but for the whole time I was The Beast, I never ate, nor since."

"Well, we must clear the cobwebs from your stomach."

Scott rubs his chin in thought.

"Let me think. Where should we go? Oh, I know this great spot on 68, just past St. James, The Palace! *Lots* of ambiance. My treat." Looking up, he grabs Peter's hand saying, "Scotty, beam us there."

"You know, it's not that late. And since you mentioned mortals, let's travel like one, in *my* car."

"Your *car*?"

"Yeah. Like you said, 'all work and no play,'" says Peter, motioning to the elm. "In the eighty-seven years under that tree, the world passed me by. After becoming a benefactor, besides my apprenticeship training, I decided to study modern lifestyles. I even allowed myself to feel mortal sensations. Did fieldwork like going to movies, microwaving popcorn, driving a car. I found the research *most* interesting. If I'm gonna work with folks as a benefactor, I need to experience the current mortal condition."

"Now *that* shows initiative. But zapping popcorn is one thing—how did you learn to drive?"

"Invisibility is really convenient," says Peter, inflating with pride. "Take driving. I just picked some drivers at random and sat next to them as I watched. You'd be surprised how many different techniques there are for operating an automobile. Then, when they weren't using the car, I managed to 'borrow' their keys. Took some practice spins," he says, smirking. "There were a few minor 'incidents' but after returning the car, I made sure there was enough cash on the front seat to cover repairs, plus a little extra for the inconvenience."

"Okay, you can drive. So, I assume you are parked at the prison a *mile* away?"

Scott glances at the leather-clad volume.

"Well, the sunset *is* beautiful. I thought we could walk. Of course, I'd be happy to carry *that,*" says Peter, nodding at *The BOOK*.

"This must be *some* car."

"Thank you," whispers Peter to the elm as he rises from the bench.

Scott hands Peter a leather satchel into which they shove *The BOOK*. Peter straddles the bag. Lifting, he grunts while sagging like a swayback mule under the load. They weave down the trail through the woods with two gaunt, guardian shadows leading the way. A few hundred feet later, Peter, exhausted, sets his burden down. The path sinks under the weight.

"Darn thing must weigh fifteen pounds per code," he says.

Peter rubs dirt on his hands for a better grip.

"Quit your griping and act like a good mule."

"Why all those different types of writing in this thing?" asks Peter, his fascination overpowering his fatigue. "Funny, when I was alive, I couldn't read plain ol English, but I can read all of this. What's the first part called again, the one with all those triangular marks?"

Peter catches his breath.

"If you would complete your homework, you would know all this. That section is the *Ancient Text*. The triangular writing is the cuneiform script of the old Akkadian language, over four thousand years old."

"No wonder this thing's so heavy. Didn't they write on clay?"

"The second part," says Scott, rolling his eyes, "is the *Contemporary Text* which contains the more current languages. They number more than a hundred, all in their original form."

Peter leans against a tree, mopping his face with a handkerchief.

"Why'd they keep all that old stuff?" he asks.

"*The BOOK* chronicles the history of humanity, including the evolution of conscience."

"Some of the sections remind me of the Bible."

"You sound surprised," says Scott.

"You mean, benefactors wrote passages in that?"

"In addition to the Torah, the Qur'an, and the Bhagavad-Gita, all the religions, my son."

"So, why not change em all into one language, like the Bible?"

"Even the Bible was originally written in three languages," says Scott, opening the satchel. "*The Book* remains in its original scripts, thus eliminating any mistranslations. We like to think this adds a little style, an ego thing."

"So, there's a lot more stuff in this book besides the twelve statutes?"

"Yes, wondrous 'stuff.'"

"Such as?"

"Such as Jesus was one of us, a benefactor. He even *looked* like us."

Knees buckling in disbelief, Peter slides down the tree.

"You're kidding?" he says. "Jesus was Black? What else is in it?"

"Things like where to find Noah's Ark and the remains of Jimmy Hoffa."

"Well, I'll be . . . "

"We take pride in staying current. But when you get your copy," says Scott as concern narrows his eyes, "*never* let it fall into mortal hands. *The Book* documents human history through the millennia, dispelling many popular myths. Mortals are not ready for the whole truth and nothing but the truth."

"And when do I get *mine*?"

"When *I* say so."

"Really? Well, a while ago even *you* said the way I handled last night's meeting was ingenious."

"Funny," says Scott, slapping Peter's back, "just before I said it, you complained how the meeting was a failure.

"Yes, your initial solo with the committee was impressive. But fledglings do not soar with eagles on their first flight from the nest. You shall get your Book when *I* decide, not before."

Scott breaks into a toothy grin.

"We better get going. I want to see this vehicle of yours while there is still light."

For twenty minutes, Scott saunters forward. Peter plods behind, leaving a wake of furrowed gravel. Finally, the path leads them to the prison's parking lot. Surveying the black sea of boiling asphalt, they take a breath, then forge across. Peter's sweat strikes the pavement, erupting in columns of steam. Approaching the object of Peter's pride, Scott's face slumps with awe.

"Well, I can see why you were willing to play pack mule."

Before them, flaming red in the sunset's light gleams the sleek silhouette of a topless Corvette convertible. Scott shades his eyes from the reflective brilliance.

Peter beams like a cat that has dropped a mouse at its master's feet. Sweat dripping on the upholstery, he leans inside, opening the car's center console. Pressing a button, he unlocks a rear deck lid which he opens, then pulls up the white cloth convertible roof.

"What are you doing?" asks Scott.

"Putting the top up."

"Why? You afraid of messing up your do?"

"No. There's only one place big enough to fit this book—in the convertible top's storage well, but the top has to be up."

"Why not in the trunk?"

"What trunk?"

"How convenient," says Scott as he inspects the passenger compartment. "Hey, there is enough room up here. If we put this book on the floor up against the seat, I can squeeze my legs over it."

"Yeah, I suppose, but why?"

"Hey, if we are going to play mortal, let us do so in style, with the top down!"

"Alright," says Peter, "but we'll have to put the satchel in the well under the folded down top. Won't fit by the seat with *The BOOK* in it."

He takes one of the satchel's two looped handles as Scott takes the other. They sling it onto the front seat floor. The car creaks under the weight like an overloaded Radio Flyer wagon. They remove the satchel and place it in the well.

"Where *did* you get this car? Let me guess . . . Fillmore Motors."

Peter's lips curl with pride. Opening the driver's door, he drops into the white leather cockpit. Invigorated by the new-car scent, he tugs at the steering wheel, happy as a baby shaking its crib.

"You know, we are not allowed to exploit our clients," says Scott. Innocence consumes Peter's face.

"I paid full price," he says, "well, almost. Last night I humiliated Fillmore in front of the committee. I wanted to make amends. So first thing this morning, I went over to his dealership. Yesterday, refreshments materialized out of thin air when I snapped these fingers," says Peter, holding out his hand. "This morning, it was one-hundred-dollar bills, three hundred and eighty of em."

Scott glares with disapproval.

"I know *we* don't need money," says Peter, slapping the dash, "but when dealing with mortals, a bulging billfold's like having God in your pocket. You should've seen Fillmore's reaction. After that, *I* got *this*."

An exhausted Peter releases an infectious yawn as his head slumps against the dash.

"Cut that out," complains Scott.

But his warning falls on sleep-deafened ears. Scott climbs inside. Squeezing over the tome, he soon follows Peter's lead.

* * *

A 9:30 p.m. tumult awakens the duo. The monthly meeting of the prison's correctional officers has just ended, littering the area with exiting olive drab uniforms.

The two bolt upright in their seats.

"Look at the time," says Peter, eyeing the dashboard clock.

With a flick of his wrist, he awakens the 350-cubic-inch V-8 which growls to consciousness. The thirty-two-hundred-pound beast strains with the anticipation of an escape.

"Immortal or not, fasten your seatbelt," says Peter

The warning is heeded with a pair of metallic fasteners clicking followed by Scott's fervent prayer. Simultaneously, the driver's face contorts in a devilish grin as his hands arm themselves with black, leather gloves. Grabbing the dash, Scott's prayers grow less distinguishable but more fervent.

"Hang onto your hair!" screams the driver.

The accelerator pedal spanks the floorboard. Rearview mirrors fill with blue smoke, then gray exhaust. With a monstrous squeal, the beast's hindquarters drift to one side, preparing to leap.

The commotion captures the guards' attention. They watch a blurred specter bolt out of the parking lot, passing cursing car horns and insulted stop signs.

"Damn rookie!" complains one officer to another.

Absent any fear of death, Peter's only excuse for holding the road is the dread of a dent. Headlights like burning meteors approach on the left growing larger, then breaking in two as they hurl by. Fleeing taillights shrivel into specks of red. Bugs explode on the windshield. Into the black horizon the car races when after another meteor flashes past, the rearview mirrors reflect a glowing, crimson cloud of dust. The deep mosquito's drone of a siren pierces the growling air.

"Ah, shit, a state trooper!" says Peter. "He made a u-ey on the shoulder. Damnit, now he's turned on his flashing lights!"

"What the hell are you doing?" asks Scott, sucked against the seat as the Corvette accelerates.

"Outrunning im!"

Behind them, the trooper's flashing display dims. In front, taillights approach, bright as crimson-eyed devils, bellowing threats as the beast screams past. Forward the Corvette scurries, leaping through traffic. Forty minutes and sixty miles into the flight from the law, a nearing blush of light congeals into a red neon sign, The Palace.

"This is the place!" shouts Scott.

Peter hits the brakes. Reluctantly, the beast yields to the

command, turning from the two-lane highway onto a gravel lot. The only thing this ragtop fears more than a Porsche or a state trooper is kicking itself with stone. After tiptoeing across the aggregate hardscape to the farthest parking stall alongside The Palace, it waits in the darkness.

"Get down," says Peter.

Three minutes later, a wailing, flashing-light patrol car streaks past, disappearing into the night.

"Wasn't that a blast!" says Peter, bounding out of the car.

Scott extricates his fingers from the dashboard and crawls out, kissing the ground on bent knees, a few more strands of gray added to his silver hair.

"Pussy!" says Peter, slapping the keys in his hand.

The pair install the convertible top, shove *The BOOK* into its satchel, place it in the storage well, and lock the doors. After sauntering across the building's boardwalk, Scott waits for Peter at the entry. Peter hurries to the road, searching for the trooper. Confident they are safe, he returns through a parking lot occupied by a menagerie of rusted pickups, station wagons, and sedans. Of particular interest, bathed in the glow from the establishment's lone front window, waits a black Lincoln Continental. Last night, Peter saw it in front of City Hall where the committee met. He knows this is the same car for its rear bumper bears the sticker *From my cold, dead hands*. Peter steps up to the entry.

A relic from a Tom Mix western, The Palace has not been painted since the horse trough, overflowing with beer cans and whisky bottles, went dry. Inconsistent with the building's primal past, on the roof in red neon flames "The Palace" like an enormous bonfire igniting the night sky. A smoky gale of noise blows through the establishment's doorless entry, doorless because The Palace *never* closes.

"You look troubled," says Scott. "Something bothering you?"

"I don't know. Just got this strange feeling like something bad's gonna happen."

"Alright. Do you want to leave?"

"No, because I also got this feeling Mary Cook is here," says Peter, his face weathered with concern as they walk inside.

* * *

Choking on the odor of stale beer, the pair enter the pine-paneled cavern where illumination is as scarce as sanitized tableware. On their right stands an L-shaped bar, its short leg paralleling the entry wall. The fluorescent glare from the under-counter lights illuminates the only hurried activity in the room, the bartender's. To their left glows a red, white, and blue jukebox screaming country music. In a distant corner of the bar, a party of around twenty people seated at two end-to-end tables competes with the harmonic commotion. Mingling with their celebration, a fog of cigarette smoke churns under the blades of two wobbling ceiling fans. No other patrons occupy the room.

First Scott, then Peter, plop themselves in the room's center on either side of a tabletop which looks and feels like it fried this morning's bacon.

A pinecone-complexioned waiter approaches. Wearing an apron an auto mechanic would not touch, the employee arrives without menus or an order pad.

Peter eyes the man. *Either this guy's memory is very good, or the establishment's menu isn't.*

With arms akimbo, the waiter glares down at the pair.

"I'm Jake. Whata ya wanna drink?" he yells above the jukebox.

Peter asks what food they serve.

"Kitchen's closed," says Jake, throwing a thumb over his shoulder at a rearward dark doorway.

"Oh. I hear your burgers and fries are to die for. I was really hungry," says Peter in what sounds more like an apology.

From another table, Jake grabs a bowl of stale peanuts which he tosses in front of the two.

"O-o-o-kay, we will just have something to drink," says Scott. "I would like . . . "

"Two beers, Leroy!" shouts Jake to the Black bartender, then limps towards the bar.

Peter raises his hand as though to question the order.

"If you want to change that to a glass of milk," says Scott, "I am out of here!"

Peter pries his elbows from the sticky-as-flypaper surface.

"You know," he says, "I last ate only eighty-nine years ago. I'm not really that hungry."

Leaning back in his wooden chair, Peter questions his decision to experience earthly sensations. As his eyes sting in the acid air, they focus on the revelers in the back. They look familiar, especially the portly man seated at the head of the tables. And when not overpowered by the jukebox, the revelers *sound* familiar. Throwing his chair back, Peter leaps up, motioning Scott to follow him outside.

"What seems to be the problem?" asks Scott, stepping onto the boardwalk.

Peter peeks back inside through the front window. Planks creak as he staggers back, pointing at the two tables.

"It's . . . it's . . . them. See?" he says.

"Who?"

"The Citizens for Justice Committee!"

Chapter 28

Any Car Will Do

Peter aims a finger at the hazed window to the celebration inside.

"Why didn't I know the committee'd be here? I'm their bene-factor!"

Scott shrugs. "Well, as an apprentice, you are restricted from knowing your clients' entire future. But you are correct, you should have known about this." He leans down, peering through the glass.

"Yeah, you're damn right I should've!" Back to the window, Peter reels, eyebrows furrowed in disgust. "Just like I thought, Mary's here. Hell, everybody's here! There's Wilson sitting at the head table. I see Mary's husband, Kevin. Hell, even Fillmore, the guy I bought the Corvette from this morning."

At this moment, a battered, yellow pickup rumbles off the high-way, parking in the gravel lot. Squealing in pain, its doors pry open. Two rotund brothers, Henry and Benny in dirt-infested over-alls spill out, surveying the area through suspicious eyes. The red Corvette parked around the corner of the building hides from their view. Tramping to The Palace, they step onto the boardwalk, stop-ping at the sight of two stooped men, one white, one Black, peer-ing through the bar's window.

"What you lookin at, boy?" says Henry, approaching the Black man.

"Uh, just seeing if there are some folks in there we know," says Scott, straightening up.

Peter stands, turning to the brothers as he steps to Scott's side.

"We can go in an ask for ya," says Henry. "Who shall we say is callin?"

"Thank you, but that is not necessary. We were just leaving," says Scott.

Flicking his head, Scott motions to Peter they should depart, *now*. They back away from the window.

Henry slithers to the side, blocking their path.

"You're not from around here, are ya? You them two fellas we seen ridin in a fancy red car?" he asks, squinting in an ice pick glare.

Henry's hand slides into a bulging hip pocket which sags from something heavy inside.

Peter, pondering a reply, eyes his partner.

"No, we are riding in this," says Scott, pointing to the black Lincoln with the *From my cold dead hands* bumper sticker. "It belongs to my friend here, why?"

Scott added the owner's statement suspecting the brothers would assume only a white man and not a Black person would own such an expensive car.

"Cause," grunts Henry, "they fuckin near ran us off the road tonight."

"Yeah," says Peter, continuing Scott's charade, "they passed us, too. Car must've been stolen cause a trooper was chasing em."

"Musta been. We just seen the passenger. He was Black an I bet the driver was too." Henry's hand relaxes, rising from the pocket. "Come on, Benny, let's get us a beer. Maybe someone inside seen that car."

"Thought you'd never ask, Henry!"

The two rotund overalls disappear into The Palace.

* * *

The parking lot, in homage to The Palace's sign, cloaks itself in shades of crimson and black. Through this surrealistic setting, the two walk to the Corvette. As they round the building's corner, The Palace din diminishes, replaced by a cricket's two-tone melody. Approaching his car, Peter requests a few moments alone. Scott nods in agreement.

In a heavy thud, the car door slams shut. Peter settles into his seat, gazing into the sleeping day's black dream. His mind churns in thought. The dark amorphous area beyond reminds him of the forbidding expanse he has wandered in the decades of his spiritual journey. Just when he finds a familiar landmark, a respite, like tonight's sojourn with Scott, he stumbles, falling again into the one constant of his supernatural existence—turmoil. *Is there no peace?*

The car's slamming passenger door interrupts Peter's thoughts.

"Don't you dare say it," he warns Scott.

"Say what?"

"You know, something like, 'Well, thanks to your reckless driving, we damned nearly got ourselves shot.'"

"I would not have used 'damned.'"

"But *you* had to know the committee'd be in there. All your talk about having a beer at The Palace was just a ruse to get me here!"

"Yes, I knew they would be there," says Scott, slapping Peter's leg, "but the question is, why didn't you?"

"You deaf from the music? I already asked that."

"Peter, all our abilities, including those to foresee our client's future, come from the light of God. But you are staggering in the dark. Any idea why?"

Peter gazes into the night's void, his hands twisting on the steering wheel. He knows why the lights are out. He is still imprisoned in the same hate he had nurtured in the shadow of the elm: hate for the mob, the committee, and even sometimes himself. Hate's lead curtain blocks the light.

"Your expression says you realize the problem lies not in your loving tolerance," says Scott.

"Yeah, I've got my problems, but I became a benefactor not out of hate, but a desire to serve justice, help Jerome as well as his family. Doesn't that balance things out?"

"We do not want everything *balanced*. We want it crushed by love. And right now, you need a ton more of that love."

"I wish you would've told me they were here. I wouldn't have stopped."

"Had you known or not is immaterial. God's will has brought you here. We benefactors serve His desires, *not* ours, no matter how noble *ours* appear to be."

"Again, with the 'Him.'"

"Maybe you would be happier in Sanctuary."

"Yeah, that so-called place of eternal, non-eventful bliss?"

"You can always revert to The Beast. But a blessing awaits should you accept everything that has and will happen: the lynching, the committee, yourself, Jerome's fate."

"And what is this 'blessing'?" asks Peter.

"The bloom of forgiveness which sprouts from the seed of acceptance."

"Fancy words, but what if this flower turns out to be a *weed*?"

"The answers are in *The BOOK*," says Scott as he points back to the car's storage well.

"I don't dislike *everyone* in the committee. There's Mary. Remember, I had a hunch she'd be here. Yeah, she voted for Jerome's death, but did it reluctantly, not like the rest of the mob crying for his blood. Because of that, she might need my help."

"My son, you had a hunch about Mary because you respect her and accept her failings. Some light is getting through. Anything else on your mind?"

"Well, yeah. This thing about accepting God's will. In life, the white man's will was what I had to accept. When I rebelled against that will, killing Thornton, I paid the ultimate price. If it hadn't been for my pride, I would've just walked away. Like I've confessed, his death haunted me, a nagging echo in my conscience. But tonight when I saw Mary, the echo, for a while, stopped. For the second time since my transformation from The Beast, the thought of helping someone consoled me. The first time was with Jerome. Maybe I *am* reaching for the light."

"I could not have said that better," says Scott. "The mere thought of helping Mary filled you with joy. Service is the path to light. But *everyone* has done something worthy of respect, even Oscar Wilson. One day you will learn his story. And speaking of stories, what is the story with this car?"

"I knew you'd bring that up," says Peter.

"Why such an extravagance?"

"Though this may sound frivolous, this car's a symbol of the freedom I never had; liberation from my mortal poverty. Driving here like a fox chasing a hare was a harmless expression of that liberation. But the icing on the cake? Outrunning the state trooper, thumbing my nose at the law that had thumbed its nose at me!"

"Symbol, huh? Funny thing, symbols. The more lavish, the more they deceive."

"Don't worry, it's just a car."

"So why not a Plymouth?"

Absent any self-defense, Peter's gaze drops to the floor mat.

An approaching sedan interrupts the moment, parking next to the Corvette. A man and woman exit. They join hands, strolling to the bar's entrance, gravel playing under their feet. Peter leans forward, adjusting the overhead mirror, watching them snuggling as they walk. He tingles from a long dormant longing.

Still focused on the mirror, Peter drifts into a fantasy of imagined romance. *Glad I'm not touching Scott so he can't read my* thoughts. *I'd be a little embarrassed. After all, it's been almost a hundred years since I've . . .*

He keeps the pair in view for as long as possible. Settling back in his seat, Peter watches them disappear around the building. *I wonder if Mary finds me attractive? Where the hell did that come from? When I was alive, I'd never consider such a thought about a white woman. This white disguise is having a strange effect.*

"Getting a good look?" asks Scott.

"Uh, just trying to see if our yellow pickup is still there," says Peter, turning the mirror back.

"Uh-huh. You feeling some romantic stirrings? Be not concerned. It is only natural for old mortal sensations to arise."

Peter fidgets in his seat. *Damn! I swear he knows my thoughts even without touching.*

"Anything involving Mary?" asks Scott.

"Why'd you ask that about a married woman? A white one to boot!"

"Well, you are no longer a repressed Black man. Mary *is* a beautiful lady, both physically and spiritually. Plus, for a white man, *you* are attractive."

"You saying she finds me good-looking? Uh, I mean, uh, I was just curious."

"Remember what curiosity did to the cat. Beware of mortal romances."

* * *

A blast of noise from The Palace penetrates the car. Scott elbows Peter.

"Duty calls, son. Back to the salt mines."

Climbing out of the Corvette, the pair stroll to the boardwalk.

Thunder growls in the distance. As they approach the entry, the two brothers emerge. Seeing Peter and Scott the brothers stop.

"You two still here?" asks Henry, the elder. "We been askin inside and that there black car ain't yours . . . is it?"

Peter steps forward, but Scott grabs his arm.

"Gentleman," says Scott, "believe what you wish. Now, would you two please step aside?"

"You real polite ain't ya?" says Henry, stepping closer. "For a Black, you talk good as your white buddy."

Henry's face buckles in a smile as the brothers step onto the gravel.

"Yeah, we'll let ya pass, but you two gotta have to leave sometime. Me an Benny gonna be waitin to see what ya drivin. If it ain't the black car," he says, patting his bulging pocket, "we gonna have us some fun. Come on, Benny."

The brothers waddle to their pickup, exiting the parking lot in a turmoil of dust and burning oil. As the yellow wreckage sputters down the road, a passing telephone pole struck by lightning explodes, splintering into flames. The Palace lights flicker.

"Damn, did you see what happened?" says Peter. "And it came outta nowhere!"

"Yeah, I saw it. His aim was off."

* * *

Upon entering the room's haze of pollution, Scott and Peter notice something is missing—the screaming jukebox. Violating the momentary serenity, Jake curses then pounds the dark and mute electronic musician.

"Damn ligthnin shorted it out!" shouts Jake to the bartender. "But them lights ain't out. It's a wonder we got anything still workin!"

"Thanks to that bolt of good fortune, we will hear the committee's every word," says Scott.

He and Peter pick a table having a clear view close to the gathering. Several heads in the committee turn with no apparent concern, noticing the pair. Jake approaches.

"Two more beers please," says Scott.

"Gonna finish em this time?" grunts the waiter.

His boot steps fading, Jake tromps to the bar. Gripping a dripping mug in each hand, he returns, slapping the drinks on the table.

"You two fellas the ones the Banger brothers was askin about?"

The duo trade glances.

"I do not know," says Scott. "Depends on what they were asking."

"What kinda car you're drivin. How long you been here. Shit like that." Wiping his hands on his apron, he adds, "I seen ya drive up in that Vette. But I didn't say nothin."

Jake stands motionless, his gaze dancing from one man to the other, waiting for something.

"Oh, excuse me," says Scott.

He pulls a twenty from his pants. The waiter grabs the bill which he stuffs in his trousers before Scott can say "keep the change."

"If I was you," says Jake, trudging to another table, "I'd trade them fancy wheels for *any* car in the lot."

"Sounds like good advice to me," says Scott.

"I'm *not* trading my Corvette for somebody's piece of shit!"

"Whatever . . ."

Arms folded against his chest, Peter leans back in his chair. He forces his attention on the committee, but his eyes keep drifting to Scott. Then from the corner of the room, the two hear a committee member speak:

"And here's to our beloved chairman, Oscar Wilson, whose unceasing efforts have sent a clear message to Judge Daring that we, the Godfearing people of Barkersville, want that murderin nigra dead!"

The haze fills with cheers. After congratulations, everyone raises their glasses in a toast, everyone except Mary Cook.

* * *

In the twenty-four hours since the Citizens for Justice Committee meeting, Mary's world has decayed from challenging to insufferable. Her uncertainty about a death vote for Jerome resulted in an avalanche of phone calls. Some were genuinely concerned with her well-being, but most expressed hatred over her hesitation to have her son's killer, killed.

Kevin has not helped. He sulks around the house, refusing to answer the stampede of calls while avoiding her as though she were a leper. Conversation has withered to grunts. He demanded she attend tonight's meeting at The Palace as "requested" by Mr. Wilson. When she pleaded she has "done enough to satisfy that asshole's demands," the resulting skirmish cost her all her Sunday china. It has become absolutely clear that Kevin's love of "their" clothing business exceeds that of her. Mary has made up her mind.

* * *

From the agitated foot of her crossed leg, a black high-heeled shoe swings like an erratic pendulum. Her chin resting in the palm of her hand, Mary stares into the smoke-choked emptiness. Her countenance screams with disdain. All, especially Kevin, notice Mary's demeanor. Smiling and looking straight ahead, Kevin leans close.

"Stop it. People are watching," he says.

"I don't give a *damn* who's watching!"

Her eyes burning like embers in a potbelly stove, Mary makes no attempt to subdue her contempt. The high heel takes a wild swing, somersaulting off her toe. She bends down, retrieving the acrobat then sits up. Kevin grabs her forearm. The shoe falls to the floor. Silence slams the room while all attention lurches in the duo's direction.

Chapter 29

The Celebration

The committee's membership grows quiet as a firing squad awaiting the fatal command.

In shallow breaths, Mary's chest constricts. A throbbing pulse echoes in her head, the same sensations she felt at last night's committee meeting when after she succumbed to these same murderous eyes, she voted for Manning's death. But unlike last night, Mary now rebuffs these glares, including those of Kevin whose hand crushes her wrist, warning her of an obedient wife's duties. At first, anger blocks the ache of his grip, but as she stares at her hand's protruding veins, her emotions yield to pain. She tries to wrench free. Kevin's cinch tightens.

Before Timmy's death, Kevin's controlling disposition had ruled the family to suit what he thought was in everyone's best interest. When his anger flared, he resorted to sarcasm, nothing more, but his annoyance quickly cooled. Now, aided by the increased drinking, his displeasure rises to physical intimidation and broken china. His voice alone summons fear. Privately, their pastor told Mary this new pattern of aggression is probably a manifestation of the guilt Kevin feels about Timmy's death.

Though Mary has tried to make allowances, her thoughts flame with anger. No parent should suffer the horror of burying a child. But damnit, Kevin's not the only one hurting! Where's the we in our relationship? He won't see a counselor. "We'll work it out," he says. Then the next minute I'm ducking a Wedgewood flying saucer.

God knows I've tried. Talked to people. They say they know

how I feel. Shit! Nobody knows how I feel. They say I have to stick by Kevin's side. He needs my support. My pastor says the same thing. What the hell do they think I've been doing? Crocheting doilies as our lives disintegrate like tissue paper in a hailstorm? When I confided to Cynthia that Kevin was hurting me, she said it must be something I'm doing. Some friend. So, I keep to myself while my life withers in a drought of love. Dear God, help me. I feel so damn alone.

Mary's attention wanders across the room. She notices two strangers sitting at a table watching her. One of them looks vaguely familiar, the younger one with wavy brown hair. He leans close to his older companion, a Black man, says something, then looks at her. Mary is sure the younger fellow is talking about her, though she cannot hear. For a moment she feels an unanticipated sense of calm.

* * *

"Did you hear that?" Peter asks Scott.

"Keep your voice down, they are looking at us."

"Yeah, I know, but did you hear *that?* A prayer, a cry for help. It sounded just like Mary."

"It *was* Mary," says Scott.

"But I thought you had to be touching someone to hear their thoughts."

"Normal thoughts, yes, but prayers are an exception. They are cast into the infinite for any benevolent spirit to hear. Akin to pulling a fire alarm."

"Will her prayer be answered?" asks Peter, staring at Mary.

"Why do you think *you* are here?"

* * *

Kevin is now the bull's-eye of the audience's attention. Glancing at the head table, he sees a red-faced Oscar Wilson glaring at him. Kevin must do *something* to prove his committee solidarity even if doing so embarrasses Mary. Throwing his chair back, he leaps up, dragging Mary from her seat. Stumbling backward, she grabs the tablecloth. Tableware and bottles crash to the floor.

"Take your hands off me, Kevin!" says Mary, regaining her balance.

Through concealed satisfaction, the gathering watches.

Wrenching her arm free, Mary grabs her purse, then hobbles on one high heel towards the exit.

In clutched-jaw anger, Kevin watches.

After three single-shod steps, Mary stops. Removing the orphaned patent leather pump, she hurls the footwear at Kevin. He ducks. The somersaulting, black missile streaks past, striking Oscar's wine glass which explodes in a purple plume of fermented fluid. Eyes focus in horror on their stained leader. As Oscar sautés in his juices, sycophants scramble forward, patting the foul fluid with napkins, handkerchiefs, and shirtsleeves.

Disgusted by the fawning over their soggy sire, Mary prances to the bar. She sits on a stool, glaring in the backbar mirror at Kevin's reverse image. As the Black bartender approaches to take her order, she notices *Leroy* stitched above his shirt pocket.

"Scotch and water, Leroy."

Blushed as a priest who passed gas at communion, Kevin empties his tumbler on the floor. From a wine decanter, he floods his glass with burgundy, pitching the contents down his throat. He belches as the deluge strikes a fire in his gut. Dropping into his chair, he glares at Mary, raises the empty glass in a toast, then shatters his glass on the table.

Mary examines the reflection of Kevin's displeasure as Leroy serves her order. Swirling the golden drink in her glass, Mary returns Kevin's toast. She empties the liquor in her mouth with a flick of her wrist, then shatters *her* glass as she slams it on the varnished counter.

The bartender watches, making no effort to wipe the demonstration.

The committee watches, making every effort to protest through their silent scorn.

Meanwhile, Mary notices the brown-haired stranger's stare continues. She struggles to divert her eyes.

* * *

Arms folded, Peter rears back in his chair, glaring at the defiant woman at the bar.

"What are you doing?" asks Scott.

"Homework."

"You are supposed to sit here unnoticed."

Peter smiles.

* * *

Oscar stands. He taps his water glass.

Mimicking their leader, the room chatters like a wind chime in a gale.

"I appreciate everyone accepting my invitation on such short notice. Thank you for making the long drive to this *elegant* establishment."

Oscar chuckles.

All laugh on cue.

"I apologize for my guest's behavior," he says, glancing down at his sour suit. "One would expect Mrs. Cook would show a little gratitude for we who are striving to secure justice for *her* son. But I suppose a distraught mother's rantings must be tolerated."

Mary's teeth grind at Oscar's every word. The committee nods in approval.

"At Judge Daring's request, we met in private today regarding the Manning case," says Oscar.

The room descends into the silence of a morgue.

"He said due to the *unanimous* concern for justice from Bark-ersville's leading citizens, that Black man's good as dead. I in re-turn pledged our committee's *substantial* financial support for his upcoming reelection."

The chatter of dragging chairs fills the room as all stand, erupt-ing in applause.

Into the early morning, the committee's drunken brawl contin-ues while each clap of celebration punches hard as a fist in Mary's gut.

Mary aches from regret. Barkersville's leading citizens, unan-imous. It sounds so evil. If I had voted differently yesterday, one vote for life from the mother of the murdered child, would that have changed anything? Coward! I was afraid of Kevin, of being an outcast. Then those awful dreams last night. I saw Jerome in the gas chamber like I was actually there! My God, I've never imagined anything so horrible, including that voice in the background repeating over and over, "May you rest easy with your decision." I can't get the nightmare out of my head.

Glancing into the mirror, she orders another drink. No wonder Oscar chose this old bar. It's over an hour's drive from Bark-ersville and away from any town. But why's he so bold to *announce his conspiracy with the judge in front of the two men working the bar and those two strangers at the table? Bold, hell—arrogant! I bet Oscar and probably the whole committee think nobody would pay attention to those four. Possibly. But those guys at the table, for some strange reason though it makes no sense, I trust them. Damn this is weird.*

Pride weeps from Oscar's eyes at the committee's display of affection.

"I want you to know," he says, raising his hands for silence, "that I couldn't have done this without your kind support. Let this be a message to those who'd dare defile our town by their immoral deeds: We will hunt you down and have our vengeance!"

"We otta go over to that jail, *right* now! Lynch the nigra just like we done in the ol days," shouts an elderly man.

The committee howls their approval.

Mary stares at the mob's reflection, a boiling caldron of hellish brew spewing hate on all who draw near. With the rising fury of a thunderhead, Mary slaps her glass on the bar.

"Give me another, Leroy," she says.

"Beggin your pardon, ma'am," Leroy says, pushing a chilled soft drink her way, "but considerin the ones you had before the meetin, I think you've had enough. This one's on the house."

His comment, added to the cool, dripping glass of soda, distracts Mary's anger. She realizes her behavior only adds to the commotion behind her. Calming herself, she sips her diet cola, returning Leroy's thoughtfulness with a nod.

In the committee's exuberance, all except the Cooks rush to the head of the table, vying for Oscar's attention.

Mary watches the obedient display, reminding her of flies swarming on horse shit.

Shoving the well-wishers aside, Oscar plows straight ahead to Kevin who sulks in his chair.

"Mind staying when everyone leaves?" says Oscar, shunning Kevin's extended hand. "*We* need to talk."

Unable to hear, Mary scrutinizes the pair's body language as they converse.

"Uh, sure, Mr. Wilson. I . . . I know this is about Mary, Sir. Ever since Timmy's death, she's been acting . . . different. Hasn't done housework, irritable, crying at the least little thing. Sassing back. A real bitch! But until tonight, she's only pulled this stunt at home when . . . "

"Kevin, for Christ's sake, have *some* pride! I don't give a shit what your wife does at home, just don't wash your dirty shorts in public!"

Like the prideful calm in the center of a groveling hurricane, Oscar turns, then joins the crowd. After the last of the committee staggers outside, Oscar, as though summoning a bellhop, beckons Kevin.

"Yes Sir, Mr. Wilson. You wanna finish talking now?"

Mary, watching master and servant, cocks her head. One eye squints at the scene. One ear strains on the conversation.

"Young man," says Oscar, placing his hand on the subordinate's shoulder, "*we* seem to have a little situation here." He nods in Mary's direction. "I'm concerned about you two."

Kevin's blush flashes to a siren's red.

"I, uh, thank you for your concern, Mr. Wilson."

"Yes, indeed, *very* concerned."

Kevin's gaze falls to the floor. Mary's stomach wrenches with disgust. Peter and Scott swap glances.

"This evening's 'performance' was an embarrassment. I didn't ask for your wife's attendance just so *she* could do her little fucking show! Being Timmy's mother, she's something of a celebrity. That woman could ruin everything I . . . uh . . . we've, worked for. You need to keep her in line just like any man would. Get it, Kevin?"

"Y-y-yes, Sir. I certainly do."

Kevin's blush retreats, leaving a chalky void.

"Wonderful," says Oscar.

He marches to the exit, but after an abrupt stop, he saunters back.

"Oh, by the way, I hear you and the little lady have a business, Cook's something."

"Y-yeah . . . a men's clothing store, Cook's Clothing. It's coming . . . "

"Did you know most small businesses fail within the first three years?" asks Oscar.

Mary's ears swallow every word as Oscar's face creases in a smile, glaring at his wine-soiled suit.

"One needs word of mouth," continues Oscar, "especially in a small town like ours. *Especially* when one's competition is an old, established business like Kensington's Apparel where *I* and all *my* friends go. Just how *is* business, Kevin?"

Oscar again inspects his dirty attire, sighs, then fires his eyes at Kevin.

Mary prickles with apprehension. Though she is infuriated by Kevin's performance tonight, their economic survival hangs on the business which is struggling. She prays Kevin will tell the pompous ex-mayor they will replace the suit. But Kevin stands dumb as the bar's short-circuited jukebox.

"Tell you what," says Kevin, his eyes flashing bright as a new light bulb. "I have a dry cleaner that'll clean your suit good as new."

"*Kevin*, I'm throwing these clothes in the trash. The stain of what happened here tonight will *never* wash out."

Oscar stomps to the exit. Mary's eyes roll in defeat. Kevin's face drops limp as spaghetti from a toddler's spoon.

"Damnit," says Mary in a whisper. "If I could only tell Kevin to give Oscar one of our new lines of clothing, a suit that would smear jealousy on the chairman's minions."

Eyes screaming for attention, she turns to Kevin, pointing in Oscar's direction, her lips exaggerating "Armani!"

Finally, Kevin understands.

"Mr. Wilson, wait!"

Flashing a victorious grin, Oscar stops.

"What I meant to say was, I'll replace your suit with the best line of clothing I have—Armani. I'll also throw in a pair of shoes, a shirt, plus two ties. A new wardrobe is the *least* I can do after all the humiliation you've been through . . . Sir."

Mary's attention returns to the mirror. *The Scriptures got it wrong. God made man from the rib of a woman. Those clothes are gonna cost around thirteen hundred bucks, but maybe Oscar's fashion fetish friends . . . maybe this is just what our business needs.*

"See you Monday," says Oscar, walking away while flicking a thumb over his shoulder at Mary. "And don't forget what I said about that woman."

"Asshole," mutters Mary.

Leroy nods in agreement, wiping the bar.

"Thank you, Mr. Wilson!"

Kevin's words bounce off the walls, dancing through the room with the mockery of a performing monkey.

Except for the waiter and barkeep, the two strangers at the table, and Kevin and Mary, no one else occupies The Palace. It pulses with Kevin's slow, deliberate steps toward the bar where Mary sits. As Mary watches Kevin's approach, his expression reminds her of "that look" before he breaks something.

"Get ready," says Scott.

Chapter 30

Kleenex

Standing behind the counter opposite Mary, Leroy watches Kevin's approach.

"Don't you worry none, Mrs. Cook," says Leroy, leaning forward. "Just say the word. Me and Jake'll take care of im."

He motions to the burly waiter across the room.

Encouraged by his words, a smile breaks the concern on Mary's face.

Leroy winks. Pretending to dry glasses, he glances at Jake, flicking his eyes in Kevin's direction. Cleaning tables, Jake nods, keeping one eye on his work while the other watches the husband who now hovers behind Mary.

"Well, I hope you're satisfied!" says Kevin, slamming his fist on the bar.

Mary flinches.

"I'm speaking to you, *Mary*!"

Kevin's so close that Mary's hair rustles in his breath. Fear's icy finger crawls up her spine, a familiar feeling when he is in one of these moods. Kevin grabs her arm which she yanks free, his wine-stale breath blowing in her face.

"If you grab me like that again, you'll be pissin blood!"

Eyes locked and loaded, the couple take aim at each other.

Like children watching a schoolyard fight, Peter, Scott, Leroy, and Jake glue their attention to the confrontation.

"Mary, you got any idea the problems you've caused Mr. Wilson? You know what he said?"

"I don't give a damn what that fool said. He might have the whole town and you kissing his ass, but not me!"

Mary turns. Facing Kevin in the mirror, she feigns a smile. Though she is aware Oscar *is* someone to fear, pressing Kevin's button feels good.

"He's *very* upset, Mary, from your little performance tonight!" Mary lies with a shrug.

"Now, that may seem unimportant to *you*, but he can ruin *us*! One word from Wilson, and our store's blacklisted. People are watching you, but it's not just your little display tonight. It's your whole attitude. You act like you're above all this and it could jeopardize everything the committee's worked for. Everything *we've* worked for!"

Mary glares into the mirror but fears her eyes may betray the emotions seething within.

Kevin stumbles to a greasy stool in the middle of the bar, throwing himself on it. Tossing a handful of dollar bills at Leroy, Kevin twists to his left, staring at Mary sitting near the end of the counter. He is so emotional his voice almost squeaks.

"Scotch over rocks . . . make it twins," he orders.

"Sir, do ya think ya really need another?"

"What really I *don't* need is some fucking barkeep's advice!"

Observing Jake's intimidating reflection growing in the mirror, Kevin grunts a racist insult, grabs his money, then storms to the table from which he crawled. Grabbing a wine decanter and empty glass he returns, taking a stool on Mary's left. He guzzles a glass of wine. Pouring another, he bats the drink between his hands like a cat playing with a mouse.

Mary sneaks a sideways glimpse at Kevin. She worries the booze will again unclasp the chains restraining Mr. Hyde.

Kevin's dancing glass slithers to a stop, its wet streak on the counter drawing a stain of resentment.

Mary watches a familiar kaleidoscope of fear and anger tumble across Kevin's face. I feel the same emotions, but I'll be damned if I let him see it. My "display," my "attitude." What the hell do they expect? Timmy's only been gone seven months. I'm just as afraid as Kevin that our store will be blackballed.

Clenching her teeth so hard her ears ring, Mary shifts on her stool. You'd think those fools in the committee would be fawning all over me instead of that asshole Oscar. If I or Kevin, if he weren't such a pussy, threatened to go to the newspaper about Oscar and the judge, everyone'd be splattered in the shit storm!

She twirls the soda Jake gave her. There must've been others in the committee who went along, like me, out of fear. Maybe they weren't as vocal as me, but then they weren't cursed by the heartache of losing a child. Yeah, I'm angry with them almost as much as I am with myself. But I've grown up alongside these folks. Some were, could still be, friends. Damn. I don't know what to do.

Mary gazes into the twilight of the mirror. Heartened by the reflections of Leroy and Jake's supportive eyes, she smiles an ear-to-ear smile, a smile which since Timmy's death has been as rare as a hug from Kevin. But the joyful expression bounds off the mirror, striking Kevin harder than a line drive.

"What's so funny?" he asks.

"Oh, I was just thinking about what you said about my attitude, being watched by people. That was a big help. I now know just what to do."

By the fear on Kevin's face, she knows he is buying the lie.

"What do you mean 'big help'?" he says.

"You'll see."

"I don't think I like your tone, Mary!"

From her purse, Mary grabs some loose change, including a packet of Kleenex. Throwing them, they skip across the counter, landing in front of Kevin.

"What are these for?"

"To call me on the pay phone when you've decided about my *tone*, and to wipe Oscar's skid marks from your nose."

Kevin's face reignites in flaming rage. Sliding from his stool, he approaches Mary. Leroy sidesteps closer. Jake, cleaning a table, drops his towel. Scott, then Peter, look on.

Her back tingling with apprehension, Mary watches Kevin's reflection when terror explodes through her body from the impact of his fist against her brow. In a helpless sensation of falling, she reaches out to grab anything that will stop her descent. But that thing is the soda glass which she clutches in her hand before the blunt impact of the bar's counter on her skull hurls Mary into a black, silent void.

Chapter 31

The Beast Returns

Mary lies motionless on the floor. Outside, thunderclouds rumble like stampeding black stallions. Lightning flashes.

Bar lights flickering, the jukebox rises from the dead, roaring its joyous resurrection with a favorite selection: "There's a yellow rose in Texas, that I am going to see. She's the sweetest little flower . . . "

"You knew Kevin was gonna hit Mary," says Peter, his gaze snapping from Mary to Scott. "Why didn't you tell me? Why didn't you stop it!"

"You know as well as I that intervention with fate is forbidden."

Scott's tone, intended or not, reminds Peter of a dispassionate mortician. *I wonder if I'll ever act or do things with as much detachment to my clients.* Peter agonizes at the sight of a motionless Mary lying face down on the floor. Blood trickles through her tangled hair, gushing from the hand holding the broken glass.

A dazed Kevin kneels beside Mary when the crash of overturning tables shatters the silent stalemate. Jake charges like a bull at the husband. With vice-grip hands, the waiter clamps Kevin by the shoulders. Leroy, already on the phone with the sheriff, summons an officer, including an ambulance.

"I can't stand it any longer!" shouts Peter above the jukebox's roar.

"Here we go," mutters Scott.

Throwing his chair, Peter races to Mary and kneels, feeling her neck. Scott follows.

"There's a pulse!" he says.

Kevin cries with relief.

"The ambulance and sheriff will be here in fifteen minutes," says Leroy.

Peter stands, his gut burning in a flame of rage followed by a tingling throughout his body. As he grabs the bar to steady himself, the room's rear window explodes from a lightning strike. The building rattles in fear, falling into ozone-permeated darkness.

Kevin screams.

"Don't let go of im, Jake. I'll get the fuse box!" says Leroy, stumbling through a disheveled maze of chairs and tables.

The chaos intensifies Peter's prickly sensation. Swelling in size, he feels himself grow in strength.

"Peter, this way, *please*," says Scott, tugging Peter's arm.

"I wanna stay here with Mary!"

"There is nothing more you can do. We must leave before they fix the lights."

"Why?"

"*Please*, just trust me," says Scott, dragging Peter to the men's room.

After they enter the seclusion of the bathroom, the electricity returns, along with the jukebox's scream.

* * *

Scott bolts the door, then flicks the light switch. The room glows with the feeble light of a forty-watt bulb as a screaming exhaust fan sucks urine-fouled air. Scott points at the mirror.

"Go look at yourself!" he says.

Peter stumbles to a rust-stained sink. Above it hangs a mirror etched with names and phone numbers. Having grown two feet in height, he stoops to see the reflection of an enormous black spider, The Beast. He sinks to the floor.

"God help me!" he says.

Crouching beside the sobbing specter, Scott whispers, then closes his eyes.

"What are you doing?" asks Peter.

"Praying."

"What's happening? I'm falling back to the hell of that beast. If you hadn't dragged me away, I'm scared of what I would've done to Kevin. God help me!"

With a deformed, black arm, he embraces Scott.

"Huh, do you realize you have beseeched God's help twice in as many minutes?" says Scott. "Funny how desperation drags us back to Him."

"I don't understand what's happening," says Peter, prowling about the room.

"Since the committee meeting, you have teetered on the edge of the black abyss, denying The Almighty. Should you fall, you may never return."

Scott shoves Peter to the mirror.

"Is this what you want *Mary* to see?"

"No, but He can't help me!"

"Then why call out to Him, twice?"

Peter answers with silence. Why the hell did I call for Him?

"My son, you want to be a benefactor. Your client, Mary, for whom you have great fondness, lies bleeding on the floor. She is the only one who will help Jerome. Meanwhile, as The Beast, you cower in this cesspool."

From his shirt pocket, Scott removes a business card. Its golden letters glow with a yellow radiance legible in the dingy light:

Leader of the Pack
I.M. Emmanuel
12 Grace Way, Barkersville, MO 65043

"Here, take this. See the man."

Peter grabs the card.

"Grace Way, that's down by the river. A guy could get killed in that Black slum," says Peter. "Uh, I mean, what good could this Emmanuel guy do?"

"Trust me. Just pay him a visit."

"Well, okay. If you say so . . . "

"Thank you for your enthusiastic consideration."

* * *

Howls of approaching sirens overpower the screeching fan and jukebox.

"Great," says Peter, "help's arrived."

Pounding fists bruise the bathroom door.

"You two okay?" yells Jake.

"We are fine. My friend was shaken up by the fight and sight of blood. How is the young lady doing?" asks Scott.

"She's come to. A medic's checkin her."

"Good. Just give us a few minutes."

Jake leaves, followed by the sudden silence of a muted jukebox.

"I hope they ripped out its vocal cords," says Scott.

Peter faces the mirror. In its reflection, he observes a fully re-stored human form. *Hmm. Look at that. Maybe those prayers worked.*

Seconds later, the two hear authoritative voices outside.

"You ready to go back, son?"

"I guess so," says Peter. "But keep your fingers crossed I don't lose it again."

"Better than that—pray."

* * *

Opening the door, Peter surveys the room. The walls around the bar's front window echo the flashing red lights of an ambulance and the sheriff's car outside. Subhuman voices squawk from the parking lot. Mary sits in a chair beside a round table, holding a cold compress over her eye. Like mummy's rags, bloodstained fabric wraps itself around her head and hand. Kneeling before Mary, a paramedic examines her as he shines a flashlight in her eyes. Another paramedic stands behind them. Behind Mary towers Jake. He steadies her by the shoulders, his arms a dike protecting her from another wave of abuse. On the table's opposite side sits Leroy. Arms folded, he leans back in a chair, focused on Mary. Kevin slouches on a bar stool facing the mirror, hands cuffed behind his back. Standing near him, a brown uniformed sheriff scribbles in his notepad.

The poison of Mary's appearance sickens Peter. Like a snake shedding its skin, he twitches with the writhing of The Beast within, yearning to be unleashed. *Dear God.* The spasms subside. His human form remains intact. But instead of joy, Peter reviles his weakness which summoned the deity he so distrusts.

Peter follows Scott to Mary's table. Scott sits next to Leroy. The pair confer about this evening's events which include Kevin's arrest for assault.

Peter sits next to Mary. Rubbing his knees, his awkward demeanor attracts Jake's attention.

"You feelin all right, mister?" asks Jake, still standing guard behind Mary.

"I'm doing fine, now," says Peter, finally confident in his dominion over The Beast. "Thanks for asking."

"You city guys look kinda squeamish. Ya shoulda been here when we had a fella hit someone upside the head with a whisky bottle. Damn near cut off his ear. Blood . . . "

"Jake!" says Leroy, nodding at Mary. "Enough."

Jake is as comforting as a root canal. But Peter likes the burly employee. I wonder what "squeamish" looks like.

Peter's gaze bounces between the bandaged Mary and her attacker. Once more, Peter's emotions flare, but the flames are of concern, not hate. If that bastard's gonna beat her, better here in public where he can get arrested. At home, it's just "domestic" violence. But why do some guys abuse women, especially those they supposedly love? I remember Scott saying when a man feels worthless outside his home, he's more likely to abuse his wife because she's the only one he can dominate. Kevin must feel that way because of that pompous ass Oscar. I felt worthless as a mortal with whites. We're both punching bags. But punching bag or not, I was taught to respect the fair sex.

Just look at Mary. Even though she's in pain, bleeding, she holds herself with pride. And to think she's still going to help Jerome. . . Of all the mortals I've met, I admire her the most, even if she's white.

Peter wants to set Mary at ease, but to do so he must touch her. He scoots closer as Jake casts a wary eye.

"Mary, you don't know me, but may I put my hand on your shoulder? You look like you could use a little hug."

"I was barely conscious, but weren't you the one who knelt by me, feeling for a pulse?"

Peter nods yes.

"What's your name?"

"Peter."

"Peter who?"

"Just plain ol Peter."

For the first time this evening, Mary lifts a smile, disregarding his lack of stating a last name.

"Well, plain ol Peter, I'd be honored if you gave me a hug."

After flashing a reaffirming grin, Jake takes a chair at the table.

Peter nurses his arm around Mary's shoulders. Sensing her anguish and pain diminish, he revels in his benefactor's ability to comfort others. A barrage of her thoughts flees through his hand into his awareness. One thought surprises him; she still loves Kevin but vows their future relationship will be different. Something else Peter failed to expect. Her anger is the fruit of disappointment, not the decay of hate. *I must get to know this mortal better.*

Everyone smiles as the sheriff shoves a weeping, stoop-shouldered husband into an awaiting squad car. After locking the vehicle, the sheriff returns to take statements.

A highway patrol pursuit vehicle slides into the gravel lot. Leaping through the mushroom cloud of dirt and dust, a blue-uniformed state trooper storms into The Palace, his Smoky-the-Bear hat littered with heaven-sent debris.

"Need any assistance, Roland?" asks Trooper Brandon, surveying the scene as he brushes dirt from his hat.

Sheriff Roland assures the officer that the situation is under control.

"I've been patrolling up and down 68 all night looking for some clown in a red Vette that passed me doing close to a hundred. When I turned around to give chase, that crazy bastard turned off his lights like he could see in the dark! He disappeared like spit in Niagara Falls. I was in pursuit for nearly half an hour. Figured he pulled off somewhere around here.

"When I noticed your car out front I slowed down," he says to Roland, "then pulled in when I saw that Vette parked on the side. That guy in your back seat, what's he driving?"

"The BMW parked next to me. He's this lady's husband."

"Shit," says Brandon, staring at Mary. "I . . . uh, excuse me. Is he responsible for *this*?"

Everyone nods yes, except Mary.

Brandon scrutinizes the four men huddled at the table.

Peter avoids Brandon's searching eye. Though immune to mortal law, his car is not. The Vette can be confiscated. He hopes his tattletale sweaty brow goes unnoticed in the pale light.

"I would've had every trooper within fifty miles in pursuit of that son-of-a-bitch and roadblocks if only my radio hadn't gone out. Damnedest thing."

With a self-satisfying grin, Scott glances at Peter.

"Which one of you owns that Corvette?"

"Well, sure the hell ain't mine," says Jake. "I wouldn't be caught dead in no fancy-ass car like that! I got me a pickup."

"It's not mine neither. I suspect it belongs to one of these two gents," says Leroy, pointing to Scott and Peter, "but they been here since early afternoon."

"Yes Sir, Officer," says Peter, expanding Leroy's unexpected lie, "since around 2 o'clock. That's *my* car. My name's Peter and the guy across the table is my friend, Scott."

Scowling, Brandon faces the parking lot with a skeptical stare.

Freed of Brandon's piercing eyes, Peter slinks around the table, then leans behind Scott.

"Why's the bartender sticking his neck out for us?" whispers Peter.

"Leroy told me how much he admires Mary's courage. Of all the people here tonight, you and I were the only ones who showed her any kindness. I guess this is his way of saying thanks."

"Well Leroy, if you say so," says Brandon. "But if any of you see another red Vette pull in here, call the patrol. That guy's goin to kill someone."

Once more, Peter dodges Brandon's suspicious stare.

"Rest assured, Officer, we will," says Leroy.

Trooper Brandon exits the bar, leaving in his patrol car in a thunderhead of dust.

* * *

"She refuses to go to the hospital," says the paramedic to the four men. "Her pupils aren't dilated, nor different in size. She's not nauseous. But someone otta stay with her all night. Don't let her sleep, then get her to a doctor first thing in the morning."

"You sure she'll be okay till then?" asks Peter.

"I'm pretty sure. But if she starts vomitin or passes out, get her to emergency, *fast*. That car of yours otta get her there quick enough."

"Where's the closest hospital?"

"PCRMC in Rolla, about fifteen miles from here."

The medic hands Peter a card with the address and phone number of Phelps County Regional Medical Center.

All thank the medics who leave after packing up their gear. An hour later after taking everyone's statement, the sheriff leaves. The Palace is now reduced to five occupants all bunched around a circular table—Leroy, Jake, Peter, and Scott, all glaring at a self-conscious Mrs. Cook.

"You guys remind me of vultures waiting for a meal," she says. "I may look like a sideshow freak in all these bandages, but enough with the eyes!"

"Mary, never say you're a freak!" blurts Peter, blushing as he realizes his over-exuberance.

"It's almost two in the morning. Why don't we all take turns in keepin Mary up?" says Jake, after spending several moments staring at his watch. In a concentrated frown, he counts his fingers. "There's four of us. If we all take one-an-a-half-hour turns, that'll get us to eight. I'll start off. That okay with you guys?"

"Jake, if I'd known you were that good with numbers, I would've put you behind the cash register," says Leroy.

All agree on the waiter's plan. Soon three men lie slumped on the table, sleeping. Jake sits beside Mary, entertaining her with tales of bar fights, large-busted waitresses, and pool sharks.

An hour passes. Mary finds herself the only one conscious. She will not awaken a soul. They have all been gentlemen in their own way. Besides, the roar of snoring makes sleep impossible. Surrounded by the slumbering security, she sits patiently awaiting the horizon's announcement of a new day.

Chapter 32

The Morning After

Through the hole which used to be The Palace's rear window, the one blown apart by last night's lightning bolt, scattered beams of sunlight churn the room's smog of cigarette smoke into a boiling thunderhead. Ceiling fans blow the swirling cloud throughout the room in a carcinogenic fog.

An old grandfather clock standing behind the bar—the slender servant of Father Time— sounds its hourly chore with eight chimes. A rustling is heard at the circular table as three slumped men awaken from their failed good Samaritan efforts. Mary's chair sits empty.

Leroy's internal timepiece awakened him two hours ago. Besides being the bartender, during typically slow periods such as this Sunday morning, he fills in as the cook. Silent as a ghost, he prepares for breakfast. He now waits on a stool by the kitchen stove for the trio at the table to stir.

The clock's chime stirs Jake from his sleep who responds to the 8:00 a.m. summons with his ritual of cigarette coughs. Next, Peter and Scott having no need to sleep, pretend to yawn and stretch though absent mortal discomfort from their night of contortion.

"What's for breakfast?" asks Jake between gasps of air.

"The usual," says Leroy.

His announcement races over the kitchen counter's grease chased by echoes of cracking eggshells and aromas of fried bacon churned with acrid cigarette exhausts.

"We're lucky we're already dead. Between the cholesterol and smoke, we wouldn't have stood a chance," says Peter to Scott, then asks, "Where's Mary?"

"Must be in the lady's room."

Peter's nose furrows in disgust.

"Now what?" asks Scott.

"That smell."

"*Which* one?"

"Rancid beer."

"You sure?" says Scott, eyeing the floor's litter of beer mugs and crumpled Bud cans.

"Not *those*," says Peter, waving his arm at the alcoholic chaos, "*This*," he adds, pointing at his shirt's large, yellow stain.

Sniffing, Scott leans forward.

"Coors."

"Damn, must've spilled some last night," says Peter, taking another whiff. "Damnit, I gotta wash it out."

He shuffles to the men's lavatory but finds the door locked. Turning, he checks the room. Sure enough, three guys. He rattles the doorknob.

"Just a minute," says a feminine voice from inside.

Scott and Jake swap amused glances.

"Mary, is that *you*?"

The bathroom door crashes open. Within the dark opening stands a woman's slender frame. Under the unraveling dressing around her head, bruised and bloodshot eyes glare at Peter.

"Yeah, it's *me*!"

"What are *you* doing in there?"

"I had to pee last night. The room was so dark that I couldn't tell His from Hers. But once inside, I knew." She fans her nose. "Why can't you guys stand closer to the target?"

Peter wheels around at the sound of Scott and Jake laughing, then falling off their chairs.

"Anyway, I was so tired that I fell asleep on the toilet."

Shuffling to the table, Mary sits. Still chuckling, Scott and Jake climb back in their seats. Peter storms into the restroom. Soon he sits back in his chair, the stain's odor invigorated by the drink of water.

Her right hand still wrapped in a pink-stained gauze, Mary sits half-dozing in her chair. Her left hand supports her head. Above her eye, a bruise peeks through the separating bandages.

"How you feeling, Mrs. Cook?" asks Scott.

"I don't know which aches more, my hand, my head, or my bruised pride. Other than that, thank you, gentlemen, for all your help last night, but please, call me Mary."

"Tell her she's welcome an that I'm sorry for not stayin awake," shouts Leroy, still in the kitchen. "Ain't none'a you leavin without first havin this breakfast."

Jake lumbers into the kitchen. He returns with Leroy, carrying plates of food plus coffee. After gorging themselves, Scott pulls out a twenty-dollar bill. Mary rummages in her purse for the same.

"Your money ain't no good here," says Leroy.

"Thanks, Leroy. You too, Jake," says Mary.

Scott and Peter echo Mary's affirmation. The two ask if they can drive her to see a doctor somewhere. Mary says there is one in Rolla. She dumps her handbag on the table, picking through grocery receipts, lipstick, and a pound of loose coins.

"What ya lookin for?" asks Jake.

"Keys to the BMW out front. But just remembered they're with Kevin—in jail."

"I could hot-wire it," says Jake.

"Or we could take Peter's car," says Scott.

"*We*? My car only holds two."

"We can use my ol pickup out back," says Jake.

"Yeah, but gotta first shovel out that load of manure," says Leroy.

"You gentlemen've done enough. I'll call a cab."

"No cabs way out here," says Leroy.

"Well, that settles it. I'll just have to take you myself," says Peter, seeing an opportunity to be alone with Mary.

"But what about your friend?" she asks.

"Oh, don't worry about *him*. He'll grab a ride from a friend in Rolla, won't you, Scott?"

"Sure," sighs Scott. "Leroy, may I use your phone?"

"Help yaself."

After faking a call, Scott strolls out to the parking lot.

Mary grabs her purse, giving Jake, then Leroy, a kiss on the cheek. Jake's weathered face blushes, resembling a ripe, bird-pecked plum. Turning, she follows Peter to the exit.

"Hold on a minute, Mary. We can't let you go lookin like a war refugee," says Leroy.

He disappears into the room's storage locker. Following a crash and profanity, he emerges with a red, paisley bandana, sterile gauze, and bandages. After changing her dressings in a blur of hands and fabric, he winds the bandana around her head.

"Now *that* looks better. Fifteen years of patchin up drunks comes in pretty handy."

Mary parades to the bar mirror, admiring the red headpiece.

"And if you happen to be passin by one day, drop in and have one on the house."

"If I do, I'll return this," she promises, touching the bandana.

"We ain't taking it back. It's a gift," says Leroy. "And don't you worry none about that car. We'll take good care of it till you pick it up."

"That's Kevin's. *He'll* be coming for it."

"Don't worry none. That car'll give the place a fancy look. Beats em ol pickups that's always breakin down out front," says Jake.

Peter watches from the boardwalk. He realizes his prediction of her aiding Jerome Manning, begins to unfold. The Palace lies on the road Mary will take to IMCC where Jerome will await execution.

"Thanks again, fellas," says Mary.

* * *

"Peter," says Scott as they stand outside in the gravel. "Is *The BOOK* still in the car?"

"Behind the passenger's seat, but I'll return it later after I get Mary to a doctor."

Peter starts to the boardwalk but stops and faces Scott with a worried expression.

"Yes, what is it?" asks Scott.

"I've been thinking. I'm concerned with what's going to happen, especially with Mary. Why am I not allowed to see all of my client's future? If I could, I could better prepare myself—think about what powers I'll need to use and what action to take."

"There is not an apprentice who has failed to ask that question. We withhold certain future knowledge so you will learn to use your judgment, your wits, to react to unforeseen circumstances. That way you will build confidence in your judgment. As for deciding when to use your powers, *that* will be one of the biggest challenges you will face. Again, experience will be your greatest teacher."

Peter, deep in thought, looks back at the entrance for Mary.

"Well, alright . . . When will we meet again?" he says, turning back.

Silence answers. Scott has disappeared, walking towards the main road.

* * *

Mary shuffles onto the boardwalk. Peter steps from the gravel, walking beside her. "Where's your friend?" she asks.

"Already got his ride."

By her halting stride, Peter can tell Mary is hurting. But the late morning sun offers an appreciated massage. In empathy with each step of her discomfort, the building's planked walk groans with the discomfort of an arthritic old man.

Peter sneaks a glance at Mary. Her dancing, long, auburn hair twirls below the bandana, bouncing with each step, flickering with reds and browns under the spotlight of the adolescent day's sun. Though scolding himself for his amorous feelings, he burns with carnal images.

Unlike last night, Peter dares not touch Mary out of respect for the privacy of her thoughts. He would like to confess his feelings for her, but they have only just met. His lips wilt with hesitation.

I wonder if my real identity hidden under this white disguise would offend her. I dare not reveal my true self until I'm sure, just like I didn't expose it last night at the committee meeting. A Black man at that all-white gathering would've been thrown out, or worse. And God forbid the consequences of a Black man walking alongside a married, white woman. So, I'll continue this bleached charade. Damnit, even in death I'm still a slave of the white establishment, including their God.

Peter's earlier joy at Mary's side sours like milk on a hot summer day.

"You alright? You're so quiet," says Mary, stopping.

"I'm fine, Mrs. Cook."

"Remember, *Mary,* and I don't believe you."

"Mary, we need to get you to the car."

Their walk resumes. Mary tires. Tripping, she grabs Peter's forearm for support. Her thoughts slam into his mind. *I hope he lets me hold on. Yeah, he's moody, but that wavy brown hair, those bowling ball shoulders. God, he's gorgeous. I know I've met him before. Was it at the City Hall committee meeting? Is that why he was here last night? But if so, why didn't he and his friend sit with us? They both sat at that table, looking at us like . . . like we were a pack of rabid dogs. How true.*

Stopping, Peter stares through Mary as though she is made of cellophane.

"Peter? Peter!"

As though waking from a stupor, Peter shakes his head. The fog of thought congeals into consciousness.

"You say something, Mary?"

"I asked if you're alright."

"No, before that, something about us meeting before?"

Peter was so concentrated on Mary's thinking that he forgot they were thoughts, not an audible conversation.

"Peter, I didn't say anything about us having met," says Mary, her expression creasing with concern. "But I *was* thinking it. You . . . you one of those psychics?"

Silence.

"I'm waiting."

Peter sighs. *What the hell. We're alone. Why not tell her who I am? An unbelievable truth is as safe as a lie.*

"Yes, as a matter of fact, I *can* read your mind. Not only that, I can foresee some future events!"

The suspicion in Mary's smile fades. She squeezes his arm.

"For a psychic, you're awfully cute."

Peter's face ripens with embarrassment. Both continue side by side down the wooden walk. Mary's curls stroke Peter's cheek, and tickle his soul, while teasing his manliness. Her surging emotions add to his.

Rounding the corner of the building, the two encounter the blackened wreckage of The Palace's neon sign dangling from the roof.

"So, this is what that bolt of lightning hit last night," says Mary. "Guess He didn't like what was going on here. Can't say I blame Him, God I mean." She faces Peter. "You think there's a God?"

"Yeah," he answers but withholds his negative feelings.

"You believe in an afterlife?"

"Yeah," repeats Peter. "Do you?"

"Sometimes, but when I see what people like Wilson and the judge get away with, I wonder. But let's say there's something spiritual out there. Let's say this something involves an afterlife. A lot of folks think so, believing if you're 'good' you'll go to your reward. But what if your reward is *here,* this life, now, is as good as it gets, no afterlife? Or if there is, what if it's *worse* than this one?"

"Worse? Interesting," says Peter, remembering his years as The Beast.

"I guess what I'm saying is, in either case, shouldn't we make *this* life the best we possibly can?"

Mary's reasoning for mortal altruism intrigues Peter. He is ashamed to admit that in her, more than him, glows the spirit of a benefactor.

* * *

The chatter of the wooden walk yields to the crackling of gravel. Finally, the two stand beside Peter's gleaming, red carriage wearing Fillmore Motors license plate frames.

"So, *you're* him," says Mary.

"Him, who?"

"The guy who bought the Corvette from Fillmore Motors."

"Yeah, Albert was happy as a baby with a new rattle when I drove it off his lot," says Peter.

"I'll bet. His sales are nearly dead. Wilson ordered a boycott of Albert's business because he called Wilson a bigot at the committee meeting. Wilson was *very* upset."

"'Pissed' is the word, Mary," says Peter. "And I'm gettin to really like this car. It's gonna be seen in town, a lot."

"Is this the car Trooper Brandon was looking for last night?"

The roar of a rusted yellow pickup racing through the parking lot ends their conversation as abruptly as a head-on crash. In boiling dust, the truck skids to a stop opposite Peter's car. Henry and Benny roll from the truck. They waddle to the driver's side of the Corvette, eyeing the red chariot with the determination of hogs at a feeding trough.

"Yep, this's it!" says Benny.

Each drawing a pocketknife, they pry open a blade.

Peter recognizes the pair from last night, looking for the red sports car that had cut them off on the highway. Peter, trying to think over Mary's distressed thoughts as she squeezes his arm, yanks the passenger door open.

"Take these keys, Mary. Get in. Lock the doors," he says, pushing her inside, then faces the men. "Can I help you, gentlemen?"

Henry and Benny trade narrow-eyed glances. Benny squints inside, chuckling.

"You and the missus have a little disagreement?"

Peter glares, expressionless as stone.

"This here your car?"

Peter's first thought is to answer no, we're stealing it, you fat fart. But with Mary inside . . .

"Who wants to know?" Peter asks.

"*We're* the Banger brothers," says Henry, puffing up his chest as he points the knife to himself and his brother. "The Marauders of Maries County!"

"Really?" says Peter. *I wonder if I should bow or offer my condolences.*

Frustrated by Peter's impassiveness, the man waves his knife over the Corvette.

"This fuckin thing near ran us off the road last night. We came by to pay our respects."

Peter searches his mind for an answer that will appease these rotund idiots. *Damn! I wish Mary weren't here.* He finds the reply in a corner next to his survival instinct.

"Oh, *that* car. Trooper Brandon was by last night telling us about some clown joyriding. Apparently, there's another Vette out there just like ours because *we've* been here since early yesterday afternoon."

The brothers trade another narrow-eyed glance.

"Go inside. Ask Leroy and Jake. They'll tell you the same thing," says Peter, sincere as a used car salesman.

"Benny, you go in. Check it out. I'll stay here."

Peter leans down, reassuring Mary with a smile through the rolled-up window.

"It's okay, honey! These gentlemen are inquiring about that *other* Corvette Trooper Brandon told us about. I told em we've been here since yesterday afternoon."

After checking the doors are locked, Mary nods, signaling she gets the scam.

Minutes pass slower than a pregnant snail when Benny finally returns.

"Yeah, Henry, these two was here just like he said. Been here with them folks from Barkersville, you know, the ones that want that murderin nigra dead. What's his name . . . Manson?"

"Manning," says Peter.

"That right?" asks Henry.

"Yeah, we were here, but not with them."

"That's too bad," says Henry, scratching his cheek with the knife. "You know it weren't that long ago a nigra would'a never made it to no trial."

Peter's face flashes like a brake light. He storms around the front of the car, eyes nailed on the two brothers as The Beast within claws for a confrontation. *Yeah, I bet you two miss the good ol days.*

Intimidating as a bull before its charge, Peter glares at them. Then, through the windshield, he catches Mary's terrified expression. He struggles to keep the monster within chained.

Henry, oblivious of his salvation, grins, revealing a rotting picket fence of tobacco-stained teeth.

"Ain't I seen you before? Last night out fronta the bar with that nigra?"

Peter denies the statement reminding the brothers how dark and noisy it is at the bar's entry.

"It could've been anyone," says Peter.

"Uh-huh . . . " grunts Henry as his hand slides into a bulging pocket.

At that moment, a carload of brawny construction workers from a highway project pulls up beside them. Henry quickly removes his hand as both brothers close their knives.

"Ya'll take care, now," says Henry. "An if ya plan on stayin round here, might wanna grow eyes in the back'a your head."

Benny leans down again, staring inside the car.

"An we'll be keepin an extra eye open for you too, missy!"

Squeezing back into their pickup, they tear from the lot in a storm of dust and gravel.

Chapter 33

Farewell

Mary watches the pickup accelerate north, zigzagging a path memorized by a white exhaust contrail. Through the truck's passenger window, a frankfurter appendage extends, firing a pistol skyward. Screaming cars dive to the shoulder fast as cowardly matadors as the rusting hulk charges past. Long after the yellow turmoil vanishes, the gunfire crackles in the distance.

Though Mary sits safely in the Corvette, fear's icy tentacles entwine her. She stares rearward at the commotion when startled by a knock on the passenger door. She snaps around.

"Thank God it's you, Peter," she says through the window.

"You all right?"

But Mary's relief fades like cheap paint in the summer sun. A storm rages behind her crumpled brow. Last night's contentious committee meeting, and Kevin's assault followed by the threat of those two brothers thunder in her mind.

"You *all right*?"

"I'm okay," she says, concealing her throbbing head pain with a lie as she unlocks the doors.

Peter slides into his seat. He flicks the ignition, summoning the two hundred and forty horses from their slumber. Seatbelts lock.

Peter notices Mary's tenseness and shivering like a cornered mouse.

"I'm a little chilly. Mind if I turn on the heater?" he asks.

Consoled by the obvious lie, Mary snuggles into her seat. She closes her eyes, hoping the darkness blinds the pain.

Mindful of the delicate cargo within, the Corvette tiptoes

around the gravel lot's potholes and steps onto the highway. Eyeing for the yellow intruder, the car slinks northward towards Barkersville. Soon, a pack of four-wheeled exhaust-suckers tailgates the Corvette, their taunting horns biting Mary's ears. Opening her red evening handbag, she grabs four Valium, popping them in her mouth as though they were pebbles cast down a well.

"How can you take those without water?"

"A survival skill I learned from living with Kevin," she says, then glares at her handbag. "I *hate* this damn purse. Kevin *makes* me use it. Says it's more 'ladylike' than that 'leather cabinet' I carry. But this thing's as useless as high heels in bed."

Finding a small mirror after more rummaging, she inspects the black and blue crescent moon sinking below her bloodshot eye.

"Great, that's all I need!"

Her stomach growling, courtesy of the waterless drugs, she catches Peter's sideways glance.

"What are you lookin at?"

"Oh, nothing."

"Well, instead of *nothing*, shouldn't you be looking at the road?"

Peter's attention shifts to the approaching highway while the tailpipe-lickers yip behind.

"Doesn't that honking bother you?" asks Mary.

"I'm doing the speed limit," says Peter, glancing at the speedometer which reads double nickels.

"Peter, I'd like to get home before my first Social Security check arrives."

Peter's jaw muscle bulges when he notices Mary's pale face. He veers to the shoulder, stopping as the horde stampedes past.

"You look a little pale, Mary. Should I take you to emergency?"

Though her nauseous stomach does not, her throbbing headache ignores the Valium. She worries that this plus a growing sleepiness might be the delayed symptoms of a concussion. Mary leans to the side, her hand barely supporting her head.

"Yeah, better get me to one."

"That medic said there's one in Rolla— about fifteen miles. We'll be there in a few minutes."

Ignoring its rearview mirror, the Corvette leaps into traffic and jumps the double yellow line, sprinting past the horde whose once impatient horns now cry with the whimper of frightened children. Three minutes later, the car slams onto Route 63, then turns south, bolting for Rolla, impatient as a thoroughbred to the finish line.

As Mary slides into semi-consciousness, the passing country-side assumes a surrealistic blur. Wooden sentinels, tall and slender, stand at attention, guarding the red chariot's passage. Homes chained to barns by decaying wire fences flee past on rolling fields of browns and greens. Then, breaking the roar of wind, road, and car, a rearward siren screams.

"Shit!" says Peter, staring at the mirror. "A trooper. Looks like the same one at The Palace last night."

Skidding to a stop on the shoulder, the Corvette shakes from agitation. Sated by the capture of prey, the patrol car grows mute, but its flashing lights watch the Corvette, as intense as a red-eyed dragon. Exiting a white Ford Mustang, the blue-uniformed officer strolls to the driver's side, motioning to roll down the window. He peers inside.

"Well, well, look who we have here!" says the trooper.

"Hello, Trooper Brandon. We're in a hurry . . . " but his explanation stops when Mary loses consciousness, slumping forward.

Mary awakens to another wailing siren. Ahead in her vision's fog, she sees a white patrol car under a bar of flashing red lights, leading the way as cars, semis, and a rusting, yellow pickup, scatter before them like frightened deer. Mary's drifting consciousness deadens the sensation of the Sunday afternoon ninety-mile-per-hour chase.

Minutes later, the Corvette, its tires squealing from exhaustion, follows the patrol car to the Phelps County Memorial Hospital emergency entrance. Peter races inside. Two male nurses return with a gurney, lifting Mary from her seat. Though still insensible, she is aware of pressing voices announcing an impelling urgency.

* * *

Mary lies in bed feeling caged as a toddler in a crib, surrounded by institutional green walls. Overhead, a monitor echoes with the beep of a monotone sparrow. A plastic cord dangles from above, shackled to her wrist by coils of tape. On the wall hangs a clock, its black hands pointing to 8:03. Daylight, too intense for sundown, spills through a window on her right. To her left, a stand supports a plate of fried eggs plus toast beside a bowl of fruit. Folded neatly beside a cup of coffee lies a red bandana. Her attention shifts to a marker board which reads:

Patient: Mary Cook
Today is: Monday, September 5th, Labor Day
Nurse: Beatrice

Mary's head throbs with confusion. What happened to Sunday? And who's that guy sprawled out in the chair?

"Kevin, is that you?"

Grunting, the figure squints at her through red, spider-webbed eyes.

"Morning, Mary. How you feeling?"

Though the face and voice are familiar, they are not Kevin's. Mary strains for a memory.

"Mary, it's me, Peter, remember? We drove here yesterday from The Palace. You fainted."

Hazy as an out-of-focus movie, a cloud of visions drifts across Mary's mind. Moments pass as she assembles bits of memory. Her eyes flash with recognition.

Rushing to her side, Peter grabs her hands but diverts her thoughts out of respect.

"Peter!" she says, sitting up.

"Mary, everything's all right. Just stay calm. They want you to rest."

"What happened?"

"Remember two days ago? The Palace? Kevin? You hit your head on the counter. They say you suffered a mild concussion. You've been in and out of consciousness. They took a scan. No internal bleeding, but they want you here for another day or two."

"Where am I?" asks Mary, her eyebrows folded with confusion.

"Phelps County Memorial."

"Has Kevin been by?"

"No. He's still in jail."

"Good. I need to check out of here."

Releasing Peter's hands, Mary flings the sheets aside. Peter flushes, turning away from Mary's unveiled legs. Noticing his embarrassment, she re-blankets as she reaches up, turning his chin toward her.

"Why Peter, you're blushing. How cute. How long've you been here?"

"Since we checked you in," he says as his ripe cherry cheeks fade.

"We?"

"Trooper Brandon and myself."

"Brandon. I seem to remember. He's the officer who pulled us over."

"Yeah," says Peter. "The minute he looked inside, seeing you unconscious, he told me to follow im to the hospital. He even smiled and asked if I could keep up. Never asked for a driver's license or anything. The nurse said he's been by at least once asking how you're doing. Apparently, you've made *quite* an impression on him."

"Huh, can you believe that?"

"Oh, *I* certainly can."

Like a cat batting a ball of twine, Mary's thoughts play with Peter's tone.

"And you've been here the whole time?" asks Mary.

"Yeah, sleeping in that recliner."

Mary pats his cheek. Its cherry glow has a power surge.

"You poor thing. Thank you for staying by me," she says, followed by a pause. "Your old offer to take me home still good?"

"Sure. When they say you can."

"No, I mean *this* morning."

"Like within the next ninety minutes? What's the rush?"

"Because the sentencing phase of Jerome's trial starts tomorrow. I *have* to be there!"

"Why? Remember what Wilson said at The Palace? Jerome's gonna get the death sentence sure as a bear sh . . . , I mean there's no more that can be done," says Peter.

"The prosecuting attorney asked Kevin and me if we'd say something before the court. Wilson even asked. Well, I plan to do *just* that! I'm going to ask that they spare Jerome's life."

With a twinkle in his eye, Peter says not a word.

"You hear what I said? I'm going to ask that they spare the life of Timmy's killer!"

"Oh, I heard," says Peter.

"What's with you? You don't seem surprised at all."

Suspicion tingles in the back of Mary's neck. *Ever since I* first saw Peter at The Palace, I've had a feeling he's "different." He seems too cool under pressure. Take the way he handled the Banger brothers. How he drives that Corvette like he's immune to harm. But his reaction to my decision about Jerome is really strange. It's like he already knew.

"Mary, you're right, I'm not that surprised, because you're more courageous than anyone I've ever met," says Peter, taking her hand again.

The shiver shrinks to a tingle inching down Mary's spine, but this time the sensation is void of fear.

"Your decision's gonna twist a few shorts. Does Kevin know?"

"We've had no discussion. In fact, we haven't *discussed* much of anything since Timmy died, unless you call shouting, discussing."

Peter releases Mary's hand. She rolls over, eyes locked in a vacant gaze out the window at a maple tree.

"I'll plea for mercy; life imprisonment. Taking Jerome's life won't bring my Timmy back," she says, turning to Peter. "You think hearing something like that from the mother might get their attention?"

"Yeah, like an earful of hornets," says Peter. "You realize what you're letting yourself in for? They're gonna call your testimony the rantings of a deranged mother. But you do seem quite at ease. What made you decide this?"

Mary returns to the view of the maple. She notices two doves perched side by side. They snuggle, drawing Mary into a mindful refuge.

Though I've been unconscious, I was aware of things. Just like those two doves nestling together, something, someone, was beside me, touching me. I'm sure it was Peter. Then it started—the dreams. But they were more than dreams. I was transported back to the first committee meeting. I felt

Peter's presence there, though I don't remember actually seeing him. I saw Jerome's life flash before me clearly as a movie. Everything, especially the Mother's Groceries holdup . . . I watched Jerome's gun explode as his partner fell on him. He never meant to hurt Timmy.

Timmy, my beautiful Timmy. Dear God, how I've wished for one last moment beside him. But in my dream, I did.

I walked up to the pickup in front of the store and saw him. The window's rolled down so I knocked on the door. He smiled and we talked.

"Hi, Mom. What ya doing here?"

"I've come to say goodbye, my darling."

"Goodbye?"

"Yes. You're going on a long trip."

"You comin with me, Mom?"

"Not now, my precious. But I will, later."

"Where am I going?"

"To a beautiful place."

I lean inside. Kiss his forehead. Touch his hair. I'm overcome by a sense of loss. Not only for me and Timmy, but all humanity. The joy, love, and yes, even the pain Timmy will never feel. What beauty, great deeds will mankind never see? But I am grateful for the time I shared with him. Then, BANG! All goes black.

I'm cast into the future as I watch Jerome's execution. That's when the remorse hits like Judgement Day. I voted for his extermination at that damn meeting. If only I'd seen Jerome's death before my vote. Nothing could've made me . . . But then, this was just a dream, wasn't it?

Dear God, is death Jerome's only fate? If not, can I put myself through the hell I know awaits? Then I remember a voice much like Peter's in the background, saying, "Not the

destination, but the journey is the measure of one's being."
That's when I decided to testify. I've wondered, should I tell
Peter about these visions? I think he already knows.

"Yes, I am at ease," says Mary, turning to Peter. "Mind taking
this ranting, deranged woman home?"

"I'd be honored."

Chapter 34

Helping Hands

Outside the hospital room window, the morning breeze tickles the maple tree. Peter, half-asleep, lies in his recliner watching the giggling ball of branches. Through a half-open bathroom door behind him, a growling exhaust fan rattles the ambient serenity.

"Mary, you about ready?" asks Peter.

In the bathroom, Mary peers into a vanity mirror.

"You know, this thing doesn't look that bad," she says.

"What thing?"

"What do you think? The bandana the boys gave me at The Palace. Pretty cute, huh?"

Mary slips on a pair of sunglasses a nurse gave her. But Mary seeks assurance, not the truth, that even wearing a turban of bandages over a quarter-moon bruise rising above her cheek, she still looks attractive.

"Oh, that. Yes, Mary, very nice."

"Men," she mutters, grabbing her purse. "'Nice' is what Kevin says after I've preened all afternoon for the theatre."

Peter climbs out of the recliner as nurse Beatrice barges in.

"There's an Officer Brandon in the lobby who wishes to speak to you," she says, looking at Peter.

"Did he say what it's about?"

"No, but he *didn't* look happy."

"It's getting late," says Mary, checking her watch. "I'll go with you. We can leave . . . "

"The officer said *just* him," interrupts Beatrice, then stomps out of the room.

The exiting physique reminds Peter of the north end of a south-bound cow.

"That old broad's charming as a cold bedpan," he says.

"Go on and see Brandon. I'll wait here. But *please* hurry."

Flinging sunglasses and purse on the bedsheets, Mary plops on the bed, staring at the maple whose leaves have lost their laughter.

After Peter leaves the room, Mary briefly waits. Removing her high heels, she slips on her hospital slippers, then follows him.

* * *

Peter enters the lobby. It echoes with the stomping of Trooper Brandon's pacing boots. Brandon's face increases with concern as he and Peter talk for a few minutes. Mary hides behind a column, trying unsuccessfully to hear their conversation.

Brandon has learned Peter and Mary are returning soon to Barkersville via Route 63, the same road they traveled to the hospital. He offers to unofficially escort them twenty miles to the town of Vienna because he has learned the Banger brothers are searching that road for them. Vienna will place them beyond the brothers' prowl.

Peter tells the trooper about the Bangers' confrontation at The Palace.

"Trust me," says Brandon, "you *don't* want another run-in with those two. Benny's brain doesn't fire on all cylinders makin im prone to irrational behavior. Both of em carry a gun but Henry's smarter. Worse, he's a dead shot. So do this; meet me here in an hour and don't tell anyone."

Mary scurries back to her room.

* * *

"Wait how long?" asks Mary, sitting on the bed with crossed arms.

"Only an hour or so. That Brandon seems like a nice fellow but he's worried about those Banger guys," says Peter, sitting on the bed. "Mary, I've got this premonition something bad's gonna happen if we don't wait like he says."

Mary's brow wrinkles with concern. Premonition, huh? Yesterday he said he could foretell some future events. At the time his claim sounded like a joke, but now I wonder . . .

"Is there something you're not telling me?" she asks.

"I . . . I've just got this feeling."

"Peter, I'm getting out of here *now*! If I don't get home today, I'm gonna miss Jerome's trial tomorrow. If you don't wanna take me, fine. I'll rent a car and drive myself!"

"What if you pass out again?"

"Then that'll be on *your* conscience!" Then, placing her hand on his knee, her voice softens. "I need to get home. Tomorrow's gonna be a long day. I wanna be rested. Besides, what are you so worried about? I know what those two roughnecks are like, and it's not like we're walking down some dark ol alley at midnight. This is Labor Day weekend. The roads are full of cars. Those two won't try anything in full view of everyone. Besides, if you can't outrun that yellow heap of theirs in your Corvette, get an Edsel."

Peter slumps in defeat.

Mary springs off the bed. She tosses the sunglasses over her bandanna and snatches her purse. Pulling Peter to his feet, she drags him down the hall.

An hour later, Brandon stands at the lobby desk listening to the receptionist's answer.

"Yes, Sir, *quite* sure. They left an hour ago in a red Corvette. Can't miss a car like that!"

Grumbling, Brandon marches to his car. He stares across the

white-lined checkered parking lot when his radio squawks a dispatch about a disabled red Corvette with a male driver parked on the southbound shoulder of Route 63 at County Road 522.

"Where's the woman!" he shouts.

Leaping into his Mustang, Brandon grabs the mike, responding to the call. With blazing red eyes and a siren's wail, the car pounces onto city streets, vehicles leaping to the side while the white crusader gallops to I-44, then north on Route 63.

* * *

One hour before the police dispatch, Mary sits reclining in the Corvette, trying to nap. Through the corners of her dulled vision, she watches Peter, his eyes fixed on the rearview mirror as though stuck on fly paper. *He's making me a nervous wreck! It's a beautiful day, why can't he just enjoy the drive?*

"Look out!" she says.

"What?" says Peter, his attention whipping forward.

"Oh, nothing."

"Then why'd you say that?"

"Because you haven't looked at what's ahead, or me, since we left Rolla."

"I'm sorry," says Peter. "Guess I'm a little worried about what Trooper Brandon said."

"A *little* worried?"

Mary watches the passing countryside. *I suppose I should be grateful. No one's been this concerned about me since I was pregnant. Oh, how Kevin doted over me like I was a princess. God, how I miss those days.*

"You seem preoccupied about something, Mary. You alright?"

"Oh, just thinking how gorgeous the day is. Let's put the top down."

She flicks off her sunglasses, leaning through the open passenger window. Her auburn flag of hair waves in the wind.

"Yeah, this beauty would like a tan," says Peter, pulling on the reins.

The Corvette drifts left across the two-lane highway to a widening at a dirt road intersection. The car stops, still pointed toward Barkersville. Peter climbs out. He opens the storage well lid behind the seats, ready to fold down the top, and sees the leather case containing *The BOOK* in the compartment.

"Uh-oh."

"What's the matter?" asks Mary.

"I forgot, Scott left his briefcase."

"Well, can't you leave it there?"

"It won't fit with the top down. I'll have to take it out. It'll fit under your legs if you don't mind."

"That's stupid! Must've been designed by a man. Okay, if that's what it takes to ride in the sun."

Mary exits the car. Peter grunts, slinging *The BOOK* into the passenger compartment. He removes the book from the satchel, then returns the satchel to the well. After the top disappears into the bowels of the car, Mary climbs in, arching her legs around the brown monolith.

"It's alright," she says. "Not too bad. What's in this thing, anyway?"

"*Promise me* you'll never open it to find out!" says Peter, glaring down at her.

Shocked by the outburst, Mary nods yes. Pouting, she turns to the traffic, counting cars.

Ninety-seven vehicles later, they are still stuck on the shoulder, unable to cross the traffic.

"You know, you don't look very comfortable," says Peter, his hardened demeanor thawing.

"Better this than missing the sun on my face. Turn on the radio."

Eager as a child in a confessional atoning for a sin, Peter complies. The air reverberates with:

"There's a yellow rose in Texas,

that I am gonna see.

She's the sweetest little flower . . . "

"That's what they were playing at The Palace! Turn it up, Peter."

Led by the music, Mary's thoughts wander back to The Palace's committee meeting. It's only been two days, but that night seems as distant as the stars. I didn't realize it then, but when I walked away from Kevin and the committee, I was walking away from my old, and I thought comfortable, life. But what I mistook for comfort was really denial. It was like I was wearing sunglasses which I dared not remove. They blinded me to the truth, to the pain, letting me see just enough to survive.

Radio singing, Mary twirls the sunglasses dangling in her hand. Then folding back her arm, she catapults them over the driver's side into a field, her hand slightly touching Peter. During the brief contact, Peter hears a flash of Mary's thoughts. He turns off the ignition.

"No sense wasting gas. I have a feeling you just started," he says.

The remark tickles a smile on Mary's face. Digging through her purse she finds, then throws a plastic bag of tranquilizers. The bag lands in the same field, bursting open like a ripe opium pod scattering its seeds of oblivion. Dumping the contents of the cursed, red handbag on the mat, she removes her high heels, flinging shoes and purse behind her out of the car. She laughs with liberation as the trinkets of her past servitude summersault out of her life.

Peter watches with a grin.

But their bliss withers fast as a tender sprout in April's frost. The metallic thud of leather's impact upon sheet metal turns their heads rearward. To their shock, behind them, inches from the Corvette's bumper looms a rusted, yellow pickup. The Banger brothers, in blue overalls, glare through a cracked, bug-splattered windshield. A door squeals open. Out waddles the driver, Henry.

Instead of the cold squeeze of fear, Mary burns with anger over her inattentiveness of the approaching truck.

"Gun it!" she says. "You can outrun those bastards!"

Henry nears. The Corvette roars awake. Peter pops the clutch as the red beast strains to escape but shutters and stalls. Panicked, he tries again, but the herd of horses under the hood sputter, choke, and die.

As Henry hovers at the door, Peter looks up, his face a swirl of despair and embarrassment.

"Got car troubles?" says Henry, scratching his groin. "Me an Benny's damn sorry bout the way we scared the both of ya the other day. Maybe we can make it up ta ya. I know somethin bout cars. Be happy ta check under the hood."

He extends a leathery, brown palm. The two men shake hands.

Mary chills with suspicion, remembering Brandon's warning that Henry carries a gun.

"Best take that key outta the ignition. Don't want ya accidental like runnin me over," says Henry with a chapped-lipped grin.

After Peter complies, Henry lifts the hood, leaning inside the engine well. The vehicle jiggles, followed by muffled snapping noises as Mary sinks in her seat. Grabbing her wallet from the mat, she removes her driver's license, Visa card, Social Security ID, plus a folded document. She slips them into her panties. The wallet, still holding a Macy's credit card and seventy-three dollars cash returns to the mat.

Henry straightens up clutching a fistful of spark plug wires. They dangle like black worms. "This here's your problem. Ya ain't firing on all cylinders," he says with a decayed-tooth grin as he slings the wires towards the truck, then approaches Peter.

Henry yanks a gun from his overalls. Standing behind the door, he lowers the weapon, aimed at Peter, concealing it from traffic.

"Turn on them flashin emergency lights. Both of ya's smile like ya happy we're here helpin. Don't want no passersby gettin the wrong idea. And gimme them keys and your wallets."

Peter surrenders his keys. Mary hands over her wallet.

"Ain't gonna ask ya again. Gimme your fuckin wallet!" he says, leaning close to Peter.

"I . . . I don't have one. Lost it somewhere."

"For God's sake, Peter, give him your damn wallet!" says Mary.

"I don't have my wallet," answers Peter, twisting between the two. "Really, I *don't!*"

"You must think I'm pretty stupid," says Henry, pressing his gun on Peter's temple.

Mary stares in terror. *Please don't answer that.*

"I said I don't have the damn thing! Let me outta the car. Search me yourself."

Henry backs away, lowering his gun from passing prying eyes.

"Alright. An don't try *nothin.*"

Peter exits the Corvette, standing at attention as Henry searches the driver's empty pockets.

"Well, Benny, if that don't fuckin beat all. He ain't got nothin!"

Peter sits back in his seat. Laughter rings behind from the pickup.

"But I got the missus' wallet and these," says Henry, waving the ignition keys. "They ain't goin nowhere. Get your ass over here! Cover em while I look around."

Fear glues Mary to her seat. It's bad enough about those brothers, but Peter, no driver's license? No money? How can he drive a car, pay for anything? Is he some kinda fugitive? And that book. Dear God, is there anyone I can trust?

Chapter 35

Escape

In the passenger's rearview mirror, Mary watches Benny spill from the pickup with the consistency of warm Jell-O. Unlike his brother, Benny's bald head carries a frayed straw hat, its once white hue now blotted in browns. An empty Bud can falls out the door, rattling under the truck. Mary forces her attention from the reflection.

A smile cracks Benny's cue-ball face. Sauntering to the Corvette, he retrieves a woman's red shoe, twirling the footwear by the heel. He stops beside Mary, tapping the door with the footwear as his other hand strokes a side pocket which sags due to the heavy contents inside. Benny's gaze slithers between Peter and Mary's bandaged head.

"You look like *shit,* lady. That why you an that trooper passed us like a bat outta hell a couple a days ago?" he asks.

Meantime, Henry turns his back to the car, digging through Mary's red billfold with a starving dog's eagerness. Removing seventy-three dollars plus the credit card, he backhands the wallet onto the snarl of spark plug wires.

"You two don't seem to take no fuckin hint," says Henry, slamming his pistol against the driver's door. "We don't take kindly to nigra lovers hangin round here. Ya see, I know it was *you* with that nigra at The Palace that night even in the dark."

Leaning over Mary while his brother rants, Benny roots like a pig through the car's center console. His eyes slip to Mary's exposed legs under his sagging belly. Nauseated by the pressing soiled body's odor, she yanks her dress down.

"You was sure throwin a lot a shit outta the car. Anything else you wanna take off beside them shoes?" asks Benny, his eyes still drooling on Mary.

Mary squirms under his gaze. Thank God we're at least in full view of Labor Day traffic.

"Nothin in here but some sales paper shit," he says handing over documents from the console to his brother.

"I'll be damned," says Henry, slipping his gun into a pocket. "Ya gotta see *this*, Benny!"

"See what?"

"Where it says 'name,' it only got 'Peter.' And where it says 'address,' it's blank. What the hell's goin on?"

Henry cocks his head, eyeing Peter. Benny straightens up, prying his eyes from the bare legs. Mary strains to listen, her concern swelling with every word.

"I assure you, Mr. Banger, everything's legal. I bought this a few days ago at Fillmore Motors, just like those papers say."

Stuffing the documents in his overalls, Henry leans down, inches from Peter's face.

"There's somethin funny about ya. Who the hell are ya, where ya from, and what ya doin here?"

Mary wonders the same thing as six anxious ears await an answer.

Breaking the silent stalemate, on the two-lane highway behind the Corvette approaches a red tow truck. The vehicle crosses the oncoming lane, skidding to a stop beside the disabled car. The driver's window lowers from which erupts a plume of tobacco smoke, followed by a hand flicking cigar ashes.

"Can I help ya?" shouts the sun-glassed driver underneath a greasy baseball hat.

Benny glares into the fume-filled cab. So does Mary. With exaggerated eyes, she flicks sideways glances at Benny, trying to signal the driver that something is wrong.

"Naw, we're fine," says Henry. "These two folks thought there was somethin wrong with their car, but they just ran outta gas. We're givin em enough to get em inta town."

Mary continues her visual plea.

"Might be a problem startin that Vette after she's run outta gas," says the driver.

"Thanks, but we're fine," says Peter as Henry's hand crawls into his gun pocket.

Without a response, the tow truck departs. Mary watches the driver's curious stare in his side-view mirror as he leaves the scene.

"Smart thinkin, mister," says Henry.

"Let's get the hell outta here! Don't like the way that guy was lookin at us."

"Hold your shit, Benny. We can't go and leave em with this here flat tire. An ta fix it, I gotta get in the trunk," says Henry walking to the rear of the car.

"What flat?" all ask.

"This one!"

Henry draws his pistol. BANG! The left rear wheel falls to its knees.

Mary's gut wrenches in an avalanche of fear released by the gunshot. Peter's knuckles bleach white as he grips the wheel. Benny's eyes bounce like ping-pong balls, inspecting every passing car. Henry shoves the revolver back into his overalls.

"How ya get in the fuckin trunk?" asks Henry.

"Doesn't have a trunk," says Peter, his eyes flashing at Henry in the overhead mirror.

"Hear that Benny? Ain't got no trunk."

"Yeah, just like he ain't got no wallet and driver's license!"

"Then how do ya carry anything in this fancy piece of shit?" asks Henry.

"With the top up there's space," answers Peter, flicking his thumb behind him.

Strolling to the passenger's side, Henry points to the cover lid behind the seats.

"That where ya keep the top?" he asks.

Peter nods yes. He pushes the console button, unlocking the cover, which Henry lifts. He sees a folded layer of white cloth and under it the edge of the leather satchel.

"Looks more like a diaper to me." Then noticing the large book under Mary's legs, he asks Benny, "What's that?"

"What's what?"

"That! Looks like one of em Bibles. You ain't seen *nothing* past this broad's legs you horny bastard!" Then, with a face shriveled in suspicion, Henry asks Peter, "What's with the book and the bag in the back?"

"They's gotta be somethin important, ya can see it in his eyes," says Benny. "Maybe there's a buncha money in the bag. That's it! This guy's on the *run*! That'd explain why he ain't got no license or nothin. An maybe this gal is . . . is his *partner*, like a regular Bonnie an Claude."

"*Clyde*, you stupid fuck!"

"I wonder if they gotta a reward on em?"

"Yeah, dead or alive," says Henry, slapping his gun pocket.

Mary wishes she never heard any of this. Maybe they're right. Maybe Peter is a fugitive. Maybe that guy with him at The Palace is his accomplice. What's his name? Scott?

"Hate to break your shoelaces, guys, but there's no cash in there," says Peter. "It's just a satchel for that book."

Immediately, Benny yanks out the satchel and opens it.

"Shit! Ain't nothin in it."

"What kinda book?" asks Henry.

"A reference manual for my work."

"What kinda work?"

Mary again pays close attention.

"I'm in public relations."

"Public relations, huh? Hear that Benny? Bet it's some kinda damn government job. Must pay pretty good to be drivin this fancy car."

Opening the door, Henry orders Mary out so they can remove the reference manual. Sensing an opportunity, she complies. After Mary walks to the pickup in her stocking feet, she sits on the passenger side with the door open. Rubbing her knee, she slides her hand up her skirt, retrieving the driver's license and Visa card she had removed from her wallet. Concealing them in her hand, she watches the brothers.

"Benny, keep an eye on her," says Henry, tugging on the manual. "Damn, this fuckin thing's heavy. Gimme a hand."

Squeezed together tight as two hotdogs in a bun, the pair lift the manual from the car.

Henry grabs it with both hands, shuffling around to the driver's door where he drops the volume, safe from traffic's eye. Kneeling, he inspects the leather-clad tome upon which is inscribed in bold silver letters, *The BOOK*.

Henry notices Peter's attentive stare. He opens the volume, flipping pages like a six-year-old with a comic book. But void of pictures, Henry loses interest. Standing, he leans against the door.

"That a real funny book ya got there. Some of it's got American writin. Some of it's that hydroglific stuff they got on them pyramids. And there's a lot of writin *I* ain't never seen before. What's it all say?"

Mary leans out of the cab to hear. All three, again, eagerly await Peter's response.

"Like I said, that's just a reference manual about some job regulations."

"I know!" says Benny, struck by a thunderbolt of thought. "Them's secret codes. He's a *spy*!"

"Benny, shut the fuck up. Mister, this here 'manual' looks old as my granpappy's Bible. It ain't nothing the government would give ya."

Mute, Peter stares at a yellow bug smear on the windshield.

"I *said* it ain't no fuckin government book! Where'd ya get it?"

Mary watches the three men as they obsess over *The BOOK*. Here's my chance! Quick as a scared rabbit, she leaps from the cab, sprinting away on the pavement's shoulder, gravel stabbing her stocking feet. The urgency of escape overrides her pain as she trips, falling on her knees. Mary staggers to her feet, license and credit cards still grasped in her hand. Feet and knees raw as skinned tomatoes, her flight continues, marked by a freckled trail of blood. Waving her arms, she tries to stop a car. But like spawning salmon, the holiday traffic whirls past, briefly slowing from curiosity of the frantic spectacle. They gawk at the barefoot woman in torn nylons whose cries barely penetrate their boxes of streamlined steel.

"Stop . . . Stop!" she shouts. Dear God, please have someone help me!

But all speed up again, fleeing the scene and their conscience when a passing sedan slows down. The old, brown sedan leaking white fumes from the hood, rolls to a stop on the opposite side of the road. Vehicles rush by, honking displeasure at the motionless clunker cluttering their lane.

The sedan's window lowers, through which a portly, spectacled, Black man poor with hair, peers. Observing the Corvette, he sees three men, two of whom, jaw-dropped, stare at the woman.

"Need a lift!" the man shouts.

Mary strains to catch the driver's remark, but through the traffic's roar, the words are obscure as a prayer on a battlefield.

"Lady, you want a ride!"

Mary hears the request. But she eyes with hesitation the decrepit vehicle and its Black driver.

"Yes! Please!" she answers, shaking herself into reality.

"Get in!" he says as he leans over, pushing the passenger door open.

Amid screeching tires and screaming horns, Mary dodges two lanes of speeding traffic. Sprinting around the sedan, blood dripping from her injuries, she leaps into the car.

"Get me the hell out of here!"

The sedan lumbers off as Mary rejoices, watching the Corvette sink in the distance behind her. But joy fades as blood boils through her bandana and pain slaps her unconscious.

* * *

"Shit, Benny, how'd that fuckin broad get down the road? Told ya to keep an eye on her!"

"Me? You coulda look too!"

"Get in the fuckin truck an grab them shoes and purse. We're gettin outa here before someone calls the patrol!"

For once, Benny does not argue. He toddles to the truck, retrieving the two items. Throwing them in the bed, he climbs into the cab, slamming the door. Like a goldfish in a bowl, he glares at Henry through the bug-encrusted windshield.

"If you want to see this fuckin book again, bring three hundred bucks tomorrow mornin to The Palace. An if ya real polite, I'll even give ya your keys back," says Henry, flashing another display of decayed enamel. "An don't bother tellin the police. The sheriff's a good friend of us, and he don't like no strangers poking around here neither."

Henry grabs the satchel into which he shoves *The BOOK* for

ease of carrying. He shuffles to the pickup, lugging the leather bundle between his legs. Into the bed he slings the case, followed by a tangle of sparkplug wires plus Mary's wallet. The driver's door bangs shut.

"Let's see if we can catch us that getaway car, Benny."

Spitting rock and dust, the pickup sputters onto the road, disappearing in a shroud of exhaust.

Chapter 36

The Brown Sedan

pproaching a gravel driveway marked by a rusting mailbox, the sedan turns off Route 63. The vehicle inches up the drive, turning left onto a rutted trail just wide enough to pass. Bucking along, the vehicle penetrates a vine-infested maze of trees hidden from the main road, but close enough to watch highway traffic. After stopping, the driver turns to the unconscious female slumped in the bench seat beside him, propped against the door.

The fresh patch of blood on her bandana has lost its luster, a sign the bleeding has stopped. However, the floor mat mottled with fifteen years of soiled soles cannot hide the blood from the woman's injured feet and scraped knees. Reaching over her, the driver locks the door. From under his seat, he removes an unmarked metal box which he sets on his lap. All the while, he makes frequent glances at the highway while squinting in the mirror for a rearward intrusion.

Awakened by the jostling, Mary sits up. With a puzzled squint, she inspects the surroundings of a dense woodland from the interior of an obviously old car driven by a Black man. Slowly, the cloud of confusion in her mind parts, allowing the sunlight of memory to ignite the events of her escape from the Banger brothers.

"How long've I been out?"

"Oh, about fifteen minutes. You fainted. Must've been your wounds and all the commotion."

Draping his arm over the backrest, the driver glances in the mirror, then down at the highway.

"What are you looking for, and why are we parked here in the woods?"

"I pulled off the highway in case those guys back at the car were trying to follow us."

Mary pushes against the passenger door. Slipping one hand behind her, she clutches the door lever.

"How long are we gonna be here?"

"Till I'm sure they're not looking for us."

Mary presses harder against the door. *I wonder how he'll know that?* She stares at the shoebox-size metal container between his legs.

"What's in that?"

"Something that'll ease your pain."

Fondling the box, he flashes a crooked smile, checking the mirror and the road again.

Mary stares at the driver. *Why in the world was this Black guy the only person to stop? For all I know, he could be that serial killer I read about prowling the roads for victims. That box could be where he keeps the gun. 'Ease my pain . . .'*

Mary yanks on the door lever. Nothing happens. A nauseous fear consumes her.

"All this shouldn't take more than a few minutes," says the driver. "Oh, I locked the door so you wouldn't fall out."

Mary's heart bangs against her chest. She pulls on the lock button.

"Wouldn't do no good," says the driver, "the button's stuck. Gotta unlock it from the outside."

Mary feels her head spinning, near to fainting again as the driver's crooked smile expands. He opens the box. Then drawing out a shining round barrel of plastic-wrapped gauze, he hands it to Mary.

Mary almost wets herself with relief as she rakes up the scattered leaves of her motion. For the first time since stepping inside, she draws an easy breath. But in the excitement, she has forgotten about her injuries which burst into awareness with a painful vengeance.

"You look awfully pale, Ma'am," says the driver, pointing to her feet. "They're not bleeding much, but I'd get a tetanus shot. Some antibiotics. If you get an infection, you'll be wheelchaired for God knows how long. Not to mention lockjaw."

"Any more words of encouragement?" she says, flipping the overhead rearview mirror toward her. "God, I look like a war refugee. Don't suppose you've got anything for the pain?"

"Yes," he says, watching as Mary fumbles to redress her wounds. "Here, let me help with that."

Blushing, Mary lifts her skirt as the driver winds gauze and tape about her knees, then her head. She chuckles. *A few minutes ago, I was scared of being the breaking evening news.*

"What's so funny?" asks the driver.

"Oh, nothing."

"Open the glove compartment," he says, then pulls a wad of bleached towels from under the seat which he slides under her feet.

Pulling her blood-spattered dress over her knees, Mary opens the compartment from which spills a dozen pill bottles. Remaining inside is a horde of containers reminding her of a hypochondriac's treasure chest. The driver points to a pink container rolling on the mat.

"Take two from that one, they'll help the pain. I've got water in the back."

"You some kind of a doctor, mister . . . mister . . . ?"

"Oh, I'm sorry. The name's Seymour, Seymour Lesterman. Pleased to meet you, Ma'am," he says, extending his hand. "I'm no doc, just an insurance salesman. You can tell by this heap that business ain't too good."

Mary remembers her adventures in fancy cars—Kevin's BMW and Peter's Corvette.

"It's a pleasure riding in something modest," she says, shaking his hand.

"Any more modest, Ma'am, and we'd be walking."

"Please, call me Mary."

"Anyway, *Mary*, my wife Nancy's a nurse. She's got one of those bottles for every occasion. Have pill will travel."

From the mat, Mary lifts the pink, unlabeled bottle which she rolls in her palm. Only an idiot would take this from a stranger. Dropping the container, she tries to brace herself against the pain, but the knife of distress severs her determination. Peeking inside the glove box, she finds something familiar, Excedrin, and shakes out four tablets. Waterless, she chokes them down. Seymour shivers at the sight.

"I know, but I've had a lot of practice with my husband's driving," says Mary, cramming the rest of the bottles inside the glove box.

"No signs of a pickup or that Vette," says Seymour, checking the mirror and road.

"Then let's make a run for it!"

"We're not *runnin* anywhere in this. Best wait for that sports car. It should get here before that pickup, then we'll decide."

"Won't be a sports car," says Mary, informing Seymour about the day's events.

"Holly horny toads! We gotta call the police!" he says as blood oozes from Mary's feet on the floor towels. "And get *you* to a hospital."

"No! Hell no! Not another one of those! Uh, I mean, I'm all right, really."

Seymour's face shrinks with confusion.

After an hour passes with no suspicious vehicles, both decide to return to the highway. The brown sedan struggles with the Labor Day traffic, pulling over to let more able-bodied vehicles pass. Mary peers out the passenger window at the passing scenery.

"Where we heading?" she asks.

"Barkersville."

With both hands, Seymour battles the steering wheel, keeping the wandering wreck pavement bound. Releasing one hand to shove the first aid box under the seat, the vehicle wanders into the oncoming traffic. Horns holler. Seymour, blasé about the impending head-on catastrophe, tugs on the wheel, coaxing the vehicle to its lane. Mary nails her eyes on the approaching asphalt. *I wonder if I'm any safer in this rusting roller coaster than with those two brothers.*

"Sure you don't want a doctor?" asks Seymour. "Those towels are getting pretty bloody."

"Sorry for the mess, but I've *got* to get home!"

"Where's that?"

"Barkersville, and since you're headed that way, I wonder if you could . . . "

"Any place, anything you want, Ma'am," says Seymour, but notices Mary's agitation persists even with this reassurance. "Relax, Mary, you're safe. Okay?"

"If only I could . . . "

Mary then informs Seymour that the boy in the newspapers who was killed in the Mother's Groceries robbery was her son. She must arrive in Barkersville today. Tomorrow, Tuesday, she will testify at Jerome's sentencing phase of the trial but fails to mention she will plea for Jerome's life.

"My condolences on your loss, Ma'am. Nancy and I've been following the story. Can't imagine what you've gone through," says Seymour, shaking his head. "But about the trial, sounds like you haven't heard."

"Haven't heard what?"

From the rear seat, Seymour snatches today's copy of the *Gazette*. He hands the paper to Mary. Catching the headline "Manning Trial Delayed," she reads the column under the headline:

"Jerome Manning, the Black man found guilty last Friday of murdering Timmy Cook during an attempted robbery of Mother's Groceries, was attacked in jail last night by two white prisoners. Manning was beaten unconscious. The attending physician said the head injuries were severe and the resulting trauma to the brain could hinder Manning's comprehension of courtroom proceedings. The doctor recommended delaying the sentencing hearing of the trial until at least Thursday."

She stares out the side window. *Poor Jerome. I can't imagine what he's goin through. I bet those assholes in the committee are having a good one about this. Damn! I hope I can still make a difference.*

"So, Mary, you've got a couple of more days. I've heard you're involved with that Citizens for Justice Committee. I bet you're pleased about what's happened to that Manning guy."

Mary yearns to unload her weight of emotions on some trusting soul, possibly Seymour. After all, he was the only one willing to give her a ride. But what if he reacts no better than most of Barkersville's good citizens and kicks her out of the car at fifty miles an hour?

"You want to tell me something, don't you?" asks Seymour, resting his hand on her shoulder. "Now I may look like a loser salesman and a *Black* one at that, but I might be able to help."

"You already have . . . "

Mary then unveils her story, a story of regrets for her involvement with the committee plus a desire to atone by testifying for

Jerome's life. The sedan veers off the road. Seymour's midnight eyes shift to Mary. She waits for his response, her expression impassive as hardening plaster.

"If you'd like, you're welcome to stay with me and Nancy. Isn't she the prettiest thing you ever did see?" he says, pulling out his wallet, then flipping to his bride's picture.

The proposal softens Mary's expression. She stares at the wallet's photo of a blond, Caucasian woman who reminds Mary of a chubby Marilyn Monroe.

"Yes, she is beautiful," Mary answers, containing her disbelief.

"Offer still goes."

"You know, I might take you up on that, but only till my feet get better."

"Stay as long as you want. We don't get many folks from town."

With water from a plastic bottle Seymour pulled from under his seat, Mary swallows two more Excedrin. They seem to be helping. She settles back, propping herself against the door. Freed of fear, her mind wanders, thinking about Peter stuck in his car with the Banger brothers. But something about Peter, a certain mystery, tells her he'll be alright, the same mystery about him which frightens her. *I should be glad to be free of him. But still, I'm grateful for the kindness he's shown. Helping me at The Palace. Staying with me every day at the hospital. But the way he acted in the car today with those brothers was . . . different. Even though I was scared, I would've stayed with him. If only he'd been more reassuring, protective like before. You know, it's almost like he wanted me to leave. Get me out of harm's way? I wonder . . .*

* * *

The sedan pulls back onto the highway. More miles pass.

"Uh-oh," grunts Seymour, his attention fixed on the rearview mirror.

"What?"

"There's something blowing smoke coming up behind us . . . fast."

Mary looks out the back window. Seeing a yellow pickup, her eyes explode with fear.

"Damnit, it's *them*! They must've been waiting somewhere off the road the whole time! Can't you go any faster!"

"The pedal's already dentin the floor."

Horrified, Mary watches the pickup, white exhaust swirling behind as though it was on fire, pulling within feet of the sedan. Patient as a hawk, the truck hovers there ready to strike its prey. For miles, the brothers stalk the sedan, their sinister smiles piercing through the windshield.

"What are they waiting for?" asks Mary.

"Probably a break in the traffic, so there won't be any witnesses."

And just as Seymour predicted, when the highway clears ahead, the brothers make their move. The pickup's horn blares like a wounded goose. Then a hand holding a gun extends through the driver's window, motioning the sedan to pull over at an approaching gravel drive. As the pickup's horn shouts, followed by an overhead gunshot, Mary grabs Seymour's arm.

"Dear God, Seymour! What are we going to do now!"

Chapter 37

The Red Tow Truck

The cloud of exhaust trailing the yellow pickup melts in the distance. Peter slumps in his seat, cursing his indulgence with Mary. They never should have left the hospital this morning without Trooper Brandon's escort. Short of tying Mary to her bed, what more could he have done? He had an ache in his gut that *something* evil loomed ahead. But since apprentice benefactors possess limited precognition, the extent of this evil eluded him.

The sky darkens as black as Peter's thoughts. Rumbling clouds announce an approaching storm. Peter exits the car, pulls out the convertible top, then slips back inside. Beaten by the wind-driven rain, the roof pounds like a bass drum. But its unruly rhythm is soon interrupted by a siren's howl as a white Mustang from the patrol slides to a stop behind the Corvette. In the mirror, Peter watches an agitated state trooper, minus his rain gear, leap into the downpour. Peter recognizes the scowling face of Trooper Brandon.

"Ah shit," says Peter, bracing for the approaching officer's verbal assault.

Water sheeting from the brim of his Smokey the Bear hat, Brandon taps the door, motioning the driver to lower the window.

"I figured that dispatch about a disabled Corvette with a lone male occupant was you! Where's Mrs. Cook?" asks Brandon, his words striking with a baton's impact.

"After she sneaked away, she ran down the road, fell, and banged herself up pretty good," says Peter, relating the calamity with the Banger brothers. "An old, brown sedan stopped. Mary jumped in the front seat. Can you call and have em look for that car? She'll need a doc."

An enamel vice of teeth clamps on Brandon's lower lip.

"I'll make the call. *You* stay in the vehicle. Remember anything more about the vehicle?"

"Just that the driver's Black."

"Why didn't you say that before? Can't be that many brown sedans driven by a Black man with a white woman sitting up front," says the trooper, then plows through the mud to the Mustang to send an alert.

Rain slices through the open window as Peter glares in the side mirror. Shame shadows his face. How could he forget the impropriety of a Black brother helping a white woman?

Meantime, a red flatbed truck rolls backward to the Corvette's front bumper, the same tow truck which had offered to help earlier this afternoon. Its door creaks open. Tobacco smoke boils from the cab. The driver, draped in a yellow rain jacket, slides out. Steam spits from a cigar wedged in his hand as he saunters through the deluge and pulls open the sports car's hood. Removing his sunglasses, he inspects the engine compartment, barren of ignition wires. He slams the hood. Sliding back his shades, he walks to the rear, observing the flat tire.

"Need a tow?" he asks through the open driver's window.

"Hello Scott," replies a soggy Peter.

Sun burning through a tear in the retreating clouds, the rain stops. Trooper Brandon completes his call which includes a tow request. He slogs to the Corvette. In the sunlight, mist boils from his waterlogged uniform as he eyes the truck driver.

"How the hell did *you* get here so fast?" asks Brandon.

"I was here before," says Scott, sucking a drag from his cigar.

"Humph," grunts Brandon, then fires his attention at Peter. "Your brains musta got windburned from all that topless drivin. I warned you about the brothers. Asked you to wait an hour so I could give you an escort. Hope those sixty minutes you *saved* were worth it!"

Brandon grins at the vehicle's condition. He and Peter lock eyes.

"Come on guys, enough with the stare wars. I have to get this car into town," says Scott.

"I'll hang around till you two leave, just in case the Bangers stop by again."

Mumbling, Brandon trudges through the slop of soil to his car. Halfway there, he kicks at an empty beer can, courtesy of the brothers. Missing the mark, his feet sail skyward as he falls backward into the wet clay.

"Shit!" he says, wobbling to his feet, then lands in the patrol car with a squish.

"Looks like he's been fondued in mud," says Peter.

His attention shifts to the winged, yellow smudge on the windshield. *I wonder if helping Mary's been as futile as that bug's attempt at crossing the road.* His musing erupts in anger.

"Scott, I wanna talk to you, now!" he says, throwing open the door.

"Stay inside. Brandon is watching."

Scott grabs a scissors jack from the truck and changes the flat tire. Then, opening the front hood, he leans into the engine well pretending to work. With the hood hinged at the vehicle's front, Peter can see him through the windshield.

"Alright, what's happened to Mary?" asks Peter.

"Keep your voice down," says Scott, gazing at the engine. "After she got in the sedan, she passed out from the pain. The driver pulled into a remote wooded area several miles up the highway, then . . . "

"She's . . . she's been abducted by some kind of pervert. We'll never see her again!"

"Quiet. Before you write her obituary, Peter, let me finish. Mary is going to be just fine. She is in the company of Seymour."

"Seymour? Who the hell's *Seymour*?"

"One of the boys, a benefactor who drove the sedan *we* sent for Mary," says Scott.

"A sedan *we* sent for Mary? Isn't that altering fate? We're not supposed to do that."

"You have been paying attention in class. Technically, sending the sedan is not considered altering, more like offering an *opportunity*, especially when it is in answer to a prayer. We send lots of 'sedans.' Some are ours, some are not, but the mortal has to decide to get in or send it away."

"Is . . . is Mary . . . alright?" asks Peter.

"Well, after she regained consciousness, Seymour returned to the highway. But the Bangers caught up to them." Watching Peter's face darken, Scott adds, "Remember, Mary is responsible for this predicament. *She* refused Brandon's escort."

"Yeah, she sent that sedan away."

Scott continues to fidget with the engine.

"Son, I know how you used Mary's fear to make her distrust you, leaving her with no option but to escape you and the brothers. As difficult as that was, you behaved in a manner befitting a benefactor. I am proud of you."

"Yeah, I suppose I did," says Peter, his face flushed with crimson pride. "But why send a Black man driving an ol wreck?"

"We *already* sent a white guy in a fancy red sports car."

"Me? You mean everything I've done for Mary was part of a plan—preordained?"

"Uh, preordained sounds so controlling. Consider it another *opportunity*. We knew once you got to The Palace and witnessed Kevin's assault, you would come to Mary's aid. The rest is history," says Scott.

"I remember you suggesting we go to that bar. I feel like I've been used."

"You *have*, but we would not use just anybody when it comes to helping a mortal like Mary."

For the first time in days, instead of the cold, empty ache in his gut, Peter feels the warmth of service well done. *All the world's a stage, and sometimes I get to ad-lib.*

"Who's this *we* you keep talking about?"

"Another benefactor. A guy named Emmanuel," says Scott, pretending to tighten a sparkplug.

Peter remembers the name. It was on the card Scott gave him in The Palace lavatory. Peter still carries the card in his shirt pocket. He yanks it out:

Leader of the Pack,
I.M. Emmanuel
12 Grace Way, Barkersville, MO 65043

"Like I said in the bathroom, you should pay him a visit," says Scott.

"Been busy."

"Yeah, so was the *Titanic's* priest. You know where the name Emmanuel comes from?"

Peter shrugs as a string of cigar smoke drifts around Scott's head.

"It is Hebrew, meaning 'God is with us.'"

"Wait a minute. God?" says Peter, leaning close to the wind-shield. "You said all benefactors were once mortals. So, if this guy Emmanuel was once flesh and blood like us, *how* can he be God?"

"Good question. You must ask him yourself. Oh, concerning Seymour, this time I wanted Mary's savior to be someone whom she subconsciously distrusts, a Black man."

With the words "distrusts a Black man," Peter's previous good mood dissolves faster than Alka-Seltzer. *What made me think if*

I ever revealed my Black identity it wouldn't be a problem? Lucky I didn't. Wait a minute, lucky? Will it never end? Does goodness and hope always have to come wrapped in white?

"By accepting help from the only one who stopped," says Scott, "Mary will be forced to address her fear. She will survive. She will be stronger for it."

"Lots of people *survive*, but the hell she'll endure," says Peter, slumping back in his seat.

"Do not worry. Mary has the attitude of a three-hundred-pound linebacker in high heels."

The image tickles Peter's imagination. But staring at the vacant passenger seat, he feels profaned by the thieves of loneliness.

"Bastards! Wait till I get hold of those brothers! I'll use all my abilities and . . . and . . . "

"And *what?*" says Scott. "Remember, when we get hold of those brothers tomorrow our only goal is to pay their ransom and get *The BOOK* back."

Completing his masquerade of repairs, Scott ambles back to the patrol car.

"You can leave now. I just have to winch the car onto the bed. Then we are off to Rolla."

"Like I said, I'll hang around till you leave," says Brandon, then squints an eye. "You two talked like long-lost buddies."

"Just car stuff."

With a suspicious grunt, the trooper rolls up his window.

Scott informs Peter that Brandon did not hear a thing, "though he is skeptical."

"You know, Scott, I'm impressed. You're really into this towing thing. But why this flatbed and not a regular tow truck?"

"Another benefactor who did this coached me. A regular tow truck would tear up a Corvette's front end. He suggested this flatbed. Just winch you up, no scrapes, no bruises," says Scott, then peers over the top of his sunglasses. "By the way, how do you like my disguise?"

"Very convincing. Where'd you find it? A Goodwill dumpster?"

"Borrowed it. Right now, some poor mechanic is changing oil in his shorts."

Scott tilts the tow bed. After dragging up the Corvette, he chains it in place.

"You have to ride up front with me."

"Uh, I'll just stay in the car," says Peter, avoiding the lecture he knows awaits in the cab.

"Against the law to ride in a towed vehicle," says Scott, nodding at the patrol car. "We *do not* want a ticket on top of everything else, now do we?"

Just then, Peter catches the mirror's reflection of a scowling Trooper Brandon speaking into his handset. The patrol car door flies open.

"We've received a call about a brown sedan up the road with its back window shot out!"

The Mustang's engine roars awake.

"I'm comin with you!" says Peter, flinging open the door.

"Not allowed. Where you gettin towed?"

"To Main Street Chevrolet," says Scott.

"Wait for me there!"

Peter watches the Mustang fishtail onto the highway, wailing northward on Route 63.

Chapter 38

Pimples and Pork Chops

Fast as a bumble bee in a tornado, Trooper Brandon's car flies out of sight. The siren's wail lingers in the evening air.

"Good thing you're already dead. This stuff would kill you," says Peter, climbing into a thunderhead of cigar smoke in the truck cab. Fanning the choking haze, he glares out the rain-streaked passenger window.

"Immortal or not, fasten your seat belt," says Scott.

With a turn of the ignition key, the engine barks to life. The truck U-turns into the river of Labor Day traffic, the Corvette strapped behind, snug as a trauma patient on a gurney.

"Smile, enjoy the ride," says Scott.

"Great," mumbles Peter, "marooned in this red tuna can beside Mr. Happy Face."

"You say something?"

"No."

The truck splashes down the road, time resonating with the rain's metallic beat. Peter ignores the flurry of the driver's sideways squints.

"After all that has happened to your client Mary, know what the guys at the office are calling you?" says Scott.

"What *guys*?"

"The other benefactors."

"Not really," says Peter.

"Sherman."

"Sherman?"

"Yes, as in Sherman's March to the Sea," says Scott.

"Great, now I'm the butt of everyone's jokes! But I feel like shit about what's happened."

"I know you are feeling lower than the *Titanic*, but I am just trying to make light of things. Yeah, Mary *is* a little scraped up, but no need for a mortician."

Peter watches the rain crawling up the windshield like a herd of snails.

"You know, I remember the frustrations of apprenticeship, trying to save the world through our limited powers. Kind of like facing Goliath, clutching a slingshot armed with marshmallows. That is when we have to turn it over to *Him*."

Peter's tinder box of emotions ignites at the mere mention of Him.

"Just who is this *Him* anyway? First, you say *He's* a Higher Power, a Universal Authority. Back at the ridge, you said I could find Him by tapping into the 'spirit of the elm.' Then there's this Emmanuel guy, who's some kinda 'God is with us.' Damnit, make up your mind!

"And what's this *it* we're supposed to turn over to Him? From all I've seen, *it* is the grave. He's got *it* planned for Jerome and his girlfriend. He's already sent Timmy to *it,* and me. And what the hell was He doing when I was kicking at the end of a rope? Don't tell me. I was lynched on a Saturday. He had the day off!"

With pallid hands, Scott's grip tightens. Wrenching the steering wheel, he yanks the vehicle to the shoulder so quickly that not one passing horn shouts in anger.

"When you were kicking at the end of a rope," says Scott, "what the hell was *He* doing? He was crying . . . crying. Who in all His sorrow, do you think sent *me*!"

Scott accelerates onto the road. For the next twenty minutes, more conversation echoes in a graveyard at midnight than in the truck's cab. In the verbal silence, interrupted only by the windshield's patter of rain and the engine's roar, Peter's rage sinks into shame.

Peter stares through the windshield. *Well stupid, happy with another of your little God outbursts? What if he's right? What if God really did send him? Look how I troubled Scott and after all he's done for me.*

"I see we're coming to I-44. Be at the Rolla dealership pretty soon," says Peter, attempting to warm the refrigerator of silence.

"Yes, but before we arrive, we must talk about our meeting with the Bangers tomorrow," says Scott, his eyes nailed to the road.

In all the excitement, Peter had forgotten about the brothers' morning engagement at The Palace. Relieved to hear any breaks in the verbal stalemate, Peter grins, hearing *our* meeting. He did not relish encountering those two hoodlums a second time alone.

"You know, instead of paying their ransom, we could use our special abilities and just take *The BOOK*," says Peter. "Confronting those two idiots as The Beast, watching them stain their shorts, is as tempting as Satan's apple."

"Calling mortals' attention to our abilities is forbidden, but we must retrieve *The BOOK*. You know how unscrupulous people could misuse this book's secrets, like Area 51 aliens, and who really shot Kennedy. Since you seem a little edgy lately, I will do all the talking."

At 7:15 p.m., the tow truck turns into Main Street Chevrolet, weaving through the parking lot to the back of the dealership. The vehicle stops alongside a gray overall-clad young man. He ignores the truck's approach, turning his back to lock the last of the service bay doors. Scott lowers the driver's window to speak.

"We're closed. Come back tomorrow!" snarls the employee.

"Shit," says Peter. "What'll we do now?"

"I did not trouble myself getting here to be stalled by a pimpled-faced kid. Watch and learn.

"Excuse me, young man," says Scott, jumping from the cab as he points to the Corvette. "Is there *any* way we can get that car repaired by the morning? This is an emergency."

"No way!"

Pocketing his keys, the teenager turns to see a folded, crisp one-hundred-dollar bill scratching Scott's chin. Stitched in white on the employee's lapel appears the name *Warren*.

"Tell me, Warren," says Scott, waving the Benjamin in front of the young man, "if there *was* a way to fix this car by 6:00 a.m., how many of these would be required?"

"I'm just a summer worker." But after a sideways glance confirms their solitude, Warren asks, "What's wrong with it?"

Turning, Scott winks at Peter. Warren scrambles onto the tow truck's bed for a quick inspection of the four-wheeled patient. After four more conjured Benjamins, Scott lowers the car to the pavement, then climbs into the cab. Warren pushes the Corvette through the reopened shop door.

"The car'll be ready by 6:00 a.m. before anyone comes to work," says the mechanic.

"Why you going to all this trouble?" Peter asks Scott.

"This is *no* trouble. I love haggling, especially when the money is His."

Just as the shop door uncoils to the floor, Trooper Brandon's Mustang squeals to a stop in front of the truck. Brandon slides out, his mud-caked uniform replaced by a clean one. Sunglasses dangling from his buttoned shirt, he strolls to the driver's side of the truck.

"Glad to see you made it," says the trooper, then recounts his afternoon's encounter with Mrs. Cook.

"She's a gutsy little lady, all right. When those brothers forced em off the road, even with her injured feet, she and the sedan driver, a Black guy named Seymour Lesterman, jumped out and ran into the woods. Considering all the witnesses from the Labor Day traffic, the brothers didn't follow. They waited for a break in the congestion, shot out the sedan's back window, and fled the scene. Cook damned near got herself killed flagging down a car. Luckily, it had one of those new car phones and called 911. I was the second trooper on the scene. Cook looked pretty banged up but refused medical treatment. She left with Lesterman, headed to Barkersville."

Peter slumps in his seat, heavy with worry.

Then in an abrupt change in tone, Brandon steps back. His right hand pressing against his gun holster, he orders Scott to approach the rear of the truck, "and bring the vehicle registration papers."

"Maybe you've got a burned-out taillight," says Peter.

"If Wyatt Earp here shoots me, I hereby empower you to turn him into a frog."

Scott exits the cab. Escorted by Brandon, he walks to the rear of the truck. Peter, deaf to their conversation, adjusts the rearview mirror, watching two heads bobbing over the tow bed.

"You're Scott, Peter's 'friend,' right?" asks Trooper Brandon.

"Yes."

"May I see your driver's license and registration?"

Scott hands over the fake documents. After a quick review, Brandon pulls a note from his pocket.

"I remember seeing you with Peter last Saturday night at The Palace," says Brandon, shaking the note. "Mrs. Cook wanted *you* to have this and wants *you* to give it to Peter in the morning."

"Hmm."

"She remembered you from The Palace. Said she recognized you in the tow truck the first time you stopped and figured you'd come back." Eyes narrowing, he says, "How long've you and Peter known each other?"

"A while."

"What were you doing at the bar?"

"Officer, are we under suspicion for something?"

"Not *we*, *you*. I find it quite a coincidence you just *happened* to be passing by in a tow truck when the Bangers were assaulting those two. I watched you from my patrol car talking to Peter this afternoon. Whatever you said seemed to upset him a great deal. You know the Bangers? You ever tangle with the law?"

The trooper steps closer, popping off the holster safety strap, ready to pull his weapon.

"No, I have not. Look, officer, I was with Peter that night at The Palace because he wanted me to ride in his new car. Among other things in my line of work, I drive this tow truck. Lucky for all of us I happened to be passing by today. Check those papers again. Everything is in order."

After a final inspection, the trooper snaps the safety strap as he slaps the three documents into Scott's outstretched hand.

"Now, about Mrs. Cook's wish," says Scott, "why wait to give her note to Peter?"

"Don't know exactly. Something about tomorrow being a long day and she wanted Peter to get a good night's sleep. Sounds like a 'Dear John,' huh?" says Brandon, taking a step back. "This long day tomorrow, anything to do with the Bangers?"

"Officer, do you really think we would be foolish enough to get tangled in another altercation with those two?"

"Uh-huh. I'm gonna get those two sons-a-bitches. The only thing they're gonna get tangled in is leg chains."

"Thanks for all you have done, Trooper Brandon."

Slipping the note into his shirt pocket, Scott climbs inside the cab. The patrol car scrambles back to the interstate.

"What was all that about?" asks Peter.

"Like you said, bad taillight."

Twilight creeps from the east.

* * *

Crimson webs wrap the mechanic's eyes.

"She's running fine," says Warren, puffing up like a banty rooster. "Didn't have tires in stock to change the flat. So, I swapped em all with ones off another Vette. Looks even better, huh?"

Peter nods with approval. They all shake hands.

Wearing its top hat, the Corvette strolls into The Palace parking lot.

"Don't see the pickup. Maybe they're not coming," says Peter.

"It is only seven o'clock. They have not climbed out of bed yet," says Scott.

"Bed? They probably slept in the truck."

Peter rolls down the window, gazing outside. His concentration drifts to Mary. Concerned for her safety, he is unaware of the jail inmates' attack on Jerome which resulted in the two-day trial delay. *I hope she makes it to court today. She'll be the only one at the sentencing to testify against the death penalty.*

"You seem quite distracted. Mary, I presume?"

"You readin my mind?"

"No, just the worried furrow on your face. It has Mary written all over it," says Scott, handing Peter the note. "Trooper Brandon gave me this last night. Said it might interest you."

Expecting Brandon's official report of yesterday's events, Peter slides the folded paper into his shirt pocket when *Peter* written across the top in a feminine hand snags his attention.

"This from Mary?"

Scott nods yes, relating last night's tailgate conversation with Trooper Brandon.

"So, Brandon's looking for the brothers? Why don't we go

inside and call the cops right now? I'd love to see those two pork chops' expressions when someone pulls a gun on *them*!"

"You are still forgetting *The BOOK*. We retrieve that first . . . "

"Yeah, *then* we'll fry their fat!" says Peter, eyeing the note, when a vehicle approaching from behind lifts his attention to the rearview mirror. "That's em now!"

A rusted pickup stops several stalls behind the Corvette. Doors grinding open, first Henry, then Benny, plop out. They hit the ground, followed by empty beer cans plus a dirty pair of shorts. Waddling across the lot, they point at the Corvette, mumbling inaudibly. Henry leans to one side, lugging the satchel containing *The BOOK*. The two disappear into The Palace haze.

"Read that note later," says Scott, and snapping his fingers, three crisp one-hundred-dollar bills materialize in his palm. "I got the grease. Let us see what is cooking."

Chapter 39

The Note

Through the silence of an adolescent day drifts a dove's lonesome tune. Violating this quiet melody, the gravel parking lot crackles under Scott and Peter's approach to The Palace. Like the broken stones scattered by Peter's feet, memories of the Bangers' previous encounters tumble in his thoughts. Despite Peter's supernatural forces, his forbearance is no match against the brothers. Stopping, he observes the sun squinting low on the horizon through the nearby woods. I wonder what will've happened the next time that burning eye stares at me.

Ahead, Scott waits in a fog of tobacco smoke exhaling from The Palace's never-closed doors.

"You coming?" he shouts.

"Yeah!"

Inside, the brothers exit the men's room. Weaving through the scattered tables and chairs, they approach the bar. With the consistency of horse manure, they plop onto a pair of stools at the corner of the bar nearest the entry. On Henry's left lies *The BOOK*. On his right squats Benny. Facing away from the entry, each brother huddles over a glass of beer. Leroy, his head lowered, stands opposite the duo behind the counter performing his bartender's ritual of wiping glasses. Jake, shifting his duties from waiter to janitor, swabs the floor at the far end of the bar. He lifts his gaze from the mop which he wrings into a bucket of drifting cigarette butts as Scott and Peter enter.

"Hi fellas!" says Jake.

Nodding in response, both approach the bar.

"Nice seein ya both again," says Leroy, hearing Jake's greeting.

Two bar stools moan as the brothers twist around, glaring at Scott and Peter

"Well, look what the cat drug in," says Henry. "Where that missus of yours? We heard from that janitor she might be stoppin by here real regular like."

Jake, struck by Leroy's angry eyes, blushes from a sudden awareness of his verbal blunder.

"Yeah, hear she's visitin a prisoner up at Iron Mountain. We gonna like meeting up with *her* again!" says Benny, grabbing his crotch.

Watching Benny's gesture, a rage burns in Peter's gut, the same rage which summons The Beast. Peter stops, sensing a change in his body when a hand touches his shoulder.

"Peter, *please,* not now. Just go sit at the counter."

Though emotions blaze, Peter dreads a repeat of The Beast which occurred the last time he occupied this room. Taking a calming breath, Peter marches to the bar as the inferno inside subsides. Glaring at the disgusting duo, he takes the corner stool diagonally opposite Henry. To Peter's left sits Scott. He sets on the counter the ransom comprised of three one-hundred-dollar bills. Peter grabs the money, then slings the bills to Henry.

"That price just gone up!" says Henry, slapping the cash.

"What's the deal," says Peter. "We had an agreement!"

Chairs chatter at a distant table from which the bar's two remaining patrons scurry to the entrance.

Henry's smile resembles a decaying oak barrel missing half of its staves. Pushing *The BOOK* towards Peter, Henry flips open the front cover, exposing a folded piece of paper which he waves as though a victor's flag.

"That was before I seen . . . *this*," he says, flinging the paper, a note, at Peter.

With the flutter of a somersaulting bird, the article lands on the bar face up, exposing a name—Peter.

Leroy dries his hands. Jake leans on his mop. The brothers trade glances. Scott darkens with concern. Peter sits stone still. Patient as Pandora's Box, the note waits to expose its contents.

"It ain't gonna bite," says Henry. "Open it. It real sympathetic."

"Yeah, it real sympathetic!" echoes the brother.

"Benny shut the fuck up!"

Aching moments pass when to everyone's surprise, Scott breaks the stalemate as he slaps the paper, dragging it towards him.

"I gotta take another piss," says Henry, stuffing the three hundred dollars in his overalls. "That'll give ya two time to think how much more ya wanna pay."

The brothers slide off their stools. Henry orders two more beers, then snaps at his brother.

"Ain't you forgettin somethin, Benny?"

"What?"

"*That*, stupid!" he says, pointing to *The BOOK*.

Benny drags the leather-clad manuscript off the counter, cradling it in both arms on his protruding belly. They parade to the bathroom.

"See? It's goin even better than I thought. Told ya so," says Henry.

Setting two beers on the counter, Leroy wipes the bar. With each towel's rotation, he inches closer to Scott. Jake shuffles nearer, pretending to mop. Staring at Scott, Peter wonders what lies buried under the hand which is so important, even the brothers realize the significance. With a slam, the bathroom door opens. The Bangers approach, their footsteps growing louder, culminating with the thud of *The BOOK* upon the varnished bar. Climbing on their stools, they glare at Scott through hungry eyes.

"Okay, Henry, in light of this new circumstance, what would *you* consider a fair price?" asks Scott, patting the note.

Happier than finding a half-full whisky bottle in the garbage, Henry turns to his brother.

"What'd ya think, Benny? Ya know, it isn't just this here book. Seeing em in that fancy car out there, I know it was them two that ran us off the road a couple a nights ago. I think we all otta go outside and . . . "

Henry reaches for the gun in his overall pocket when Leroy slaps a revolver on the bar.

"Enough, gentlemen!" says Leroy, then turns to Scott. "How much more you willin to pay for this damn thing?"

"Two more of these!" says Scott, flipping a pair of Benjamins at Henry.

Peter blinks in disbelief. *What the hell is written on that damn piece of paper?*

"Gimme them other three bills," says Leroy, waving his pistol at Henry.

The bartender gathers the money, arranging the five bills face up. He slides the collection to the portly patron. As a further enticement, he casts a six-pack of Bud on the counter.

"Well, Henry, that's five hundred bucks and free booze," says Leroy. "Why don't you boys take your loot an go play gangsters in somebody else's sandbox?"

The faces of the dead statesmen glare up at Henry. He gulps the rest of his beer. Slamming down his glass, he grabs the money, the six-pack, and with Benny in tow, waddles out of The Palace.

"Thanks, Leroy," says Scott.

"Don't mention it."

Leroy sets the pistol under the counter. In erratic swirls, he wipes the bar. Jake resumes his pretense of mopping. Outside, the brothers finish the six-pack. Then as gravel explodes to the rear, their yellow pickup rattles off while gunshots punctuate their exit.

"Damnit, I was gonna call the police and tell em the Bangers were here. Now they're getting away!" says Peter.

A smile creeps across Leroy's face.

"What's so funny?" asks Peter.

"They ain't gettin far."

"How do you know?"

"Remember those two guys in back who left? Last night they was here sayin how they'd heard of some fellas in a yellow pickup that shot up an ol car. Said the police was lookin for em. I knew it musta been the brothers, so when Henry and Benny got here this mornin, I called the patrol. It wasn't what ya'd call a good business decision, but those brothers've been on my shit list for years."

Leroy's concentration returns to his circling towel as a siren's wail drifts through the door.

"An drivin drunk'll add six months."

Another one-hundred-dollar bill drops on the bar.

"That should cover the six-pack," says Scott. "The rest is a bribe to keep *us* off your list."

Though glad to be free of the Bangers, Peter sulks about this morning's events. Why didn't Scott tell me about that note? I feel like a damn fool the way this came up in front of everyone. Real sympathetic, huh? Whatever it says, the brothers probably told everybody about it. I bet even Jake and Leroy. That Leroy, setting the brothers up, calling the patrol. Shit, sometimes I feel useless as a flat tire.

"You and Jake have been so kind," says Scott, taking the note and leaning over the bar to Leroy. "Would you do us another favor by giving us a few moments alone?"

Nodding his head, Leroy disappears into the kitchen, motioning Jake to follow.

"Son, shall we go sit where we can have some privacy?"

Ambivalent, Peter retreats to a distant corner of the room. His back to the bar, he plunges into a chair beside another bacon-greased tabletop while his eyes scour the wall before him. Grunting, Scott follows, lugging *The BOOK*, which he drops on the table. It groans under the heavy burden. Sitting, Scott slides the note forward. Peter's gaze lowers to the folded paper. Eyes squinting in the pale light, he reads the note, drops it, and storms out of the bar.

Peter's eyes well with despair as his head throbs with torment. For eighty-nine years I've allowed this spirit named Scott to manipulate me. Spirit, hell! More like a demon. Had I known his real identity, never . . . never would I have joined the benefactor's ranks. I always wondered why he took me under his wing. Why, I bet the son-of-a-bitch even expects forgiveness! How could I've been so stupid? Better to have suffered death than to be spared its pain by the likes of him. Better to have remained in the hell of The Beast than to have lived this benefactor's lie.

Peter's agitation leads him from the boardwalk across the gravel into the grove of trees circling The Palace. There, absent prying eyes in the wood's solitude, he recalls his days as The Beast. Though they were trying times, he worried not about fate. He engaged in no philosophical ping-pong about justice, God's will, good or evil. It was just him, the elm, and his vengeance. Simple, uncomplicated, honest. Raising his arms, he scowls skyward through the canopy, shouting to the cosmos with its indifferent Gods:

"Damn You! Damn all of you!"

* * *

After watching Peter's exit, Scott retrieves the note. For the thousandth time, he reads the painstakingly phrased document which closes with a salutation he has held secret for years.

Dearest Peter:

This book is my gift to you. My benefactor passed this down to me decades ago just as his benefactor passed it down to him. Anonymously inscribed on the borders, including the blank pages in the back, are my insights and individual experiences plus those of previous benefactors. You will notice these pages of notes exceed the original text, for our forebears knew the experiences shared by generations of benefactors would be as important as the theology contained in this book.

This collection is a treasure, but not a treasure to be hoarded. Give this wealth away, for only by giving that which we have so arduously acquired, do we keep its riches.

Use this gift with my blessings, and my beloved son, add to the pages.

Your loving father,
Scott

Chapter 40

A Beautiful Lie

S hedding its infant morning hue, the sun climbs above the woodland, glowing in mature brilliance.

Gravel scurries before Peter as he crisscrosses the parking lot. He contemplates the truth revealed by *The BOOK*'s secret note. Scott is the spirit of Peter's dead father.

Peter remembers at an early age asking his mother about his dad.

* * *

"Where's Daddy?"

"He up an gone away," was his mother's consistent reply.

"How come them white babies got a momma an daddy, an I only got me a momma?"

"Maybe the Lawd he gimme twice the lovin than them white folks got," she would answer, followed by a shortbread bribe for his silence.

If his father's disappearance had resulted from a deadly accident or a lynching as was common for male slaves, Momma would have told him. So young Peter blamed himself for Dad's absence, something bad that Peter must have done. Years passed. The childhood doubt gnawed at his soul like a starving rat, doubt which festered into hate. Hate allowed Peter to rationalize his dad left for another's love or simply grew tired of the family.

Peter's mother never expressed bitterness about the absence. She had faith, a faith which could turn a flour sack blouse into Cinderella's evening gown, a faith Peter never inherited.

* * *

Leroy and Jake remain secluded in the kitchen. Pots clang. A faucet gushes water.

Scott still sits at the table. After slipping the note back into *The BOOK*, he taps the table, staring at the entry, anticipating Peter's return. A half-hour crawls by when his son's shadow fills the doorway followed by approaching steps. Peter hovers over the table.

"God Damnit, we need to talk!" says Peter.

The acrid smell of stale smoke and booze adds to Peter's irritation. He throws himself into a chair, staring at Scott, when wrapped in a fresh apron, Jake appears, holding a plastic serving tray.

"Excuse the interruption, but you fellas look like ya got some serious talkin to do. Ain't somethin ya wanna do on no empty stomach."

Setting down the tray, Jake unloads sugar, cream, a thermos of coffee with mugs, plus a plate of pastries. He licks his finger after pulling it from one of the gooey delights.

"I picked em myself. The ones with the gob'a jelly are my favorites," says Jake, then leaves.

"Before you say anything, have one of these," says Scott, shoving the dessert dish at Peter.

Peter bites into a sugar-caked roll. His cheeks stinging with a sweetened stab, he takes another bite, followed by a second roll. Reared back in his chair, he stares at Scott with an expression that has faded from the red flame of anger to the whitewash of disdain.

"Son, I do not blame you for being upset."

"How dare you call me Son after what you did!"

"I have always called you Son."

"I know, but I thought it was just a figure of speech. Why the hell didn't you say you were my father years ago? If you had to say this in a note, why not in the privacy of the car? Why humiliate me in front of everyone, especially those asshole Bangers. You couldn't have picked a worse time!"

"Okay," says Scott. "If I had told you in the car, you would not have come inside for *The BOOK*. So it would still be in the Bangers' hands, God forbid. You do not know how often I wanted to say I was your father. But what if I had told you years ago when you were The Beast? Would you have rejected that hideous existence, followed me as a benefactor?"

"Hell no!"

"Alright, if you hate me so much and what I stand for, you can always claw your way back to the good ol days cowering in your den of webs," says Scott as he bites a Danish. "But you can forget seeing Mary again, driving that red chariot of yours, and sweet rolls."

Confused, Peter remembers his anger in the black lair under the elm with the never-ending isolation. If it wasn't for his patience and support, I'd still be there. Maybe he was right not exposing his identity. Maybe his silence about the note was the best decision. His armor of pride softening, Peter gazes at his father as he wipes the emotion raining from his eyes.

"Tell me the truth. Everything you've done for me, was it out of a guilty conscience? Or was your help because you felt sorry for me?" asks Peter, rejecting Scott's extended hand.

"Neither. All I have done was . . . is . . . from love. I thought often if I should dare end that note with 'your loving father.' I was afraid those words would stir up a cauldron of boiling memories."

"More like a cesspool!" says Peter as he sits in his chair stoic as a post.

"Sweets for your thoughts?" says Scott, pushing back the pastries.

"My thoughts? I don't know. It's like two guys are boxing in my head. One wants to reach out and hug you, my benefactor, who's helped me all these years, the father I never knew. But the other wants revenge. He wants to hurt you for what you did to our family, the silent lie you've kept."

"Who do you want to win?"

"The guy with the hug," says Peter, surrendering with a smile.

"I'd pick him over a black eye."

"Why, then, did you abandon us?"

"Well, your momma's story about how I just 'up an gone away' was not exactly the way it happened. *That* is what she and I decided you should remember. We were afraid if you knew the truth, one day when you were older, you might seek revenge, get yourself hurt, or worse."

Peter squirms in his seat. Sounds like my rationalization about my father's desertion was wrong. Peter wants to bolt for the exit again, escape the truth, but it was pointless before. He grabs a jelly roll.

"Seek revenge on *whom*?" asks Peter.

"Master Boyers."

"The white man who owned us as slaves?" asks Peter, strangling the pastry he holds in his clenched hand.

As though a captive in a nightmare, Peter is forced to learn of his father's suffering. How Scott as a slave was a troublemaker. As a result, Boyers sold him to a Southern plantation for a huge sum of money when Peter was three years old. On the day of the sale, Boyers gloated, telling Scott of his sexual intentions for Peter's mother. Scott made a vow to Boyers. If he ever touched her, somehow Scott would return to make Boyers rue his birth.

Scott died a year later, during which time Boyers made good on his sexual threats. Fulfilling his vow, Scott came back as a spirit. Discovering he was endowed with the same supernatural abilities Peter had as The Beast, Scott decided to seek revenge on

Boyers. But instead of assuming the form of a monster, Scott returned as himself, tormenting Boyers with nightmares and all manners of evil, making Boyers' life a living hell. Boyers' sexual advances stopped. Scott continued protecting his family until the Civil War freed them from slavery's chains.

For an hour, Peter endures the hellish images this tale conjures. Then, as though awakening from a trance, he drops the emaciated jelly roll to the floor.

"I can't believe that after those years, Momma never told me about all this."

"You going to hate her too?"

Silence.

"After you two left Master Boyers at the end of the war, I grew weary of my ghostly existence. I worked through my hatred of him, became an apprentice benefactor, rising to master benefactor. I appeared before you the day of your lynching, thirty-six years after my own death."

"If you protected Momma from Boyers," says Peter, "why not *me* from the lynching?"

"I tried to, but I failed. You became my Jerome."

The words pierce as sharply as a sword. Peter knows Scott the benefactor acted appropriately. He also knows Scott, as his father, deserves respect. But this moment's introspection explodes in rage.

"Boyers, that son-of-a-bitch! If I'd known all this, I would've . . . "

"Would have what? Looks like Momma and I made the right decision," says Scott, leaning back in his chair, sipping coffee with a smile. "But you did have your revenge. He was one of the men in the mob you tormented as The Beast. Boyers was the mastermind of your lynching, leader of the mob, The Accuser."

Vomiting obscenities to God, Peter leaps to his feet. Throwing his chair aside, he circles the table like a spider stalking its prey in a web. His gut churns, a twisting nauseous sensation as he feels himself succumbing to The Beast.

"You did not recognize Boyers because over three decades had passed since you fled with Momma, and you were only six. But he remembered *you*," says Scott, his gaze slumping to the table. "Which brings me to a final confession, the one I have dreaded the most all these years."

"What the hell could be worse than what you've already said?" asks Peter, his surprise distracting The Beast's metamorphosis.

"When I haunted Boyers, I let him know it was me, and those years of tormenting instilled a vengeance of his own. He would get even with *me* by punishing *you*. When you and Momma left Boyers, he knew I would accompany both of you. He also knew a rebellious Black man like you would step out of line someday. He as a privileged white would use that as an excuse to extract *his* revenge. His patience was rewarded. He lynched you. My retribution had coiled the noose from which you hung."

Peter drops into his chair, staring into the hazed darkness of The Palace. Confusion, doubt, and shame tumble in his mind. The walls he had constructed in the past have crumbled in a lie. Worse, just like his father, Peter chose vengeance at the unintended expense of a loved one, his momma. The supernatural forces used to torment his murderers could have been used to ease her suffering. Instead, she died the year after Peter's lynching, her death hastened by his. By her bed, friends found a photograph, the one the newspaper took of Peter standing in the buckboard before his lynching.

This hateful battle tires Peter. Should he raise the white flag of forgiveness, surrender to love?

Scott approaches Peter, hugs his child, and kisses his beloved's cheek.

"I have waited too long for this moment. Love you, my precious son," says Scott, his words wet with emotion.

Peter's arms dangle limp as melancholy ropes. They rise, wrapping around his father. As each caresses the other, their tears fall soft as spring rain, melting Peter's heart.

"I love you too, Dad."

Jake and Leroy peek from the kitchen . . . and smile.

Chapter 41

Dear John

Through the choking tobacco smoke, Jake approaches Peter and Scott's table. Tray in hand, he eyes the ravaged remains of pastry.

"You fellas ate them rolls like ya was vultures," he says.

Clearing the table, Jake lumbers into the kitchen. He reappears carrying a breakfast-laden tray. In his usual style, he sets the table using horseshoe-pitching finesse. The clatter of dishes scrambled with the aroma of coffee plus fried cholesterol distracts Peter's mental mayhem of the Banger brothers and his father's reunion.

Sated after the meal, Peter rears back in his chair pondering the unbelievable; across the table sits the parent he thought he would never see again. His once boiling stew of emotions now simmers in appreciation of the spiritual realm. But feeling a rustling against his chest, Peter's momentary bliss shrivels quicker than cheap bacon in a frying pan. He remembers the note in his shirt pocket, the one from Mary which Scott gave him in the car. Chair slapping the floor, Peter withdraws the missive, sets it on the table, and stares at Scott.

"Have you read it?"

"No. I can only handle one note at a time. Even we immortals have our limits."

"What if it's a Dear John?" says Peter, unable to cast his eyes on the writing.

"One way to find out, but you have to look at the words. It is not written in braille."

The wildfire of yesterday's disaster with Mary and the brothers still smolders in Peter's mind. He stretches the note between his hands and reads the hastily scribbled text:

Dear Peter:

I'm fine. Trooper Brandon says you're okay, too. He'll tell you what happened with the Bangers and Seymour, the Black man who picked me up. I'm staying in the home of Seymour and his wife in Barkersville, address on the back. Forgive me for running away. I was so scared. Like to see you again. Need to talk about some things.

Mary

P.S. Jerome's trial was pushed back to Thursday.

Flicking the note on the table, Peter flounders in a sea of emotions. Just like Scott said, Mary's safe, thank God. She still wants to talk. But why the hell was the trial delayed?

"Jerome's punishment phase was supposed to start today," says Peter, tapping the note. "That's why we were in such a damn hurry getting back to Barkersville. You knew about this, didn't you?"

"Yes, I did. Jerome was beaten by a gang of white inmates. His injuries necessitated the two-day postponement."

"Damnit!" says Peter, beating the table. "It also says something happened to Seymour. What's that about?"

"After they made that 911 call, the patrol arrived. Seymour was handcuffed, then thrown to the pavement by the first trooper on the scene; suspicion of a Black man kidnapping a white woman. Brandon arrived. After explaining how the man lying on the pavement actually helped Mary, they released Seymour."

"Why the hell haven't you told me all this before?" asks Peter.

"You had enough on your mind. Besides, what could you have done?"

Peter stiffens in rage at the image of a bloodied Jerome and a handcuffed Seymour lying at their attacker's feet.

"Damnit, all this shit just because they're both Black, and I didn't know a damn thing about it! I know as an apprentice I have limited power to foresee these events, but . . . "

"Yes," says Scott, shaking his head, "but we have discussed this. Even as a journeyman, you cannot foresee all future events, only God can. But your anger is blocking what limited powers you do have."

Peter's gut twists like a wet rag. *Some good these powers are doing me.*

"I know that part of town," says Scott, reading the note's address from across the table. "A nice, older neighborhood. Mind if I read the whole thing?"

Peter grunts yes, stuffing the paper in his shirt pocket after Scott finishes.

"Mary must care deeply for you to write this after all she had been through."

The knot in Peter's stomach loosens.

"You know, you might consider accepting her offer and pay her a visit."

"I think I'll give her a few days to calm down," says Peter as his fork stabs a sausage.

"From what she wrote, she seems pretty calm right now. You prefer comatose?"

Glaring at his father, Peter drops his fork.

"Just what *are* your intentions for Mary, anyway?"

"I like her . . . a lot. She's beautiful, caring. Three days ago, out there on the boardwalk, she held my arm going to the car. I could hear her thinking how much she liked me. You've warned me not to get emotionally involved, but damnit . . . " says Peter, his eyes begging for help.

"Concerns of the heart will always be an issue. You aid mortals when they are most vulnerable. It is only natural they will develop strong attachments for you and sometimes, you for them. But romances between us and mortals are doomed. This path you must walk alone."

"Yeah, but the way is so steep, Dad.

"What's so funny?" Peter asks, perplexed by the sudden smile creasing his father's cheeks.

"You realize this is the first time you have called me Dad?"

"Yeah, it does feel a little strange."

"Not from where I sit," says Scott, then turns, shouting to the kitchen. "Check please."

Jake lumbers toward them. He hovers over the table.

"Ain't no charge," he grumbles.

* * *

Exiting the bar beside his father, Peter lugs *The BOOK* into his car. Book on the floor with the satchel in the back, he settles behind the steering wheel. Apprehensive about his destination, he slaps the empty seat.

"Dad, I think I'll take a drive and see Mary this afternoon. Hop in. I could use the company."

"I think it best you have some time to yourself."

"Uh, when will I see you again?"

"After the trial. I will meet you at the ridge."

Peter hesitates, his face clouded by childhood memories of abandonment.

"You . . . you're not going with me to the trial, Dad?"

"Son, you are no longer that little boy waiting for daddy's return. Let go of the fear. Let Him lead."

Peter flicks the ignition switch, provoking the Corvette to life.

"I'll forego my God tirade," he says, "but I still don't trust nor will I follow Him down another path to abandonment."

Scott's face lifts in a smile.

"Problem with trust? Fear of abandonment? Funny, just a few minutes ago, you felt the same way about me."

* * *

With the top down, Peter bounds northward on Route 63, the scorching wind hotter than a dragon's breath. For the past hour, his thoughts have obsessed over today's events. Learning The Accuser and Master Boyers are the same person is shocking enough. Add to this the revelation that Scott is his father. But what troubles Peter, what rattles in his head as loudly as marbles in a tin can, are concerns about trust, love, and hate. Will I ever have the self-assurance needed to become a benefactor? How I hated my father for abandoning our family. Hated the mob, hated the committee for their hideous acts. But in my father's case, my hate was unjustified. He hadn't abandoned us, he was sold. When I learned the truth, the hateful bloom I had nurtured withered, then died. What other truths am I unaware of? What other fields of thorns have I cultivated and watered with self-righteousness?

* * *

The road summons the Corvette north across the Missouri River as Jeff City, which moments ago filled the rearview mirror, shrinks from sight. Peter checks the address on Mary's note: 1316 River Shore Road, Barkersville. He swings onto Highway 94. Minutes later, he turns onto River

Shore, poking down the street between rows of white picket fences towards the waterfront. Arriving at 1316, he observes a small, two-story, white-trimmed cottage fenced by green hedges, including a red bougainvillea weaving into the front porch trellis. He pulls to the curb. In the cottage, after a window curtain separates and then closes, the front door opens. A plump, middle-aged white woman wrapped in a red, checkered apron wearing a crown of straggly blonde hair, stands in the opening. She raises her arm, motioning the driver inside, but Peter hits the gas. In a squeal of haste, he accelerates down the street. Afternoon fades into the dark sleep of night.

* * *

The next day, Peter stops his Corvette again in front of the cottage. *What the hell's a white woman doing standing at the door of a Black man's residence? Ha, ha, ol Seymour must be doing pretty good to afford a maid and a white one at that.*

Peter waits in the car, building his confidence before seeing Mary. Reaching up, he tilts the rearview mirror, observing the reflected morning's red glow on the horizon. He brushes back his hair when the house's front door opens. The same woman motions him inside. Peter exits the car. His eyes bouncing between the brick walkway and the lady, he trudges through the doorway into the living room.

"Hello. My name's Peter. I've . . . uh . . . come to see Mary. Hope I'm not intruding. I wasn't gonna come in til later . . . "

"Been up an hour," interrupts the woman, slamming the door. "Recognized your car from Mary's description." Then nodding at the stairs, she says, "She's up in the guest bedroom."

Peter examines the dwelling decorated in Early American Goodwill, with fading wallpaper overlooking frayed braided rugs. But the oak crown molding, the ornately carved trim framing doors and windows, speak of a once stately home built with craftsmanship plus a deep pocket. Peter continues his inspection, ignoring the woman's gaze nailed to his eyes.

"Like I said, Ma'am, my name's Peter. And you are . . . ?"

"Nancy," she replies, crossing her arms as her stare bores a hole in Peter's forehead.

"Glad to make your acquaintance," says Peter, his extended hand refused. *Kinda uppity for hired help.* "Uh, is *Mr.* Lesterman home?"

"Nope."

"Is *Mrs.* Lesterman home?"

"Yes."

"Can you go get her?"

"No need."

"Why not?"

"Because she's standing in front of you."

The room hangs in silence as Peter's stammered attempt at an apology fails.

"Forget it. Happens *all* the time," says Nancy, staring at the damp, hairy mop on Peter's head. "A little early in the day to be driving with the top down, isn't it? You need something hot to drink."

Not waiting for a reply, she marches to the kitchen and pours two cups of coffee. She sets them on a faded oilcloth tabletop. Slapping the table, she offers a seat. Nancy sits facing the living room.

Peter sits opposite Nancy in a cracked, vinyl chair tucked among avocado green appliances and chipped Formica counters. On the wall beside him clings a framed photograph of a young lady in an austere wedding dress, hair pulled back in a tight bun. She holds a red rose at her side. Standing beside her in a black and white suit topped by a high, rounded collar, a Black man, arms to his side, stands straight as rigor mortis.

The hues in the photo's background of yellow and pink flowers in beige vases look unnatural to Peter as do the two people. *Never seen a wedding picture of a mixed-race couple.*

"I noticed your interest in the photo," says Nancy.

"Yeah," says Peter, sipping his coffee. "It reminds me of those old hand-tinted photographs from the 1800s. Use to be a guy in town who did those reproductions. That where you found it?"

"We didn't *find* it. That's an original of *our* wedding."

Upon hearing the unexpected revelation, Peter spills his drink. Wiping the splatter, his thoughts churn like a blender.

"That's right my dear, I'm over a hundred and twenty years old, a fellow benefactor," says Nancy, nodding at the picture. She leans closer. "Seymour's told me all about you. How under your white facade there hides the soul of a Black man. I can sympathize with the storm that must rage within, including the cloud that hangs over you and Mary."

With these words, Peter quivers in remorse. Never will a wedding portrait of him beside Mary adorn any room. But also with her words, all walls between Peter and Nancy crumble faster than sandcastles at high tide. For an hour they talk. Nancy repeats Seymour's narrative of events about escorting Mary, battling tears about his handcuffing and being thrown to the pavement.

The two talk shop, swapping tall tales, alternately joyful, then solemn. Since becoming a benefactor, excluding Scott, this is the first time Peter converses openly, freed from the chains of his identity.

"Nancy," asks Peter, aching for the right words, "you don't have to answer this, but why did you and Seymour decide . . . "

"To get married then continue our relationship after becoming benefactors?" she says, smiling. "Why, and *you* don't have to answer, did you choose to disguise yourself as a white man?"

"To work alongside white folks, I had to look like em," he says, eyes cast down. "But I feel like I've betrayed my heritage, because though I hate to admit it, I've liked being one of *them*."

Peter catches himself saying *them*, forgetting Nancy is white. Clearing his throat, he sits erect.

"I can stand," he says, "where I please without being harassed for loitering, run down a street without being detained for fleeing the scene of a crime. Why, I can even escort a white woman, free of being arrested or worse."

"Peter, I know what discrimination's like," says Nancy. "When I'm not by my Seymour's side, people treat me like any other white woman. But when I'm with *him*, they look at me as though I'm a whore. You seek justice by working within the white establishment. Seymour and I confront it. Together we all affect change in the world."

Peter drinks in Nancy's words of support.

"But there are other benefactors who challenge injustice by being its victim."

"How does that change anything?" asks Peter.

"When good people witness persecution long enough, they will act against it. Victims are mighty forces for change."

"Uh-huh, victims . . . Sounds like a bunch of Jesus wannabes."

"One could do worse. But many benefactors, such as Seymour, are *Black* like Jesus was."

"Yeah, Scott told me Jesus was Black. Won't that tie a knot in a lotta white shorts!"

Peter grins with the knowledge that white folks have no monopoly on a deity's skin pigment.

"So, besides yourself, Seymour, and Scott, how many other benefactors have I met who are masquerading as mortals?" asks Peter, his face wrinkling with suspicion.

"I'm forbidden to give those details. However, there's one who's definitely *not* a Jesus type."

Breaking free of Peter's penetrating stare, Nancy's eyes wander about the kitchen.

"Besides," she says, "it's best *not* knowing who's a benefactor."

Just then, hard-soled shoes descend the living room's stairs. Footsteps ceasing, Peter yanks around, staring at a face in the doorway, a face impassive as an erased chalkboard.

"Thought I heard a man's voice," says Mary.

"If you'll excuse me, I've gotta pull weeds in the back," says Nancy.

Throwing her apron in a cupboard, Nancy scrambles from the room, the bang of the screen door proclaiming her retreat. Peter's attention ricochets between her and Mary.

"You can't leave without telling me who that not-a-Jesus guy is," says Peter, sprinting to the screen door. "Nancy . . . Nancy!"

"*Who* are you talking about?" says Mary, watching Peter's erratic behavior. Then in a voice cold as the Artic, she says, "Aren't you glad to see me?"

"Uh, yeah, of course. Hi . . . uh, hello, Mary."

Composing himself, Peter brushes back his disheveled hair. He trudges to the table, his chest a heaving volcano ready to explode. Above his shirt pocket peeks a corner of folded paper.

"See you got my note."

Chapter 42

The Wedding Picture

Following Nancy's hurried departure, the kitchen festers in silence.

Standing by the table, Peter stares at Mary waiting in the doorway, her gaze glued to the note peeking above his shirt pocket.

Mary's eye, injured by Kevin, flowers in a black and blue bloom. Tied around her head, a black wrap covers Leroy's red bandana used to conceal her bandages. Encircling her neck like a napping cat, she wears a crimson scarf borrowed from Nancy. Together with the loaned midnight-black jumpsuit, Mary resembles the Red Baron in drag. Her hostile expression matches her attire.

Peter, anticipating a confrontation, takes the offensive.

"Uh, about this letter," he says, slapping his pocket, "it says you needed to talk. Well, here I am, and all ears."

"With nothing in between," she replies.

"What's with the Frigidaire tone, Mary? I drove all the way here yesterday because your note said you wanted to meet. I spent the night in the car so we could talk this morning. Sorry if I've been an annoyance!" he says, slapping the note on the table, then turns to walk out the door.

"Peter, please sit down. I'm sorry, but the past few days have been awful, and I'm takin it out on you," says Mary, seating herself at the table. "I need to get to the bank by nine o'clock. Nancy's offered to drive. But we've got a whole hour before I have to go."

Mary hands back the note. Slipping it into his shirt pocket, Peter grabs a chair.

"Mary, I didn't mean to come in so early, but Nancy insisted."

"When it comes to 'No,' she needs hearing aids. Guess you know who pulls the oars in *that* boat," she says, flicking a glance at the wedding picture. "But strange thing about that photo. Nancy said they got it at some carnival. The photographer had em put on some mid-1800s costumes and printed it out to look like an old hand-colored photograph."

"What's so strange about that?"

"It's the *only* wedding picture they have."

"Mary, what is it you wanted to talk about?" asks Peter, avoiding any discussion about the picture.

"Folks around here think it's *very* inappropriate for a white woman, especially a married one, to be seen in the front seat of a car beside a Black man whether he's driving or not. I should've been sitting in the back."

"Mary, what are you getting at?"

"My stopping that sedan driven by Seymour, getting in. How do you feel about that?"

Peter twists in his seat. How do I feel? Before meeting the Lestermans, I thought benefactors had to blend in, go unnoticed as a drop of water in the Great Lakes. But as Nancy said, she and Seymour "confront." I guess just like mortals, there's no such thing as normal in the spiritual realm.

"Damnit, Mary, you were running for your life! What difference does it make whose sedan you got in or where you sat? For all I care, you could've perched on the front hood pretending you were an ornament!"

"I was hoping you'd say that," she replies, but the brightness of her smile fades. "You'd think I'd feel the same way, but I didn't. I say this because I want you to know how I felt when I escaped the brothers, then flagged down that car. Because even though I was feeling all that terror, when I saw the only person who stopped to offer me a ride was a Black man, I almost didn't get in. Can you imagine?"

Peter recalls Scott had intentionally sent a Black benefactor to challenge this fear Mary harbors.

"At the risk of being recaptured and those brothers doing god knows what to me, I actually considered waiting for another car."

Mary tells Peter about her experience in the sedan. She ends with Seymour's arrest, then his release after Brandon's arrival.

"Brandon," she continues, "said he was gonna meet you and Scott later in Rolla. That's when I scribbled *that* note," she says, pointing to Peter's shirt pocket, "and asked him to give it to you.

"Through all this, I've learned something about myself. I've always thought I was an upstanding member of society, special, a few even say, an angel. After all, hadn't I forgiven Jerome? Why, I'm even willing to testify on his behalf for a life sentence instead of the death penalty.

"Then there's Seymour. If I'd been him, I never would've stopped to pick up a wild-eyed white woman waving her arms, let alone share my home with her. Even after I got here, instead of gratitude for Seymour and Nancy's hospitality, all I felt was fear my friends might see me in the company of this 'mixed' couple.

"Well, I've surrendered my halo. I've never met two people so in love, so supportive of each other while caring for others. Some contrast to respectable white couples like Kevin and me."

Mary walks to the counter, her eyes drifting to Nancy in the backyard. After pouring a cup of coffee, she returns to the table.

"Nancy and Seymour have offered me their home for as long as I want. They've inspired me, given me courage. I've decided to call the ACLU and ask if they could investigate the Manning case. I'm leaving Kevin. While I'm here, I'll look for a job and another place to live. I'm gonna visit Jerome in jail, if he'll see me, and I want to help Alice and Nathan any way I can."

Peter shakes his head in reverence. Fulfilling their role as bene-factors, the Lestermans have worked their magic defying the norms of society, confrontation as Nancy called it. Peter realizes he has much to learn.

"And Peter, there's something else," says Mary. "Ever since we've met, I've had a strange feeling about you. Like what happened with the Banger brothers. I've never been more scared in my life. There I was in the car with Benny, pawing me like I was some kinda whore. I felt dirty. Threw away my clothes when I got here. That's why I'm dressed like this. Anyway, it wasn't just the brothers I feared. I was also scared of *you*."

"Me?" *Here it comes.*

"Yeah, you didn't carry a wallet or any money. Your car registration didn't include a last name or address, just 'Peter' as the owner, not to mention that strange book you carry around with all that weird writing.

"So there I was in your car, between the brothers and their guns, while the person I had grown to trust, *you*, I began to doubt," says Mary, folding her arms. "You know, I think the way you acted in the car was deliberate. You *wanted* me to escape. Right?"

Peter's gaze breaks from Mary and wanders about the kitchen. *She's right, the way I acted was deliberate although at the time I didn't have a clue how she could flee. What was I thinking? I had no idea Seymour would show up. Best I keep my mouth shut. No matter how I answer, it'll just raise more questions.*

"Okay, don't answer, but there's something else about you that bothers me. The night after the City Hall committee meeting, I started having a dream about it. Someone walked out of the darkness from the back of the room, then took control of the meeting from Mr. Wilson. This someone or something has no shape; more like a ghost. He, it, or whatever showed movies of Jerome's past, tried to get the committee to feel compassion for him. Every night I have the same dream." Hesitating, Mary asks, "Peter, was that someone *you*?"

Fear's metallic taste sours Peter's mouth. He had erased all memories of his attendance at the committee meeting. However, he warned all that they would be haunted by nightmares of the evil they had done. But how had Mary guessed that "someone" might be him?

"What makes you think that?" he asks.

"Because of the odd things that've happened after the meeting. Take your friend, Scott. He just happened to show up in a tow truck offering to help after the Bangers disabled your car."

Peter opens his mouth, but the lie he tries to speak sticks like a cactus in his throat.

"And don't tell me it wasn't him!" says Mary, shifting back in her chair, her eyes rifled at Him. "Let's not forget my miraculous escape from the car. Seymour, conveniently stopping to give me, a white woman, a lift. Then there's the conversation you had this morning with Nancy. I was standing on the stairs. Heard you two talking like long-lost friends about some people called 'clients.' It all seems so suspicious, contrived." Mary then asks, "Am *I* one of those 'clients'?"

Peter's wrinkled brow gleams with sweat as Mary jumps from her chair. Grabbing the wedding photograph, she shakes it in front of him.

"Take this picture. One of Kevin's annoying hobbies is collecting old photographs. Our home is a garbage dump of things like this. This one looked too real to be something made at a carnival, so I decided to take a closer look."

Mary turns the picture around, pointing to a red stamp imprinted with the face of George Washington glued to the back.

"See this stamp with the date of 1866 written in faded ink?"

she says. "It's a tax revenue stamp. All photographs sold between 1864 and 1866 were taxed to help pay for the Civil War. This photo is the real McCoy, which raises some interesting questions about Nancy and Seymour."

Mary rehangs the picture, then takes her seat.

A hush foreboding as a tomb fills the room. Peter stands, pacing around the kitchen, avoiding Mary's scowl. *How do I explain the realm of the supernatural to a mortal? She's analyzed the situation methodically as a detective, no, a prosecuting attorney, and I'm guilty.*

"Mary, I . . . " says Peter, dropping in the chair.

"Please, don't say a word. Knowing the hard truth about all these strange events would ruin everything. I want it to be a mystery, kinda like what faith is. I have faith that there are angels and spirits at work for good. I also have faith we mortals are capable of kindness and love without being manipulated by those supernatural beings."

Hearing "manipulated," Peter's head cocks with surprise as Mary leans closer.

"I realize I've been manipulated all my life, but it's getting worse: Kevin, the committee, Oscar Wilson, the townspeople, the culture. Told to behave, for my own good, in the way 'they' expected. But it wasn't for *my* good, it was for *theirs*.

"Peter, you and your friends, sometimes at great risk, have helped me through difficult times. But there's something unnatural about all of you. I'm frightened . . . frustrated. My head thinks I should run out that front door. But my heart feels you can be trusted."

"Which is it, Mary? Heads or hearts?" asks Peter.

"Too much thinking. Time to follow my heart," she says, then reaches out and holds his hand.

Afraid of what he might hear in her thoughts, Peter blocks her mind's conversation.

"Peter, I need a favor, actually several."

Chapter 43

Independence Day

"It's okay Mary, Seymour's running late anyway. Go on with Peter to the bank," says Nancy.

As Mary exits the house, she grabs the black purse plus the sunglasses Nancy gave her. Peter follows, carrying a black leather briefcase, also on loan.

Approaching Peter's car, Mary sees *The BOOK* on the passenger floor mat.

"How'd you talk the brothers into leaving *that*? Just before I ran away, they seemed quite interested in it."

"They didn't leave it," says Peter.

Omitting Scott's involvement, he tells Mary about meeting the Bangers at The Palace and the ransom ending with the patrol's apprehension of the two hoodlums.

"Sounds like those two are gonna end up in jail. Can't say I'm sorry."

"Yeah, everybody wins. Compared to what they're used to, jail will seem like a resort," says Peter as he lifts the convertible's top.

"Please, Peter, don't put the top up. I'll be warm enough thanks to this outfit."

Wearing Nancy's black jumpsuit, with sunglasses plus all the trimmings, Mary hops into the Vette.

"Mary, you sure you're up to going out? You're feet and knees were skinned up pretty badly from your escape, and that was only two days ago."

"Thanks for asking, but I'm doing fine. Nancy's a nurse. She's been rubbing my wounds with one of her 'Loving Ointments' that's almost got me back to normal. Strange, I've had less severe cuts and scrapes, but they've *never* healed this fast. Like I said, there's something unnatural . . .

"Well, what are we waitin for?" she says, lips coiled in a devilish grin as she buckles her seatbelt.

The Corvette U-turns, ascending River Shore Road. Then, freed from the leash of residential speed limits, the roadster roars down the highway, Mary's scarf stretching in the wind. After a mile, they exit onto Acacia Boulevard.

"May I ask what you paid for this red beast?" asks Mary.

"Out the door, just over thirty-seven thousand. Pretty good considering all the extras. I bought it at Fillmore Motors last Saturday. Albert's face lit up like candles on Methuselah's birthday cake as I drove it off his showroom floor. You remember, that was the first day of Wilson's declaration blackballing Filmore Motors—revenge for Albert's insults at the committee meeting."

"Who could forget Albert Filmore calling the former mayor a bigot for wanting Manning executed? That took guts. Everyone knew Wilson would retaliate against his dealership," says Mary, flashing another devilish smile. "Can't believe the committee meeting was just five days ago."

"What's the grin about, Mary?"

"Oh, nothing."

They roll into the parking lot of Barkersville First National Bank.

"Could you accompany me inside?" asks Mary after they park safely away from a threatening station wagon from which explodes five door-slinging children. "Oh, don't forget the briefcase."

Eager as a puppy, Peter complies.

Mary struts through the bank's entry of varnished oak and polished brass just as the doors open for business. Like a general approaching his troops, Mary marches straight to the assistant manager's table. Sitting down, she slings her purse onto her lap and grabs the leather case, motioning Peter to sit. She gazes through her sunglasses at the bank's turn-of-the-century wood-paneled walls surrounding two-story high marble columns.

The assistant manager approaches from the manager's office. They shake hands.

"I'm Mr. John Davidson. How may I help you?" he says, sitting behind his desk.

"I'm Mary Cook. I want to withdraw some funds from my and Kevin's joint savings account."

"That's fine, Mrs. Cook," says Davidson, motioning to a teller's window. "I'm sure she can be of assistance."

"Thank you, but this is for a rather large sum."

"How much?"

"Thirty-six thousand."

Peter slouches in his chair, pretending to admire the architecture.

"Kevin, uh, Mr. Cook, you haven't said much," says Davidson, eying Peter.

"He's *not* my husband, John. How much will that leave in the account?" asks Mary.

"Just a minute."

John heads to a cashier's booth. He returns, holding a slip of paper.

"Twenty-two dollars and forty-nine cents."

"That's fine," she says, turning to Peter. "I wouldn't want to appear greedy."

After John's manicured hands rifle through a pile of papers, he shoves a yellow form at Mary.

"We'll need Mr. Cook's signature."

"That'll be difficult," says Mary. "The son-of-a-bitch's in jail."

Davidson gawks at Peter.

"Don't look at me. I'm just the chauffeur!"

"Besides," says Mary, removing a legal document from her purse, "his signature's not needed."

"N-n-no, Mrs. Cook, I can see by this you don't. May I please see some identification?"

"Certainly," says Mary, handing him a driver's license and social security card.

"Everything appears to be in order. After you complete these forms, I'll get a cashier's check."

"That won't be necessary, John," says Mary. "I want it all in cash. One-hundred-dollar bills, except for a thousand in twenties." She then slaps the briefcase on the desk.

Peter pushes himself to a vertical position in the chair. *Things are getting interesting.*

"You want thirty-six thousand dollars in cash?" asks the almost manager. "Uh . . . Just a moment, please."

Davidson scurries into the manager's office. Official-sounding mumbling emanates through the partially closed door, followed by two pairs of eyes peeking through the doorway. One hour later, Mary strolls out of the bank, a wad of fifty, twenty-dollar bills stuffed into her purse. Behind her, Peter clutches the leather case which swells from the three hundred and fifty, one-hundred-dollar bills crammed inside. They slide into the car. Peter lays the case on Mary's lap.

"Finally! I've won my independence from that bastard Kevin!" says Mary, slapping the black leather bank.

Peter flinches, surprised by the outburst.

"You must think I'm an awful person for taking all this money, Peter."

"Mary, there's nothing you could do that would make me think any the less of you," he says as a blush flashes across his face. "Uh, I mean, uh . . . "

"Peter! What a sweet thing to say. You know, I feel the same about you."

Mary returns the blush.

"Uh, about this money. It's the amount of an inheritance I had when we got married. Kevin didn't have a dime. We used my inheritance to start our clothing business. I consider this thirty-six-thousand payback on a no-interest loan, made due in full when he knocked me to the floor."

Tears peek from the corners of Mary's eyes.

"Uh, what next? Want me to take you back to the Lesterman's?" asks Peter. *But what I really want is to give her a hug.*

"You're a darling. One more stop. Keep going down Acacia, but before you do, I have one last favor to ask. Could you accompany me tomorrow at Jerome's sentencing phase of his trial?"

"I'd be honored to, Mary."

Smiling, Mary leans over the counsel and hugs Peter.

As they touch, Peter overhears her next exploit. He chuckles at the coming attraction.

* * *

"Turn right, here," says Mary, thrusting her finger at an upcoming driveway.

Peter yanks the steering wheel.

A man in a rent-a-cop uniform dives from the path of the careening car, dropping a sign reading:

"DO NOT PATRONIZE THIS ESTABLISHMENT!
BY ORDER OF FORMER MAYOR OSCAR WILSON"

Skidding to a stop, the red invader parks in front of the

showroom window of Fillmore Motors. Taking a deep breath, Mary climbs from the vehicle, asking her accomplice to bring the money case.

From behind his desk, Albert Fillmore observes the crimson arrival. Peter and a peculiarly attired woman wearing sunglasses, climb out. Albert approaches the pair entering the showroom.

"Peter, uh, how nice seeing you again. Having fun with that new baby?" says Albert, his usual sticky-sweet voice soured with concern.

"Don't worry, Al, the car's running fine."

"Who's your lady friend?" asks Albert, his tone replenished with sugar.

"Al, this is Mary Cook."

"Oh, Mrs. Cook. I didn't recognize . . . "

They shake hands. Albert's gaze twitches to one side, questioning Mary's bandana-covered head dressing. Mary wanders the showroom, hands clasped behind her back, holding her purse.

"You got any more of those, Albert?"

"Those?"

"Yes, those," she says, pointing outside to Peter's car framed in the display window.

Albert's chin dents the floor. Peter, aware of Mary's plan, plays along, displaying surprise.

"Boys," says Mary, her arms akimbo, "I asked if there's another red convertible for sale on the lot, just like that one."

"W-w-well . . . Mrs. Cook . . . I, uh . . . where's Mr. Cook?"

Peter braces for the response.

"Mr. Cook is rotting away in some jail," says Mary, her purse dangling from her folded arms. "I've asked Peter to bring me here so that I can purchase a red Corvette convertible just like his. I'm prepared to pay thirty-five thousand in cash. Peter, show the man."

Cradling the briefcase in one arm, Peter opens the black leather

container into which the salesman drools. Mary's foot taps, awaiting a response, but Albert's attention locks on the Benjamin
Franklins staring up at him.

"Peter, let's go to Barkersville Chevy. They'll have one," says
Mary, stomping to the exit.

"Mrs. Cook! Wait!"

* * *

During the three hours in which mechanics and clerks scramble
to complete the details of Mary's purchase, not one customer enters the showroom. Though the former mayor's no patronage decree is just five days old, bankruptcy looms.

After Peter takes a bathroom break, he and Mary wait for her
car in a public garden next door. With Mary by his side, Peter
glows with contentment. Her presence warms him like a spring
day's sun while they stroll through the shade of the Acacia trees.
For what seems an eternity to Peter, they walk quietly, side by side.
Then, as if in answer to a prayer, Peter feels Mary's hand in his.
Out of respect, he wills himself deaf to her thoughts. Now, in the
pleasure of the moment, they amble hand in hand through the park
to a bench where they sit.

"Thank you for your help today, Peter. I didn't want to ask Seymour or Nancy. They've already done so much. Besides, I much
preferred *your* company," says Mary while Peter nods with a grin.
"You seem awfully quiet. If you're worried I'm broke after this,
don't be. Thanks to a rich uncle who never trusted Kevin, I have
a little nest egg of my own."

"Glad to hear that," says Peter, but inside he itches with questions.

"Peter, I can tell something's troubling you. What is it?"

"Mary, of all the cars, why's it so important you have a
Corvette exactly like mine?"

"It's a symbol of my independence, my escape from Kevin. And the car reminds me of you."

Peter blushes with the praise, but the warmth within chills due to other nagging doubts.

"Mary," he says, releasing her hand, "this morning before we left, you said there was something about me that felt unnatural, like I was some kind of spirit. You said it started when you began having dreams about a 'ghost' at the committee meeting. Then there's the day the Bangers stopped us. The fact that I had no wallet, money, or legitimate registration really concerned you. But yet you've said you still trust me."

While Peter's eyes scour the park, Mary's hand touches his knee.

"Peter, yes, something about you does bother me. But first, you should know I couldn't have done anything at the bank or the dealership without you. Hell, without you I probably wouldn't even be alive! All my life I've let men control me. You're the first who's let me . . . be me."

"Mary, I care deeply for you," says an emboldened Peter.

"The word is love. It's alright to say it, Peter, because I love you too."

Hearing the 'word,' Peter's knees weaken.

"But I'm filled with guilt because I'm still married. I'm afraid of the future and what might happen to Jerome. And though I'm a moth drawn to your flame, who or what you are puzzles me. Peter, what should I do?"

Mary rests her head on his shoulder. Her sobs, damp with sorrow, plus the brush of her hair on his shoulder, melts Peter's soul. Wrapping his arm around her, Peter joins in her tears.

* * *

"Cook, your car is ready!" sounds from the dealership's loud-speaker.

Severing their entwined affection, the pair rise. While Mary squeezes Peter's hand, they trudge back to the waiting lounge and the reality of a callous world.

Albert bursts in holding two large envelopes in his hands. He hands Mary one containing the papers for her car and the keys. Then turning to Peter, Albert opens the second.

"Peter, look what I found in my desk: your wallet. I also found these, the completed registration papers for your car. I don't know how all this got into my desk drawer or why I hadn't noticed them before. I guess I haven't been myself because business has been so bad."

Peter congratulates himself. During his men's room break, he conjured up the fake wallet and papers. When no one was looking, he slipped them in Albert's desk.

Peter catches Mary's curious smile. I wonder if her expression is a sign our love might endure or a gesture that this sudden discovery seems a bit contrived. Maybe, both.

Chapter 44

The Old Man and the Dream

A Monopoly board of city blocks passes by while Peter drives up Acacia Boulevard on his way back to Phantom Ridge. He congratulates himself for his car document ruse. Mary's reaction to Albert's convenient discovery of these oddly missing items remains to be seen. Meantime, Peter has safely stowed the papers and wallet in the center console of his Corvette.

Peter cannot wait to tell Scott about today's events with Mary. Pulling over to the side of the road, he gazes through the windshield, remembering how only five days ago he first encountered Mary amid the turmoil of the Citizens for Justice Committee meeting here in Barkersville. Though she had voted in favor of Jerome Manning's death, she did so only under pressure from Oscar Wilson and the committee. Due to Peter's ability of clairvoyance, he foresaw Mary would later renounce her participation, proceeding to give aid and comfort to Jerome. Praising Mary, Peter told Scott she represented, "the light of goodness and love—a new moon's reflection into darkness." Never would have Peter attended the second committee meeting at The Palace were it not for his premonition Mary might be there needing his help.

According to Scott, Mary was part of God's plan, a statement which infuriated Peter. "Plan" was just another word for divine interference. But despite his resentment of being manipulated, Peter's affection for Mary grew. As he aided and accompanied her in a convoluted series of events, he embarked on an odyssey of self-discovery.

Now this affection has blossomed into a full flower of love.

Peter admires Mary's fighting spirit, and he believes she has been a turning point in his spiritual experience. In amazement, he has watched her capacity for acceptance, and notably her absence, unlike his, of blaming a Supreme Being for life's evils.

Sitting in his car, his thoughts drag back to the garden earlier today. There, Mary said she loved him though who or what he was puzzled her. She questioned what to do about their relationship.

I also questioned.

Taking Mary's note from his shirt pocket, he opens the center console, removing his wallet. Into the wallet, he slips the note.

When I was alive, how I longed for a woman's affection. But since I was a poor Black slave, I was too busy scraping a living for Momma and me to have any kind of romance. Now that that's changed, then why not have a relationship with Mary?

I could give up my immortality, experience the fear and pain of death again. That I'd do without hesitation, but I'd have to resign as a benefactor, surrender the supernatural powers I use to help others suffering the persecution I once did.

Who am I kidding? No spirit's ever returned to a mortal existence. I've had my chance. However, could I remain a spirit while still being by Mary's side? I could tell her everything about me. How I'm a Black man, lynched almost ninety years ago. A spirit once in the form of a monstrous spider roaming the earth, now assuming a white man's disguise. She suspects there's something different about me anyway, but would she accept something that different?

Maybe there's another way, an elaborate charade. Since as a spirit, I can alter my appearance into a hideous spider or a white man, surely I could make myself age like a mortal. Yeah, it'd be a challenge, but I could do it. Slowly gray a few strands of hair while pulling some out. A wrinkle here, a limp there . . .

Peter chuckles at the thought of standing before a mirror and making himself look old, quite the reverse of his mortal efforts. All that goes with this sham could be possible, but the relationship would be based on a lie. What would happen if someday he forgot a little detail of his deception? He is not a god or an infallible spirit. Right now, Peter's very comfortable in his white disguise. He has had over a year to acclimate to it and gives it no thought. But with Mary, he would constantly be making delicate alterations. What if one day instead of thirty years' worth of wrinkles, he only added ten, or forgot the limp or cane? He groans under the weight of this deception. It could work for a while, but, eventually, the truth would rise like the living dead.

And what about Mary's mortality? The phrase "grow old to-gether" in mortal terms strikes a romantic chord. But having to watch her age and die might not be so charming.

Exiting his car, Peter paces along the sidewalk. His eyes settle on an elderly couple sitting on a curbside bench waiting for a bus. Anchored in orthopedic shoes, their stone column legs rest on the concrete. A pair of wooden canes leans against their bench. As they sit side by side, their vein-embossed hands intertwine.

Peter stops his pacing. Do I really want to take the chance of hurting Mary? Is this the way of a benefactor? After all she's been through, isn't Mary due the blessing of aging with her mortal beloved and not some imposter?

Peter decides to set Mary free and avoid the temptation of fanning her love into a regrettable flame of desire. He will comply with her request and accompany her tomorrow at Jerome's trial. But afterward, he will let her affection cool by a self-imposed exile. He knows this intention is best for her, but the ache in his heart will not be stilled by any logic of his mind. In tears, Peter realizes never will he play the role of the old man on the bench.

Trudging back to the car, Peter falls in his seat, his soul a boiling stew of emotion. He squints into the rearview mirror for the vision of Fillmore Motors which had disappeared behind a bend in the boulevard. He slumps back in his seat. Moments pass as his face slowly blooms in a smile. He imagines Mary driving away in her Corvette, her red scarf a victory banner flagging behind. Slowly, the image fades from his mind like the light of a setting sun.

Chapter 45

Dissension in the Ranks

Commanding the corner of Acacia Boulevard and J Street for over thirty years, Wilson's Jewelry overlooks Barkersville City Park. The boulevard roars with afternoon traffic visible through the front window of Oscar's office and the adjoining showroom window. Void of personal effects except for a desktop photo of Oscar's grandson, Michael, the room begrudges its ensemble of furniture: two oak chairs, and a cherrywood desk including a leather executive chair. Pictures of his deceased wife, Sherise, and his estranged son, Sherman, decay face down in the desk's bottom drawer. Tacked to the wall behind the leather chair, is a 1988 calendar upon which tomorrow, Thursday, September 8, is circled in red around a hand-scribbled *Jerome Sentencing Phase*. Within the same wall stands the steel-clad door to the Buying Room. Spartan diversions adorn the remaining green, plastered walls.

Meantime, Peter continues his cruise up Acacia Boulevard. Wilson's Jewelry looms ahead in the Corvette's windshield. Peter observes Oscar's black Lincoln Continental parked in front of the store. A premonition overcomes him—a premonition with sensations similar to an alcoholic's irresistible craving for a drink. Such a craving now consumes him, an insatiable urge to visit Oscar's private office. Peter parks blocks away, out of sight.

Cloaked in transparency, he materializes inside the office beside the front window, observing Oscar on the opposite side of the room reclined behind his desk, engaged in a phone call. Oscar's eyes dart from the front window to a man crouched in a seat across the table, a man who sits with his back to Peter.

* * *

Kevin squirms in his chair in front of Oscar's desk, eyeing a three-day-old copy of the *Gazette* on the table's top. Kevin's gaze lifts to Oscar, still engaged in a telephone conversation, then again drops to the newspaper. Its headline reads:

"COOK CUFFED AND CANNED"

Fifteen minutes have passed since Kevin walked to the office from the Greyhound bus station where he recently arrived from Maries County Jail in Vienna. For eighty hours he was incarcerated, awaiting formal charges by Mary for assaulting her at The Palace. As no charges were filed, he was released this morning. However, during his discharge, Kevin received a phone call from Oscar, demanding Kevin's presence before him, "in a fucking hurry!" Since Kevin's BMW was still marooned at The Palace, he grabbed a bus, his joy of freedom fading with each mile closer to Barkersville.

Leaning back in his chair, Oscar continues talking while glaring at a fidgeting Cook.

Oscar hangs up when the phone rings again.

"What is it?" he answers.

"Uh, Sir, excuse me for the interruption, but there's another call for you. Line two," says a salesman's voice.

"Who is it?"

"Wouldn't say. Just that it's about some campaign contributions. Sounds like a real ass."

"I'm not giving any money to . . . " Oscar stops in midsentence. Campaign contributions? Real ass? Shit, must be Judge Daring.

"Sir?"

"Have im hold. Say I'm taking a shi . . . uh, that I'm indisposed," he says. Slamming the receiver down, Oscar nods at the door to the showroom. "Gimme a few minutes, Cook, and shut the fuckin door on your way out."

In a fester of thoughts, Oscar assumes the judge's call concerns the fifteen thousand dollars of election contributions which Oscar has not yet acquired. Oscar itches for an excuse.

"Uh, Sir, the gentleman's still on hold and getting very impatient," says the salesman.

"Damnit, put im through. Hello?"

"It's me."

"Oh, Charles! How nice to hear your voice this fine Wednesday afternoon!"

"Cut the shit, Wilson. Where's my money?"

"Yes, Your Honor, the contributions. Well . . . I *am* working on it."

"Yeah, the check's in the mail. Uh, wait a minute . . . "

Oscar hears voices in the background.

"I'm putting you on hold, Wilson. Be on the line when I'm finished."

Oscar presses the receiver to his ear. Sweat drips down his neck. Waiting for the judge, Oscar's thoughts drift back to the last conversation with His Honor. The exchange occurred at the judge's residence on a Saturday morning, the day after the Citizens for Justice Committee meeting at City Hall.

* * *

The hallway of The Honorable Charles A. Daring's home still reverberates with the doorbell's drone as the brass-trimmed oak door opens. Standing at the threshold, the maid inquires what business the man on their front porch has with the judge.

"I have an appointment with His Honor."

"Whom shall I say is calling?"

"Tell im it's Oscar."

"Oscar who?"

Oscar's grip on his black leather briefcase tightens.

"It's alright, Tina, I'll take it from here," says Charles, approaching from behind. "Please bring coffee and some pastries to my office."

The maid exits. Charles has known the visitor since the second grade. He shares Oscar's middle age and thinning black hair. Though both men's eyes stand at the height of an average man's Adam's apple, Charles' sharp physique cuts a stark contrast to Oscar's watermelon figure.

"Oscar, you're punctual as usual."

The nonchalant tone unnerves Oscar.

"That you parked out front?" asks Charles, stepping onto the porch as he surveys the manicured neighboring estates.

"Yeah."

Charles points to a dirt driveway down the road used by his gardener.

"Use that. Tina will meet you at the tennis courts, then escort you inside."

"Uh . . . alright," says Oscar.

After moving his car, Tina escorts Oscar across the backyard, through the rear delivery door, and into the judge's private office.

"Have a seat," says Charles. "You said on the phone you have something of interest for me." Both men settle into carved French chairs. Oscar places his attaché on the floor. Peeking through the curved bay window behind Oscar, the morning sun massages his shoulders. Between the two men poses a spindly cocktail table upon which Tina, after asking permission to enter, sets coffee, pastries, and ornate, white China.

"I'm afraid to touch the cups and saucers," says Oscar.

Charles flashes a thin smile.

Setting down a petite, silver bell, Tina departs, closing the office's double doors.

Munching on a croissant, Oscar inspects the Persian rug spanning the distance between him and the judge's mahogany worktable, which itself seems half the size of Oscar's office. Proud he's above such vulgar displays of wealth, Oscar removes a large, red envelope from his briefcase.

"A Valentine's card? Oscar, you shouldn't of," says Charles, sipping coffee from his porcelain cup.

"This is the petition from last night's committee meeting that I . . ."

"I know damn well what it is. It's splattered like vomit all over this morning's *Gazette*!"

Oscar removes the petition from the crimson cover. Pushing aside the tableware, he sets the envelope down, then spreads the petition on top. The document consists of a brief, typed statement above a worm field of scribbled signatures.

"You know, Oscar, considering what the *Gazette* wrote about this declaration, I shouldn't be seen with you," says Charles, setting down his coffee. "It could jeopardize my judicial impartiality. That's why I told you to go in the back entry just in case any neighbor's watching.

"Can't read a word of it without my glasses," he says, eyeing the document, "but see *your* John Hancock well enough. How many signed it?"

"The whole committee—all twenty of us!"

"My, haven't we been a busy ex-mayor?" says Charles, then leans forward. "Do you suffer from some sort of memory impairment?"

"What do you mean?"

"Don't you remember our meeting here weeks ago before the start of Jerome's trial?"

Relying on their years of friendship, Oscar had requested that meeting. He asked Judge Daring to withhold certain facts from the forthcoming courtroom proceedings, facts such as Oscar's purchase of a stolen ring from Jerome. Plus the gun which Jerome had stolen from Oscar's desk was the gun he used to shoot Timmy Cook. Oscar would deny all this, but he knows how small-town folks love to gossip.

"You confided in me," says Charles, "how you fenced stolen jewelry to pay for your grandson's medical bills. Cystic fibrosis, I believe?"

Oscar nods yes.

"Noble cause, but not a get-out-of-jail free card."

Oscar's face furrows in a self-righteous scowl. *Jail, hell! I'm too careful. Besides, I don't deserve it. If the fucking insurance would've paid like it was supposed to, I wouldn't of dealt with scum like Jerome. I sure as hell didn't tell im to steal that damn ring or commit murder. And if I've gotta send that Black son-of-a-bitch to his death to protect my family, so be it!*

"Ah, your expression says your amnesia's clearing. Good," says Charles, grabbing his cup. "You know, Oscar, you and Jerome have something in common."

"What the hell you mean?"

"You both were engaged in criminal activities to support your families. The only difference is Jerome's Black, so *he* got caught.

"Now," says Charles, filling his cup, "let's continue our stroll down memory lane and reminisce about Mr. Manning's trial. He was defended pro bono by an inexperienced attorney just starting his practice. However, Jerome's partner in crime, Anthony, in case you've forgotten his name, was defended by a seasoned criminal lawyer, paid for by an anonymous donor. Anthony's plea bargain with the court was accepted; in exchange for his testimony against Jerome, Anthony received a reduced sentence of manslaughter. Additionally, Jerome's failure to testify on his own behalf made him look guilty as sin, another nail in a coffin in which he and your dirty little secrets will rot. All those nails; how convenient." Charles sips his coffee.

"Convenient? Hell! I paid for it, just like *you asked*, by finagling that fifteen thousand dollars' worth of contribution commitments at your County Fair fundraiser!"

Charles leaps from his chair, throwing his cup to the floor.

"Don't you ever say *asked* again!" he shouts, aiming a finger at Oscar. "That donation was *your* idea, you son-of-a-bitch!"

Charles storms to his desk. From a drawer, he removes a folded clipping he snipped from this morning's *Gazette*. Reading glasses perched on his nose he returns, looming over Oscar with the hungry stare of a vulture about to dine as he reads:

"We want Judge Charles Daring to know what the voting citizens of this community are thinking. We, under no circumstances, will tolerate anything less than the death penalty. Judge Daring should be mindful of this considering his reelection is only two months away."

"It says this was a quote taken from *you* at last night's meeting. That true, Oscar?"

"Yeah, and that's pretty much what this petition says," replies Oscar, china scattering off the tea table to the floor as his hand pounds the document.

"Don't worry, Tina will clean up the mess," says Charles, returning to his seat after flashing that same thin smile.

"You know Oscar, at first, the committee's flaming rhetoric

about that murdering Black was a benefit. It stirred up the public—good fertilizer for my political hay. But you couldn't leave it there. No, you had to go and make it a personal attack against me!" Shaking the clipping, Charles adds, "*Not* the sort of thing a judge running for reelection wants to see in a paper. *Not* the sort of thing a person in your delicate position ought to be saying. So this mess is something *you're* going to clean up."

The judge removes his glasses. After folding the article, he slides both into his shirt pocket.

"Oscar, you have the finesse of a pinecone tampon. But since you're here, pass this on to your twenty committee members. Say if each one finds five friends who'll donate a hundred and fifty dollars to my campaign, that would go a long way in removing this boil from my reputation."

"You serious? They won't do that!"

"Then, Oscar, I guess *you'll* have to make up the difference."

"That's another fifteen thousand dollars!"

"You always were good with numbers," says Charles, folding his arms. "Ever consider asbestos shorts? Because every time your ass gets burned your wallet goes up in flames."

Realizing all profits from his illegal business will not be spent on his grandson, Oscar's teeth grind hard enough to crush diamonds.

"Smile," says Charles. "The extra funds will buy more nails." The scowl on Oscar's face inverts into a grin.

"Alright," he says, "I'll call *another* committee meeting, tonight, somewhere far from town. There's this dump in Vichy called The Palace Bar and Grill. I'll say it's gonna cost em plenty, but you're going to make sure Manning gets the death sentence."

"I never said *that*. And concerning you and me, we have never met, talked, or exchanged written communication about anything regarding Manning. As far as this fucking suppository of a petition goes, use it as you see fit because I've never seen it! Likewise, during the trial, I've stopped delivery of all my newspapers. Like the jury, I've sequestered myself from all television and radio. There shall not be the slightest doubt that the court has, in any way, been prejudiced by outside influences.

"Oh, about the money," says Charles, crossing his legs and leaning back in his chair, "make sure not one penny is contributed by any committee member. I want *nothing* connecting me with your bloodthirsty mob. Two weeks should be sufficient time, don't you think?"

"But won't that look . . . suspicious? Me and the committee giving all this money to strangers, then telling em to donate it to your campaign?"

"Oscar, you're a former elected official, no virgin to the nuances of fundraising."

Charles shakes the silver bell. A knock sounds at the double doors.

"The maid will show you to the back door, and don't forget your petition. Have a nice day."

* * *

A screaming horn outside Oscar's office summons his attention to the present. Fifteen minutes have passed since he has been on hold for the judge with the receiver pressed against his aching ear. Finally, the phone vigil ends with an abrupt:

"You still there?"

"Yes, Sir."

"Something's come up that could affect Jerome's sentence," the judge says in a tone absent its accustomed arrogance. "We must meet *today*. Some place private, far from town."

Oscar glances at his watch, 4:53 p.m. More tense words are exchanged.

"When you get to Vichy, call me," says Charles, as a dial tone ends the conversation.

With a crash, Oscar throws the receiver into its cradle. Like an ambulance rushing to a car wreck, he races from the room, locking his office door.

"Meet me back here tomorrow, 9:00 a.m., sharp!" Oscar says to Kevin in the showroom.

"Tomorrow? But what about the trial?"

"It's been pushed back to Friday."

Glass doors nearly shear from their hinges as Oscar flings them open, bowls down the stairs, then leaps into his Continental.

Kevin stands, straining his neck to observe the antics. The black car explodes from its parking space. As the Lincoln horns obscenities at those in its line of fire, a red Corvette follows.

Chapter 46

The Abyss

Tossing his sunglasses on the dash, Peter unfolds himself from his Corvette. For the past hour this Wednesday afternoon, he followed Oscar's speeding Lincoln from Wilson's Jewelry to a pay phone here in Vichy. Peter parked behind a gas station in front of which stands Oscar in a phone booth. Cloaking himself in invisibility, Peter eavesdrops on the conversation:

"Can't make it to The Palace," grumbles the judge. "Something's come up. Meet me at Phantom Ridge tomorrow morning, nine o'clock, sharp!" The conversation ends with a click.

"Asshole!" Oscar shouts after pausing to confirm the line is dead. "To think I got a damn speeding ticket getting here. But now, only fifteen minutes from The Palace, I got an hour and a half fuckin drive to Potosi in the morning!"

He slams the receiver which ricochets off the payphone, flopping at the end of the cord, helpless as a hooked catfish. Exiting the phone booth, he checks into a motel where Oscar spends the night amid a battalion of bed bugs. Meantime, Peter, under stars pristine as scattered diamonds on black velvet, drives the seventy miles of snaking road from Vichy to IMCC behind which ascends Phantom Ridge. He parks in the prison lot, far from the ridge's trail entry, to avoid Oscar or the judge's attention.

* * *

The horizon's fluorescent red ribbon proclaims another day.

Peter gazes at the ridge looming in the distance over the penitentiary's gray walls. Only five days ago, he and Scott had walked the one-mile, twisting trail descending from the ridge to where he is now parked, where a proud Peter had shown Scott his new Corvette. *Strange, since becoming a spirit, events flip by faster than pages of a book in a hurricane. I could materialize on the ridge. But, just as I enjoyed the serenity of last night's drive, I think I'll walk. Oscar and the judge won't be here for three hours; plenty of time for a stroll.*

Gravel groans as Peter arrives at Phantom Ridge, the commemorative park at the crest of the knoll. He watches a deer leap over a bench, sprint past the giant elm, then bound over a granite tombstone inscribed with *Unknown* marking the memorial's grave. Peter sits on the bench.

In the solitude, images of the mob, the lynching, and The Beast haunt Peter's thoughts. Closing his eyes, he composes himself as the ridge's mystic turmoil engulfs him. In his last appearance here, Peter complained to Scott about the disastrous Citizens for Justice meeting. Despite Peter's supernatural forces and devices like the black button, his efforts failed to thwart the committee's deadly goal. Chairman Oscar Wilson, with unanimous approval, pressed the button, initiating the fate of Jerome's death. Peter wonders how a "loving" God tolerates such evil.

Doubting the benefit of his early arrival, Peter stands, pacing about to the rhythm of his agitated heart. He then notices someone standing in front of the *Unknown* tombstone.

That guy wasn't there when I sat down.

He approaches the man dressed as a Highway Patrol trooper. Head bowed in reverence, the officer holds his gray Smokey the Bear hat in one hand. In the other, he holds a flower bouquet wrapped with a yellow ribbon. Peter watches the trooper drop to one knee, set the flowers at the foot of the grave, and make the sign of the cross. The trooper, alerted by Peter's footsteps, rises.

"Trooper Brandon! What are *you* doing here?"

"Waiting for you, Peter," he says with blue-uniformed confidence, twisting his hat into place.

"Waiting? How'd you know I'd be way the hell out here?" asks Peter, twitching with suspicion.

"I know lots of things about you. Like the *Unknown* is you, a Black man lynched here eighty-seven years ago. You once lived here as, how shall I say it, a bug with an attitude.

"How do I know all this? Wait here while I get out of this disguise," he says, stepping behind the elm.

"Disguise?" asks Peter, his face bleached with astonishment.

"Remember now?" says Brandon, reappearing in blue jeans, a sweat-stained Stetson, a plaid shirt, and boots, all vintage late 1800s. A silver star deputy's badge sags from his shirt.

"Deputy Monroe!"

Peter twinges with a kaleidoscope of emotions. His thoughts retreat to the night decades ago when at the deputy's dying request, Peter went to visit him in the shack. Scott said Monroe wanted to make amends, then asked forgiveness for his part in Peter's lynching. So what the hell does he want now?

"My presence must be upsetting, Peter. But trust me when I say I've come here to help."

"Help? I trusted you once, but it led to that!" says Peter, pointing to the grave.

"Yes, but you're no more receptive to forgiveness now than you were then. Will your storm of wrath never calm?"

"Storm of wrath? Did you think of that yourself or was it something you heard at Sunday school?"

"Peter, words can't erase the harm I've caused, but they can ease your pain. Like you, I had issues in the spiritual realm. My suffering didn't end with my last breath."

"So, we have something in common, huh? Okay, as a spirit, did you ever haunt a person or *persons*?"

"In a way . . . " says Monroe, the furrows of his brow deepening.

"I knew it! You went after the mob, just like I did!"

"No, I *went* after myself. My spirit was crushed under a weight of shame and guilt, a regular Marley's ghost. If only I had set you free. Yeah, I would've been jailed, become an outcast, but that would've been the end of it, no eternal guilt. But now, just like Marley, I appear before you with the sincere desire to help."

Monroe steps forward. In a cloudburst of tears, he hugs Peter, soaking the embraced shoulder in a torrent of sorrow.

Rigid with uncertainty, Peter remembers other emotions he felt the night at the shack. *I knew Monroe wasn't an evil man. He had no hatred for me and genuinely tried to protect me from the mob.* Peter then experiences the unexpected. As the deputy's tears fall, they seep through the cracks of Peter's distrust, trickling to, then melting Peter's heart's icy core.

"Peter, I've wanted to do this since that night you stood by my bed in the shack. But I was too weak."

"So why now?" asks Peter. "Why this visit after all these years?"

"I doubt as The Beast you would've been receptive. So I waited until the time was right when my help would be accepted, starting as Trooper Brandon which led to this visit."

"I wondered what happened to you. I even asked Scott, but he said he wasn't allowed to say." Peter steps closer. "You know, I never thanked you for helping Mary and trying to protect us from the Banger brothers. So, thank you." Peter pauses, then asks, "Are, are, you a benefactor?"

Monroe nods yes, his tears flowing into the valley of a growing smile.

"*You're* the one Nancy was talking about. I remember her exact words: 'However, there's one who's definitely *not* a Jesus type.'"

"Yeah, I'm the one," chuckles Monroe.

"The Lestermans and I are called the 'Dynamic Duo' by the other benefactors. The Lestermans, with their mixed marriage, a boil on the nose of social norms. Me, an uptight police officer, the epitome of Midwest conservatism. Together we have more fun than throwing stones at glass houses like Wilson."

"Wait a minute. Was it *you* who gave Oscar the speeding ticket yesterday?"

Monroe smiles.

"Oh, how I liked the insult of a sobriety test. Watching that pompous ass walk a straight line in front of commute traffic did my heart good."

"To serve and protect," says Monroe, snapping a salute.

Peter wishes he were having as much fun as this Old-Western-clad benefactor, which prompts another question.

"I remember Scott was at the shack. Are you doing your apprenticeship under him too?"

"Uh, well, actually, I've finished all that."

"So, you're already a full-fledged *journeyman* benefactor?"

"In full plumage."

The warmth of Peter's amusement shivers under jealousy's frost. How the hell did Monroe make journeyman so damn fast?

"Oh, well then, congratulations," lies Peter, extending his hand. "Glad you came by to tell me."

If Peter were Pinocchio, his nose would have knocked Monroe to the ground.

"Thanks, but I'm not here to brag," says Monroe. "I want to return the favor you extended to me at the shack."

"What favor?"

"You told me the truth I didn't want to hear."

Uh-oh, I feel a lecture comin and bet it's something about my problem with The Almighty.

Turning, Peter stomps back to the bench, followed by Monroe. With each step boils a volcano of dust mirroring Peter's emotions.

"As I said, I had my issues in the spiritual realm," says Monroe, sitting next to Peter. "You remember the three choices Scott offered for spiritual existence: the eternal bliss of Sanctuary, revenge on those who had harmed me, or become a benefactor. Well, I took something related to revenge, The Abyss."

"I *knew* there was something else! That's why you made journeyman so fast," says Peter, slouching lower on the bench.

"Peter, I didn't suffer in life like you had: slavery, prejudice, violence, and even death at the hands of a mob. I was spared the anger accumulated over a lifetime of that atrocity. So it's only natural it's taking you *longer* to trust Him. Nothing's wrong; whatever time it takes is the right time. But if I had suffered as much as you, I honestly don't know if *I* could trust God either. But I *do* know trusting Him—faith—is the *only* way I ever become a journeyman."

Placing a hand on Peter's shoulder, Monroe blocks both of their thoughts.

"Faith's a funny thing. Adversity and time strengthen it. So I pray your faith has strengthened, for you'll make one hell of a benefactor."

Monroe releases Peter.

Frustrated, Peter folds his arms. Spoken just a like white guy. Trying to put himself in my place and then questioning how he might have acted. No way in hell can any white fathom what we Blacks go through.

"All right, I'll bite. What were *your* 'issues' in the spiritual realm?" asks Peter.

"Well, they weren't with God because I never really gave Him a thought. They were all about me. When I died and became a spirit, I was consumed with guilt. I slid into a deep depression.

Being removed from those who had shown me love, the people who had taken me in when all others turned me away, just added to my sadness. I didn't have an ever-present source of strength to lean on."

"Go on, say it again—God," says Peter.

"Call It what you want: Jehovah, Higher Power, Universal Authority. Now like I said Peter, of Scott's three choices, I chose the vengeance of The Abyss. I had no one to blame my problems on. Yes, I hated the mob, hated The Accuser who lynched you, but I already knew how they would act if they ever caught you. It was the culture, the culture I grew up in, the culture I had sworn to protect. So the hate for the mob was exceeded by the *loathing* of myself because I had brought you to them. And there's a spiritual place reserved for souls of the self-loathing. They descend into The Abyss."

"Haven't heard of that one."

"The Abyss is something like a deep chasm," says Monroe, fighting back tears, "only worse. Imagine being alone, in despair, imprisoned in an endless void. But the truth that tortured me as much as the emptiness that imprisoned me was I could leave at any time. *I* chose to stay."

Peter recalls his self-imposed isolation here as The Beast. But he was fortunate. He had the occasional luxury of crawling from his lair to torment his victims.

"How long were you there?" asks Peter.

"Thirty years."

Sounds to me like Monroe's bragging since I was The Beast for eighty-seven.

"How'd you finally escape?" asks Peter.

"It wasn't an escape. Like I said, I could've left any time. The whole time I was there, above the void on the ridge stood a white-robed figure enveloped in a golden glow. One day, don't ask me why, I decided to investigate that aura from above. For days I crawled up the stone-faced cliff of The Abyss until I reached the top."

From his shirt pocket, Monroe removes a tattered piece of coarse fabric from which emanates a golden radiance. As a cloud wanders overhead casting a shadow over the bench, the cloth's glow intensifies.

"Strange isn't it? The darker its surroundings, the brighter it gets."

"Where'd that come from?" asks Peter.

"From the hem of the gown of The One who lifted me from the darkness," says Monroe, sliding the fabric back in his shirt.

"Who's . . . ?"

"Hear that?" says Monroe, his head cocking towards the path.

"What?"

"Footsteps. Someone's approaching."

"Must be someone for the meeting."

"Whoever it is, Peter, by the way he's gasping, I'd say he's a couple of steps short of a coronary."

"That's gotta be Wilson," says Peter. "Coronary . . . Great. Just what we need, another surly *spirit* stirring things up."

At that moment, Monroe pulls out his pocket watch.

"My how time flies. I gotta go," he says.

Reassuming his trooper's disguise, Monroe heads towards the path.

Peter runs after him, tears swelling in his eyes.

"Stop! Thank you, my friend, for caring enough to visit me. Also, the flowers. Do you know no one's ever put those on my grave before or knelt, or prayed? You did the same thing years ago when I hung from the end of a rope. You're the only white man who's ever shown me kindness."

In a steel embrace, he hugs the trooper, then steps back.

"You know, I'm ashamed of how I treated you on your deathbed," says Peter. "Even now, I've judged your capacity to help me simply because you weren't born Black. Maybe if I'd been more loving . . . "

"Don't go there. You are now as you were then—hurting. You couldn't help yourself. Besides, there was nothing you or God could've done to save me from myself."

Brandon hands Peter the cloth from his pocket.

"Remember, don't drink and drive," he says, flicking the brim of his hat, then evaporates.

Oscar's footsteps grow louder . . .

Peter inspects the frayed luminescence shining in his hand. From his shirt pocket, he removes the card Scott had given him inscribed with a name:

I.M. Emmanuel

Just like the fabric on his palm, the card glimmers.

Chapter 47

Bugs, Beast, and the Bitch

Entering the IMCC parking lot, Oscar hunches forward, squinting through the windshield. Morning's light through the insect graveyard smeared across the windshield makes visibility impossible.

Where the hell's this fuckin park, Phantom Ridge, anyway? I know it's around here somewhere.

The driver's window of the black Lincoln Continental rolls down. Out pops Oscar's head, his eyes straining across the asphalt when he stands on his brakes, squealing to a stop. Two monstrous, green pickups soaring five feet off the pavement, horns blaring, scream around him, prison guards rushing to their eight o'clock shift change.

"Assholes!" he shouts, flipping the bird.

Oscar is about to give chase when he observes an assault rifle mounted on a gun rack in each truck's rear window. Considering the puny Saturday night special stuck under his dash, he decides the odds of seeing another sunset are best achieved by blowing his horn.

He drives up to a gate in a chain-link fence opening onto a gravel path advertised by a sign:

"PHANTOM RIDGE—ONE MILE"

Head stretched out his window, Oscar eyes the path which resembles a rising wisp of gray smoke fading at a distant hill's summit.

You gotta be kidding. Way the fuck up there?

To save himself a thirty-foot walk, Oscar parks in the area's lone handicapped stall, designated by a sign atop an eight-foot post. On the dash, he places a blue placard he extorted from a doctor. The extra space should protect his beloved black beauty from any Jolly Green Giant's door. As Oscar rolls out of his car, it creaks with relief, rebounding six inches.

Oscar trudges up the path. His daily coffee and donuts breakfast punctuated by a twenty-five-foot aerobic walk from car to office chair has taken its toll. Between gasps for air, he claws at wounds from last night's bed bug assault. *I would've slept better on poison oak!* He then eyes his uphill destination. *I know the judge wants privacy, but way the hell up there? That son-of-a-bitch's as paranoid as a bug in a chicken coop!*

Oscar hears gunfire from below. Grinning, he thinks the shooting is the two guards target practicing on inmates when he sees a Missouri state trooper approaching from the ridge.

"That's the prick who gave me the ticket yesterday!" he mutters. "What's he doing here?"

The trooper passes, brushing the brim of his hat in a polite gesture, then disappears around a bend. Oscar flips a bird. The gunfire repeats.

* * *

At the summit, Peter leans against the elm, cloaked in transparency. He watches Oscar's arrival for his meeting with Judge Daring in which they will conspire to ensure a death sentence in the forthcoming sentencing phase of Jerome Manning's trial. Peter's unobtrusive observation of evil troubles him. However, Statute XI of *The BOOK*, the Benefactor's Bible, states:

"A client's free will is supreme, therefore, benefactors shall never coerce a client, mortal or spirit, into an act regardless of the consequences, nor shall a benefactor directly intervene to alter fate. A benefactor shall influence behavior and situations solely as an appeal to the client's conscience, and all powers and devices bequeathed to a benefactor shall be used only as a means to that end. Such powers shall include prophecy, telepathy, time dilation, teleportation, shapeshifting, polyglotism, invisibility, and conjuring material commodities."

Yeah, but appealing to those two's consciences is like asking a snake not to slither.

* * *

Oscar collapses on the bench, his heart beating with the frenzy of a thimble bailing out a bathtub. He checks his sweat-drenched watch: 9:20 a.m. Still no judge. Shit! Then his lips arch in a grin as he imagines the delay possibly, hopefully, is due to a vehicular confrontation with the trooper.

Pulse slowing, his attention turns from his fatigue to the park's surroundings. A coin's toss behind the bench, Oscar sees a three-foot-high marble pedestal supporting a massive bronze plaque. Fifty feet farther back stands a granite tombstone marked *Unknown*. At the stone's base lies a fresh bouquet wrapped in a yellow ribbon.

Between the marble pedestal and tombstone, stands the elm. The trunk, with its gnarled bark, grasps a shoe-box-size bronze placard. Just another stupid historic site. However, having untold minutes to kill, he approaches the marble pedestal and its weighty plaque with a patina inscription:

PHANTOM RIDGE PARK

In memory of the unnamed Black man lynched at this site in 1899. Dedicated on Veteran's Day, 1986, by the estate of the late Bartholomew Cummings, former Senator from Missouri.

July 22, 1899: A Black man in the custody of Washington County Deputy Louis Monroe was en route to Potosi to stand trial for the murder of a white man, James Thornton. A twenty-man vigilante committee, the mob, seized the Black man. He was brought here as a crowd of hundreds followed, and was lynched from this elm.

Oscar then approaches the elm. There awaits a still invisible Peter who touches Oscar's sleeve, hearing Oscar's thoughts as Oscar inspects the tree's placard:

In memory of one who died here:
"The only thing necessary for the triumph of evil is for good men to do nothing."
Quote attributed to Edmund Burke

"Humph, 'In memory . . . '" mumbles Oscar. So, what's the big deal? Evil wasn't allowed to triumph. A Black guy killed a white man so they lynched the son-of-a-bitch. Blacks've been hung for a hell of a lot less, and if they built a shrine for every one of em, we'd be littered with more tombstones than Big Mac wrappers!

Oh, how I wish I could've been here, shouting the order that killed the Black man, watching the son-of-a-bitch twist in agony, reaping the evil he's sown. I only pray I can do the same for Jerome!

He returns to the marble pedestal:

For eighty-seven years after the lynching, bizarre events were recorded: An enormous apparition in the form of a black spider was rumored to lurk by the elm. Strange noises emanated from the knoll. Witnesses reported that vigilantes on their deathbeds screamed in horror about the unseen presence of a ghastly black beast. The site was thus christened Phantom Ridge.

These phenomena ceased after the last living participant in the lynching, the same Bartholomew Cummings who created this memorial, died.

"Mob, hell," says Oscar as though speaking to the Citizens Committee. "It was just a committee of citizens doin what the courts would've done anyway, hung the bastard! Implying his spirit terrorized the mob's fucking ridiculous! I wonder if the senator's grandkids like how their inheritance was spent."

* * *

Peter aches in anger that the number of vigilantes, twenty, escapes Oscar's attention, the same number who participated in the Citizens Committee. Also, Oscar's contempt for the supernatural enflames The Beast within. Just as the apparition did at The Palace, the monster begs to be released. But though he subdues The Beast, Peter wants Oscar to appreciate the supernatural presence in which this memorial is cradled. Remembering *The BOOK*'s passage about appealing to a mortal's conscience, Peter decides on a more subtle approach. He summons all his strength . . .

* * *

Darkness drifts across the knoll as Oscar watches a single cloud stretch across the sky, blocking the sun. Except for this thin shroud, the sky expands from horizon to horizon in an unobstructed blue dome.

That's weird.

Then Oscar hears the shouting of a distant crowd. Swelling into the screams of a mob, the uproar draws closer, surrounding him. The morning's breeze erupts into a gale. Quivering from the cold ache of fear, Oscar stumbles back, his arrogance fleeing before him like leaves sheared from the elm. Through the hurricane of debris, he envisions a black silhouette darting through the shadows. Fragments of silken filament fanned by the storm skip across the soil. In this gloom of gale and ghoul, Oscar trembles with terror. There's something sinister here. Could it be . . . the Black man trying to escape? Could it be . . . that black beast hovering nearby? A twig snaps behind him. Then another. Slow as opening a mausoleum's long-sealed door, he twists around when in the tornado of haze, he sees . . .

"Oscar? You look like you've seen a ghost!"

A mute, whitewashed-faced Oscar stares back at the voice.

"Oscar?"

Shaking his head, Oscar closes his eyes. As they open, Judge Daring comes into focus.

"Oscar, what the hell's . . . "

"Some . . . some kinda storm, huh?" says Oscar, rubbing his quivering chin.

"What storm?"

Releasing Oscar's sleeve, Peter grins.

To Oscar's amazement, the park is bathed in the same gentle light as when he first arrived. Had the storm been some kind of horrific dream? With all the worry about today's meeting plus just three hours of sleep, shaking his head, Oscar quickly changes his demeanor and the subject.

"Damnit, don't sneak up on me like that, Charles!"

"I *never* sneak," says the judge, surveying the knoll. "You know, I used to come here when I was a kid, before it was a park. Before they cleared that weird canopy of branches and spider webs. Place gives ya the willies, doesn't it?"

"Don't know what ya mean," says Oscar.

"Right."

Pinning Oscar in a half-eyed inquisitive glare, the judge flicks his thumb at the bench. The two sit. Behind them by the marble monument stands Peter, still transparent.

The judge says they are meeting in this remote location because yesterday he was in nearby Rolla visiting Franklin B. Hayes, the lawyer who got Jerome's partner in crime, Anthony, off with manslaughter. After meeting Oscar, the judge is visiting his family here in Potosi.

"Have a nice visit," says Oscar. Why the hell did the judge see Hayes? Anything to do with the big bucks for Anthony's defense?

"Frank and I go a long way back. We both graduated from WashULaw. He's one of the best, most expensive defense attorneys in the state. Anyway, I've asked him to stay involved in the trial on a 'consulting basis,' if you know what I mean," says the judge, elbowing Oscar. "His thumb's in a lot of pies and he's pulled out quite a plum. So, what do you want first? The bad news, or the worse news?"

"I guess the bad," says Oscar.

"Mary Cook. Frank says she's called the ACLU in St. Louis. They're sending out a couple of lawyers to investigate Manning's case. That's why I called you yesterday for this meeting."

Oscar stares into the distance.

Peter chuckles.

"You look like you've seen another ghost and rightfully so. Those ACLU guys," says Charles, "are persistent as mosquitoes in spring. They'll ask a swarm of questions. If I were you, I'd bathe in bug repellent. So, stay low for a while."

"For how long?"

"I'd give it two weeks after tomorrow's sentencing."

"Two weeks? I can't go underground that long. I'm in charge of the committee! Besides, how's that gonna affect those reelection contributions you want?" asks Oscar.

"Oh, I *still* expect the fifteen grand. You'll have almost two weeks left to pound on doors before the election, but your inflaming rhetoric that Manning has to die . . . has to die *now*. And I better not hear you're still fuckin with stolen jewelry!"

"Uh-huh, but what's those ACLU assholes gonna find anyway? Jerome's *not* gonna talk. Everything was done nice and legal. Plus *you're* the presiding judge. You can throw one roadblock after another into their investigation."

"I'm glad *you're* so confident because *you're* the one who stands the most to lose. Yes, you've intimidated Jerome. But you won't be able to intimidate the ACLU. If they turn up anything about that gun he stole from your shop or stumble onto something else concerning your fencing operations, *you're* in deep shit!" says the judge, reclining against the armrest, glaring at Oscar.

"Me, huh? I'm not the only whore in this bordello, *Charles*!"

"I see you're still suffering from memory impairment because that sounded like *another* threat. But this time I won't ask for money. I'll have my pound of flesh. I'll contact the police. Have them compare merchandise you've sold over the past ten years with their records of stolen jewelry. After I'm finished, Wilson," Charles says, pointing down to the prison, "*that's* where you'll be getting your mail. Even if you try to accuse me of payoffs and courtroom misconduct, who do you think they'll believe? A criminal like yourself or a respected public official boasting of an unblemished twenty-one-year career on the bench? Get the picture, or would you like to experience the real thing in living Technicolor?"

Stiffening from rage, Oscar reminds himself this partnership with the judge serves only one purpose: to allow Oscar's continued financing of his grandson's medical bills by illegal profits. Though his pride is bruised as an over-ripe banana, he keeps his mouth shut.

"Now for the worst news: Mary Cook," says the judge.

"That broad again? Any catastrophe that she's *not* involved with?"

"Oh, I forgot. Before we talk about her, there's some other bad news. It's your car. I assume it's that black Lincoln parked down in the handicapped stall?"

"Yeah, what about it?" asks Oscar.

"Well, the handicapped signpost is sticking through your front windshield. It also looks like someone used the other windows for target practice."

"Ah, shit! That's what all the gunfire was about!"

"It must've happened just before I arrived. Sorry," but the judge's grin betrays his sincerity.

A tear zigzags down Oscar's cheek as he envisions his black beauty defaced by a thorn in its eye and shattered pride.

"Oscar, you irritate people, the olive pit that breaks a tooth. How the *hell* did you *ever* get elected mayor?"

"I've got friends in low places," says a grinning Oscar. "They found more dirt on my opponent than he did on me. So, what's this worse news about Mary?"

"At tomorrow's sentencing, she's gonna testify *against* a death penalty. She's going to plea on Jerome's behalf for a life sentence. Manning's attorney told me."

"Fucking bitch!"

"Fucking bitch is right. You remember how the jury was hung on a murder conviction?"

"Yeah, they stayed in there for almost a day and a half," says Oscar. "Hell, they were just milking it for the free room and board while sequestered."

"Well, some bleeding hearts, don't know who or how many, weren't quite sold on Anthony's testimony that Jerome was the mastermind behind the robbery. Imagine that, someone doubting Anthony's credibility, who having two years of college, including a police record as long as Rapunzel's hair, naively followed his partner who could barely write his name and had never been arrested."

"But they did arrive at a murder conviction," says Oscar.

"Only after I told them how important it was they reach a verdict. If they didn't, we'd have to retry the case, with all the court costs, time, and effort. But tomorrow, due to Mary's plea for Jerome's life, I guarantee those bleeding hearts will be emboldened just like David against Goliath. They could infect the whole jury with compassion, and kill a death sentence. Don't forget how *your* Citizens Committee has whipped *my* constituency into a frenzy for the Black man's blood. If it's a life sentence for Manning, it's a death sentence for my reelection!"

A moment of dead silence passes.

"So, what do we do, Charles?"

"Not 'we,' *you*. Keep your ass away from Mary. Don't say anything to the press and for God's sake throw some cold water on that Citizens Committee of yours if Jerome gets life. It's only a month until the election. In the meantime, pray to The Almighty that justice is served and the jury sends that Black son-of-a-bitch to his death!"

* * *

So as not to be seen together, the judge ordered Oscar to leave the knoll fifteen minutes after him.

Oscar, though bloodied, has survived the morning. But now, after he drives his half-blind car back to his office, he will have to browbeat Kevin just as the judge did him.

Oscar stares at his watch. *That asshole trooper's probably waiting, a regular Wyatt Earp ready to law-and-order me with another ticket. All in all, another shitty day.*

After the required fifteen minutes, Oscar leaves. Peter follows, delight gleaming in his face.

Oscar marches downhill in long strides. With each step, the prickle in his spine from the morning's imagined storm continues, including the feeling he is being followed. So every few minutes he peeks behind him, seeing nothing. During one of his back glances, he falls over a root.

"Shit!"

As Oscar pushes himself up, the tingle in his back explodes with the force of a grenade striking the base of his skull. Around his shoes and trousers, tangled like dust-encrusted hair nets, clings a slivery maze of spider webs.

Chapter 48

Exhausted

Gravel's angry growl ceases as Oscar steps off the path, through the fence, then onto the prison's parking lot. He approaches his car. Just as the judge said, someone had shot out the Lincoln's windows and harpooned the front windshield with the handicapped sign pole. Even though his blue placard (illegally obtained) hangs from the mirror, someone possibly questioned his vigorous exit from the car. Teeth grinding, his eyes rake the parking lot for the prison guards in the two monster pickups he encountered earlier this morning. Perhaps they grew a little miffed when he flipped them the bird. Perhaps they targeted his car with the assault rifles gloating in their trucks' rear windows. Fortunately, Oscar's search for the culprits fails. Another confrontation would leave him worse off than his car.

Hands clamped around the wooden post, he yanks it from the windshield, heaving it over the fence. A splinter pierces his finger.

"Shit!"

He discovers two folded slips of paper clamped under the wiper blade. One is a fix-it ticket for the shattered windshield, courtesy of Trooper Brandon. The other is a parking violation for occupying a handicapped stall with an expired placard, courtesy of a Washington County sheriff's deputy. Resembling a blue Frisbee, the placard skips through the air, somersaulting to a stop atop the crippled handicapped sign bent around the pole.

* * *

Preceding Oscar's arrival at his disfigured car, Peter reassumes his human form and drives back to Wilson's Jewelry. Once there, he again cloaks himself in transparency, standing in Oscar's office by the front window facing Acacia Boulevard. While he awaits the next event, a meeting between Kevin and Oscar, Peter reflects on the uncensored behavior of Judge Daring, Oscar, and Kevin. In the full bloom of their ugliness, Peter has witnessed the hatred, bigotry, and conspiracies against Jerome, including his beloved Mary. As he stares through the window, tears trickle down his cheeks, the sorrow flooding his soul.

* * *

After battling over three hours of traffic, Oscar parks in the alley behind his business. Unlocking the two deadbolts on the back entrance, he enters the building, throwing a backward glance at his battered black beauty.

What a fucking morning!

Into the Buying Room, he trudges, secures the alley door, and flips on the light. He stares at the room's only decorations—photographs of Michael. Oscar reflects on Judge Daring's threat this morning to stop "fuckin with stolen jewelry." Oscar's brow wrinkles. Yeah, it'll stop for a while, but nothing on earth is gonna come between me and Michael. Not that pompous-ass judge. Certainly not that Black bastard Manning!

He unlocks the steel-clad door to his office, enters, then drops into his leather chair. Staring at the crooked, partially drawn window shade, he contemplates his next move, unaware of Peter. Meantime, since nine o'clock this morning, as ordered by Oscar yesterday, Kevin has been waiting in the adjacent showroom.

Like a wooden drum, Oscar's desk vibrates under his tapping fingers. When they are not drumming a rhythm, his fingers claw at the still-itching wounds from last night's bed bug onslaught.

Hopefully, the sores won't get inflamed, but after the past twenty-four hours, if they do, a private hospital room would be a vacation.

Oscar glances at his watch, 3:30 p.m.

"Dammit, I forgot about Cook!

"Cook still there?" he says, yanking the receiver from the desk phone.

"Yeah," says the salesperson.

"Tell im to get his ass in here!"

Oscar slams the receiver. *Fucking worm. I gotta dump that Mary crap on him like the judge did on me. But at least this time, I'm the one shoveling the shit.*

Apprehensive as a mouse, Kevin creeps in, sitting at Oscar's desk with his back to the window.

"You wanted to see me again, Sir?"

Oscar locks his concentration on the minion across the table. One can almost hear the drum rolls of Kevin's heart.

"That wife of yours is a problem, Kevin, a real fucking problem!" he says. Stopping his tapping, Oscar hunches forward. "Remember The Palace? We had an understanding. You were gonna show Mary who's boss like any *man* would. Like I did with my . . ."

But Oscar stops mid-sentence as an image flashes in his mind—the body of his wife on the bathroom floor, her hand clutching the smoking revolver.

"Uh . . . Mr. Wilson . . . Mr. Wilson?"

Silence lingers as resolutely as a child's nightmare.

"Uh, Sir, I *tried* to do like you said, but I think it might've pushed her over the edge. And for all *my* trouble, I got thrown in jail."

"Excuses!" says Oscar, regaining his senses. "Well, you're *too* late. I've just learned that she's got a couple of ACLU lawyers comin over from St. Louis, stickin their noses in the Manning case.

Worse than that, she's gonna testify at the trial tomorrow on Manning's behalf for a life sentence."

Standing up, Oscar stomps around the desk. Deliberate as the grim reaper, he hovers over Kevin.

"If that Black asshole lives, I'm blamin you, *Kevin*!"

As Oscar storms back to his chair, Kevin's downcast gaze lands on Oscar's cobweb-encrusted shoes and trousers. Conscious of Kevin's attention, Oscar sweeps off the debris with a brush from a drawer. The heat of his anger chills as his mind wanders back to the ridge, conjuring this morning's images of an aberration under the elm, the screaming mob, and a black silhouette fleeing in the shadows of an imagined storm.

"Sir . . . Sir . . . ?" says Kevin, sinking lower in his chair.

Oscar shakes his head. For the second time, he had drifted into a daze.

"Sir, w-what're we gonna do?"

"W-what're we gonna do?" says Oscar, scrambling back to reality. "I'll tell you what we'll do. Nothing!"

"Nothing?"

"Leave her alone. That wife of yours is a mad dog. No telling who she'll bite next!"

His face glowing red as a winter's furnace, Oscar glances at the *Gazette* rotting on the desk. The publication's sordid details of Kevin's attack on Mary at The Palace summons as much anger now as the article did four days ago. Grabbing the newspaper, Oscar flings it, striking Kevin in the chest.

"Have it framed, *Kevin*, so you don't forget how you fucked up!"

At that moment on Acacia Boulevard, visible through the office window, a sight screws Oscar's face into a scowl: a speeding, red Corvette convertible brakes hard, parking on the opposite side of the street from the office. The female driver, sporting sunglasses, her head crowned with a black and red bandana, just sits there. Leisurely as a movie star, she adjusts the rearview mirror while applying lipstick. Around her neck, a crimson scarf sags behind her seat, a deflated flag waiting for the wind. Oscar leans forward, recognizing the celebrity as Mrs. Cook. Taking a writing tablet, he heaves the pad at the window. The glass pane reverberates from the paper explosion.

"Bitch!" Oscar says, pointing to the window while glaring at Kevin. "Take a look at what's happened to your life savings!"

"Oh God," says Kevin, twisting around, his face turning pale as talcum powder.

Peter smiles as the last shred of the tablet spirals to the floor.

"Heard she bought it yesterday after cleaning out the cookie jar," says Oscar, laughing. "Got it from Fillmore Motors, even though she *knows* I had im blacklisted. My boy, that bitch's got no respect."

"I . . . I'll see what I can do, Sir."

Kevin pushes himself up, a schoolboy ready to hightail it from the principal's office.

"Haven't you heard a fucking word I've said?" asks Oscar, as the words he is about to express sour like vinegar in his throat. "If I hear you're bothering Mary, that store of yours, Cook's Big an Tall . . . "

"Kevin's Clothing, Sir."

"What?"

"Kevin's Clothing. My store is called Kevin's Clothing."

"Yeah, whatever. I'll blacklist *that*, too. You'll have less clients than a priest preachin to a congregation of atheists. Now get the hell outta here and take your fuckin newspaper with you!"

Dismissing Kevin with a sweep of his hand, Oscar drops his head, pretending to concentrate on paperwork. Kevin, wringing the newspaper in his hands, slinks to the door.

"Oh, I'll stop by after six to pick up my new wardrobe."

"Wardrobe?" says Kevin, reeling about.

"Yeah. The new duds to replace the suit your wife threw wine on at The Palace."

"Uh, yes, of course. A new suit. How could I forget."

"No, not just a suit," says Oscar, lifting his head. "A *wardrobe*. You know, jacket, slacks, shirt, ties, and shoes, *including* laces. Don't forget the cashmere socks and silk shorts—seven pairs."

"Yeah, uh, stop by any time. I'll squeeze you in," says Kevin, his Adam's apple bouncing as fast as a ping-pong ball.

"'Squeeze'? A mortician sells more clothes . . . "

As Oscar locks eyes on Kevin, Peter glances outside. His face rises in a crescent moon grin at the sight he beholds. He yanks on the roll-up shade. The sharp slap of the recoiled curtain pulls the two men's attention to the window and the scene beyond. Outside, Mary's Corvette pulls away from the curb, stopping at a red light. Flicking her scarf, she glances back at the office, her freshly glossed lips twisted in a smile. The light turns green. In a flashing red streak, the Corvette squeals away, leaving behind Oscar and Kevin's pride to suck the convertible's exhaust.

Chapter 49

The Prosecution Rests

Spellbound as an audience before the final act's rising curtain, the gallery of the Barkersville courtroom rustles in excitement. Seven days ago, Jerome Manning was convicted of first-degree murder in the death of Timmy Cook. This Friday morning, the trial's sentencing phase begins to determine Manning's fate of life imprisonment or death in the gas chamber. Originally scheduled to convene three days ago, the proceedings were continued by Judge Daring, allowing Jerome's recuperation from wounds inflicted by a gang of white inmates in the Barkersville jail. All twenty members of The Citizens for Justice Committee are seated, including reporters, spectators, and witnesses.

Peter, in mortal disguise, sits in the courtroom gallery consisting of pew-style benches on either side of a central aisle. In front of him stands a three-foot-high oak rail, the "bar," separating spectators from the well where the trial will proceed. Arriving early, he sits at the right end of the front row, furthest from the aisle behind the defendant's table. Mary wants him here. As a benefactor, Peter knows he must endure the often painful manifestation of fate. But still, three days ago at The Palace when he had learned Scott was his long-dead father, Peter had asked for his companionship at the trial. Scott declined, saying, "Son, you are no longer that little boy waiting for daddy's return. Let go of the fear. Let Him lead." God at the helm is just what Peter is afraid of, another *Titanic*.

On Peter's bench wait witnesses who will testify for moderation of Jerome's punishment. To Peter's left sits Ms. Pinch, supervisor of the closed daycare facility, Open Arms, where Jerome once worked. Next to her, Alice Smith, Jerome's live-in girlfriend of six years, twists nervously, her arm coiled around her thirteen-year-old son, Nathan. Seated beside Nathan, Seymour and Nancy Lesterman watch the proceedings. The pair flick a wink at Peter. He returns their salutation, consoled that as fellow benefactors they share the knowledge of Jerome's fate. At the end of the bench next to the aisle sits Mary Cook, her hand nestled in Nancy's.

Peter waves at Mary who feigns a smile. He still marvels how she, after testifying this afternoon against the execution of Timmy's killer, will tolerate the community's loathing. Never has Peter met someone who has such compassion and courage. *Oh, if only I was human again, sharing ten thousand tomorrows with her. But I only have a few days until I start my self-imposed exile from her. I hope she'll forget me, find love in mortal arms, but I'll never forget her.*

Testifying in aggravation of punishment, a two-man firing squad sits across the aisle: Kevin Cook, and the owner of Mother's Groceries, Dale Peterson.

Peter scans the courtroom. Through the audience's din, he can hear journalists scratching on paper like chickens clawing for food. Reporters fill a third of the pews; no surprise. This is the dirt in which supermarket tabloids grow: two parents in court, one testifying for, and the other against capital punishment for their only son's murderer.

Into the well shuffles the defendant, Jerome Manning, his turban of bandages a testament to his beating. He winks at Alice through his non-swollen eye, smiling at Nathan who sniffles, trying to hide his tears. Alice, cheeks wet with emotion, squeezes Nathan tighter. Both stare in horror at their beloved. He sits at the defendant's table to their right in the well.

Bernard Stockmeier, the court-appointed defense counsel, talks to Jerome. Stockmeier, a five-year law veteran, is a young, blond-haired, narrow-framed man of angular features, whose only previous attempt in defending a capital punishment client is nothing of which he brags.

On the opposite side of the well sits the state prosecutor, Zackery Thurman, arms folded across his chest as though a Confederate general. The counselor's graying hair atop his military countenance hints at his twenty years' experience, including a 92 percent conviction rate.

Peter has never entered an arena of law. The polished marble walls accented with oak panels arouse a discomfort of callous intimidation as cold as the courtroom's décor.

The jury box, an oak bleacher filled with a white inquisition of ten men plus two women, rises at the defendant's right. The court clerk takes his place in front of the judge's bench which looms above the court as though a high priest's pulpit. The door to the judge's chambers opens. A gray-uniformed bailiff exits, followed by the black-robed judge.

"Please rise for the honorable Charles A. Daring of the 13th Circuit Court, State of Missouri," says the bailiff.

"Be seated. All parties ready to proceed?" asks the judge, taking his place at the bench.

Both counsels reply yes.

The judge states this is the sentencing stage of the trial. He reads the jury its instructions. Afterward, Mr. Thurman will open with arguments for the state followed by Mr. Stockmeier for the defense.

Thurman makes his opening statement to the jury.

"As you have already heard during the guilt phase of this trial, on Friday, February twelfth, in this year of 1988, Jerome Manning, during his commission of an armed robbery of Mother's Groceries, did shoot to death eleven-year-old Timmy Cook. You, the jury, have convicted Mr. Manning of first-degree murder for this heinous act. Due to the three aggravating circumstances of this murder—the use of a gun during the commission of a felony, the endangerment of persons other than the victim, and the young age of the victim—the state will be asking for the death penalty.

"I shall call two witnesses to these aggravating circumstances. They have previously testified in the guilt stage: Kevin Cook, Timmy Cook's father, and Dale Peterson, proprietor of Mother's Groceries. Mr. Cook will tell us of the horrifying crime scene when he discovered his son's lifeless body. Mr. Peterson will tell us about two previous robbery attempts in his establishment, comparing them to the much more vicious crime of Mr. Manning. As the nature of Mr. Manning's actions is so important in determining his punishment, I shall ask your patience as Mr. Peterson repeats some of his prior testimony about that terrible night. It was only through his heroic efforts that he and Mr. Cook themselves survived the violent crime.

"Ladies and gentlemen of the jury," says the prosecution, pointing at Jerome, "in the name of God and His Almighty justice, send that monster to his death!"

Thurman marches to his chair. "Death" reverberates from the polished walls as though uttered by a chorus from hell. The gallery explodes in applause, followed by a pounding gavel.

"Order in the court!"

Stockmeier slaps Jerome's thigh, then approaches the jury for his opening statement.

"Ladies and gentlemen. We shall ask for life imprisonment, which in Missouri means the defendant will not be eligible for probation or parole for fifty years. We will present three witnesses to testify in mitigation of punishment. That means they will testify for the lesser of the two punishments. I will first call Ms. Betty Pinch, a supervisor at the Open Arms daycare facility where Jerome had worked for three years as a janitor before its closure.

I will then call Ms. Alice Smith, Jerome's live-in companion for over six years. For our third witness, the defense will call Mary Cook, Timmy's mother."

As Stockmeier names the last witness, the jury glares at Mary. The gallery's gasp of surprise sucks air from the room in a vacuum of disdain. Mary sits quietly, her face impassive as porcelain.

The prosecution calls Dale Peterson, who takes the stand. The clerk reminds the witness he is still under oath.

"Where were you on Friday night, February twelfth this year, around 7:00 p.m., the time of the robbery and murder?" asks the prosecution.

"I was at the store."

"And as you have previously testified, you were working the cash register. The only other person in the store was Mr. Cook, who had parked his pickup out front while his son waited in the vehicle. Is that correct?"

"Yes."

"Mr. Peterson, would you again briefly tell the court of the events that followed."

"Well, Mr. Cook was payin for some ice cream when two men with stockings over their heads busted in. Both had guns and aimed em at me. I felt like a bullseye in a fuckin shootin gallery!"

"Mr. Peterson," says the judge, "please refrain from profanity."

"Sorry."

"Please continue," says the prosecution.

"One of em walked up and stuck his gun in my face. Told me to put both hands on the counter. He was wearin a short sleeve shirt. I could tell by his arms that he was a Black guy," says the witness, wiping sweat from his forehead.

"That Black man was Mr. Manning, correct?"

"Yes, Sir."

"Mr. Peterson, have you been robbed before?" asks Thurman.

"Yes, Sir, twice."

"How would you describe those first two robberies in comparison to the one by Mr. Manning?" asks the prosecution, facing the jury.

"Those fuc . . . clowns, in the first two holdups, were real amateurs. You could tell they were scared by the way they talked—nervous like—hands twitchin. The first one was a white guy. I keep a gun under the counter. When he asked me for the money, I opened the register with one hand, then grabbed the gun with the other. When he seen it, he ran off like a scared rabbit. Same thing happened in the second robbery. He was a Black guy. Only when he started runnin, I got a shot off. Hit the bast . . . I mean the man . . . in the arm. But he got away."

"Seems you are quite proficient with a pistol."

"I got three shootin trophies. An in the army, I was a sniper in Nam; seen *lots* of action with Charlie," says Peterson, puffing himself up in the chair.

"Considering your military experience, being under fire, your competency with weapons, why was the robbery involving Mr. Manning so different from the other two?"

"That Black guy," he says, pointing to the defendant, "was real cool. He held that gun at me steady as a rock. I remember thinkin you never hear the shot that kills ya. His partner was shakin so bad I didn't know if he was gonna accidental-like pull the trigger or crap in his pants. The Black guy says, 'Cover me while I get the cash!' But that's when we heard the police car siren. Guess he thought someone had seen what was goin on and called the police because that's when the Black guy changed his mind an took off runnin."

"You said earlier that this first patrol car went on past."

"Yeah. I couldn't believe it didn't stop."

"Tell us what happened next," says Thurman.

"I grabbed my gun, then shot the Black guy in the leg. He hit the floor; blood all over."

"What was Mr. Manning's partner, Anthony Gallon, doing while all this was going on?"

"He just stood there like a deer in the headlights, his gun aimed at my head. Then *he* started runnin, slipped in the blood, and fell on top of Manning. That's when both guns fired at once."

* * *

"Why they keep lying like that?" says Jerome, leaning over to Stockmeier.

"Don't worry, Jerome. I'll get to that, again."

* * *

"You then covered the two men with your weapon while Mr. Cook called the police," says the prosecution, his knife-sharp eyes dissecting the jury.

"Yeah. After makin the call, Mr. Cook ran out to his truck. That's when I heard im screaming after findin his son was dead. The police showed up about three minutes later."

Crying, Mary buries her face in her hands, a waterfall of tears flowing through her fingers. Nancy hugs her. Sobs stained with muffled curses punctuate the pall shrouding the room. The judge's gavel raises to command order, hovers, then lowers quietly to the bench.

"No more questions," says the prosecution, then sits.

Peter, observing the courtroom's reaction, notices Oscar sheds not a tear. Quite the opposite, his cheeks swell, plump as overripe tomatoes above his smile which is no surprise to Peter. He understands Oscar knows all about the store owner's lies. All as planned.

All as part of Judge Daring's conspiracy. A murder conviction with a death sentence assures Daring's victory in the upcoming reelection.

Peter sighs. *Justice is dead, a ghost, just like it was eighty-nine years ago at my death sentence. This vaulted stone and varnished oak is no different than a gallows of bark and limbs.*

"Objection!" says Stockmeier. "The witness is grandstanding. This testimony isn't relevant!"

"Overruled!"

The defense, walking to the witness stand with a document clutched in his hand, begins his cross-examination. Every eye in the courtroom follows.

"Mr. Peterson, may I call you Dale?"

"Yeah."

"Dale, tell me, when Jerome Manning was running away, did his accomplice, Anthony Gallon, still have his gun aimed at you?"

"That's what I just said!"

"That's interesting," says Stockmeier, holding up the document, "because it says in this transcript of the guilt phase, you testified, and I quote, 'the other guy,' referring to Anthony, 'lowered his gun and looked out the glass door when he heard the siren.' So which statement is correct?" asks the defense, glaring with a hawk's eye.

"I, uh, I guess I was a little confused. He *did* have his gun aimed at me, even after the siren."

"Alright, let me get this straight, Dale. Jerome's running away, no longer a threat, and Anthony's still aiming his gun at you. How far away was Anthony?"

"About fifteen feet."

"And with that gun aimed at you, you still dared to pull your weapon from under the counter and fire at Jerome who was no longer a threat to you?"

"Yeah!" says Peterson, his face in a scowl.

"Dale, I'm impressed by *your* coolness. Possibly you were also 'a little confused' in your previous testimony as to *who* was in charge."

Stockmeier walks back to his table. He returns, clutching another document held up high.

"You'll remember this. Anthony's criminal record. Impressive, huh? His wrists must be callused from handcuffs."

The attorney slowly reads the ten accounts of suspected criminal activity. The eleventh, armed robbery, resulted in a twelve-year prison term.

"Jerome has *no* criminal record. As I stated during your first testimony, it seems odd to me, Dale, that Jerome would suddenly acquire the expertise and cold-blooded nature to conceive and commit this crime such that Anthony, a felon who's committed such an offense, just stands there shaking so hard you thought he'd soil himself?" says Stockmeier as he returns to his chair.

"Wait a minute! You're making it sound like I got it all mixed up like I was scared or something. I should'a killed the Black son-of-a-bitch. Would've saved us all this trouble!"

"So, what you failed to do then," says Stockmeier, leaping to his feet, "you'll finish now, even if you have to lie! No further questions, Your Honor."

The counselor sits, winking at Jerome. Peterson stomps off the stand, exiting the courtroom.

The state calls Kevin Cook. He is reminded he is still under oath. Thurman approaches.

"Mr. Cook, I realize this will be difficult, but could you please tell the court what *you* saw that Friday night of February twelfth this year as you returned to your vehicle at Mother's Groceries."

"Your Honor, with due respect to the witness," says Stockmeier, "I object to this line of questioning. We already have this information from the police reports."

"Overruled, Counselor. This is cumulative evidence. Mr. Cook, you may answer the question."

Kevin grapples for words as all watch the father struggling to speak.

Initially, Kevin's reaction saddens Peter, but Peter's pity decays to contempt. All through the trial, Kevin has upheld Peterson's lies. Kevin could alter fate, redeem his soul, and save Jerome's life by exposing the truth. But bankruptcy due to Wilson's boycott threat and fear of perjury outweigh Kevin's salvation. Justice rots within this marble mausoleum.

"It's alright, Mr. Cook, take your time," says Thurman.

"I still have nightmares about it. I have to take pills to sleep, but they don't help. The two masked guys are lying on the floor. Both of their guns had just gone off. Peterson had his gun pointed at em. After calling the police, I ran out of the store to the pickup. The passenger's window on Timmy's side was rolled down. At first I didn't see him. Thinking he's hiding on the floor from all the shooting, I looked inside. The radio's playin, and it's dark and hard to see. I see Timmy lying on the seat sideways like he's sleeping. That's funny, I thought, him sleeping through all that commotion. But as my eyes adjusted to the dark, I saw *it*. The driver's window, all cracked with a hole in it. It's covered with blood an . . . an pieces of . . . I . . . I . . . see more blood on the seat. I don't remember anything after that except screaming."

As Kevin breaks down, sobbing, Peter leans forward, looking at Mary. She is crying too. He pulls a handkerchief, but Seymour has already offered his.

"Mr. Cook, if you'd like to be excused while you compose . . . "

"No! I want to tell the rest!" he says, lifting his head as he tells how he and Mary are getting a divorce. "I'm seeing a psychiatrist. He says separations after something like this are common. And," he shouts, pointing at Jerome, "it's all that bastard's fault!"

"The prosecution rests," says Thurman and settles in his chair, arms folded.

"No cross-examination, Your Honor!" says Stockmeier and turns to Jerome. "Best Cook gets the hell off the witness stand."

The witness is permanently excused. Judge Daring declares a ninety-minute noon recess. Spectators exit the gallery. In the hallway, the committee congregates around Kevin, offering condolences. Mary, tears streaming down her cheeks, enters the hall escorted by Peter. The committee blocks their way.

"Would you please let us pass?" asks Peter, holding Mary's hand.

Through a crack in the crowd, Mary, Peter, and Jerome's supporters run the gauntlet of hate.

Chapter 50

The Punishment

Noon recess ends. The static of shuffling feet fills the gallery as reporters, spectators, and witnesses retrieve their seats. The bench behind the defendant's table swells with Jerome's friends: Peter, Ms. Pinch, Alice, Nathan, Mary, plus the Lestermans. Behind the prosecution on the opposite side of the aisle, Oscar, Kevin, plus the Citizens for Justice Committee huddle like vultures on a limb. Gavel pounding, Judge Daring summons the courtroom back into session.

Stockmeier calls his first witness, Ms. Betty Pinch. After she is sworn in, the defense asks:

"Ms. Pinch, do you know the defendant, Jerome Manning?"

"Yes, I do," she says, casting Jerome a smile. Betty testifies she first met him thirteen years ago at the First Baptist Church of Barkersville where she ran their daycare facility, Open Arms. Jerome was homeless. He begged for food, sharing it with his fellow homeless companions. Betty grew to trust Jerome, then persuaded the church elders to hire him as janitor. They soon allowed him to help in daycare. Sleeping in the basement, he received meals and a small stipend as he worked for nine years until the city closed the facility. "But his real talent was the way he treated the children."

"And how did Jerome treat the children?" asks the defense.

"He was polite and kind and played all kinds of games with them. It was like he was a kid himself."

"Would you say Jerome was someone who could be trusted?"

"Yes. We were *very* careful who we let work with the children. The mothers trusted Jerome, too."

"Ms. Pinch, tell us about the mothers," says Stockmeier, approaching the jury.

"They were extremely suspicious of strange men. Many were victims of abusive relationships. But not one *ever* said they felt uncomfortable with Jerome. In fact, one of the mothers, Alice Smith, started dating him. They began living together, planning to get married."

The defense ends the questioning. The prosecution begins his cross-examination.

"Ms. Pinch, were you a staunch supporter of Open Arms?" asks Thurman.

"Yes, I was."

"Do you know why Mayor Wilson, with the City Council, closed it?"

"They said it was a concern about public safety. They said the center brought in quote 'undesirables and people with questionable character.'"

"Yes, but you still fought to keep it open, knowing it was endangering the lives of the neighborhood's good citizens."

"Objection, Your Honor. Hearsay," declares the defense.

"Sustained. Strike Mr. Thurman's last comment from the record. The jury will disregard the prosecution's statement."

"No further questions, Your Honor," says Thurman, marching to his table.

Stockmeier throws his chair back, approaching the witness for a redirect examination.

"Let's get something cleared up, Ms. Pinch. How long was Open Arms in business?"

"Almost eleven years."

"And in all that time, was there ever any violence or criminal activity at the center?"

"Never!"

"No further questions."

The witness is permanently excused. The defense calls Ms. Alice Smith.

"Wish me luck," Alice whispers to Nathan as she rises from her seat,

She takes the stand. After swearing to tell the truth, she states her name.

"Ms. Smith, do you know the defendant, Mr. Manning?" asks the defense.

"Yes, I do," she answers, wiggling her fingers at Jerome who wiggles back.

"And how long have you known him?"

"Bout six years. Me and Jerome we met at Open Arms, the one Mis. Pinch just talked about."

"Would you please describe the relationship you had with Jerome."

Peter watches as Alice straightens up, her sight aimed at the jury, just as instructed by the defense when all the witnesses testifying for Jerome met earlier this morning.

"It was wonderful, specially the way he and Nathan got along. Nathan, he was six then and them two played a lot of checkers. Jerome, he always let my boy win. Nathan, he liked Jerome and that was how I come to like im too. After a couple'a months, Jerome, he came to live with us. It was real nice havin a man around. He never got mad at us or nobody else; always real polite. Jerome, he tried helpin us with the money and even though we was poor, he always got us something for our birthdays. My boy loves im like he's his real daddy, don't you, Nathan?"

Alice winks at her son in the front row.

Nathan nods in agreement.

"Ms. Smith, did Jerome ever talk about his childhood?" asks the defense.

"He ain't the kinda man that say much bout himself. But he did say it wasn't good." Alice relates how Jerome often left his abusive, drug-addicted mother after she beat him "an go see his Auntie Helen for a couple'a days. She live someplace outside'a Jeff City. She weren't really his aunt, but she treated him like kin. One day, Jerome, he made up his mind to stay for good."

"Ms. Smith, it's all right if you say exactly why Jerome decided to stay for good."

Alice stares at Jerome who nods his approval.

"He say he went to live with her cause his momma done been killed by one'a her boyfriends."

"How old was Jerome when he went to live with Auntie Helen?" asks Stockmeier, pacing in front of the jury.

"He didn't exactly say. I suppose he was around eight."

"What happened next?"

"Jerome, when he got older, he got himself a part-time job and bring the money home. Auntie Helen, she make im go to school but she died before he finish."

"Do you know what grade he was in?"

"Don't know. He say he was around fifteen when she passed."

"Probably the ninth grade," says Stockmeier. "What happened after Jerome's aunt died?"

"Jerome said the sheriff, he come by and was gonna take him some place for kids that ain't got no folks. Jerome, he ran away and ended up west'a town down by the river where all them home-less people stay, that place they call Camp Hilton. He got to know a lot of folks there; they all helped each other. They liked Jerome cause he always bringin em food and tarps and things from that church Mis. Pinch belong to. She gave im that job. He and Mis. Pinch, they got to be good friends, and well, you know the rest from what she said."

"Thank you, Ms. Smith. No further questions."

The defense sits, slapping Jerome's knee as Thurman, tucked in his profession's typical glum demeanor, approaches the witness stand.

"Ms. Smith, where is Nathan's biological father, or do you even know who he is?"

"Objection!" says Stockmeier. "I request that remark be stricken from the record."

"I'm simply trying to establish the witness's character."

"Objection overruled," says the judge, turning to Alice. "Please answer the question, Ms. Smith."

Peter feels Alice's public humiliation. Stockmeier warned her the prosecution would sink to this line of questioning. When asked if she still wanted to testify. Alice answered, "Yes, I do!"

"Sir," says an erect Alice, "I ran away from home, too. I was gonna have me a baby. It was because of what my daddy done . . . He the bastard that done rape me when I was fourteen."

The courtroom sinks into a mire of silence. Through a pool of tears, Alice stares at Nathan.

"I done hate to be tellin this in front of all these people, but dear God, I had'a try an do somethin up here to help the man that's been the daddy my boy shoulda had."

"Your Honor, the witness is obviously distressed. Could we have a brief recess while she regains her composure?" asks Stockmeier.

After Alice declines a recess, Peter cringes at the next line of questioning.

Thurman describes the couple's six-year relationship as, "sinful relations out of wedlock." He emphasizes Jerome's inability to obtain employment after the daycare closed, all over Stockmeier's futile objections.

Ms. Smith," says the prosecution, "we've heard sworn testimony earlier in the trial that Jerome participated in several home burglaries during the time he lived with you. Were you aware of these criminal activities?"

Alice lowers her head, paralyzed for words.

"Ms. Smith," commands the judge, "will you please answer the question."

"Didn't know exactly, but I suspected he was."

"Did you inform the police of his unlawful behavior?"

"No, but . . . "

"Do you realize that could make you an accessory to his crimes?" says Thurman, walking away. "No more questions."

Stockmeier raises to redirect his examination.

"Ms. Smith, did Jerome search for employment after losing his janitor's job?"

"Yes, Sir. First he try every day. But nobody gonna hire a Black man that got no good schooling, specially one that useta work at that daycare that Mr. Wilson shut down. Folks they scared'a what Mr. Wilson gonna do if they did."

"And Ms. Smith, regarding *your* character, do you have a job?"

"Yes, Sir. I'm a waitress at the Howard Johnson's. Been there almost eight years."

"Do you attend church?"

"We go to The West Side Baptist Church *every* Sunday," says Alice, sitting high. "I sing in the choir. The director, he say I'm pretty good. He let me sing 'Gather by the River' all by myself."

"And your son, Nathan, do you see that he goes to school?"

"Yes, Sir. He in the seventh grade an gettin A's an B's."

"No further questions, Your Honor."

The witness is permanently excused. She takes her seat next to Ms. Pinch. Jerome flashes a smile at his beloved.

"You did just fine," whispers Betty, taking Alice's trembling hand.

But Peter abstains from the moment's joy, watching a sour-faced

Oscar Wilson scribble a note. Oscar's frown twists into a smile. As a result of today's testimony, Alice will become unemployed.

"The defense now calls Mary Cook," says Stockmeier as he winks at Jerome.

With the hiss of serpents, whispering wriggles through the gallery. Peter's spine twitches. He surveys the audience, seeing the Citizens Committee collectively narrow its eyes, glaring at Mary as she takes the oath.

"How are you this afternoon, Mrs. Cook?" asks the defense, approaching the witness stand.

"Fine, thank you," she says, but her quivering betrays her answer as she sets her purse down.

"Mary, I know your presence here is difficult, and excuse the questions I must ask for the record. Will you please identify yourself?"

"Mary Cook, mother of Timmy Cook, the boy killed in the Mother's Groceries robbery."

A collective hush envelops the courtroom.

"Do you personally know Jerome Manning?" asks the defense.

"No, not personally."

"Have you been threatened to testify on his behalf?"

"No."

"Do you stand to gain monetarily or in any other way from your testimony?"

"No."

"Mary, considering your husband's earlier testimony, your presence on behalf of the defendant is *highly* unusual," says Stockmeier, walking to the jurors. "Tell us, Mrs. Cook, what *is* your motive for appearing before the court?"

Only the scratching on notepads disrupts the silence. Judge Daring shifts closer to the witness. Peter can almost feel the room tilt as all lean forward.

"*My* motive?" asks Mary, straightening up. "The question is, what's the *court's* motive?"

"Objection!" shouts the prosecution, springing to his feet.

"Let me redirect. Mrs. Cook, what do you think's the purpose of these proceedings?"

"I still object," says Thurman. "The witness' opinion of these proceedings is immaterial."

"In consideration of the special circumstances of this witness," says the judge, "I'll allow this question. But be careful where this leads, Counselor. You may answer the question, Mrs. Cook."

"The purpose is to determine if Jerome committed murder, and if so, what's his punishment."

"Mrs. Cook," says Stockmeier, "the defendant's been found guilty of first-degree murder. The state wants the death penalty. Capital punishment, some say, acts as a deterrent for murder. What are your thoughts about capital punishment as a deterrent?"

"You mean killing to stop killing?"

"Yes, you could put it that way."

"If executions were a deterrent, instead of sitting in this witness stand, I'd be home waiting for Timmy to come back home from school," says Mary, staring at the twelve people to her left.

Not an eye blinks in the jury box.

"Mrs. Cook, what punishment would you prefer?"

"The law says since Jerome used a gun in the robbery, the *only* options for punishment are life imprisonment or death. I choose life! I *know* that's what my Timmy would want, and shouldn't his desires be considered too? He had no lust for blood like a lot of people in this town. If my son were here in this room, he'd walk up to Jerome and say he forgives him—that life imprisonment *was* a just punishment. This trial isn't about justice. It's about vengeance; making sure the Black man dies.

"That testimony from Anthony, saying Jerome was the

mastermind of the robbery, I don't believe a word of it!" she says, glaring at Wilson. Then her gaze shifts to the jury. "And I'm worried what'll happen to Jerome's adopted family, Alice and Nathan, especially Nathan without a father figure."

Thurman objects, saying Manning should have considered this before committing the crime.

"Overruled, Mr. Thurman." With eyes flashing hard as the marbled walls, the judge glares at the defense. "You may continue, Counselor."

"What would you say to those also thinking Jerome should've thought about Nathan before he committed the crime?" asks Stockmeier.

"I believe Jerome's basically a good person. He only committed the robbery because nobody'd hire him because they were afraid of Oscar Wilson. Killing Jerome only adds more suffering for Nathan, Alice, and *me*. And it sure doesn't help Jerome. Is any law that causes that much more suffering, just?"

"Your Honor," says Thurman. "We're not here to justify the law."

"Your Honor, the witness is simply asking a rhetorical question," says Stockmeier.

"I'll allow the testimony, but again, watch where this is going, Counselor."

Peter leans back on the bench. *I'm no lawyer, but I've done some research. Daring's gotta be very tolerant. This case, especially the penalty phase, will be appealed before Missouri's Supreme Court. To avoid a new trial, he's gotta be fair and impartial, even at the risk of over-leniency.*

Stockmeier approaches the jury box.

"'Only adds more suffering . . . ' But how else shall we protect ourselves from crime?" he says, resting his hands on the railing.

"What about the crime of children like Jerome growing up in

fear of violence? Why can't we be a society of love? Love needs no law. Without love, we commit the crime of indifference. And *our* punishment? More dead Timmys," says Mary, tears seeping into the corners of her mouth.

"I *must* object to the witness' statements about the law," says Thurman. "They sound more like the defense's closing argument than testimony in mitigation of punishment."

"Your Honor," says the defense, "Mary's testimony on behalf of Mr. Manning is highly unusual. But I ask for the court's continued leniency, even concerning her opinions."

"Objection sustained," says Judge Daring. "This has gone far enough. You will confine further inquiries to matters specifically concerning the defendant."

"Yes, Your Honor. Mary, is there anything more you'd like to add about Jerome?"

Peter, knowing what Mary is about to say, again pushes himself against the bench.

"Yes, Sir, there is. But first," she says, staring straight at Jerome, "I want you to know I forgive you for what happened. I hope you can forgive *us* for allowing the injustice of your childhood." Turning her attention back to Mr. Stockmeier, Mary says, "A moment ago, you asked if I was threatened to testify on Jerome's behalf, and I said 'no,' but I've been threatened *not* to!"

The room rattles in subdued chatter.

"Order!" shouts Judge Daring, slamming his gavel.

"Threatened! By whom?"

"I don't know . . . anonymous letters . . . phone calls. It started a few days after a secret meeting of the Citizens for Justice Committee that Kevin and I attended. It was held last Saturday at a bar called The Palace. Wouldn't surprise me if one of those letters came from Mr. Wilson."

"Your Honor," says Thurman, "Wilson is not on trial!"

"Mrs. Cook," says the judge, "I said further testimony must only concern . . . "

"And at that meeting, Wilson said the judge had personally assured Manning would die."

The courtroom erupts in a volcano of shouting. Reporters claw over each other, scrambling to the exit. The prosecution shouts objections. The gavel slams like a sledgehammer breaking stone.

"Order! Order in the court!" says the judge. "Strike that last comment from the record! Members of the jury, you will disregard the last statement!" Then aiming his oak mallet at Mary, he says, "Mrs. Cook, given the stress you've been under, you're obviously not of sound mind. I'll disregard that last outburst, but *one* more word from you and you're in contempt!"

"Your Honor, the defense rests!"

Thurman declines cross-examination. Permanently excused, Mary marches back to her seat.

Declaring a fifteen-minute recess, the judge storms into his chambers. After the courtroom regains composure, he returns. Ordering the court back in session, he gives the jury several legal instructions. The prosecution's closing arguments then follow, again citing the three aggravating circumstances for capital punishment: the victim's age, the use of a gun in commission of the crime, plus the endangerment of other lives. The defense argues against the death penalty, reminding the jury the bullet which killed Timmy was never found. The round could have come from Anthony's gun, who is only getting manslaughter. After the judge gives the jury their final instructions, they retire to deliberate a verdict.

Hours pass as friends and foes of the defendant cluster outside the courtroom. Panting journalists return. The curious leave, remaining within earshot of radio and TV. All await the jury's decision. At 6:58 p.m., the bailiff announces the jury's return.

"Mr. Foreman," asks Judge Daring, "have you reached a verdict?"

Alice grabs Nathan. With her other hand she grasps Ms. Pinch. Mary clasps her hands as if in prayer. Stockmeier's hand rests on Jerome's shoulder. Peter's gut churns in anticipation of the pre-destined announcement.

"Your Honor," says the foreman, "we're unable to decide on a sentence."

The courtroom hums with confusion. Witnesses for the defense whisper from side to side. Jerome turns, staring at Alice. Peter cannot believe his ears. *Has fate had a change in heart? Is it possible Jerome's gonna live?*

"Order! Order in the court!" says Judge Daring, then faces the foreman. "This is the second time the jury has been hung. I remind you of the importance of reaching a decision. I ask you to think about a verdict tonight and deliberate tomorrow."

"Your Honor, further deliberations won't help. We're hope-lessly deadlocked on a verdict for life imprisonment or the death penalty," says the foreman, glaring at the two women jurors.

Thanking the jury for their service, Judge Daring dismisses them. After the bailiff escorts the jury from the room, the judge declares:

"According to Missouri law, if the jury cannot reach a decision on the sentence, the judge shall impose punishment." He then states that the evidence presented establishes the three aggravating circumstances beyond a reasonable doubt. "Let the record reflect that the jury, having found the defendant guilty of murder in the first degree of Timmy Cook, it is the judgment of the court that the defendant's punishment be fixed at death."

With the gavel's crash, fate proclaims victory.

Chapter 51

Leader of the Pack

For two hours from the bench at Phantom Ridge, Peter has waited for the sun to climb from its Friday night's slumber. He clutches a copy of yesterday's evening edition of the *Gazette* with the headline:

"Manning Gets Death"

Peter's mood mirrors the flowers on his grave, flowers placed there two days ago by Trooper Brandon, flowers wilting in September's heat.

Dad had agreed to meet me here after the trial. Hope he remembers.

Recent events have temporarily dampened Peter's joy of driving. So, Peter tele-transported himself here while his Corvette waits under the shade of a Barkersville acacia tree. Twisting the paper as though it were a wet rag, he tries to wring the cesspool of news onto Mother Earth.

"Hi, Son," sounds from behind.

"Hello, Dad," says Peter, relieved.

"I bet the last four days since we met at The Palace seem like forty years," says Scott, sitting.

"Time dies when you're feeling glum."

Scott eyes the tortured *Gazette*.

"I understand your frustration," he says, "but you knew the court's decision before the judge had slipped on his robe."

"Yeah, but knowin the future doesn't ease its pain," says Peter, setting the newspaper down. "The irony. Though Mary's testimony led to a hung jury, it allowed Judge Daring to make the death sentence, guaranteeing his re-election. Better if she'd never testified. The jury would've decided on death, but at least Daring would've been robbed of the glory."

"Some good will come from this," says Scott, slapping Peter's leg. "Take Jerome's defense attorney. At the start of the trial, Stockmeier could care less about people like Jerome. But witnessing the system's injustice, he will make a career representing the disenfranchised, though mowing lawns would pay more.

"Notice how Mary has grown in character. She confronted the committee, Kevin, *and* Judge Daring. Besides the two women jurors responsible for the hung decision, her testimony moved many in that courtroom. And her statement of forgiveness to Jerome gave him comfort. Her self-confidence will serve her and others well.

"Good *will* eventually triumph in its battle over evil, but there will be casualties."

"Casualties? All I see is an endless graveyard!" says Peter, slamming the newspaper to the ground. "As for Mary, my love's been drawn to her like a six-year-old to a puppy. But like everything else I've endured as a benefactor, it's doomed. Damnit, it's all His fault!"

Peter points skyward.

"The fault lies within you, not Him. Again, I say it is an unjust world. But what you fail to change you must learn to accept. Otherwise, you will forever live in the hell of The Beast. Learn from Mary. She has endured the horror of Timmy's death. When she helped Jerome, she knew Kevin and the community would hate her. But she accepted these misfortunes. Acceptance is not a hopeless resignation to adversity. Acceptance is a willing acknowledgment you are sometimes unable to avoid it. As eagerly as you do the light of joy, embrace the night of adversity. Both are His gifts, for in the darkness, blind and lost, is when you find Him.

"You still have that card I gave you at The Palace?" Scott asks, stroking Peter's shoulder.

From his shirt pocket, Peter removes the card. Still sticking to the paper is the scrap of fabric Monroe gave him here at the ridge, the fabric from the gown of The One who lifted Monroe from the depths of The Abyss. Both emit a yellow luminance. In gold letters, the card reads:

Leader of the Pack
I.M. Emmanuel
12 Grace Way, Barkersville, MO 65043

"Yeah, still got it, and no I haven't seen im, yet."
"You promised."
With a sigh, Peter yields to his father's request. Both agree to meet again here under the elm after Peter visits Emmanuel.

* * *

The Grace Ward, a fifteen-minute drive from Wilson's Jewelry, lies downhill in the decaying lowlands district hugging the Missouri River. However, Grace is the last thing the ward gets. When the river floods, this neighborhood drowns under three feet of turbid water.

The sun stands on the horizon's edge at the birth of its daily arch. Peter's Corvette slinks through the alley edged by discarded mattresses, overturned garbage cans, plus a prowling pit bull. *What the hell am I doin in this cesspool?*

Avoiding eye contact with the locals, he stops at a driveway identified by a rusted mailbox labeled *12 Grace Way*. He turns into a dirt clearing where twelve Harley-Davidsons are lined up parallel to a corroding chain-link fence. The motorcycles, boasting their gleaming chromed-steel frames, elevated handlebars, and high-back leather seats, starkly contrast the enclosure's decay. Peter parks behind a fifties-something pickup with a corroding bed gorged with trash. Exiting his car, he pulls the top up, then locks the doors, protecting his precious cargo. *The BOOK* still lies on the passenger floor, with its protective leather satchel in the rear well.

Surveying the area, he tries to ignore the tirade of a German Shepherd. The dog's target of attention is the pit bull lifting a leg on the Corvette's front tire. The Shepard strains on a leash nailed to a weathered building shedding paint faster than scales off a dead fish. Approaching the windowless eyesore, Peter gawks at the entry, a metal-clad door adorned with the painting of a Black Virgin Mary straddling a chopper. His lips coil in a grin, wondering how this painted heresy has escaped the townspeople's flaming wrath.

The building rattles to the beat of sixties rock and roll as Peter approaches the door, then knocks. Heartbeats pass. No answer. *Thank God!*

He knocks again, praying nobody hears the summons through the musical mayhem. If no answer this time, he can leave. At least he can tell Scott he tried. But just then, the door squeals open revealing a burly, tattooed man in a leather vest, twirling a length of chain.

"What'd ya want?" he asks, cigarette exhaust billowing from his nostrils.

"Damnit," mumbles Peter, flashing the yellow card.

"Come on in," says the greeter, stubbing his cigarette in his hand.

Glancing at his red beauty, Peter enters, wondering if the car will still be shod in gleaming wheels when . . . if . . . he returns.

Visions of The Palace congest Peter's thoughts. A jukebox

continues a rendition of sixties nostalgia, singing, "Sergeant Pepper's Lonely Hearts Club Band." The odor of stale beer mixed with cigarette smoke poisons the air. Tenacious as Velcro, the floor sticks to his shoes. The only light violating the darkness is a golden glow from the back of the room.

Peter observes two men at a pool table, each flipping a billiard ball. One looks Asian, the other is brown-skinned with angular features. The visibility of such detail in the pale light surprises Peter. The two watch Peter as he shadows his escort to the far end of the room. Therein lies a long rough-plank table littered with beer cans scattered around a green gallon jug of a Gallo Vin Rosé centerpiece. On a bench behind the table sit ten men, all but one engaged in conversation while drinking canned beer. Their tattoos, greasy blue jeans, and narrowed eyes remind Peter of Hell's Angels.

The silent guy twists a dented cup of tarnished metal between his black leather-gloved hands. Though his Black complexion plus beard seem congruent with the group, his other features are out of place as roller skates in a morgue. A spotless, white robe clothes him shoulder to ankle. In one ear dangles a gold ring. Chest-length dreadlocks drape from his head. But the robed man's most striking feature is his golden halo which illuminates the room.

Stopping at the table, the escort whispers into the robed man's ear whose blue eyes bounce between the guide and Peter. The cup's rotation ceases. Whispering matures to conversation.

"Sit. Emmanuel wants ta talk to ya."

The chaperone skids a chair in front of the table, stomps to the jukebox, then turns down the volume. Grabbing a beer from the refrigerator, he throws himself on the bench. His three feet of linked steel chain clang to the floor. The two gentlemen from the pool table join. Thirteen pairs of eyes glare at Peter.

Aching from dread, Peter wants to bolt to the door, but leaving without even a "hello" to this Emmanuel guy will incur Scott's wrath, and possibly the guard's chain. Peter sits.

"I've been expecting you, Peter," says Emmanuel. "Welcome to our humble establishment."

The target of the blue-eyed stranger's gaze, Peter squirms in his seat. Never has he seen a brother with blue eyes.

"How'd you know my name?"

"Your father said you'd be coming. Somebody grab a Bud for our friend."

"Uh, no thank you, Sir," says Peter.

"No 'Sirs' here, just me, Emmanuel.

"Oh, excuse my manners. I haven't introduced you to the gang. You've met Peter, your escort, and our sergeant-at-arms." Turning to the sarge Emmanuel says, "Peter, meet Peter."

As the sergeant's beer strikes the table, a geyser of foam lands on his calloused, extended hand. Peter shakes the hand of a forearm tattooed with a black *LOVE* across a crimson heart.

Emmanuel nods down the table. "The guy at that end is Simon, then Thaddeus, Matthew, and next to him . . . " continuing until all twelve are introduced.

A page unfolds in Peter's memory: his mother by the fireplace speaking of Apostles as she cites names from the "Good Book." *Can't be!* A muscle knots at the base of his skull.

"Boys, why don't you make your rounds? Give Peter and me some time alone."

"Okay, Boss," says the sarge. Grabbing his chain, he gulps the last of his beer as he heads out the door. Eleven pairs of boots scrape after him. While the sarge guards the door, walls rattle, and dust sifts from the rafters as eleven choppers roar to the street.

Peter cannot imagine what mischief occurs on those rounds. But alone, alongside Emmanuel, he breathes easier, confident if necessary, he can outrun a guy in a bathrobe wearing an earring.

"Kind of intimidating, aren't they? Hard to believe they're *all* benefactors," says Emmanuel.

"Yeah, benefactors," says Peter, rolling his eyes.

"Not *just* benefactors—ambassadors. Next to me, the highest-ranking benefactor. Master benefactors report to them, and they to me."

"Ambassadors, huh? Okay. Dad's a master benefactor. Which hoodlum does he report to?"

"Simon, and he said you'd be coming."

"Oh, I get it, like the game—Simon Says," mocks Peter, rising from the chair. "Something's screwy here. If it weren't for Dad's insistence, I would've left this menagerie the minute your maid, Igor, darkened the door. Then there's you in white with that halo looking like a birthday candle on steroids. What makes you the head honcho?"

"I'll answer that with another question. Why did Scott want you to come by?"

"That's what I've been wondering, but it sure as hell wasn't to watch a twelve-pack of fugitives suck beer," says Peter.

"Those fugitives travel the world on their chromed chariots assisting other benefactors. They're *my* representatives."

"And just who the hell are you?"

The room trembles. Shards of light spark from the halo, condensing in a spiraling flame. Peter drops to his chair, his mouth awash in fear's metallic taste. As the flame slips back to a subtle glow, Emmanuel slips into a grin. His sapphire eyes penetrate Peter's soul.

"Like the card says, I'm the *Leader* of the Pack."

Grabbing his cup, Emmanuel empties a mortuary of flies plus a desiccated spider onto the table. With Vin Rosé he fills, then slides the cup to Peter.

"Oh, ye of little faith could use a drink. Hmm . . . last time I used this cup was at a bon voyage dinner with the boys. Seems like only yesterday. Bottoms up!"

"But I said I don't . . . " says Peter, scrutinizing the red concoction's surface swirling in an iridescent rainbow, reminding him of metal etching acid.

"Peter, would your father have sent you if I were not trustworthy? Just a sip. The brew is rumored to have restorative properties."

His mouth puckering in noxious expectation, Peter lifts the cup. Liquid splashes onto the table from which billows a purple vapor. Saying a prayer, he sips, but instead of dissolving enamel, the liquor flows between his lips tasting of honey, followed by a sensation of warmth. Finishing the cup, he asks for a second, followed by a third. A feeling of being caressed in his mother's arms seeps into his body and soul, a shaft of light piercing anxiety's shadow. Peter's ice-caked eyes melt.

"Are you God?" he asks, cup clamped in his hand.

"No, but we dwell together in the same house. How would you like to feel as you do now for the rest of eternity?"

Eyeing Peter, Emmanuel leans forward, prying the cup from Peter's grip. Afraid any word or movement might sever this ethereal emotion, Peter matches Emmanuel's approving gaze.

"I was hoping you'd agree. But to achieve this blessing requires more than a sip from this cup. You must be willing to follow my advice, to do *everything* I ask. Are you? Are you willing, Peter?"

The rapturous buzz fades. Vinegar replaces the sweet liquor's taste. Peter slumps in his chair, sullen, angered by this psychic manipulation.

"Willing? Willing to do what?"

"To surrender your superstitions about control. Place your trust in me and a Higher Power."

"Higher Power? Just say it—God. You know how I feel about Him!"

Thunder rumbles in the distance. In a spasm of fear, Peter scans the rafters, bracing for the lightning bolt from above.

"Fear not, for I am with you," says Emmanuel, his blue eyes sparkling.

"You suddenly my protector?"

"Kind of, if He doesn't accidentally hit me."

Peter's eyes roll in a scowl.

"Lighten up, oh ye of little faith," says Emmanuel, drying the cup with his sleeve. "Considering all that's happened, I understand your anger. It was long ago, but I too had doubts."

"Sure you did . . . "

"Look, do you still want to be a benefactor or not?"

"I *am* a benefactor!" says Peter, his ego pushing him up in the chair.

"Let's be honest. You like the *idea* of being one, but you're not there yet."

"What do you mean? I've helped Mary and been trying to help Jerome. Dad even said I did a good job at the Citizens for Justice Meeting."

"All true, but the problem is you want to control the outcome," says Emmanuel. "You've decided what's right, what's wrong, then used all your powers to accomplish those ends. But when it doesn't work out the way you think it should, you blame Him."

What's with this white-robed guru telling me . . .

"Yeah, I get pissed at God, but who wouldn't with all the evil He permits?" says Peter.

The room rumbles. More dust sifts from the rafters.

"Enough! God doesn't permit evil. He *permits* you, *permits* mortals to act out of two emotions, love or fear. Out of love, your acts blossom into gratitude, charity, joy, and acceptance. Out of fear, they decay into jealousy, greed, hate, and blame. Fear sentenced Jerome Manning to death. Fear lynched you. Fear killed James Thornton."

Peter slumps at the mention of the white man he killed in "self-defense."

"When you killed Thornton," says Emmanuel, taking a chair next to Peter, "you descended into the hell of the lynch mob, Oscar Wilson, and Judge Daring. You've been trying to convince yourself you're better than these damnable associates. *That's* been the driving force in your benefactor apprenticeship."

What his ears wish not to hear, Peter's heart cannot deny. Yet, he must defend himself.

"But when I changed from The Beast to human form that day on the ridge, I really did want to help others! It wasn't *all* about me!"

"I know," says Emmanuel, rising and walking back to his bench. "Benefactor service is hard. That's why most souls avoid our ranks. Your father sent you because he loves you enough to let go and let me try to help. That is *if* you are willing to do all that I ask."

"But haven't I been working hard already?"

"That's the trouble, *you've* been doing all the work. You haven't let Him help. That too comes from fear. Free yourself from fear. Admit to yourself, to God, and to another soul the wrongs you have committed, then make amends. Accept that mortals, even other spirits like you, are all fallible. Then you can serve out of *love* and discover you're no longer fighting God; He's become a partner, a source of strength. That's how you become a benefactor."

"How the hell can I do all that?"

"You don't do it alone. You do it with me, and you do it because you *want* to."

"But what makes *you* so qualified for this?" asks Peter, standing up in defiance.

Emmanuel stands. Removing his gloves, he thrusts his palms across the table.

"*These*," he says, eyes flashing from one hand to the other. "*These* make me qualified!"

Peter's breathing quickens. In horror, he diverts his gaze, but his eyes twist back. Before him hover two tortured palms, each possessing a gaping wound.

"Are . . . are you Jesus?"

Chapter 52

Sand Gets in Your Eyes

In the darkened silence of the meeting hall, a Black Jesus cloaked in white stares at Peter.

"Why don't we take a ride?" says Emmanuel, re-gloving his mangled hands.

No answer from Peter, whose gaze is still stapled to the black pair of gloves.

"Alright, Peter, let's get this over with. No, my hands don't hurt. The reason they don't is because, just like you, I'm a spirit void of flesh, blood, and pain. Now, let's go."

Emmanuel saunters to the front entrance, his white robe a flag flowing above each stride. Still in disbelief, Peter follows obediently as a puppy.

"We'll be gone for a while, Peter," says Emmanuel to the sergeant-at-arms as they exit the building. "Anybody stops by, take a message."

The sarge fakes a salute, standing guard, resolute as a minuteman statue.

Emmanuel strolls to the German Shepard leashed to the building. The Shepard recoils from side to side with each swing of its tail. After petting the dog, Emmanuel fills the water bowl, then heads to a pickup rusting in front of Peter's car.

"Ah, shit!" says Peter upon seeing his wheelless Corvette jacked up on pallets.

He runs to, then circles his crippled beauty with a physician's attention, performing triage.

"Don't fret," says Emmanuel. "They just took the tires and rims."

"You *know* who did this?"

"The guys. They know how much you treasure this mortal status symbol. But don't worry, they'll re-shoe it after they've had their fun. In the meantime, we'll take my car."

"And where's that?" asks Peter, twisting his attention around the property.

"Right here."

As Emmanuel slaps the pickup's hood, brown dandruff falls from the fenders.

"This? But the tires are all flat."

"Not a problem," says Emmanuel, snapping his fingers as the wheels perform a Lazarus transformation into the rims and tires of Peter's Corvette.

"Adds a little class to the ol rig, don't you think?"

Peter crosses his arms. Showoff!

"And I suppose you're gonna change *that* into a camper shell including a TV, stereo, and air conditioning," Peter says, nodding at the overflowing bed of fly-infested garbage.

"Nice suggestion, but I think we'll stop with the wheels."

As Emmanuel pries the driver's door open, the hinges squeal in pain. Tucking his robe under his legs, he slides in, slamming the door. The passenger door opens, then closes in similar discomfort. Head down, Peter searches the torn Naugahyde seat.

"What are you looking for?"

"The seat belts," says Peter.

Shaking his head, Emmanuel flicks the ignition. Making a tuberculosis cough, the engine responds, farting black smoke, then brown shrapnel from the tailpipe. Shaking as though riding on square tires, the truck rattles through town, turning onto Highway 94, trash rising from the back like the dead on Judgment Day. But as the garbage ascends heavenward, the rubbish evaporates in the air. Emmanuel's dreadlocks flay about in a fury of mating snakes.

Peter twists on the bench seat, his sweaty shirt a Post-it note sticking to the simulated leather. Perspiration stings his eyes which dart between his window and the white-robed driver.

"Okay, what's with the Black disguise?" he asks.

"Disguise?" asks Emmanuel, innocent as a day-old lamb.

"Jesus is supposed to be white, just like all those pictures and statues of him, I mean you, on the cross show."

"Does my appearance offend you, Peter?"

Peter's attention drifts to the tree-bristled landscape crawling past. No, I don't feel offended. Maybe a little guilty for enjoying the perks that come with being white.

"No, it doesn't bother me, just surprised you chose to be Black."

"I didn't choose. *This* is who I am, who I've always been. Out of fear that a Black man could have been the Redeemer, others chose to bleach my complexion and make me white in their likeness," says Emmanuel, a tear rolling from the corner of his eye.

"Why don't you *do* something about this lie? Isn't that what good people, your faithful, expect? Or does everyone have to wait for your Second Coming when all will be made right?" asks Peter.

"I have faith in mankind, faith in its ability to love one another while striving for peace and justice, even in this chaotic world. My so-called Second Coming and Rapture was dreamt up by some good-intentioned zealots. But reappearing as Jesus, let alone a Black one would cause more of a mess than things are now. I've never really left, just been here working behind the scenes with the twelve ambassadors, my former disciples, not to mention bene-factors like you. That's why I've kept this identity. Who's going to pay any attention to a Black guy dressed in a white bathrobe? And as for this halo," says Emmanuel, pulling to the side of the road, "when I'm with strangers, I turn it off."

Peter nods in agreement. When I first saw Emmanuel, other than that halo, I wasn't, and still am not, impressed.

"Okay, about your disciples. Why the disguise as chain-twirling motorcycle thugs?"

"Would *you* stop one of those 'thugs' from making their appointed rounds?"

Peter sighs, staring out the windshield.

The pickup drops into low gear, scrambling onto the pavement. Emmanuel fights the steering wheel as though holding a mad dog by the collar.

"So, where we goin?" asks Peter.

"On a quest."

* * *

The truck bounces onto a dirt road. After an hour, the passing woodlands surrender to the desolation of a rockbound expanse. Through the boiling air, the sun stares intensely as a raptor's eye. The road degenerates to a narrow lane, then to a track of gravel which fades into a dirt trail snaking its way up to a distant ridge. As the trail becomes impassable, Emmanuel turns off the ignition.

"First stop. We walk from here," he says.

"I'm not setting foot outta this truck til you tell me what this 'quest' thing's about!"

"Peter, you're going to have to trust me."

I don't trust. Trust makes me vulnerable. Well, maybe Dad, a little . . .

"The quest of which I speak is a search for the strength I mentioned back at the meeting hall, the strength that comes from Him. The strength *you'll* need to become a journeyman benefactor."

"Find strength in *this*?" says Peter, sweeping his hand at the terrain, barren as bleached bones. "That'll be a surprise."

"Surprises are His way of getting our attention. Surprises make us aware of possibilities other than our 'plans.'"

This guy's wise sayings are getting on my nerves.

"To find the strength of which I speak, we shall visit three spirits."

"The Ghosts of Christmas Past, Present, and Future?"

"To make this quest, remember, you must be willing to do all of which I ask. Will you make this commitment, Scrooge? Yes or no?" asks Emmanuel, his eyes narrowing.

Peter glances up the hill. *Dad wouldn't have asked me to visit this Emmanuel guy unless he trusted him. I guess I can trust him too . . .*

"Yeah, I'll do everything you ask."

"Good," says Emmanuel, stepping out of the pickup. He points to the winding trail. "*That* leads to the first encounter."

As Emmanuel begins the ascent, Peter trails behind. *You'd think a guy who could turn water into wine would conjure something more spectacular than a cow path; Moses parted a sea.*

Peter trudges behind Emmanuel up the zigzag trail, dodging boulders scattered amongst outcrops of stone. For hours, they climb. Reaching the crest, Peter hears distant gunfire.

"Down there," says Emmanuel, pointing over the edge of a cliff, "in The Abyss."

Peter leans forward. Below him lies a deep, narrow canyon, a jagged laceration in Mother Earth's skin. The floor of the chasm seems to be a slab of pure granite blemished by swirling funnels of dust and dirt. Hot as a dragon's breath, heat rises from below where a man sledgehammers a boulder three times his height. Peter is reminded of a prisoner toiling in a chain gang, but no shackles bind this man. Behind the laborer lies a windrow of sand, straight as a surveyor's line, disappearing into the haze of the ravine. In front of him beyond the boulder, a strip of neatly arranged, smaller stones stretches to the opposite end of the canyon. Each hammer's blow blasts a minutia of stone fragments with a firecracker's blast, followed by a barrage of obscenities.

"Looks like something out of Greek mythology. Who is that guy?" asks Peter.

"Our first spirit."

"Yeah, I can see that, but . . . "

"James Thornton."

Peter prickles from apprehension. His killing of the white man in "self-defense" has gnawed at his soul as persistently as termites in a rotting stump.

"Poor old James," says Emmanuel. "What he failed to learn in life he is condemned to search for in death."

"What did he fail to learn?"

"Forgiveness."

Peter's trepidation chills, settling in his spine.

"So, what's with the rocks?"

"They're his resentments. Each stone represents a hate in his life. His mother-in-law who ridiculed him. The merchant who wouldn't give him credit. Black people. The list is endless.

"Just before you killed James, we retrieved his soul. We gave him three choices. He could go to Sanctuary, and spend eternity in bliss. Alternately, he could remain on earth seeking vengeance on those whom he hated or help other distressed mortals. Sound familiar?"

Peter's gaze drops to the ground.

"James wanted none of that 'love or help crap,' he wanted revenge. So, we showed him the stones, each laid out in the sequence he had acquired them in life. We then gave him the sledgehammer. Told him to crush the stones, and after each blow, he should try to release his anger. James asked, 'But how's that gonna get me revenge on them I hate'?"

Peter wonders the same thing.

"We said those responsible for the resentments *might* suffer pangs of conscience as he banged away. 'But,' we cautioned, 'others have pounded for years achieving no results.'" Emmanuel sighs, saying, "Know what he said? 'No results, huh? Well, they ain't been hittin them rocks hard enough. I'm gonna make *sand* out of em!' That was eighty-nine years ago."

Wafting up from the valley comes a "Fuck you!" followed by another blast of case-hardened steel against the mountainous mass.

"*That* must be *some* resentment!" says Peter.

"Yes, that one is *you*, his last resentment. He's been working on it for two years."

The prickle in Peter's back surges down his arms to his fingertips. He recalls the remorse over Thornton's death started two years ago when he transformed from The Beast to an apprentice benefactor. Peter wonders if there is something to this sledgehammer thing.

"But if that boulder's his last resentment, what's all those other rocks past it?"

"The same ones he's already broken. Until he surrenders to love, he's sentenced to an eternity of smashing stone into sand."

"Well, from where I stand, I can see he's exhausting himself for nothing," says Peter. "And from where he stands, James can only see the boulder. Well, I've seen enough," he adds, heading back to the path when Emmanuel grabs his arm.

"Not so fast. You have an appointment with James. Tell him of his futile efforts you've seen from here. Talk to *him* like Scott talked to *you* when you were The Beast. And one more thing. Tell James you're sorry for his death. It's called 'making amends.' He *might* even accept your apology. If he does, that's one less rock. You'll have eased your conscience and, at the same time, eased your portion of his pain."

"Look at im! He'll never buy an apology. Why even try?" I was afraid it might be comin to this. I'd rather play catch with a hornet's nest than humble myself before that white bastard.

"Whether James accepts your apology or not isn't your concern nor the reason you're here. You do remember *why* you're here, don't you, Peter?"

"To help me become a full-fledged benefactor?"

"Halleluiah! Remember, strength comes from Him, the strength needed to become a benefactor. Just as the rock blocks James' view, your guilt of his murder blocks you from the strength. Atone, humble yourself, and your guilt will vanish surely as the echoes of James' cursing."

"What the hell," says Peter, staring down into the void. "I've come this far . . . "

"Forget something?" asks Emmanuel.

"What?"

"Your appearance."

"Need to comb my hair? Polish my shoes?"

"You're still white."

"Oh, yeah, that."

Peter has become so accustomed to his disguise that his Black identity has become the facade. Requiring a surprising amount of concentration, Peter's bleached veneer darkens to his weather-rutted original Blackness. His clothes change to ragged pants, a tattered shirt, and half-soled boots.

Descending the jagged slope, Peter notices the sun dimming in a clouded sky. As darkness increases, so does his sense of fear, the fear he felt as The Beast trembling under the shadowed elm. He stops, cowering against a wall of rubble when Emmanuel's hand touches his shoulder.

"Fear not, for I am with you."

Emmanuel said this playfully in the hall when a superstitious Peter feared The Almighty's bolt of lightning. This time sincerity resonates in Emmanuel's words. The sky's cloud of gloom evaporates. Both spirits descend to the bottom of The Abyss.

"There he is. Go, Peter. You can do it."

Peter peeks from behind a rock. What the hell do I say to the man I . . . I killed?

"Will . . . will you help me?" he asks, turning to Emmanuel.

"We've been waiting a *long* time to hear that," says Emmanuel, his smile wiggling his beard. "Go, Peter. The words will come."

Across the hard-hearted expanse stumbles Peter. Tripping over remnants of hate and the waste of loathing, he stands beside Thornton. Stone shrapnel speeds past. Thornton stops his labor.

"Who the fuck are you?"

"I'm Peter. I'm . . . I'm the guy who stabbed you."

Callous eyes flashing, Thornton studies the intruder. Like the trembling of a hare before the coyote's fatal bite, Peter awaits the response, stunned by Thornton's lack of recognition. But Thornton turns away. He swings his hammer, hurtling skyward more splinters of stone and obscenities.

"Uh, Mr. Thornton, didn't you hear me? I said I'm the man who killed you."

With vengeance's determination, Thornton continues assaulting the igneous mass.

"You here like the other guy this mornin?" asks Thornton, his gaze impaled on the boulder.

"What guy?"

"The one sayin he's sorry for havin Charlotte evicted from our house after I died."

Peter recalls Charlotte, Thornton's wife, was dragged to the lynching by order of The Accuser. He demanded she testify Peter had killed Thornton in cold blood, but she refused.

"Well, to hell with both of ya!" he says while he continues swinging at the boulder with the fermented hate of eighty-nine years. "Take that, you fuckin son-of-a-bitch!"

Peter looks for Emmanuel, but he stands unseen at the base of the distant ridge.

"James," says Peter, summoning all his courage. "I deeply regret what I did. I should've walked away. Though I can't undo my horrible deed, I've been trying to redeem myself by helping others."

Thornton pounds away. After a frenzied flurry of blows, he stops. Stepping back, he admires his work, a puny pile of rubble at the base of his calcified resentment.

"Not bad for two years of work!" he says.

By his tone and absence of eye contact, Peter suspects Thornton is talking to himself, oblivious to or simply ignoring Peter. Staring at a pile of chips barely a foot across, Peter feels pity for him.

"Eighty-seven years I've been bustin them rocks," says Thornton, casting a satisfied glance at the row of sand behind him. "But it's worth it! I finally got to this one, that fuckin Black bastard who went an stabbed me!"

Peter steps forward, faces Thornton, then grabs his hammer before another blow.

"For your sake," says Peter, uttering the words he swore he would never speak, "may you be blessed with the peace of forgiveness."

Blind to Peter's presence, Thornton turns as though searching for a distant, indistinguishable voice. Peter hugs the impassive figure, releases the hammer, and walks away from the once all-consuming regret. Behind him, the hammering resumes, fading with each step.

Chapter 53

Pilgrim

The pickup, straddling ruts deep as the Grand Canyon, descends the road back to the highway. As though riding a pogo stick, Peter clings to the door of the bouncing truck. Staring out his window at the passing desolation of stone, he basks in a glow of peace unexperienced since reverting from The Beast. He forgets two more visitations await in his quest when a peculiar sight snags his attention. Ahead on the right side of the road stands a Caucasian gentleman dressed in a neat, brown business suit, holding a bulging briefcase in both hands. The man stares forward, reminding Peter of a commuter waiting for the morning bus.

"Give him a lift?" asks Emmanuel.

"Yeah, I guess so," says Peter, "but that guy sure seems out of place in this no man's land."

Preoccupied with the situation, Peter has failed to reassume his white disguise. And Emmanuel has failed to extinguish his glowing crown.

The truck pulls over.

"Where you headed?" asks Emmanuel through Peter's open window.

"Barkersville," says the gray-mustached man, adjusting his sunglasses.

As the man speaks, Peter shudders. That voice . . . I've heard it before.

"So are we," says Emmanuel. "You're welcome to ride in the back if you don't mind the trash."

Without a word, the stranger slings his briefcase over the side, then climbs into the bed. He flinches not an eye at the fancy wheels out of place with the rusting truck, the trash threatening to soil his suit, or the yellow luminescence encircling the driver's head.

The stranger's unconcerned behavior raises Peter's suspicions.

A grinning Emmanuel shows no reaction, stares ahead, then shifts into low gear. After several coughs, the pickup's butt-bruising ride resumes.

"What you fellas doin way out here?" asks the visitor through the glassless rear window.

"I was gonna ask you the same thing," says Peter, head twisting back. "I'm Peter and that's Emmanuel."

Peter waits for a reaction, but the man acts as impassively as watching clothes tumble dry.

"Pleased to meet you. Just call me Mr. B. I'm on my way to meet some old acquaintances."

"Business related?" Peter asks.

"Uh, yeah, you could say that."

"Whatever you're sellin," Peter says, nodding at the sterile geography, "I'd say you drew the short straw on districts. What line of work you in?"

"Well, I'm sort of a door-to-door provider of atonement."

"Atonement provider? Hmm. That some kinda lawyer, or a holly roller preacher?"

"Neither."

"What's in the briefcase?" asks Peter, continuing his inquisition.

"List of people I'm meeting."

"Looks awfully thick for just a list of names. Kinda like the Saint Louis phone book."

"Indeed. It is a ponderous list," says Mr. B.

Awkward silence and zigzagging flies fill the cab. Peter taps a rhythm on his knee. He recalls Thornton's statement earlier today about some "other guy" who had previously visited him, making amends. Peter stops his tapping. Old acquaintances, atonement . . . Strange.

"Anybody on that list I know?" Peter asks.

"Yes."

"A James Thornton?"

"Yep."

Peter swallows, struggling to expel the next words.

"Am I?"

Mr. B nods yes.

The truck hobbles to a stop.

"I'm here," says Mr. B, removing his sunglasses, "to make amends for the pain I've caused in your life. Remember? You paid me a visit in my apartment years ago."

Peter's eyes narrow, trying to picture Mr. B's face minus the moustache when his mind flashes back to a seventy-year-old memory. In a dark, one-room apartment, an old man lies asleep on a bed. Peter, The Beast, hovers over the man. In the hallway outside, a young woman pounds on the room's locked door, yelling the name Marvin.

"I remember," says Peter, rage creasing his face. "You were on your deathbed. I visited you when I was The Beast. You're . . . you're . . . "

"Yes, Peter," says Mr. B, tears soaking his mustache, "I'm Marvin Boyers, the man who owned your family as slaves. The man who tore your family apart by selling your father to a slave trader. The man who led the mob that lynched you. I'm . . . The Accuser."

A volcano of emotion erupts from the caldron of Peter's past as Boyers touches Peter's hand.

"To say I've caused you pain diminishes the hell you've suffered," says Boyers, coughing to clear the emotion wedged in his throat. "I've come to express my sincere regret for my actions."

But Boyers' touch feels hotter than crematorium embers. Glaring at Emmanuel, Peter yanks the handle of the door which opens with an aching grind. He strikes the ground as the pulsating ache of The Beast claws to be unleashed.

"Bless you my child," says Emmanuel, taking Boyers' hand. "I feel the heartfelt sincerity of your confession. Both you and Peter shall benefit from your loving act of humility."

They shake hands. A sobbing Boyers descends from the bed and trudges down the road, disappearing in the distance. Exiting the pickup, Emmanuel approaches Peter.

"I can't believe it," says Peter, contemplating his feelings of betrayal. "Why the hell didn't you *tell* me I was seeing The Accuser next?"

"A quick, clean confession was best for both of you. Will you accept?"

With a boxer's determination to throw the knock-out blow, Peter searches the truck for Boyers.

"Where'd he go!"

"That's not your concern. He did what he came to do and left. Further conversation would decay into pointless reprimands on your part."

"Pointless?" says Peter, his mind blistering with the image of his body hanging from the elm.

"Yes. This meeting was painful, but it was for your benefit . . . and his. Will you accept his apology, forgive him?"

"No! Hell No!" says Peter, his voice as hard as the barren terrain. "I don't give a damn whose benefit this meeting was for, much less *his*. *He* put the noose around my neck. Chained us as slaves, tore apart our family! How can you possibly ask *me* to forgive *him*!"

"I ask nothing more than I have done to those who nailed me to the cross."

"That's easy for you to say. You're Jesus!"

Emmanuel's halo erupts like Fourth of July fireworks.

"It's nice to know my efforts have been so inspiring. I suffered a mortal's pain of death. But you, we spared that pain and took your soul before the snap of the rope."

The needle-prickling sensation of Peter's spine returns.

"You don't hold the Nobel Prize on suffering," says Emmanuel. Cocking his head, he scans the landscape. "You know, if I listen real hard, I can hear Thornton pounding away. Here, you'll need this," he says, and in his clinched, outstretched hand materializes a dangling sledgehammer.

Emmanuel slings the hammer into the bed, then climbs in the cab. Peter follows. Verbal silence consuming the interior, the truck stumbles from the gravel road and onto the highway back to Barkersville.

Pondering today's events, Peter's arm rests in the opened window through which blows a gale hotter than a rocket's exhaust. With a drunken snake's unpredictability, the pickup weaves back and forth across the center line when an approaching sedan yells with alarm. The oncoming car dives to the shoulder while the driver, still turned rearward, gawks at the pickup driven by a halo-capped Black man.

"A penny for your thoughts," says Emmanuel, oblivious of the near head-on which would have sent the sedan's driver to Emmanuel's father.

Peter sulks in his seat, his resentment over The Accuser's encounter growing with each sideways spasm of the pickup. *How could Emmanuel have been so callous? But I did agree at the start of this damn "quest" to trust and do everything he asked.*

He glances at Emmanuel fighting the steering wheel as though boxing Mohammed Ali. Chuckling at the performance, Peter breaks his silence.

"Alright, we need to talk."

The pickup slows, stopping behind a row of trees. Emmanuel's attention shifts to Peter.

"After my amends to Thornton, I felt a sense of peace I haven't experienced in years . . . like a heavy burden was lifted. Even surprised myself when I pitied him in his hell of resentment. But after The Accuser's visit, that weight's back, heavier than before because *my* executioner is probably feeling as good as I did after making *my* amends. That pisses me off! He doesn't deserve it!"

"*I* decide who deserves *it!*"

Helpless as a tumbleweed in a tornado, something snaps in Peter.

"Funny thing, Emmanuel, just being in your presence has affected me. I . . . I . . . can't explain it, but yeah, I can actually say I *should* forgive that bastard Boyers and that fuckin mob, something I couldn't have even imagined until after spending time with you in this rusted wreck. But I'm discouraged. Feel like a knight in shining armor tryin to swim."

"To bask in the light of forgiveness," says Emmanuel, embracing Peter, "one must leave the darkness of pride."

Peter's mind races with thoughts. He recalls the day he changed from The Beast to a human form. Out of pride, he could have remained the apparition, living forever in darkness, nurturing his hate like Thornton's endless pounding. But having never filled the void in his soul, Peter had grown weary of vengeance's turmoil.

"Fear not, I am the light," says Emmanuel.

A wave of love floods Peter. *What I did to Thornton was no better than what the mob did to me. To escape the fate of a voluntary hell, I have to shed my hammer and forgive. I'll be a provider of atonement for The Beast's vengeance. But how? Where will I in the eternity of the afterlife, find everyone I've tormented?*

"If we hurry, we can still catch Boyers," says Emmanuel. "But concerning the rest of the mob, they still cling to the hate they embraced in life. They have not agreed to see you."

"But Thorton did. Why not them?"

"Remember Thornton didn't recognize you? That's because his hate is so strong it blinds him to any effort of redemption. Though those in the mob hate you, they are not yet blind to redemption's light. They may still see."

Emmanuel starts the engine, ready to circle back to Boyers.

"I'll walk the five miles," says Peter, switching off the ignition. "Kinda like a pilgrimage of penance. But what about the rest of the mob?"

"Pray they also find the light."

The pickup door squeals open. Peter slides out and trudges up the road.

* * *

Shadows lengthen across the fields as Peter hurries up the knobby dirt road.

"Marvin, Mr. Boyers, hold up a minute. It's me, Peter. I'd . . . I'd like to talk to you."

Boyer stops, sets down his briefcase, and faces Peter.

"I was hoping to hear you say that," he says. "What's on your mind?"

Yeah, what is on my mind? What do I say to the man who planned my death? The man I haunted on his deathbed?

"I'm wondering," says Peter, "why you decided to make amends to me and all those others on your lists."

"Good question, but first have you decided to accept my apology?" says Boyers. "I'm not asking for your forgiveness— I've already troubled you enough—it's your choice. But forgiveness can lighten the burden of hate, and we could all lose a few pounds."

Peter hesitates.

Yeah, when I left the pickup, I intended to tell him I'd forgive him. But the funny thing is, it was easier to make amends, like I did with Thornton, than it is to forgive someone for the harm they did to me. Why? Forgiving is kinda like saying what they did was Ok. Well, it wasn't OK! So why am I here? For that matter, why am I on this whole "quest" thing with Emmanuel?

Peter feels the twinge of The Beast stirring within. Just then, in the distance, he sees the headlights of Emmanuel's pickup approaching in the evening twilight.

Hey, wait, those lights. Of course! The light of redemption. What the hell have I been thinking?

Peter reaches forward, grabbing Boyers' hand.

"I thought I'd never hear myself say this, but yes I forgive you, Marvin. By forgiving you, in a way, I'm forgiving myself for the sins I've committed. Bless you for coming here and making your restitution."

* * *

Scattered trees and rutted earth flash in and out of view of bouncing headlights until the truck rolls onto the highway.

"Where to now? Peter asks Emmanuel.

"To Barkersville and our third and final visit."

Chapter 54

The Cellar

The morning sun climbs from night's nocturnal retreat, casting shards of light between pillows of clouds.

Peter, propped against the door in Emmanuel's pickup, contemplates yesterday's ordeal with Boyers, The Accuser, the second of three visitations in Peter's so-called "quest" arranged by Emmanuel. Staring at the road unwinding before him, Peter wonders what purgatory awaits in his third and final visit.

Lurching through the western outskirts of Barkersville, the smoking pickup enters a residential neighborhood. An odd assortment of cars hems the street: Fords with wood spoke wheels, Studebakers, even a Packard, a few gleaming as though they just rolled off the showroom floor. On one side of the road, a white-uniformed man steps into a delivery truck. He carries a metal basket chiming in a symphony of clanging milk bottles. Across the street, two children play cops and robbers.

* * *

"Bang! You're dead, Bonnie Parker. Fall down!" says the boy.

"No, I ain't! Ya missed. I ain't gonna play dead," counters the girl.

"I'm the sheriff and I say I got you and your partner, Clyde," says the boy, then throws down his toy gun. "Ah, shucks. This ain't gonna work. Bonnie was white; you're colored, Lizabeth."

"Oh yeah? Well, I can still outrun you, Oscar!"

The two run squealing between two houses. Streaking around

a rear porch, they disappear into a backyard followed by a small, yapping, black and white dog.

* * *

"Where are we?" asks Peter.

"Back in Barkersville."

"Yeah, I figured that, but these cars, that milkman in his old panel truck," says Peter, rubbing his forehead. "I bet it's been fifty years since I've seen those things. Not to mention those kids playing Bonnie and Clyde. Don't tell me, we're back in the thirties?"

Nodding yes, Emmanuel pulls to the curb in front of a shabby residence, its dead lawn consistent with the dwelling's splintered siding and rust-infected screens.

"Here we are," says Emmanuel as the pickup sputters to a stop.

Peter glares at the decaying house which the two children ran behind. *I wonder what's so important about "here."* He notices beside the curb a crumpled mailbox inscribed:

Wilson, 16 West Channing Street

"Oh, shit! Is this where Oscar Wilson grew up?"

"Oh, ye of abundant intellect, yes. That boy you saw is Oscar, eight years old," says Emmanuel, grabbing the door. "Shall we make our entrance?"

"Wait," says Peter, still hearing the laughter of the two children from the backyard. "That can't be *him* playing with a *Black* girl . . . can it?"

"Like I said, shall we make our entrance?"

"We can't just show up unannounced. Two Black guys in a white neighborhood stepping from a truck over fifty years in the future. What the hell will they think?"

"They won't think anything. They can't see or hear us."

Emmanuel exits the cab. Sauntering up the remnants of a concrete walk, he climbs the porch stairs to the front door. The sleeve of his robe falling to his elbow, he motions Peter to follow.

Peter watches in dread. The cold prickly sensation announcing the two previous encounters returns. What am I supposed to do with an eight-year-old anyway? Offer him a cookie, a piece of bubble gum? Oh, yeah, I forgot we won't be seen or heard, but still . . . Ya know, I think I'll set this one out.

Peter scrunches in his seat, but before he can sink behind the pickup door, he finds himself standing next to Emmanuel in an ant-infested kitchen. Through the grimy window over a sink filled with food-caked dishes, Peter has a clear view of the backyard in which the two children play. The clink of a bottle pulls his attention to the kitchen table.

* * *

Slouched in a chair, an unshaven man in a bathrobe pours himself another glass of Green River Whiskey. Glaring through bloodshot eyes first at the glass, then at the two children, he mumbles in a drunken monotone to himself with an occasional "fuckin nigra bitch" cutting sharper than a knife through his slur of verbiage. Throwing back his chair, he staggers to the back porch's screen door.

"Get your ass in here, boy!" he screams.

The two kids' joyful antics freeze quicker than two field mice at the sound of a cougar's growl. The boy whispers to the girl. She turns, then runs away.

"I said get the fuck in here! Don't make me come after ya!"

Oscar, head downcast, approaches the house slower than a man to his gallows. His father waits for the boy to slink past, then slaps him to the floor.

* * *

Peter leaps toward the boy, but Emmanuel grabs him.

"There's nothing you can do. These are images of the past."

"Then why in the hell did you bring me here?" says Peter.

"You'll see . . . "

* * *

Oscar curls in a ball on the floor. Crying, he inches away from his father. At a safe distance, after he pushes himself up, he stands stone still staring at his shoes.

"What the fuck you doin with that colored bitch? I done said stay away from the likes'a *them*!"

"She was next door helpin her mom clean the Johnson's place," says Oscar between sobs. "She came out to get somethin an I asked if she wanted to play cops and robbers."

"I'm gonna teach ya what happens when ya play with them that's below ya. Good thing your momma's not here. Spare her the shame of seein what ya done!"

"When's Momma comin back from Aunt Cynthia's?"

"Wouldn't you like ta know! Always cryin on her apron when ya get hurt. Hidin behind her every time I try teachin ya to be a *man*."

The father stumbles to, then leans under the sink. He rifles through a garbage pail, exhuming a wadded sheet of paper which he waves high over his head.

"See this? She ain't coming back. Left a note sayin so!"

"Not comin back?" says Oscar, his tears stopping in shock.

"Yeah," says the father, his snarl inverting to a grin. "Said she's ashamed of ya. Don't want no sissy for a son. An that ya better do what I tell ya cause you're livin by my rules now!"

Oscar's perceived guilt that he caused his beloved mother's departure reads like a wrinkled epitaph on his face.

"I'm sorry," he says.

* * *

"Everything the father said is a lie," says Emmanuel, stepping between the boy and Peter. "The distraught mother left out of fear for her life."

"But how can she just leave . . . abandon her own son?"

"Don't judge her. The father warned if she ever tried to take the boy, he would kill them both. Alone then homeless, she was committed by authorities to a mental institution for a nervous breakdown where she died twenty years later. Oscar later heard of her confinement, but he never paid her a visit out of hate that she had abandoned him."

* * *

Squeezing Oscar's arm, the father yanks the kitchen's cellar door open, pointing downstairs.

"You're goin back down there till ya learn your lesson about who ya play with!"

"Don't, Daddy, you know I'm scared of the dark!"

"I'll let ya out when ya become a fuckin man!" says the father, shoving Oscar into the darkness.

The door slams shut. Minutes of sobbing pass before Oscar adjusts to the darkness. In a shaft of light through the cellar's window, fireflies of dust dance and twirl. Pressed into a corner lies a soiled mattress on which rests a worn copy of "Huckleberry Finn," a half-burned candle melted onto a saucer, matches, plus a yo-yo. Oscar lights the candle, then flips the yo-yo between his hands, tears glowing in the half-light.

From under the mattress, the boy retrieves a paper pad and pencil. On one sheet he draws figures of himself, including a little girl standing beside him. His image he leaves white. The girl's he blackens with his pencil, the paper drenched in drops of tears. Then, Oscar grips the pencil in his hand like a dagger, stabbing the pointed lead into the girl's image. From the pad, he rips the wet and perforated sheet, crumples it, then flings the paper across the room, crying.

* * *

First Peter, then Emmanuel, appear in the basement. Hand extended, Peter strokes the boy's hair, knowing his presence goes unnoticed.

"Can't you do something?" Peter asks Emmanuel. "We can't just leave him here like this."

Peter withdraws his hand. Emmanuel touches his arm.

"We must leave this figment of the past. There is nothing we can do."

Once again, Peter's soul aches from the clawing of The Beast. It yearns to unleash a hideous retribution on Oscar's father. The next instant, Emmanuel and Peter are sitting back in the pickup.

"I'll ask again, why did you bring me here?" says Peter.

"To be a witness."

"That poor child. How I wish . . . " he says while rubbing away a tear as his puzzled attention turns to the old house.

"Wish what? Do I detect a chink in that armor of hate you wear for Oscar the man?"

"That *child* changed into someone horrible!" says Peter, his eyes sliding back to Emmanuel.

"But that child is still there, locked in the dungeon of his soul, groping in the void for love. We all have dark pits which harbor ghosts of our past."

"We?"

"How quickly forgotten. My dark pit?" says Emmanuel, holding up his gloved hands. "Remember these? My experience could have gone the way of revenge, but He helped me through it. Oscar isn't *all* bad. Consider his grandson's battle with cystic fibrosis. Oscar helped pay for medical treatments the family's insurance refused."

"Yeah, but he paid with money from fencing stolen jewelry!"

"If the family's insurance had reimbursed them properly, he might not have been tempted to resort to such wicked deeds," says Emmanuel, sliding closer. "Evil assumes an enticing disguise. All eventually yield to its allure. Revere the image of the boy whose head you just stroked. You can't change his childhood, but as a benefactor you *can* lovingly affect his future. With this act of love, you can open yourself . . . to the strength."

Peter looks outside. Minutes stretch into hours, hours fade into twilight. Studebakers, Packards, and milk bottles evaporate, replaced with Toyotas, station wagons, and aluminum windows.

* * *

The black sloth of night passes. Peter wakes up to the rattle of morning chores. He finds himself in the pickup alongside Emmanuel, back at the meeting hall parking lot where he met the gang of twelve motorcycle-riding disciples two days ago. The gang, though still absent, atoned for their prank with Peter's Corvette. Not only have the wheels been restored, but they washed, then waxed his beauty, and even filled the tank.

"A tip would be nice," says Emmanuel, nodding at the car. "Cash. Drop it in the mailbox."

Grumbling, Peter yanks out a twenty.

"Before I leave, there's something I gotta know. It says here," says Peter, pulling out the glowing yellow card Scott gave him, "that you're 'Leader of the Pack.' Okay, what do you do besides boss around those twelve thugs on choppers and give guided tours?"

"Besides supervising my guys and chaperoning distraught souls, I determine who becomes a benefactor," says Emmanuel. He leans close to Peter. "Do you know why I chose *you*?"

"Me? You . . . you've made a mistake! I'm not ready," says Peter, trembling as though struck by a glacier's breath. He grabs the cab door, ready to bolt.

"Made a mistake, huh? I'm known to be a pretty good judge of people."

"What about Judas?"

"I knew he would betray me. That's why I picked him, but you're not in that category. Your reluctance to become a benefactor is quite a change from when you knocked on our door. Why?"

"Uh, this may not make sense," says Peter, "but it's our 'Quest.' I've realized my hate and pride have blocked the light of His strength. You showed me how Thornton was given a choice. He could forgive those who had harmed him in life or spend eternity in a self-inflicted hell of resentment. Then there's The Accuser. The God I learned to fear as a child would've sent him straight to hell for his sins. Instead, The Accuser was allowed a chance of redemption through atonement. Thornton and The Accuser chose how they'd spend eternity, not some all-mighty deity. Then there's the visit with Oscar. Like all children, he naturally accepted people. It was only through fear of abandonment plus his father's bigotry that he became so full of hate. I came away feeling sorry for the man but loving the child. Because of all this, I *now* believe He loves us enough to tolerate our free will even when our behavior causes pain."

"And when our behavior causes pain, He weeps," says Emmanuel. "But how does this revelation *exclude* you from becoming a benefactor?"

"Like I said, this may not make sense, but when He sees all the suffering —fear, hunger, death, and more—caused by mortals' free will and does nothing about the suffering, that frightens me. So, being both frightened *and* loving of Him, how can I connect to His strength?" says Peter, dropping his eyes in shame. "I'm too weak to be a benefactor."

"Weakness makes you vulnerable to Him. Weakness is strength."

"Fancy words, but the fact is, I can't blindly trust Him!"

"Hmm," says Emmanuel. "Would you at least *like* to have that trust?"

Peter's gaze wanders about the parking lot as he ponders a response.

"Yes, I'd like to trust in *something* that would always act for the benefit of mankind, but . . . "

"I know it's hard to believe that a being who allowed your existence to begin as a slave is acting in your best behalf. God or even I could have intervened, eliminated your hardships. We could have made you white, born into privilege and rich, but you would not be what you are today."

"And just what am I *today*?" asks Peter, his grip on the door tightening.

"A reverent soul comforting those enslaved in chaos. Instead of this turmoil, you could have chosen an eternity of idle bliss in the heavens—your 'reward'. You are just one big contradiction."

Peter releases the door. This unexpected praise is more unnerving than a reprimand.

"Let's review your life—mortal and spiritual," says Emmanuel. "Born a slave, persecuted, then lynched, were all adversities that heated the metal of your soul for His forge. Hammered from the hell of The Beast was the wisdom that vengeance never heals a wound. The evil of Oscar Wilson, the Citizens Committee, and the Bangers ignited a burning desire for justice. Whereas the loving courage you witnessed in Mary and Jerome was the flame guiding you through the darkness.

"You said you have come to believe there is a loving God. Are you willing to accept everything, the blessings, even that which you have resented and feared, have brought you closer to Us?"

"Yeah," says Peter, nodding in agreement, "but I still have some concerns that trouble me."

"That is only natural. Complete acceptance will take time, but you *are* willing. So, you can *trust* even if afraid. Surrender to a strength that will guide you with eternal love. Do this and you will have crossed the last chasm to a journeyman benefactor."

The two hug. The embrace's warmth plus the morning sun on his shoulder sends Peter's spirit soaring high as a dove freed from a cage. As Peter's soul ascends, he can see the future of his clients—a future of joys, even heartaches, which as a fledgling apprentice, his dread had blocked.

"Behold the light, Peter, the *strength* from which you draw your journeyman's power."

"Will I see you again?" he says, exiting the cab as he looks back.

"Go, my child. Know I am with you, even until the end of time."

* * *

The next day, Peter drives to Phantom Ridge. The car top down, flags of his hair whip in the wind. Happy as a schoolboy with an all "A's" report card, he is eager to tell Scott the good news: Peter has obtained Emmanuel's blessing as a full-fledged benefactor. But first, Peter stops at The Palace; unfinished business awaits.

Chapter 55

Blessed Amnesia

Exiting Route 68, Peter's Corvette trots into The Palace's gravel parking lot, swerving to avoid a faded blue Plymouth charging past. Parked in the gritty yard among a half dozen fugitives from a wrecker's yard stands a red Corvette, a duplicate of his.

Yeah, that's Mary's car. Well, here goes nothin . . .

Peter weaves through the old clunkers, parking behind the bar alongside the rusting hulk of a '52 Chevy pickup. The clunker belongs to the bar's janitor, Jake, who had offered to drive an injured Mary Cook to the hospital in this four-wheeled catastrophe eleven days ago. Switching off his car's ignition, Peter grabs a pen and paper from the glove box, then scribbles a note.

After confirming he is alone, he exits his vehicle, carrying *The BOOK*. Rounding the front of his Corvette, he strokes the hood as though petting a thoroughbred's forehead. *Goodbye my beauty. You've served me well.*

Leaning through the pickup's open driver's window, he sets the note on the dash:

> *Jake: Use this the next time someone needs a ride.*
> *From a friend*

On top of the note, he sets his keys imprinted with the Corvette logo.

Lugging the leather luggage containing *The BOOK*, Peter lists to one side, entering The Palace. His eyes adjusting to the smoky darkness, Peter's gaze stops upon a nostalgic, sad sight. At a round table soiled by the cold remains of breakfast sits Jake, Leroy clutching his bartender's towel, and between them, a sobbing Mary Cook. Mary's head rests in her hands, a red scarf sags from her neck, and a black purse dangles on the back of her chair. The men's attention shifts from Mary to the figure in the doorway.

"Can I help you?" asks Leroy.

"Seems like I'm interruptin something. Maybe I should come back."

"Well, looka what the cat drug in!" says Jake, recognizing Peter's voice. "Grab a seat. Want somethin to eat?"

Nodding a polite no, Peter approaches the table.

Mary lowers her hands and raises her head. Though her head dressing is gone, a purple crescent still cradles her left eye, the last vestige of Kevin's assault.

"Hi, everyone," says Peter, sitting as his briefcase thuds to the floor.

"Hello *Peter*," says Mary in a chilly reply.

In the icy stillness, Jake and Leroy swap glances.

"How long've all of you been here?" asks Peter.

"I reckon two hours," says Jake. "Mary was on her way over to Iron Mountain to visit that Jerome fella. She stopped ta say hi. We was havin breakfast when . . . " Jake stops in mid-sentence.

"Mary's husband was by," says Leroy. "And it wasn't what you'd call a pleasant visit."

Mary blows her nose, punctuating the announcement.

"Does he drive a blue Plymouth?" asks Peter.

"Yep," says Jake.

"What'd he want?"

"He followed her this mornin from Barkersville. Leroy just finished cookin and we was just startin breakfast when he gets outta that ol car of his. He musta been drinkin; ya could smell it on im. Struts in like a damn rooster in the henhouse. Wants Mary to go outside so's they could talk private like."

Sipping coffee, Mary nods in agreement, her eyes avoiding Peter's.

"Well, Mary, she tells im real polite that she'll meet im after she's done eatin. Then she just sat there chewin her bacon like he wasn't there. Ya shoulda seen im; his face turned red as a sore ass," says Jake in an excited, raised voice. "After she was done, both of em went outside. I got up and followed cause I didn't like the way he was lookin at her. When we got to the car, he starts shriekin like some kinda screech owl."

Jake puffs himself up.

"That's when *I* stepped between em, protectin her."

"Jake, it's alright. Calm down," says Leroy, patting Mary's arm.

"Anyway, he starts callin her all sorts of things, things I wouldn't never call no lady. An says how she's hurtin their business, callin her a thief for takin their savin's. Then the damnist thing happens." Jake pauses, taking a sip of cold coffee from a mug.

"And?" says Peter.

"She says she's sorry if what she's doin about Jerome is hurtin the business. But she gotta do it anyway. She ain't gonna ask for any part of the business in the divorce. Don't want nothin more to do with it. She's gonna give im back his half'a the money she took. And then, she kisses im on the cheek, gives im back the keys to his fancy BLT, and walks away."

"It's BMW, Jake, *not* BLT," says Leroy.

"Whatever, I seen it all. Kevin just stood there, his mouth wide open like a kid who'd just seen Santa Claus. He got in his old car and did a bat outta hell. Left the fancy one behind."

"Jake, we're ignorin the rest of the customers. Better get back to work," says Leroy, surveying the room and a distraught Mary.

"Ah, let em serve themselves!"

"*Jak*e, let's *go*."

"Uh, yeah, guess I otta be gettin back to work," says Jake in a flash of awareness. "If ya two need somethin, just holler."

Resembling a grizzly rearing on its hind legs, Jake rises from his chair. Bartender, then waiter, fade into the room's haze.

Minutes of painful silence torture the room.

"Mary," says Peter, interrupting the abusive stillness, "what you did with Kevin . . . that took guts. What made you apologize to *him*?"

Mary lifts her eyes from her coffee mug.

"At Jerome's trial," she says, "I saw all those people with hate in their hearts. Then I looked at myself. Was I any better? Yeah, I've got my reasons for hating those like Oscar, Judge Daring, Kevin, Jerome. But if I can forgive Jerome, why not the others? Then it hit me."

"What?"

"Hating them made me feel good, self-righteous. But I was just intensifying anger's storm, a never-ending tornado feeding on itself. Well, I can calm my portion of the commotion. By apologizing to Kevin, maybe I diminished some of *his*. And if enough folks did that, maybe the whirlwind would shrink to a whisper's breath."

"Mary, I've got an apology of my own. I should've stopped by the Lestermans' last Saturday and talked to you. I know how upset you must've been over Jerome's sentence."

"I waited *all day* for you."

"Well, I was upset, too. Needed some time to think, but that's no excuse," says Peter.

Twisting the cup in her hand, Mary's eyes soften.

"So, Peter, what are you doing here?"

"I was headed down to Iron Mountain when I saw your car. Didn't know if you'd see me or not, but I decided to stop anyway to pay a visit," says Peter, avoiding the real reason he is here.

"You goin to see Jerome?"

"Yeah, but got another appointment first," he replies, not saying he is meeting Scott at Phantom Ridge.

"I know all that's happened bothers you too. Sorry I got mad," says Mary, taking Peter's hand.

Through their touch, Peter could listen to Mary's thoughts, but out of respect, he blocks her mental deliberations. Then, glancing at the establishment's cadre of customers, he observes most are gawking at his and Mary's demonstration of fondness.

"Mary, can we go outside? These folks aren't used to sober displays of affection."

Heading to the door, they pass Jake. Peter asks him to watch his briefcase. Mary opens her purse, offering Jake the red bandanna Leroy had given her.

"We ain't taken that rag back," says Jake.

Ambling back to their table, he grabs Peter's leather case.

"Jesus Christ, what's in this damn bag? Gold?" he says, taking it behind the bar.

"Good as, it's a reference book for my work—*most* important. And when you've got a minute, check your truck. Left somethin for you on the dash."

"Why didn't you leave the briefcase in your Vette?" whispers Mary.

"Don't own the car anymore."

"Hope you got a good price for it."

"The best."

* * *

The two round the corner of the building, distancing themselves from the patrons. They pass The Palace's red neon sign dangling from the roof.

"Amazing what's happened in a little over a week since I bought my car," says Mary.

"Y-Yeah . . . "

Again, Mary takes Peter's hand. This time he is helpless to block the avalanche of her thoughts.

"Peter, I'm glad you suggested we come outside because I want to talk in private."

Peter feels the scorpion of dread crawling down his spine. Here it comes.

"Like I said the morning when we left the Lestermans for the bank, I've come to realize there's something unnatural about them, even you. You're all kind of angels working for good. You've helped me. I wonder if you can also help with something else. After my stay with Nancy and Seymour, I began having strange dreams . . . they're all about the Citizens for Justice meeting."

Mary recaps the details of her nocturnal visions, describing how the meeting's MC, whom she knows is Peter, took control of the gathering, trying to thwart the committee's goal of a signed death petition for Jerome. She describes the movies about Jerome's life, the mysterious black button with the power to alter the future, and how she was coerced to vote for his death. Weeping, she relates the details of the movie showing his execution, her tears trying to wash away the guilt.

"And your final words at the meeting, ' . . . each of you will suffer the consequences of your actions tonight. May you rest easy with your decision.' Well, I *haven't* rested easy. Every night I dream about my part in that awful meeting, knowing all my attempts to save Jerome will fail."

She draws closer to Peter, squeezing his hand as though salvation could be passed through flesh.

"My darling, what kind of angel or spirit are you?"

"The official designation," confesses Peter, "is Benefactor, Journeyman Class, benefactor for short."

"Is that some kind of an angel?"

"Close. Angels descend from the Divine. Benefactors are the spirits of deceased mortals, but not ghosts. We help mortals, even other spirits."

Upon hearing "help," Mary's face hardens.

"You've said before that you've been trying to help Jerome and me because of Timmy's death. Wouldn't it've been better to simply have saved my son?"

Mary's face flashes in an anger Peter has not seen since the night Kevin struck her. Discovery of his identity, then interrogation by a mortal, especially Mary, has been Peter's greatest dread. Her questions are the same ones he has asked himself since he met Scott. Looking into Mary's soul, Peter decides to tell his story.

"I haven't always been a benefactor. My first act as one, an apprentice, was taking control of the Citizens for Justice meeting, before Timmy's death."

Peter tells Mary his history as a slave, being lynched, and seeking vengeance as The Beast before becoming a benefactor.

"Even benefactors have a benefactor," he says. "Mine's named Scott, the spirit of my dead father. He was that guy with me when we were all here the night Kevin attacked you."

"Couldn't another benefactor have saved Timmy?" asks Mary, removing her hand.

"Mary, I'm sure one tried. But there's this thing called self-will. That's where good and evil come from. Benefactors can't change that, but don't ask why God doesn't intervene cause we don't know."

Peter tells Mary how they are assigned clients.

"We try to influence clients' behavior by showing how their deeds affect others. We use our supernatural abilities to appeal to their conscience. Then we let the *client*'s self-will choose. That's what I did at the committee meeting. It's all up for grabs, but once the button is pushed, it starts a destiny no one, no benefactor, no power can change. So, for a destiny poisoned with evil, all I can do is try to ease the pain as I've tried to do for you."

"Ease the pain! Then why am I fighting a doomed battle to save Jerome? Why let me love you, a spirit, which will only end in more *pain* for both of us? With help like that, who needs Satan?"

"*Mary*," says Peter, grabbing her hand. "I never meant to hurt you. I'm not perfect like an angel. We spirits of the dead keep our emotions as though we're still alive. I should've kept my distance. But I couldn't help myself because you're . . . you're so beautiful, inside and out. I've *never* felt this way about a woman before."

"Really, why?"

"Because you see, after my father's death, it was just Momma and me. After the Civil War, it was all I could do to support us cause being Black, I couldn't get a decent job. Besides that, being lynched early in my prime, I never had a chance for a loving relationship."

"You poor man," says Mary, stroking his cheek.

Peter feels a passion cresting within. Releasing Mary, he draws a breath, attempting to dam desire's rising tide. Silently he curses his weakness, a mortal longing which still persists.

Her face drenched in a moist crimson glow, Mary presses close.

"Darling," she whispers, "you're different from any person I've ever known. You've suffered the horror of death, revenged your murder as a hideous beast, and finally sought salvation by serving others. You're a paradox of realities and cultures, but from all this, you've acquired the wisdom of the ancients."

"Ancients? You make me feel like something out of the *Old Testament*."

"You don't look old, but I *would* like to see you without the disguise."

"You mean, as a Black man?" says Peter.

He scours the surroundings to confirm they are alone.

"Alright, Mary, but you have to close your eyes."

She complies, squinting with anticipation.

"Okay, open em."

Before Mary under a nest of black hair with scattered strands of gray, stands a six-foot-tall man in his early forties. His arms, thick as tree trunks, hang from a mountain-wide pair of shoulders. He wears a white shirt, black baggy trousers, plus brown boots.

"My Lord, Peter, what a hunk!"

"Mary," says Peter, grinning in a self-conscious smile, "you've been an inspiration to me. The mercy you've shown for your son's murderer. Your courage in confronting people like Oscar and the committee. Forgiving Kevin. All this has been a beacon helping to guide me through my odyssey of hatred, doubt, and fear. For that I'm grateful. For that, I will always love you."

Hands intertwined tight as honeysuckle vines, they stand drinking in the sweet pleasure when twisted by a gust of wind, the Palace's neon wreckage squeals with discomfort, splitting the silence.

"Peter, about pain. *You* have helped me like nobody else. It took a dead man to restore my faith in the living. Funny thing, pain. I've spent my whole life avoiding it. Yes, I'll never get over the pain of Timmy's death, but in a way, pain's liberated me."

"How's that?"

"I'm more compassionate of others' suffering, even the suffering of Jerome and Kevin. I've even forgiven their evil deeds. Pain's also led me to you.

"And speaking of Jerome, even with all your supernatural abilities, you couldn't change the committee's mind. How do *you* deal with that?"

"Mary, until recently, I *couldn't*. But I've come to accept that

I'm *not* God. I did my best. Like you, I've been liberated. For that, I take solace."

"My darling," says Mary, throwing her arms around him, "I love you. You're at peace with yourself. I wish I were more like you."

She holds his hands for the last time.

"Peter, I haven't your strength. I don't *want* to know Jerome is doomed to die. I don't want to feel the sorrow that our relationship would never work. I don't want to know you can hear all my thoughts."

Mary releases his hand.

"There's only one solution."

Peter nods yes.

"I want all memories of the strange events at the committee meeting, all knowledge of you and your supernatural abilities removed. Dear Peter, make me forget Jerome's fate with death is unalterable," she says, her voice a broken vase of emotions.

The words claw at Peter's heart. He will always love Mary. The absence of her affection will leave a hole in his soul, a once revered portrait faded, never to be viewed again. Scott had warned romances between spirits and mortals were doomed. Worse, the mortal always suffers the most.

This was the reason for my visit today, to remove all traces of my existence from Mary's memory. But I don't think I could've done it on my own. Thank God she has the courage, but damn, it only makes me love her more.

Mary stares into the surrounding woods, then faces Peter.

"Not only am I frightened of a future without your love, but I'm worried about *you*. You won't have the blessings of amnesia," she says, as dews of sorrow drip from her eyes. "I'm ready, my love."

Peter takes Mary's hand.

Her memories begin fading, falling like petals from the autumn rose of her mind.

"Goodbye Mary, my beloved."

Chapter 56

Good Men Do Nothing

"**H**urry up, Nathan. We don't wanna be late an miss the bus!"

"I'm hurryin, Mom."

Black overnight bag in hand, Alice boards the Greyhound bus as Nathan trails behind. Upon arriving in Rolla, they meet Jake who drives them in his red Corvette to IMCC where Jerome awaits his death sentence. The journey from Barkersville to the Potosi prison totals six hours. Alice's waitress schedule including her finances only allows trips once every three months. As usual, Mary Cook has arranged for free overnight lodging. However, after checking in at the prison's visitor registration, Alice makes a phone call to Jake.

"Mr. Brown, can you come back early an pick me an Nathan up?"

"Ain't no 'Mr. Brown' here, just me, Jake. Somethin gone wrong with your visit?"

"They won't let Jerome see us cause of a fight he got into with some bald fella."

"What bald fella, Miss Alice?"

"Someone they call a skinhead."

"Bet I know who started it. Bastards! Uh, sorry Mis Alice, I meant it's too bad. I ain't able ta get there for another three hours."

To pass the time, the two decide to explore the public landmark at the nearby knoll, Phantom Ridge Park. Alice remembers this park was funded by a trust in the late Senator Bartholomew's will.

As the two trudge across the prison's parking lot to the park's gravel path, Alice's thoughts retreat to an afternoon two years ago. It was a time melded with joy and apprehension. It was a time before Jerome's nightmare at Mother's Groceries. It was a time when she, Nathan, and Jerome ascended this same hill for a picnic before the site's conversion to a park.

* * *

Twenty minutes have passed since Alice and Nathan left the prison. They trudge up the hill.

"Mom . . . Mom! Didn't ya hear what I said?"

"Sorry, my mind was somewhere else. What were you sayin?"

"Why they sayin Dad started a fight? You know he wouldn't do somethin like that. Don't they know we spent all morning getting here? The only fun I had was riding in that guy's red Vette."

Stopping, he flashes a grin.

"Mom, ya sure looked funny sittin in my lap hanging your feet out the window."

"Yeah, that was kinda fun, and that Jake fella is a friend of Miss Mary. He went to a lot of trouble drivin us here. So you best remember to say his name real polite when he comes back."

Stopping, Alice leans on Nathan. She removes her open-toe shoes, dumping gravel from each one.

"I guess we're just gonna have to wait another three months til we see your dad again."

Approaching the crest of the hill, Nathan shades his eyes.

"Mom, you sure this is the same place? I don't remember this bench or the path. Where's that big ol spider web that hung from the tree go? And remember that spooky den with all the cobwebs?"

"Nathan, I told ya they cleaned the place up since we were here a couple'a years ago. They made some kinda park out of it."

"That sign's still there on the trunk," says Nathan, then points at the granite headstone marking a grave. "And where that ol cross of limbs was, they put in a big tombstone."

Running to the stone monument, he rubs his fingers over the notched inscription:

UNKNOWN

Dirt scatters as he kicks the grave's mound of soil.

"Nathan, don't you be messin with nothin. That's the restin place of one'a our brothers, the one they hung here. I hear the senator put up that sign in the tree in memory of that poor man."

"Mom, that guy they hung. What's his name?"

"I think your dad said it was Peter."

"Yeah, so why didn't they put that on the tombstone instead of Unknown?"

"Don't know for sure. I suppose it means this memorial is more about all our brothers that been lynched, not just one man."

"Dad said that Peter's spirit didn't go to heaven. It stayed here like a ghost and turned into some kinda monster, somethin like an avenging angel. Went after those white guys that hung im. And Dad said that Peter was gonna be helping him, too."

"That's what I remember. That Peter spirit was gonna be helpin your dad. But what are you gettin at?" asks Alice.

"Mom, you think somethin like that could *really* happen?"

"Nathan, most folks say not. But I *know* the Lawd, He works in mysterious ways. *Somethin* strange went on here a long time ago cause that's how this place got to be called Phantom Ridge. But don't you fret about it. It's nothin to be scared of now."

"I'm not scared. Just thinking . . . that spirit . . . ghost, if he's still around, when's he gonna start helpin Dad?"

Tears drain from Alice's eyes. She grabs Nathan, hugging him so tight he can barely breathe.

"Mom . . . "

"All I know," she says, releasing her son, "is that Miss Mary, is tryin to help. She's got those ACLU folks working real hard. I just keep prayin they all can do somethin, even that ghost Peter."

Nathan stares at the plaque. Hate narrows his eyes.

"It says bad things happen when good men do nothing. Mom, if somethin really bad happens to Dad, I'm not gonna do 'nothing.' I'm gonna do to those white folks in the committee what that guy Peter did to the mob. Maybe worse. An I'm startin with that asshole Wilson!"

Chapter 57

Serpents in the Jungle of Time

The Palace parking lot crackles under Peter's feet as he wanders in the pre-dawn morning. Alone, he walks as though stranded on the dark side of the moon, a somber sorcerer isolated in both the supernatural and mortal realms. This sudden seclusion is due to an undesirable but necessary decision. To protect his benefactor's identity, yesterday Peter terminated his relationships with Mary, Leroy, and Jake, by cleansing all memories of him from their minds. The Citizens Committee's collective memory was scrubbed at the City Hall meeting. Then, after Peter purges Albert Fillmore and the Banger Brothers' recollections, all relevant eradications have been made. For them, Peter never existed. For Peter, this is not much different from when he was alive; white people ignored him except for their accented glares of contempt.

In a few hours, Peter will meet Scott at Phantom Ridge. Without his convertible, Peter will resort to the mundane, instantaneous mode of spiritual travel—teleportation. Mortals would wage another war to have a Scotty who could beam them up. But for Peter, the throbbing of two-hundred-and-forty horses under the hood as his hair whips in the wind are sensual experiences he has grown to enjoy, perhaps too much, just like the mortal friendships he has acquired. No longer an apprentice, Peter must dedicate himself solely to the duties of a full-fledged Benefactor, Journeyman Class. This is why he sacrificed his earthly attachments. This is why he gave his car to Jake. But one yearning that will not rest by relinquishing a ring of keys is his longing for Mary. Though cleansing her memory was best for her, his heart aches. Never again will his heart feel the warmth of her love.

Strange how my mortal cravings still linger even in death.

Slapping his hands, The Palace evaporates. In the void where the building once stood, Phantom Ridge Park coalesces.

* * *

Emerging at the park before sunrise, Peter sits on the oak bench on which he and Scott have spent many an hour. Behind looms the old elm skirted by a quilt of gray and brown leaves. Downhill stands IMCC shrouded in morning mist. Beside him rests *The BOOK* which he taps, waiting for the horizon's yellow burst of a newborn day.

Morning ages to afternoon. Sun arching across the skies, Peter wonders when Scott will arrive; probably a deliberate delay for another grand entrance. However, the respite from the landslide of recent events softens his agitation when the gravel path announces an approaching visitor who, dropping on the bench, mops his face with a handkerchief.

Between breaths, he says,

"Hi, Son, been waiting long?" He then hooks an arm around Peter.

"A few hours," says Peter, robbing Scott the pleasure of an exasperated reply.

"So, how are you doing?"

"Fine."

"Well, we agreed to meet after your visit with Emmanuel. So, how did it go?"

"Alright, I guess. I assume you know he promoted me to journeyman class."

"Wait a minute. After having finally realized your goal of journeyman, you *guess* that is alright?" says Scott, unwinding his arm. "I have seen happier roadkill. What is the problem?"

"Dad, I should be elated. God knows how much I've wanted that title. But a lot's been bothering me."

"Alright, we will get to that. But first tell me, how did everything go with Emmanuel?"

Peter talks about meeting the Black Jesus, including the twelve motorcycle-riding disciples. He describes visiting James Thornton, The Accuser, and eight-year-old Oscar Wilson.

"I said you would learn Oscar's story," says Scott. "So, what wisdom have you acquired from all this?"

Peter's eyes lift skyward, searching for words to describe his puzzle of scattered thoughts.

"We're . . . we're all shaped by our past like Oscar was by his childhood. But when we become prisoners of it, we wind up like Thornton, doomed forever to labor in resentment. Though we've been the victims of evil, we have the capacity for forgiveness. And when we've made atonement to those *we* have harmed, like The Accuser did for lynching me, like I did for stabbing Thornton, we're freed of the guilt and shame."

His eyes shifting to Scott, Peter sighs, then continues.

"I've forgiven Oscar, the committee, even the mob. I've realized my motivation as an apprentice was more about hatred of the oppressor than helping the oppressed. Vengeance was running the show. Hate blocked me from God, blocked my powers as a benefactor. The Beast was my deity."

"I never envisioned Him as an elephant-sized arachnid," says Scott, slapping Peter's leg. "These revelations are why Emmanuel proclaimed you a journeyman. I trust you appreciate the honor you have received."

Peter shrugs, strolling to the edge of the path, staring down at the prison's gray walls.

"What *is* troubling you?" says Scott.

"When I left Emmanuel yesterday, I was happy as a boy who

got his first puppy. I had accepted my and God's place in destiny. But," he says, aiming a finger at the prison, "thoughts of Jerome alone, down there frightened while awaiting the futile attempts of an appeal *still* torture me. After all that I've forgiven and accepted, why can't I get over *him*?"

"Why your concern about mourning *Jerome's* fate?"

Unable to answer, Peter continues to eye the prison.

"You have only recently become a Benefactor, Journeyman Class, including all the power plus responsibility that accompanies that promotion. Beware of any misconceptions that you must be immune to all mortal emotions. Remember XII of *The BOOK*, 'Beneficiaries . . . shall at all times be treated with *love*.' And speaking of love, how did your meeting go with Mary?"

"That's another thing bothering me."

Scott nods, stuffing his sweat-soaked handkerchief in his trousers.

"I came to realize," says Peter, "just like you've said, that our relationship would only cause pain, especially for Mary. So, without even asking her, I decided to remove all of her memories about me. Kinda pompous of me, but the strange thing is, *she* asked me to do this before *I* could, and I'm supposed to foresee my clients' actions."

"Sad as an unopened Valentine, huh? Son, we guys never see it coming. But I would not call your intentions pompous, more like concern. What better qualification for being a benefactor than loving someone enough to set them free? Anything else about Mary?"

"Yeah. I . . . I'm so damn lonely without her."

"I know the feeling. Welcome to the club of celestial celibates."

"D-a-a-d!"

"Sorry, being a spirit can be lonely. All those years after my death, I hovered beside your momma. But I could not reveal my presence. Immortality is not all it is cracked up to be."

Peter slumps on the bench, limp as wet laundry.

"Dad, when I erased all of Mary's thoughts about us, it . . . it was like I'd died all over again. Worse than that, it was like I *never* existed. And I did the same with Jake and Leroy. God, am I gonna miss them! When I walked out of The Palace with *The Book*, I looked back to see em starin at me like I was a stranger."

"You *can* spare yourself the pain of attachment. Wear a shield protecting you from any feelings of affection. Or . . . "

"Or drop the armor baring myself to the wounds of compassion."

"Shakespeare would rise from the dead to write that."

"All the world's a stage and I'm naked on it. Dad, why does this have to hurt so much?"

"I know, but in a way, I have come to appreciate the pain. It often comes from the love of service to others. So in a way, the more I hurt, the more I have loved and served."

He elbows Peter.

"What you did with Mary took guts, and was best for both of you. But do yourself a favor. Next time you decide to vacuum someone's memory, leave some dirt behind."

"What dirt?"

"Erasing *all* thoughts of yourself will leave unexplainable gaps in their memory. Take Mary. She will wonder how the hell she got from The Palace to the hospital. If you didn't drive her there, who did? Things like that. Same goes for Leroy and Jake. You might try making some of the encounters between you and Mary dreams which she vaguely recalls."

"Hell, how am I supposed to do all that now?"

"Do not worry, I can fix it. Call this a graduation present. I will handle Albert and your dealings with his auto dealership. After that, I will address everybody else's memory that needs tweaking, but let this be an example. Though it may seem contradictory, there is no room for close personal ties. You work behind the scenes—

unnoticed, anonymous. Never again act in a manner that will require an alteration of anyone's memory. Alright?"

"Yeah, thanks, Dad." *It seems with each meeting, he plugs another leak in this ship of spiritual existence. But there's another crack.*

"Now that I'm a journeyman, is . . . is your work with me finished? Do you move on?" asks Peter, fear choking his voice. *I remember as a kid seeing a slave trader dragging Dad away in chains. Maybe he'll have to leave again, this time summoned by a Higher Authority.*

"In a hurry to get rid of the old man, huh?"

"No! I want you beside me more than ever."

"Do not worry, Son. No chains, no summons, will ever take me from you again."

Relief warms Peter's soul when the sound of voices, then advancing footsteps, chills his joy.

* * *

"Why they sayin Dad started a fight? You know he wouldn't do somethin like that . . . " says a boy's voice pushed by the midday breeze.

More unintelligible words follow when distinctly a woman says, "I guess we're just gonna have to wait another three months til we see your dad again."

* * *

"That's Alice and Nathan. They've come to visit Jerome. I lost track of time," says Peter, squinting in the direction of the conversation.

The pair cloak themselves in invisibility, watching.

Alice and Nathan wander the knoll. They reminisce about their picnic months ago with Jerome, then talk about the history of Phantom Ridge. Their conversation ends when, in the event harm comes to his adopted father, Jerome, Nathan vows, "I'm gonna do to those white folks in the committee what that guy Peter did to the mob. Maybe worse. And I'm startin with that asshole Wilson!"

In silence, Alice and Nathan leave the ridge. Scott, then Peter, shed their invisibility.

"Dear God," says Peter. "What Nathan just said about Oscar. Nathan *will* follow through. I can see it in the future. Is vengeance the only legacy left in the world? It's even affected that poor child. Wait a minute. I'm *only* supposed to see the future of *my* clients, no one else's. Is Nathan . . . "

"Yes, I am giving him to you. Nathan and Oscar Wilson's fates are so intertwined they must be managed by the same benefactor. I still have Alice. Suicides are a special case."

"Damnit. I'm not looking forward to *this* future," says Peter while his foot scrapes the ground in confused thought. "Strange, though I know my clients' fates when the time comes for me to aid and comfort them, I don't know how I'll do it, what words or deeds I'll use."

"That *is* how benefactors work. If beforehand you knew your every remark, your every effort, you would simply be reciting your role in a play, each phrase memorized from a script, all gestures carefully choreographed. What would you have learned? Nothing. Better to flounder, struggle in the knowledge that when you act out of love, His strength will guide you. Be the benefactor you have trained to be, the benefactor *we* know you can be, the benefactor who summons the strength."

If Scott and Emmanuel trust me, the two souls I've loved and trusted like my own momma, then maybe I can trust myself.

"Here, you need to do some homework," says Scott, lifting *The BOOK* from the bench. "Read this again."

Handing *The BOOK* to Peter, Scott drops the tome. Instinctively, Peter lunges forward, trying to halt the descent when *The BOOK* freezes in midair.

"Thanks, Dad. I almost forgot you could stop time."

"Time's racing engine has not stopped, just slowed to an idle, what we call 'Turtle Time.' But it was not me who took the foot off the throttle."

"You mean, I can . . . ?"

"Yes, you have always had that ability. We just discourage its use by apprentices because they abuse it. Instead of homework, they will waste hours watching a fly flap its wings. Use this and your other powers wisely."

With a crimson cry, the summer sun drops behind the horizon. In the fading red twilight, father and son discuss the evil that lies ahead, evil waiting patiently as a serpent in the jungle of time. In the three years to follow, the ominous events foretold at the Citizens for Justice meeting will have taken their place in history: Mary, despised by the good citizens of Barkersville, befriends Jerome, aiding in his death sentence appeals. But the appeals fail. Alice, upon learning of her lover's fate, commits suicide. Jerome dies in the gas chamber. Nathan runs away. Homeless, he pursues a life of crime on the street.

"And being a journeyman," says Scott, "you can see into the fog of time. The avalanche of malevolence that crushes Jerome, Alice, and Nathan will crash upon all in the committee."

"I know."

Peter sighs, aching with images of events to come. But he is comforted. Never again must he act alone. Never again will he be abandoned. All he has to do is trust the power.

PART IV

THE JOURNEYMAN

October—December 1991

Chapter 58

Double A Liquor

October 1991

Rap music blasts through the windows of the four-door sedan. Holding three people inside, the car pulls in front of the steel-barred display windows of Double A Liquor in the early hours of this Sunday morning. Two people in ski masks exit the vehicle. One man, slight of frame in a hooded sweatshirt, wears a pair of black leather gloves, each with a gold embroidered star, and carries a handgun. He is known as Twig. The other man of stouter build brandishes a shotgun. Throwing open the store's glass door, they rush inside. Ahead of them stands a surprised cashier behind the checkout counter. The wall clock above him reads 12:02 a.m.

The thief brandishing the shotgun takes charge. They call him BB, short for Big Bob.

"I'm gonna blow your fuckin head off if ya don't gimme all your cash!" he shouts to the cashier. Pointing at the Halloween wall poster above the cash register, he says, "An don't ya forget that safe!"

The cashier glares at the two men, then turns to the safe.

"Two more fucking Blacks who don't know their ass from the hole in their mouth," he mumbles. "Just like Granddad always said, they're all worthless, stupid, or criminals, and aren't worth the energy to dig their graves. An to their graves is just where I'm sendin em."

Lifting the poster, the cashier twists the safe's combination dial. Opening the door, he spins around. A shotgun explodes.

"Jesus Christ! Why'd ya . . . ?" yells Twig.

"He grabbed a gun," says BB in bone-chilling calmness.

Smoke drifts from the shotgun still pointed at the safe. The smell of gunpowder creeps through the room.

"Get over there and make sure that asshole's dead. An get the fuckin cash from the safe and register!" says BB.

"What if he's still alive?"

"What'd ya think I done give ya the damn gun for?"

Twig runs to the counter and leans over, freezing at the sight of the body stretched across the linoleum. Scraps of flesh ooze down the wall behind the corpse. Dollar bills litter the floor. All dripping with blood.

"Damnit. Get ya'r fuckin skinny ass over there!" says BB.

Twig still hesitates. Finally obeying the command, he leaps over. Slipping in the splattered gore, he falls to the floor next to the clerk's body partially covered by the torn poster. Twig wonders how to make sure the cashier is dead so he lifts the poster, peering underneath.

"Fuck!" he shouts upon seeing half of the head has been torn away.

"Grab the cash and get the fuck outta there!" says BB.

Then Twig sees it—a ring on the clerk's bloody hand—a white gold ring embossed with two crosses on either side of a large diamond. In all the blood, the ring easily slides off. From the other dead man's hand, Twig grabs the gun. He shoves the firearm into a cloth bag along with the ring and the blood-drenched cash. After cleaning out the safe plus the cash register, he leaps over the counter. Running, he dives onto the sedan's front seat.

BB follows, sliding onto the car's back seat casually as if he has just bought a pack of cigarettes.

The car squeals off as approaching sirens wail in the distance.

Ripping off his mask, Twig drops the bag of loot beside him, then pukes on the floor.

Laughing, BB yanks off his mask.

"That's how ya does it!" he says, flashing a sadistic smile.

BB leans over the front seat, grabs the ring from the bag, and slides the gold band onto his puking partner's finger.

"Here, this'a make ya feel better." Slapping him on the back, he adds, "Next time, you carry the fuckin shotgun!"

Chapter 59

A Mahogany Paneled Vault

December 1991

Banners plus bunting, complete with Christmas decorations, adorn the portico of Barkersville City Hall, proclaiming the city's 1991 Citizen of the Year, Oscar Wilson. Festivities of this event will be held inside the hall this evening. All add to the merriment of this Saturday afternoon, a little over three years since the Citizens for Justice Committee convened inside to demand Judge Charles Daring impose the death penalty on convicted murderer Jerome Manning in the trial's upcoming sentencing phase.

The vine of malevolence rooted at that meeting has been carefully tended to ever since.

Judge Daring sentenced Jerome Manning to death in the gas chamber. Mary Cook, aided by the ACLU, initiated an appeal. Judge Daring stayed the execution. However, the three years of effort to reduce Jerome's conviction to manslaughter, or at least commute the sentence to life imprisonment, were denied by the Missouri Supreme Court on October 8. The next day, Judge Daring set the execution (as Mary said, "the premeditated killing") on December 14th, today.

After the judge's order, a distraught Alice Smith after learning of her lover's fate, killed herself. Her teenage son, Nathan, vowed revenge on those he felt responsible for her death and Jerome's impending execution. Nathan became a citizen of the street, pursuing a life of crime.

Meanwhile, Peter, coached by Scott, perfects his benefactor's skills.

* * *

Oscar Wilson, alone in his jewelry store, sits on one of two stools at his worktable in the Buying Room. He stares at the wall calendar. Today's date is circled in red.

The doors of Wilson's Jewelry are closed on weekends. Though normally just another day at the office, this Saturday drips with significance. On his black stool, Oscar hunches over the table, inspecting a pearl necklace through his jeweler's loupe. Lurking behind him on the wall, and following Oscar's every move, is his larger-than-life shadow, the ghoulish creation of the room's solitary light, a brass table lamp.

Thank God for the only distraction I have from this life of hell—work.

Slinging the necklace aside, Oscar rests his chin in his palm, gazing at a sheet of writing paper, a blank reminder of the letter he hesitates to write. Folding the paper, he slips it with a pen into his shirt pocket. His eyes turn up to the enlarged framed photograph on the wall covering the safe. The photo shows him and Michael at the State Fair eating cotton candy with arms draped around each other. His gaze then drifts to three pewter-framed photographs on the table, sentinels guarding treasures from the past, all reflecting Michael beginning from infancy. Marching from one snapshot to another, his attention halts on the one with the inscription he has read a thousand times:

> *To the best Granddad in the world!*
> *Mike*

This photo captures Michael with red-ballooned cheeks after blowing out sixteen birthday candles. Oscar attended that party.

The acrid scent of those smoking candles still lingers in his mind. The picture also shows a small, blue box which holds Oscar's gift to Michael—a white gold ring embossed with two crosses, one on either side of a large diamond, the same ring Jerome fenced to Oscar. His mind replays the image of Jerome standing outside at the buyer's door reaching out for payment—ten, twenty-dollar bills.

Oscar clutches the birthday photograph. The picture's fond memories briefly numb the pain of his grandson's recent murder during a store robbery where he worked as a cashier. Lowering his head, Oscar slams the picture face down, the crashing glass piercing sobs of sorrow.

This evening, Oscar will leave earlier than usual at 5:15 p.m., thirty minutes from now to attend his Citizen of the Year celebration. Afterward, he will be driven to the Iron Mountain Correctional Center to witness Mr. Manning's 11:00 p.m. execution.

Since Michael's death less than two months ago, Oscar has been absent-minded, experienced bouts of confusion, and has missed important appointments. But tonight as he vows to be punctual, the supplier's alley door rattles with a knock.

"We're closed! Go away."

Another knock.

"I said, we're closed."

Knock . . . knock.

"Damnit!"

Stomping to the door, he squints through the peephole, but a raging storm obscures the view. Twisting the handles of the dead-bolt, he raises the steel bar and inches the door open, peering into the alley. Outside, he sees a tall, muscular man standing under an umbrella. Shadows hide his face.

"Didn't you hear? We're closed."

In silence, the stranger stands motionless. Oscar's first thought is to slam the door, but the stranger's demeanor, waiting in the rain and wind, intrigues him.

"Who are you and what the hell do you want!"

Rolling thunder drowns the response.

"What'd you say? I'm just about to close up."

"I have something that might interest you," says the stranger.

Only a supplier'd be out in this!

"Since the death of my . . . I don't appraise your type of merchandise anymore. Go away."

"I know, Oscar, but what I've got, money can't buy."

Only personal friends dare call Wilson by his first name. His curiosity tweaked, Oscar pokes his head out to confirm they are alone.

"Alright, get the hell in here. Make it quick."

The stranger closes his umbrella, then squeezes through the opening.

Upon entering, the visitor's apparel seems dry as desert bones. *That's damn odd; not a drop of rain.* Slamming the door, he steps back to get a better look at the vaguely familiar intruder who offers a handshake. Slowly, Oscar takes the hand which feels too warm to have been in the cold.

"What's your name? I couldn't hear because of the thunder."

"Peter," says the stranger, smiling. "You don't remember, but we've met before."

Hearing the white man's reply, Oscar's heart unaccountably quivers.

"And everyone knows you, Oscar. You're getting that award tonight, Citizen of the Year."

Peter points to the worktable on which lies a copy of the *Barkersville Gazette* with Oscar's picture smeared across the front page.

"Yeah, so who are you to call me 'Oscar.' Only my friends call me that."

"Like I said, I'm . . . "

"Yeah, I know, Peter. You said you have somethin for me?"

Acting like he never heard the question, Peter strolls about, scanning the gloomy interior.

"Electric bill been a bitch?"

"Like *I* said," says Oscar. "Gotta close. Get ready for tonight. What's so important that . . . "

"Ah, yes, about tonight, possibly I can help."

With the phrase, 'Possibly I can help,' a spark of dread pierces Oscar's mind. His thoughts flash with an image of a man standing on a stage as movies flicker on a screen behind him.

"Why don't we go over there," says Peter, pointing to the table, "and talk."

Sauntering forward, Peter sits on the stool opposite Oscar's, leaning his umbrella against the table. He continues his survey of the dark décor.

"Love what you've done with the place. What do you call it? Contemporary Dungeon?"

Oscar follows. Sitting on his stool, he uprights the cracked pewter photograph. This guy acts like he owns the place. And his offer to help. Help with what?

"Like I said, would you like to talk?" asks Peter.

"Talk about what?"

"The nightmare, the one about Michael you've had every night since his murder."

"How do you know about *that*?" asks Oscar.

The spark in Oscar's mind flames into a wildfire of apprehension. Sitting still as stone, Oscar stares silently as a sphinx across the table. Something has not let him sleep more than three hours any night since the dreadful event. Something eats at his gut like cancer. Maybe it's because talking to a complete stranger seems easier than his minister. Whatever this something is, Oscar decides to tell Peter about the crime that took Michael's life.

"Since I'm a former mayor, the police let me have a copy of the store's security video taken the night of the robbery. I must've seen that thing fifty times, tryin to figure out who killed my grandson. Seen it so many times that I'm startin to hear sound and voices."

With a handkerchief, Oscar mops his sweat-beaded brow as the pent-up nightmares, anger, and sorrow of the robbery stream from his mouth faster than a desert's flash flood.

"And I have other nightmares, hellish visions that haunt me. Nothing helps: pills, booze, work, my minister. I'm angry, depressed, all alone. Why was my beloved grandson taken from me? Michael was more of a son than his father Sherman was . . . my own flesh and blood."

"About your son, Sherman. How did Michael's murder affect him?" asks Peter.

"Who knows? No one's seen the little shit since he deserted his family years ago."

Oscar then mentions his "appraisal service," a polite term for his fencing operation, the proceeds of which paid for Michael's cystic fibrosis expenses.

"I don't know why I just told you about my little sideline. You're the only one . . . Not even my own family knows . . . well, especially *not* my family."

"Do the police have any leads on your grandson's death?"

"Just that they're Black, in their mid-teens, and probably gang members who don't rat on their own. Like lookin for a virgin in a whore house."

Across the table, Peter extends his hand, palm up, in a display of empathy.

Oscar accepts the gesture. Thoughts squeezed between questions, he stares ahead perplexed by his confessions to someone who came in from the cold. But as he confesses, a weight lifts.

"Who are you? Some kinda priest?" asks Oscar.

"No, but we both work for the same boss. Anything else you'd like to tell me?"

Following a lengthy pause over a decision, Oscar exhumes his final burden.

"After the Citizens for Justice meetings, my fortunes began to skyrocket. Why not? Without me, that murderer Manning probably would've only gotten manslaughter. I was admired, respected by everyone in town. Rotary clubs asked me to speak about the committee. At restaurants, strangers paid for my meals. I was even asked to run for mayor again.

"Michael and I were spending more time together. Business was never better. God was finally rewarding me for all I'd done."

Lifting the shattered photograph, Oscar pauses.

"Remember I mentioned other nightmares I'm having? Well, they started after the first committee meeting."

"Oh, really?" says Peter, feigning surprise.

"Yeah. At first, they were just occasional. But unlike Michael's dreams, I can't remember most of em. But what I *do* remember has something to do with that fuckin Manning and it's *not* good. I feel nervous, scared. I have flashes of images like a stranger standing on a stage, strange movies flashing on a screen, and of all things, a big ol round, black doorbell button. Then there's things I hear: a crowd screaming like they're watchin a boxing match. A child crying. At first, I can shake em off, then go back to sleep. But they've slowly become more vivid and frequent. After I wake up, I'm like a kid too scared to go back to sleep. I roam the house, restless. That crowd or whatever they are might be coming for me! Even worse, the dreams started hauntin me in the daytime. Every day, every night's become a living hell. Business went to shit. Then, after my nervous breakdown with three weeks in the hospital, drugged out like a zombie, Michael's killed in that robbery. I closed the business for weeks. Just reopened this past Monday. I'm almost bankrupt. Kids point, callin me, 'Weirdo Wilson.' Peter, it's more than I can bear!"

Oscar slides from his chair. He lumbers over to and removes the State Fair picture exposing the safe. Spinning the combination dial, he opens the door, removing a Luger. Pistol in hand, a perplexed expression creases his face, as though considering his next course of action.

In the safe under the gun lies a folded document, a suicide letter he typed four weeks ago. However, after reconsidering his fate, he placed the farewell letter here in the safe. Should the urge to seek the ultimate solution arise again, he need not be distracted by any more literary efforts. Due to the document's incriminating confessions which implicate others, he made a copy and secured it in a secret vault at home. Oscar grabs the letter. With a heavy thud, the safe slams close. Rehanging the picture and with the letter plus the pistol in hand, he returns to his chair, slinging the gun across the table towards Peter.

A normal person would flinch at the sight of the twirling, black-steel extension of Oscar's ego. Oscar had deliberately tossed the gun, just to test this stranger's mettle. But Peter sits calmly, one leg crossed over his knee, watching the gun skid to a rest.

Oscar hunches forward, rubbing his chin. Who is this guy? He flings the folded letter at Peter.

"You sure you want me to read this?" asks Peter.

Taking the non-response as implied consent, he unfolds and reviews the document's incriminating contents. Peter then returns the correspondence and Lugar to Oscar.

Silence accumulates.

"Not a day goes by that I don't think of holding this gun up to my head." After a pause with a tone cold as a crypt, he adds, "I pray one day I'll meet those bastards who killed my grandson. One hour with em is all I ask. One hour, and I'll have em beggin for a death as quick as Michael's!"

Just then, the supplier's door erupts with a KNOCK . . . KNOCK . . . KNOCK

"We're closed!"

KNOCK . . . KNOCK . . . KNOCK

"Damnit!"

Oscar grabs his Luger.

"Is that any way to treat a guest?" says Peter.

"What fuckin guest? I haven't invited anyone!"

Raising his arm, Peter points at the steel-clad entrance.

"Open the door, Mr. Wilson. Greet the answer to your prayer."

Chapter 60

Stranger at the Door

KNOCK . . . KNOCK . . . KNOCK

The alley door rattles with the increased impact of the summons.

Oscar's desk reverberates with a rhythmic thump of his Luger.

"Answer to my prayer, huh?" he says, slapping his weapon. "Well, if they *are* those bastards who killed my grandson, do I have a little Christmas present for them!" His head turning to the door, he shouts, "What'd ya want!"

"I got some stuff they say you'll buy!" comes the answer from the landing, the words repeating themselves as they ricochet down the alley.

"I must have a neon sign saying, 'Fence Open for Business.' God Damnit!"

"That guy's persistent as gravity," says Peter. "I'd answer the door before he attracts attention."

Peter strolls across the floor. After grabbing a chair from a closet, he ambles to a corner of the room. Sitting, he leans against the wall, arms folded, pinning his eyes on Oscar.

Oscar watches with annoyance.

KNOCK! KNOCK! KNOCK!

"Don't bloody your damn knuckles! I'll be right there!"

Oscar slides the suicide letter from the desk into a drawer. Slamming the drawer close and gun at his side, he approaches the door. Through the peephole, he sees a teenage Black youth in a stained sweatshirt with a hood covering his head and sunglasses shading his eyes.

Peter looks on impassively as though he is watching an *I Love Lucy* rerun.

Peeling the door open, Oscar inspects the figure whose motionless eyes aim at him like guns.

Oscar scans the rain-tarnished alley; all clear.

"Alright, show me what ya got."

The teenager removes a pair of gloves, stuffing them in his sweatshirt. Untying a cloth bag from his belt, he empties a necklace plus two heart-shaped earrings into his hand. He holds the golden adornments up to the door's light.

"That's all?" asks Oscar.

"Yeah," says the youth, shrugging his shoulders.

"Just a minute."

Oscar slams the door.

"Fuck!"

Rolling his eyes at Peter, Oscar stomps back to the desk. He opens the drawer with the letter, tosses his Luger inside, and leaves the drawer partly open. *Just in case I get a sudden urge for my gun.* He returns to the steeled entry, opens it a few inches, and motions the youth inside.

Stuffing the jewelry bag into a sweatshirt pocket, the adolescent squeezes inside, his wet dog aroma violating the air.

Back at the table, Oscar motions the visitor to sit.

"Take off your fuckin hood and sunglasses! Show a little respect."

The visitor obeys, exposing a tangled wire of hair which has not seen soap since Halloween.

"Put what ya showed me on the table."

The youth removes the jewelry, unaware that a wad of soiled Kleenex wrapped in a strip of pink ribbon falls from the bag onto the floor.

Peter continues watching from the dark corner.

Grabbing the jewelry, Oscar examines the yellow trinkets under his jeweler's loupe.

"Don't mind the guy in the back. He's a friend," says Oscar, nodding back at Peter.

"What guy?" says the youth, twisting his head about. "No wonder they're callin him Weirdo Wilson," he mumbles.

Fortunately for the young visitor, Oscar is so concentrated on his inspection that he fails to hear the "Weirdo" part but catches the insolent tone. Smart ass! Typical Black teenager. No respect for his white elders.

"Uh-huh, this shit's junk, not worth a dime," he says, flinging the jewelry across the table.

When the visitor shows no emotion, Oscar suspects the teenager knows the items are worthless. I wonder if the little shit's just casing the place? He glances at Peter and down at the open drawer with the Luger. Looking at his watch, which shows 5:30, he remembers this evening's celebrations.

"If you've got no more garbage to show, you'll have to leave. I've got an important engagement to attend."

"I know. You're goin to that citizen award meetin."

"Yeah, that's right. And you're goin out that door."

After pocketing the jewelry bag with the "junk," the visitor holds up another golden item from the same pocket—a ring, which he slides across the table.

"That there better?" he asks.

A twirling yellow beacon casting shards of light, the ornament skids to a stop in front of Oscar. His arrogant mood implodes into curiosity as he glares at a white gold ring embossed with two crosses on either side of a large diamond.

"God damnit! This is the ring I gave my grandson! Where the hell'd you get this!"

"I done found it in the trash yesterday," says the youth.

Oscar's stomach churns with disbelief. *That's the same thing Jerome said when he brought me this ring four years ago!*

As Oscar examines the ring, the young man gloves his hands, stretching them tight—black leather gloves, each embroidered with a gold star.

Then like a foot stepping on a dead branch, something snaps in Oscar's mind. In the robbery video, the guy who jumped over the counter and took Michael's ring wore gloves just like those. Oscar's head jerks to Peter, then to the Black visitor. Erratic as tennis shoes in a dryer, thoughts tumble in Oscar's mind. *Is he the answer to my prayer?*

"My God! You're one of *them*, those fuckin hoodlums who shot my grandson!"

With a wicked grin, the visitor pulls back his sweatshirt exposing a .45 pistol secured in his waistband. The gun having waited patiently as a tiger in ambush, pounces from hiding, landing inches from Oscar's heart as the young man lurches across the table, gun in hand.

Oscar reels in an avalanche of emotion. While the nightmare of his grandson lying dead on the floor tears through his mind and oblivious to the pistol, Oscar explodes in rage. It violates his body, destroying all other sensations. Incensed, he leaps to his feet but stops upon hearing the click of a cocking pistol. He looks down at the gun. Anger's exhilaration surrenders to the paralysis of fear.

"Who are you?" he says.

Gun aimed at Oscar, the youth retrieves his bag, dumping out two crumbled news clippings.

"Read em!" says the youth, flinging the paper cutouts at Oscar.

Oscar sits. Unfolding the snippets with trembling hands, he reads the articles. One recounts his Citizen of the Year nomination for his efforts in ensuring Manning's execution. The other concerns a Black woman named Alice Smith. She killed herself after learning her lover, Jerome Manning, having lost his appeal, would be executed. The body was discovered by her son, Nathan, whom neighbors heard shouting a promise to, " . . . fuckin kill that Wilson fella . . . !" Oscar drops the clippings. Desperate as a condemned man, he faces his executioner.

"Ya, I'm Nathan," says the youth.

Flashing revenge's sweet smile of long-overdue justice, Nathan grabs the papers. He empties the earrings with the necklace back on the table.

"An this 'crap' is the only thing I got to remind me of my mamma. I took em the night I found her dead."

At gunpoint, Oscar beholds the sight of death before him. Slower than a funeral procession, an eternity of seconds passes within the room's tomb of silence. But nothing happens.

"What's the matter *boy?*" asks a perplexed Oscar. "Haven't got the guts? Go on you Black son-of-a-bitch, you're holdin the gun. Pull the fuckin trigger! Since Michael's death, there hasn't been a day gone by that I haven't thought of doing it myself."

But regardless of the insults Oscar hurls, Nathan sits immobile, a stone statue upon which is chiseled that impassive glare. Then, the unexpected happens. With his sweating hand still coiled around the handle, Nathan lowers the gun. His eyes shift from Oscar to the weapon, back and forth, slow and deliberate, a chess player deciding which move to make . . .

* * *

Nathan's thoughts flash back to the night of the liquor store robbery. "Fuck!" he shouted in horror as he pulled the poster off the dead clerk. Though Nathan had not pulled the trigger, he now asks himself if he again wants to engage in such evil, for this time, in this room, there will be no distance between him and the murderous deed.

* * *

Chuckling, Oscar senses *he* has the advantage. The fuckin prick hasn't got the balls! Lunging forward, Oscar grabs the barrel of Nathan's weapon as gunfire rattles the doors. A bewildered Oscar realizes he is unharmed. An instant before the gunfire, he felt the embrace of a hand on his shoulder. He turns to find Peter standing beside him.

"Be calm, I have slowed time," says Peter.

But Oscar, his hands still coiled around the gun tighter than a boa constrictor, can only focus on the barrel pointed at his chest. Then, Oscar witnesses the terror, a near motionless bullet spat from the mouth of the .45 trailed by a glowing red fireball. Speechless, he drowns in an unrelenting flood of fear awash in wave after wave of terror. Releasing his death grip on the barrel, Oscar tries to duck, run to the door, but as though in a dream, he remains frozen in the bullet's path.

That's it . . . I gotta be having another fuckin nightmare!

"Oh God! Please let me wake up! Please," he says, slapping himself.

"You *are* awake," says Peter, tightening his hold, "but fear not. As long as I touch you, time outside of us moves slowly as granite's decay into sand. I'll take you before the bullet strikes."

"Take me? Take me where?"

"To a place of eternity."

"Sounds like I'm gonna die. Can't you save me?"

"No more than I can save Jerome."

"Damn you, Peter! Who the hell *are* you? What do you want?" says Oscar in wide-eyed hysteria.

"I'm the stranger who intruded and took control of the Citizens for Justice Meeting. You shall now remember everything from *that* Friday night: me, the movies, Alice, the Black Button, and," says Peter, pointing to the gun-toting youth, "Nathan."

Horror howls through Oscar's soul.

"I remember . . . I remember everything!" says Oscar. "It's just like those damn nightmares!"

The storm of Oscar's fury once more swells. Reaching up, he tries to remove the clasped hand on his shoulder.

"Remove my hand and death takes your life the next instant," says Peter.

"Now I know why you're here!" says Oscar, pointing at Nathan, his voice arid with fear. "You sent *him* to fulfill your warning at the meeting, the part about consequences: 'And each of you will suffer the consequences of your actions tonight.' Damn you! Damn both of you!"

"Behold!" says Peter, waving his arm. "Your very own hell! All *this* was set in motion the night you pushed the Black Button, the fruit of your hate. But oddly, Mr. Wilson, I have come to offer you a way *out*!"

"A way out?" says Oscar, grabbing the gun again. "Fruit of my hate? Well, I'd be rude not to share that deadly harvest with my friends."

Though Oscar, straining every fiber in his body, pulls on the gun, the weapon remains immovable as the stone hand gripping the pistol. All the while the .45's glowing red eye stares upon the scene with lethal anticipation as the bullet creeps closer.

Chapter 61

Sanctuary

Oscar finds himself standing within an unbounded white expanse which glows in a brilliance intense as the setting is large. So intense, that the unaccustomed eye aches.

"What's . . . where the hell are we?" asks Oscar. "Where's Nathan and the gun?"

His eyes squinting in pain, Oscar strains to see what might be hiding in the glare of the unlimited setting in which he stands.

"Remember I said I'd offer you a way out of the hell you've created?" says Peter. "We left them behind in the mortal realm."

Upsetting as the mortal realm was, I'm not ready to trade it for an albino one . . . not yet.

Only a mirror, a massive door, plus a metal hatchway on the floor interrupt the bleached, monotonous perfection. The unadorned, black-framed mirror resembles a small bathroom vanity. But the door, as wide as a bowling lane is long, resembles the arched double-door entry of a Gothic cathedral, a door of varnished oak secured by black iron straps with massive handles of solid silver. Carved reliefs of old men in long robes decorate the wooden portal across which stretches an indecipherable inscription of golden inlaid symbols. The hatchway, a four-foot-square sheet of rusted metal secured with a padlock, lies flush with the floor halfway between the mirror and the door.

The sting in Oscar's eyes diminishes as he acclimates to the surroundings.

"Like I said, where in the hell . . . " but he stops in midsentence. Maybe I should use a different profanity.

"We're in a place called Sanctuary," says Peter.

One emotion tripping over another, Oscar turns in a circle, inspecting his predicament.

"Sanctuary, huh? Looks like the inside of a frosted light bulb."

"It's a place of peace and tranquility."

"So, is this like, uh, heaven?"

"No, Heaven lies on the other side of that," says Peter, pointing to the mountainous door.

"Okay. Heaven's over there," says Oscar. "And hell is . . . ?"

"We no longer refer to that place as hell. The name's Perdition, which in ancient times meant being lost or destroyed. Your feet are resting on the entrance," says Peter, pointing to the metal hatch on which Oscar stands.

Oscar scrambles off.

"What's the matter? Hell politically incorrect?"

"That word evokes visions of eternal fire and its pain," says Peter. "Hell's sort of a PR thing we use to entice mortals to play nice. But once they get here, we tell them the truth about Perdition."

"Which is?"

"That's best explained by a guy who's experienced both. Would you care to meet him?"

Ignoring the invitation, Oscar eyes the horizon like a scavenger searching for a meal.

"So, if this is some sort of intersection between Heaven and hell, excuse me, Perdition, I'd expect this place'd be crowded as the Bronx. Where *is* everybody?"

"Due to privacy issues, no two people can occupy the premises at the same time."

"That must cause one damn, big logjam. Where do they all wait?" asks Oscar.

"There isn't any waiting. Remember how I messed around with time? All of us here in Sanctuary do that. In the blink of a mortal's eye, we've passed thousands of souls through these doors."

An answer for everything. This guy musta held public office.

"Okay. Now that we've got the lay of the land with the traffic schedule, I'll ask one more time. What *is* Sanctuary and what the hel . . . blazes am *I* doing here?"

"Sanctuary is a dimension of serenity. Although we simply tell clients it's a place of eternal bliss or peace to avoid trying to define something that must be experienced, it's sort of a waiting room everyone enters before moving on to Heaven or Perdition. Here you'll find yourself contemplating your life. But in your case, remember, we'll *eventually* have to return to the Buying Room."

"Yeah," says Oscar. "But at least tell me where you'll be sending me—Heaven or . . . "

"That will entirely be *your* choice, Mr. Wilson."

Oscar's face brightens. "Oh? Well, gimme a minute." Scratching his chin while his eyes roll upward in thought, he says, "I'll, I'll choose . . . Heaven."

"Well," says Peter with a sigh, "some *do* choose Perdition. However, where you end up depends on your choice of certain alternatives. But all this is premature because you haven't made the final transition yet."

"Why don't we save time. Give me a damn glossary. What does 'final transition' mean?"

"Passing from the mortal realm into the spiritual one," says Peter.

"Kicking the bucket."

"Yeah."

"Then why don't ya just say 'when you *die!*'"

"Well," says Peter, "some people when they're in the situation we are now, tend to get a little fussy when they hear the 'D' word."

"Uh-huh. Damnit, we both know I'm a *dead* man so quit dancing around. What's next?"

"You need to meet that guy I was talking about," says Peter, snapping his fingers as a folding metal chair materializes. "Make yourself comfortable. Back in a couple . . . "

Oscar sits. Crossing his legs, he watches Peter saunter to the massive door. Peter reaches up, knocking on a small flap. It opens. He mumbles something, flicking his thumb back at Oscar. The flap closes. As sliding latches grind with a metallic moan, one-half of the hinged, oak monolith opens partway. Through the narrow breach, fingers of golden mist creep into Sanctuary. Peter glances back, waving goodbye. To the rejoicing of distant voices, he vanishes through the yellow fog. The door closes. Silence returns.

Oscar's pounding heart has relaxed to a rhythmic drumming. He feels like an hour has crawled by since Nathan fired his gun, but only a second has ticked on his watch. Oscar shakes his wrist. *Oh yeah, I forgot, Peter's slowed time. Who woulda thought just minutes ago I was in the Buying Room with that bullet only inches away? Strange, I don't feel frightened. I should. But the gun's flash frozen in midair. Damn, it's weird. This place . . . , Peter. Is all this really happening or just another dream? Or worse, am I already dead?*

Time marches on, slower than stampeding snails.

Oscar grows bored. His attention focuses on the mirror. *Why somethin so plain? If they can afford that door, surely they could pay for a more impressive mirror.*

He walks over to the reversed reality framed in black. A gold label fixed to the bottom reads:

GAZE INTO MY EYES AND BEHOLD THE TRUTH!

"Mirror, mirror on the wall," he says with a sneer.

Oscar peers into the glass. The reflected pair of eyes, eyes which have not slept a full night in months, stare back.

"Yeah, that's them, baggy and bloodshot," he mumbles, transfixed at his reflection.

Slowly, his image disperses in a hazy blur, condensing into the form of a shivering, crying child who lies curled on a concrete floor in a dark, stone-walled room.

"Sherman," says Oscar as the painful, decades-old memory of his son returns.

Oscar had locked little Sherman in a cellar, all night, all alone—punishment for the crime of befriending a Black boy. The same punishment befell Oscar years earlier when Oscar's father found him playing with the Black girl next door.

Next mirrored is his deceased wife, Sherise, crying, her hair recently permed, wearing her favorite Blush Rose lipstick. In a new pink evening dress, she sits alone in a dining room at a candlelit dinner table set for two. Oscar had forgotten another anniversary. Well, not forgotten. He had to address "more *important* matters" as he told her the next day.

In the next image, Sherise wears no dress for a special occasion. In her bathrobe, she lies on the bathroom floor, the smoking revolver still clenched in her hand.

Then, a succession of snapshots drift from the past: an album with an unflattering theme that reflects stabbing daggers of pain, sorrow, and fear. Faces whirl past, at first recognizable: Sherman, Sherise, Jerome, Alice, Nathan, Michael. The faces turn to a blur as they fast-forward: countless, unrecognizable, unrelenting.

"Stop!" cries an exhausted Oscar.

Dumbfounded, Oscar reels from the exposé. The kaleidoscope of images dims. It coalesces into a single face glaring from the glassy, shadowed void, a haggard face draped in sickly flesh—his face. Unable to view the mirror's hideous reflection, a weeping Oscar turns away.

His eyes seek refuge in the white expanse, too fearful to turn and behold the reflection. Never has the ugliness of his life been viewed in such crystal clarity, undistorted by the fog of time, the heat of emotion, or the amnesia of denial. Leaving the mirror, he meanders through Sanctuary.

"Damn Sanctuary! Why must I see these things?" he says, pacing in the ambivalent emptiness.

Hungry as maggots, the images eat at his decaying soul. Again, his eyes scan the expanse. Again, he wanders.

Where's that fuckin Peter? An who does he think he is . . . ? But damnit, he really does seem to care. But no one's ever really cared. I've never asked him or anyone for . . . just doesn't make sense; hell, none of this makes sense!

And in the distant Buying Room, the deadly newborn emerging from the pistol's crimson womb stalks its prey.

* * *

Heaven's door groans open. In the cascading mist stands Peter with a figure behind him.

"Aren't you going to say hello?" says Peter, nearing Oscar. "You look like you've seen a ghost."

Oscar greets Peter with a sideways scowl.

"From your pacing, I'd say you've visited the mirror. From your silence, I'd say your experience wasn't pleasant. Don't worry, that's normal. I remember my first time with the mirror."

Circling back to his chair, Oscar freezes in mid-step.

"You . . . the mirror? That means you were once alive—a mortal!"

"Yes, I was. Like you in the Buying Room, a spirit brought me here in a moment of crisis."

"Well, I'll be damned!"

Instantly the locked entrance to Perdition rattles with a subterranean disturbance.

"Just kidding!" shouts Peter at the metal hatchway. "Where was I? Oh, yeah, *my* crisis. Ninety-two years ago, I died at the hands of a lynch mob. Back then, having Black skin wasn't conducive to one's longevity. Still isn't, *especially* if you're defiant like I was."

"Wait a damn minute, you were Black? But right now, you're white. What gives?"

"My identity has always been a Black soul. I appeared before you today in my white disguise, the same disguise I used at the committee meeting. If I had shown up at your business as a Black man saying the things I did, you wouldn't have listened, or possibly worse; I could've ended up like you, waiting for a bullet."

"Damnit! You tricked me . . . played on my emotions! Just like one'a your kind!"

"Guilty!" says Peter. "But if you despise *my* kind so much, I can always cut this visit short, then take you back to your Buying Room."

Again, Oscar paces about the white expanse. He's . . . he's just a Black man, but I have been talkin to him like . . . like he's one of us. Why's he helping me? He knows how I feel about Blacks. But despite that, he really does seem to care.

Ceasing his agitated walk, Oscar faces Peter without a word.

"Let me finish my story," says Peter. "I was taken captive by twenty vigilantes. They took me prisoner, held their ritual of persecution in a buckboard, and lynched me in front of a mob. Sound familiar?"

"*If* you're referring to the twenty members of the Citizens for Justice and Manning's execution tonight, that's different! He was judged by a jury of his peers in a trial!"

"Different? Like a marble-walled courtroom instead of a horse-drawn wagon? Twelve white jurors instead of a vigilante gang? Dead . . . is dead . . . gas or noose. Anyway, before the rope snapped my neck, a spirit known as a benefactor snatched my soul."

"So, are *you* a benefactor?" asks Oscar, happy to leave Manning in the white silence.

"Yes, Mr. Wilson. I have brought you here so that I too may *help* a distressed soul."

"Well, if that's so, why all the crap with the mirror and Manning?" says Oscar, his thoughts chewing "help" to a pulp.

"Because you'll soon be deciding where to spend eternity: Heaven or Perdition. I'd like to soften your disdain for mankind, your calcified soul, so that you may be molded by the Potter's hand."

"By Potter, I suppose you mean God?" asks Oscar.

Peter's absence of a response confirms Oscar's inquiry.

"Calcified? Yeah, I was hard as the diamonds I fenced to pay Michael's medical bills. Better a hard-nosed prick and save Michael's life than a velvet-tongued jeweler visiting his grave. Potter, huh? How can I trust any son-of-a-bitch who molded the hell of my grandson's life?" says Oscar, having had his fill of a deity that sculptors clay. "So, what took you so long on the other side of that gate, and what's with the golden writing across it?"

"That writing is in the ancient text of the Akkadian language meaning, 'Gate of Forgiveness.' I apologize for my time in Heaven, but it took a while to locate the person I wanted."

"Yeah, finding a particular piece of footwear in a crowd of goody two-shoes could be difficult."

"You'd be surprised who resides on the other side, and who *doesn't*," says Peter.

Turning toward the doors, Peter waves his hand, summoning the person standing in the opening.

"Mr. Wilson, that's the guy I wanted you to meet."

Glowing with joy, Oscar recognizes the approaching figure—

his grandson, Michael. His teenage frame is wispy as a willow from his battle with cystic fibrosis. A pair of blue eyes stare from facial features reminiscent of his grandfather.

"Mike, I think you know this gentleman," says Peter.

"Yeah, Uncle Peter, I know im." Then in the monotone of a bank clerk, he says, "Hi Grandad."

Not a sound emanates from the void of Oscar's gaping mouth. *God, I can't believe that's Michael, but "Hi Grandad" like I'm the neighbor who lent him a screwdriver? An what's with the Uncle Peter? I'm the fuckin blood relative!*

"Michael, I thought I'd never see you again!" says Oscar, choking back his displeasure.

"It's nice to see you too, Grandad. Uh, are you gonna be staying with us?"

"We'll discuss that later," says Peter. "Mike, as I said earlier, I've asked you here because I'd like you to tell your grandfather about the robbery, then your experiences here since you've arrived."

Staring at the floor, Michael shuffles side to side on his feet. His gaze lifting, Michael summons all his courage:

"Grandad, though I love you more than my own father, when Uncle Peter said you were here, I . . . I didn't want to see you."

Oscar steps forward to protest, but Michael stops him.

"Please, let me explain. That night when the liquor store was robbed, the two guys with the guns, I could tell they were Black by the way they talked. I was at the checkout stand. Behind me, covered by the Halloween poster, was the wall safe where we kept most of our cash and a handgun. They ordered me to open the safe. I did. But do you know what I was thinking as I reached in, and grabbed the gun?"

Enthralled by his grandson's confession, Oscar feebly shakes his head no.

"*Not* self-protection. My thought was I finally had a chance to shoot some fuckin Blacks, show em who's boss. Just like you always said, they're all worthless, stupid, or criminals. I was gonna make you proud of me! That's when the guy with the shotgun pulled the trigger."

Oscar drops into the chair, hands cupped across his face, sobbing with remorse.

"The instant before my death, Uncle Peter brought me here. He said I could enter the Gate of Forgiveness into Heaven. Or, if I couldn't let go of my anger, I was welcomed in Perdition.

"Well, that's what I chose. Perdition's not a bad place. No pitchforks, burning pits. The only torment is what your mind creates. For me it kinda felt like the time when I was five and got lost in the woods when we went camping. I was so scared. Remember, Grandad?"

"Yeah, I was scared too," says Oscar, fighting back tears.

"Uncle Peter helped me find my way."

"How?"

Michael's eyes wander up in thought.

"I remember how happy I was when you found me. So happy that I forgot how angry I was with you for not lettin me go fishing. Uncle Peter helped me forget my anger. That's why I call him *Uncle* because here, he's family."

Oscar slumps with dejection.

"But he'll never replace you, Grandad, or Mom. Uncle Peter said Nathan was one of the guys who robbed the store, but he didn't carry the shotgun. I've heard people say, including you, that my soul would never rest until those two are dead. I once felt the same way, but not now. Since I've been here, I've seen the hell of vengeance, especially when it's in the name of justice. Take Manning's death sentence. When his girlfriend Alice learned all the appeals had failed, she killed herself. Nathan ran away to a life of crime on the street which eventually led to the robbery and *my* death. His confrontation with you tonight will lead to *your* death. Like Uncle Peter said, they're all links in the same chain of death forged in the fires of vengeance.

"I love you, Grandad. My heart will ache for your death as much as I did my mom's. But I'm tired of the chain of misery I made from hate and others make in the name of justice! Who's gonna break this chain of misery? Not me. I'm dead. You? Not from what I've seen, which is why I could barely bring myself to see you. You *are* that chain."

Taking deep breaths to cool his passion, Michael hugs Oscar then retreats through the Gate of Forgiveness.

Chapter 62

Material to Spiritual

After Sanctuary's brief excursion, Oscar, escorted by Peter, returns to the Buying Room of Wilson's Jewelry. Oscar assumes his position in a setting reminiscent of a horror movie scene: two men, he and Nathan, sit on drafting stools at opposite ends of a worktable. His arms stretched forward, Oscar clutches the pistol aimed and fired at him by Nathan. With motion slow as a glacier's crawl due to Peter's time dilation, the bullet hovers in midair, a lead messenger pursuing a lethal destiny from the gun barrel's red glow. Through the smoke of the discharged gun, Oscar glares at the approaching, unhurried hell. Releasing the pistol, he looks for his benefactor.

"Peter . . . Peter, are you here? Peter!" Oscar screams, his pleas ricocheting from wall to wall.

"Do not be afraid," answers a voice from the darkness.

A warm hand touches Oscar, briefly thawing his terror.

"Peter, thank God . . . I . . . I . . . thought you'd abandoned me."

"I'm here beside you," says Peter, his hold on Oscar tightening.

"What's happening?"

"You have begun the transition from the mortal to the spiritual realm."

"So, just like you said in Sanctuary, I'm gonna die."

Oscar lunges for the desk drawer containing his Luger. Grunting, he yanks on the drawer which remains immovable, steadfast as righteous indignation.

"Mr. Wilson, that drawer, like every other earthly object except yourself, is frozen in time. They cannot be moved or," pointing to the bullet, "altered."

Oscar releases the drawer, sagging on his stool, nauseous with terror. Though stubborn as the night yielding to dawn, the panic once more fades as Peter rubs Oscar's back.

"I've again removed your desperate feelings, but . . . "

"But what?"

"You'll keep seeking the comfort of fear, grasping it like a starving man for breadcrumbs."

"I don't do *crumbs* of anything. I'll take the whole fuckin loaf!"

"How true. You've gorged yourself hoping to be sated by a buffet of ambition, power, and vengeance; all symptoms of fear, your whole life. But this is your banquet's final course," says Peter, waving his arm at the macabre scene. "You've seldom tasted love nor nourished your soul with mercy or justice."

With the bullet just inches away, Oscar questions the timing of this smorgasbord sermon.

"What the hell ya mean? I have *too*, uh, loved . . . I've . . . " says Oscar as his thoughts condense into a memory. "I remember the first time I saw my son, Sherman, in his mother's arms. My God, how beautiful that was. That's before she . . . I . . . we were still . . . "

"Before she killed herself?"

"Yeah. Ya know, I've never talked to anybody about this. I guess I'm telling you now cause I've got nothin to lose.

"And then there's my grandson, Michael. My beautiful, *dead* Michael," says Oscar, aiming a finger at Nathan. "Damn him! *He's* one of em that killed him, and now he's gonna kill *me*! Where's your 'mercy or justice' in that?"

"Not my justice, Oscar, yours—revenge—the justice you've dispensed all your life."

Oscar slumps on his stool. So's what's with all the accusations? What good are they now?

"Do you know what separates justice from vengeance, Mr. Wilson?"

"Lawyers."

"Love."

"Love? Yeah, right, plus a gun."

"What *is* your problem?" says Peter, leaning forward, eye to eye with Oscar. "Don't you realize I'm here to help you? That as your benefactor I *love* you! But you fight me at every step!"

Peter inhales, composing himself.

"Uh, let's start over. I too fought my benefactor. As I've told you before, I wanted revenge on those who'd lynched me. Years passed before I overcame the hate. So trust me when I say I know what you're going through."

Peter points to the bullet inches from Oscar's chest.

"You're as good as dead, Oscar. And I know you're afraid— demon fear is a formidable foe. But unless you do *one* thing to save yourself, *one* act of redemption, you've condemned yourself to years if not an eternity of self-inflicted hell."

"Damnit, I'm about to pay the ultimate price! Isn't that punishment enough 'redemption'?"

"Punishment never redeems anyone," says Peter. " I'm trying to save you from the hell I went through. Didn't you learn anything at Sanctuary? Remember the mirror, the window into the past?"

Oscar's defiance deflates as the mirror's kaleidoscope of images tumbles in his mind: the reflections of Oscar's agony suffered at his father's hands, Oscar's crippled soul later seeking restitution by persecuting those he hated *and* those he loved. For the first time in his life, Oscar reflects on this suffering, exhuming the regrets he has buried under years of denial.

"Peter, I . . . you *know* the remorse I feel for the horrible things I've done."

"I know, but remorse isn't enough. To make peace with oneself, one must make atonement."

I was afraid he was leading to this atonement thing.

"Your atonement must be a sacrifice benefiting someone you feel is unworthy," says Peter.

Sacrifice for someone unworthy stabs at the one thing Oscar has left: his pride.

"Peter, I'm not so sure I can," says Oscar, flicking an eye at the bullet. "I mean, *what* can I do from here with so little time, and for whom?"

"When seeking an answer, ask the question out of love. Maybe this will help."

Peter slips his hand between Oscar and the bullet, presses Oscar's chest, then removes his hand.

A soothing warmth radiates throughout Oscar, consuming his consciousness, and liberating his soul. Never has he experienced such an awareness of self, void of ego. Once more he reflects on Sanctuary's events. He remembers this liberation had been experienced by his grandson. Michael had also expressed remorse for the chain of misery his and others' sins had made, pleading, "Who's gonna break this chain of misery?" Michael's appeal nags Oscar. I wonder how my sins, deadly as that bullet, had contributed to Michael's death?

Fingers drumming the table, Oscar glares at Nathan. The drumbeat quickens as Michael's plea pounds in his head. The drumming stops. Oscar decides. Reaching into his shirt pocket, he removes the pen and paper he had placed earlier this evening. The paper he tears in two.

Moments pass. Flourishing with satisfaction, Oscar thrusts the pen into his pocket. On the table lie two notes composed with a surprisingly steady hand, notes which until this moment he swore he would never write. He folds the two pieces of paper, handing them to Peter.

Releasing a final sigh, Oscar leans forward, grabbing the fire-breathing pistol. With Peter's gentle grip on each shoulder consoling him, he closes his eyes.

"I'm ready . . . "

The fatal momentum of the bullet concludes. All becomes silent.

Chapter 63

Gate of Forgiveness

The instant the bullet touches Oscar's chest, Peter rescues and brings Oscar's soul here to Sanctuary. A white eternity stretches before them.

"I'm going to release your shoulder," says Peter. "You'll feel a little discomfort."

Peter's grip slackens. Oscar wheels with dizziness and nausea twist his stomach as his legs buckle like flat tires. He grabs Peter for support.

"There, that wasn't too bad, was it?" says Peter.

"I feel like I've been tumbled dried. What happened?"

"You've severed all of mortal reality's ties, the final transition. You've just experienced the withdrawal from the material to the spiritual."

Regaining his balance, Oscar closes his eyes, calming his trauma of transition. Retrieving his vision, he surveys the bleached expanse which consumes him. In this white monochrome, released from mortal hate and fear, his senses awake eager as a rosebud awaiting spring. In death he is reborn.

Once more, Oscar awes at the Gate of Forgiveness towering before him. In mortal reality, less than a millisecond has expired since his initial visit. In celestial time, years have passed. During these years, a lone figure has kept watch. That lone figure stands beside the Gate. Oscar leans forward, squinting to recognize the stranger. As his eyes adjust to the brightness, the form sharpens in focus.

"Michael!" shouts Oscar, running to his grandson.

They embrace with a hug molded in love.

"Grandad, you gonna stay with us in Heaven?"

"I think that's up to him," says Oscar, pointing to Peter in the distance.

Peter saunters forward.

"What's that you said?" asks Peter.

"Michael's asked if he and I are gonna live together."

"And?"

"And I told im you'd have to answer that. Remember our first visit?" says Oscar. "You said, 'We'll discuss that later.' Well, *this* is 'later.'"

"So this is," says Peter, his eyes rolling up in thought as Oscar awaits a response . . . and waits.

"Well, where ya sending me! Heaven or hell?"

"It's not called hell anymore, remember? Perdition. Possibly you've forgotten other things about your first visit."

"Peter, I haven't forgotten a thing . . . It's just that so much's happened. I *do* remember Perdition's kinda like a minimum-security prison with a self-imposed sentence. And my crime? Vengeance. I can reduce the sentence by surrendering to forgiveness, to love."

Moments pass. All three stand in the peroxided setting, staring at each other, focused as owls waiting for the other's first hoot. Peter ends the deadlock.

"Michael, you'd be proud of what your grandad did. Remember when you asked who would break the 'chain of misery'?"

"Yeah?" says Michael.

"Well, he hacksawed a couple of its links."

"Uncle Peter, you sayin Grandad actually helped Nathan?" asks Michael, turning to Oscar. "What'd you do?"

"Grandad can brag about all this later," says Peter, then shifts his attention to Oscar. "As a new arrival, protocol requires that *you*, not me, make the choice: Perdition or Heaven. Normally, this would require some time on your part, but since this is your second visit, I assume you've already decided."

Oscar hesitates, but not due to indecision. How does he describe the longest journey of his life, the eighteen inches from the chaos of his mind to the tranquility of his heart?

Perdition allows you time to reflect on your past and consider a willingness to change your hateful way of thinking. It's all about surrender and love. There was a time when I thought surrender's just another word for weakness. And love . . . well, based on my experience, love faded faster than cheap paint in Vegas. But thanks to Peter, that's all changed.

Oscar takes his grandson's hand.

"I choose you, Michael, my sunshine in the darkness. I choose Heaven."

Then, his eyes softened by tears, Oscar faces his white-disguised benefactor.

"My friend, I can't believe how you've helped me. All my life I've treated Black people like you with contempt. But here you are, reuniting me with my Michael. I never imagined I'd enjoy such a reward after I died. Why, you even saved me from the pain of my death. My death . . . huh, I can hear all the Black folks in town celebratin."

He offers his hand to Peter, who immediately bats the extended appendage away.

"Not good enough!" says Peter, throwing his arms around Oscar.

Releasing his captive, Peter walks to the Gate. As he knocks, a hinged flap opens through which he whispers, punctuated by backward nods at Oscar. The flap closes. Grinning, Peter leans against the Gate, folding his arms.

Oscar watches Peter's odd behavior. *So far, everything's gone pretty good . . . too good. Hmm, maybe this is the calm before* the storm. Maybe there's something else I gotta do. But what if I can't or I'm unwilling to do that something? Maybe now's the time for a confession.

Oscar locks a hand on his grandson's shoulder.

"Michael, I don't know how much longer we have together, so I'll say this now."

"Say what Grandad?"

"For my entire life, I've been in a constant state of anger. It gnawed at my soul. I was too proud to talk about it. But *now* I can find the words and the courage to speak. I suppose this anger was really fear, fear I wouldn't get the things I wanted. Fear I'd lose more than I'd already lost in life: your grandmother, your father's affection, you. Fear that I'd be found out for the failure I really was.

"The only way I could handle this fear was to torment people, people who were too weak to fight back. It made me feel superior. The good citizens of Barkersville provided these people: Blacks like Jerome and Nathan. But even as I harassed them, deep down I was ashamed, scared of the consequences to come if not in life, then in death. Bigotry, shame, more cruelty, more shame, a never-ending cycle of moral sickness. To my regret, I infected you with my disease. I had to die before I found a cure. Forgive me, Michael, I'm so sorry."

From Michael's shoulder, Oscar's hand drifts to his side like the last leaf of a dead tree floating to earth.

"With those words," says Peter, approaching Oscar, "Heaven's fraternity awaits."

With the flourish of a palace doorman, Peter sweeps his arm towards the Gate. One of the paired oak doors groans open. Through the breach, golden blankets of fog flow into Sanctuary.

"Peter," says Oscar, "words can't express the shame for my deeds that led Nathan to his act of vengeance. Unfortunately, shame can't stop Jerome's execution tonight. But you know the amends I wrote on those two notes. Though they may be feeble attempts, I trust you can see they are fulfilled."

Peter nods yes.

"As for others I've harmed, I can never make restitution. I can only pray for their happiness. Pray they find the peace of forgiveness. Not for my sake, but for theirs.

"Thank you, my benevolent friend," says Oscar, wrapping himself around Peter.

Oscar steps back to Michael. Once more they embrace, reunited in the assurance their union will never again be severed.

The Gate of Forgiveness swings wide. Laughter spills into Sanctuary. Oscar and Michael, draped in each other's arms, disappear through the opened door.

Chapter 64

Hit and Run

The acrid aroma of spent gunpowder bites Nathan's nose as his face glistens with a sheen of sweat in the pale light. In front of him lies Oscar, dead on the table, blood seeping from under the edges of his lifeless form. The dead man's hands extend forward, still grasping the barrel of the pistol which lies on the table. His eyes nailed on the death scene, Nathan leans forward on the table, satisfied Oscar has finally atoned for his sins.

Nathan's thoughts flash back to this afternoon when on the pretext of having some jewelry "appraised," he coaxed his way into the Buying Room. When Nathan slid the ring across the table, he knew of the jeopardy to his life. Oscar owned a gun and would use it, especially on a Black man. But the look of terror on Oscar's face, realizing the ring lying before him had belonged to Michael, was worth the gamble. Joyfully watching Oscar's horror, Nathan drew his .45, aiming the gun at the pompous former mayor.

But then, Nathan's deadly intentions took an unexpected turn. He remembered his terror at the Double A robbery witnessing the cashier's violent death. Nathan had asked himself if he could initiate such evil.

No . . .

So he decided to let Oscar live and lowered the weapon. Nathan knew life would be crueler than a quick death; a life in which each day is another twenty-four hours endured in the hellish void of a loved one's violent absence. A life just like Nathan's.

Though he intended to spare Oscar, Nathan feels no remorse for his demise.

Why'd he go and grab the gun an yank on it after I lowered

it? He knew there wasn't no way with him bein an old man that he was gonna take it from me. Kinda like the son-of-a-bitch wanted to die! But what do I do now?

With his heart pounding louder than clanging symbols, Nathan surveys the room. He walks to the other side of the desk, gawking at the corpse draped across the table. Blood drips from the lifeless flesh to the floor. Lifting the dead body with his gloved hands, Nathan searches for the ring which should lie within the red pool. But the golden adornment eludes him.

Musta dropped on the floor when we were fightin over the gun.

Finding the ring is crucial. After Michael's murder, Oscar described it in detail to the police, though so far they are unaware of the ring's connection to Nathan. But the criminal community is well aware of Nathan's distinctive, illicit possession. If the ring ends up in the wrong thief's hand, word could leak to authorities. However, Nathan is not concerned as he has all night to find the golden evidence. He lowers the cadaver exactly into the body's original position.

At that moment, Nathan has an epiphany.

"I'm gonna make this look like the fuckin old man went and shot imself!"

The excited revelation bounces from wall to wall. Removing the .45 from the dead man's extended right hand, he turns the gun around such that the weapon is held by its handle instead of the barrel. The gun's serial numbers have been filed away. Gloves will eliminate any fingerprints. Nothing can link Nathan to the murder weapon. Surveying the place to ensure nothing other than the ring lies within to betray his presence, he notices near the body a slightly opened desk drawer which he pulls open. Nathan finds Oscar's Lugar.

Well, I'll be God damned, a trade for my .45!

As he reaches inside for the weapon, Nathan finds the suicide letter, which he reads.

"Hell!" he says, followed by hideous laughter. "The son-of-a-bitch did wanna die!"

Still chuckling, Nathan shoves the letter back inside, but as his gloved hand touches the Luger, his joy chokes with a gasp. He notices the pouch tied to his belt, the pouch which contains his mother's jewelry with the news clippings is slightly open.

Somethin's missin.

"Shit! I hope that fuckin thing didn't fall out here!"

The "thing" is a ball of ribbon-wrapped tissue, the contents of which are a birthday present to his momma consisting of a small, white, ceramic dove with the inscription:

With love: Nathan and Jerome.

On the day of Alice's suicide, Nathan took the dove, jewelry, plus the *Gazette* articles. He ran out of the apartment yelling, "I'm gonna fuckin kill that Wilson fella one day!"

Neighbors heard this threat. They informed the police, who have been looking for Nathan ever since without success.

Accordingly, if authorities find the dove in this dead man's room, the entire Barkersville police force would be mobilized. Nathan would be found, arrested, and tried. Considering all the evidence, a death sentence would be declared before the echo of the judge's gavel died in the courtroom.

Distant sirens stab Nathan's attention. Someone musta heard the gunshot and called the police!

"Shit!"

Nathan was certain the cinder block walls of the Buying Room together with the night's storm would have subdued any noise. He drops to the concrete floor. On hands and knees, he scours the dingy confines, his extended hands flailing back and forth with the frenzy of a blind man who's dropped his cane.

The whine of approaching justice grows louder. Unable to find the dove or ring, he leaves the Luger behind and runs out the back door, stopping with the presence of mind to lock the knob. Leaping into the alley to the sound of rumbling thunder, he disappears into the darkness.

Sirens scream past the store, heading to a car wreck in the Grace District down by the river.

Chapter 65

A Premeditated Killing

"Thou Shalt Not Kill" posters wave desperately as distress flags over the thirteen protesters enduring the December night at the Iron Mountain Correctional Center. At 11:00 p.m. the group will drop to their knees reciting the Lord's Prayer as cyanide gas fills the execution chamber entombing Jerome Manning.

Inside the prison, in a sterile corridor, a wall clock reads 8:29 p.m. On the hallway's opposite side, a Black clergyman claiming to be from the First Baptist Church sits on a metal folding chair in front of the Death Watch Cell. His back to the clock, he hunches forward, his attention focused through the steel bars at the prisoner, Jerome Manning, clad in an orange jumpsuit inside the drab, gray concrete confines. Jerome sits on a cot at arm's length from the bars nervously staring at the Black preacher.

For three hours, the minister and Jerome talk as casually as two kids trading their summer's escapades. But as the eleven o'clock deadline nears, the conversation grows more intense.

"Jerome, that Bible's sittin there lonesome as a lost dog. Do you have a favorite passage you'd like me to read?" asks the minister. "Miss Pinch says she used to read to you quite a bit."

Despite his present circumstances, Jerome still isn't a religious person. He saw no benefit worshipping a deity who patronized and resembled white people. But Miss Pinch and the folks at First Baptist Church were tolerant, charitable, and polite. So Jerome tolerated their God just as he tolerated Ms. Pinch's readings, some of which were quite fanciful, including that Noah guy inside his floating zoo. Besides, her stories always came with a postscript of tongue-enticing chocolate chip cookies.

"Ya know," says Jerome to the minister, "I don't remember seein ya at the church before."

"Well, my child, I'm kinda new there. Truth be told, today's my first day."

"Did ya know I use ta work there before that Wilson guy got the church's daycare shut down? He was mayor then an said that place brought in the wrong kinda people—Black folks."

"Yes, Miss Pinch told me. She's the one who asked me to come see you. 'Be sure to tell Jerome I'm praying for him.' That's what she said."

Between the minister and the cell bars stands a worn leather attaché case as large as an ice chest. He reaches inside. Grunting, he sets a large book on his lap.

"All right, give me a scripture you wanta hear," says the minister, slapping *The BOOK*.

Jerome fidgets on his cot. He glances at the hall clock which reads 9:01 p.m. *How come thirty minutes go by so fast when them seconds they drag slow as snails?*

"Why don't you pick somethin, but don't make em too long," says Jerome.

Under the clock looms the window of the Death Watch Room through which a correctional officer alongside his sergeant maintains a suicide watch. Jerome's eyes trudge from window to clock in which the hour hand relentlessly circumnavigates the final two revolutions of his life.

"My mind's mushy as Miracle Whip," says the minister, slapping his forehead. "There's a couple of things I'm supposed to give you."

Setting the weighty tome down, he checks for invasive eyes in the window, but observes none.

"That guard at the sally port," he says, slapping the briefcase, "was gonna search this when I told him there'd be *hell* to pay if he started messing with the Lord's business! If he weren't a God-fearin man, I wouldn't be giving you this."

The minister removes a small cardboard box, hunching forward to shield his activities from the Watch Room. Shaking, he slips the package through the bars, placing the box on the cot.

"Sorry. I'm kinda new at this sorta thing," he whispers.

"Me too," says Jerome, nodding at the walls. "Lyin an sneakin this in. Ain't that some kinda sin? An you being a minister an all."

"Long as I'm not swearing on the 'Good Book,' and I'm helping one of God's children, a bent truth is forgiven."

His hands trembling, Jerome opens the package. He pulls out a ring, a distinctive white gold ring embossed with two crosses on either side of a large diamond. His chest tightens.

"Ya know, this don't bring up a lotta good memories," says a shocked Jerome. He sets the ring on the blanket. "Where'd ya get this?"

"From a friend."

"Somethin funny's goin on here. You got some other stuff from this 'friend'?"

The minister then hands Jerome a wad of tissue paper wrapped in a pink ribbon.

Untying the band, a small, white, ceramic dove drops onto his lap. Immediately, tears flood Jerome's eyes.

Into his hand nestles the dove. Its ceramic-glazed surface soaks Jerome's warmth as his cheeks dimple in delight. Jerome reflects on the happiness he felt as a part of a family with Alice and Nathan. As the dimple expands to a smile, his somber face glows. But with Alice's death, he worries how Nathan will survive on the streets. Shoulders slumping, Jerome slips the dove into his trousers.

The minister slips the last of three items through the bars: a folded note, the first of Oscar's two notes composed at his desk just hours ago in the Buying Room. Elbows planted on each knee, Jerome hunches forward, reading the scribed message, bewilderment contorting his face.

"Did you *read* this?" asks Jerome.

"Yes."

Jerome's eyes wander about the barren confines, stopping at the window across the hall. He notices both officers strapping on duty belts. *Don't got me much time left alone.* Taking the ring, he twists the ornament on his finger. Sighing, he again reads the note.

"Ya know," says Jerome, his brow folded in kindly reflection, "Mary, when she come by to see me yesterday, she say she told the newspaper that what they doin ta me is nothin more than a premeditated killin. I asked her not ta come today. That Mary, she a wonderful person visitin me, considerin what I done to her Timmy.

"She even say she gonna try an find Nathan. Ya know, I don't have no blood relations an that boy he like a son. I know he gotta be feelin lonely an filled with hate, then I got ta thinkin. These things you give me, they might help im out. The ring, it represent that crime don't pay. This dove will get him rememberin all them good times we had like a family. An this letter, it might teach him that people even like that Wilson fella can change. Ya think you can get all these things to Mary?"

"It'd be my honor."

Jerome stares at the clock.

"Ya know," says Jerome, his tongue wiping his fear-dried lips, "I ain't told nobody this before, but I had a dream that I met Timmy. It was like in this big white place with nobody around. Timmy, he say the strangest thing. He say he actually forgives me even though it was my bullet that shot him. Ya know, I never did know that for sure."

The creak of the Watch Room door opening stifles any response to Jerome's revelation.

Fear distorting his sight, Jerome watches two uniformed men march forward, one clutching a set of handcuffs along with leg shackles. The clack of boots invades the concrete-walled silence.

Images of past sins boil in Jerome's mind.

"The Devil he was doin his work through me," confesses Jerome. "Now I didn't mean ta hurt that poor child. But if I had just decided not to go with Anthony, that grocery store it never woulda been robbed. An Alice she'd still be alive an Nathan he would still have his momma. So now I gotta pay the price an I'm alright with it."

He clamps the minister's hand.

"Now I ain't what ya call a true believer, but if they's a Lawd up in heaven, ya think He gonna forgive me if I'm like real sorry for all my sins?"

"My child," says the minister, returning the desperate grip, "He's already forgiven you. He's just waiting for you to ask so you can start forgiving yourself."

Trembling, Jerome slides the ring off his finger. He slips the ring and the letter into the other trousers' pocket. Correctional Sergeant Branch and Correctional Officer James Kinsley halt in front of the condemned man's cell.

"Mr. Manning, time to get you prepared," says the sergeant, opening the cell. "Please stand."

Jerome staggers to his feet. Dread bleaches his face.

"Jerome, would you like me to make the walk with you?" asks the minister.

"Yeah, I'd like you ta do that."

"After our walk, I'll see you from the Viewing Room. You rest your eyes on me, my child."

Kinsley kneels, securing the restraints. Sergeant Branch notices the bulge in Jerome's pockets.

"Mr. Manning, I'm gonna have to take whatever contraband you're hiding. Nothing other than your clothing is permitted outside this cell," says the sergeant.

"Yes, Sir."

Removing the ring and letter, Jerome hands them to Branch.

"The other pocket, too."

Jerome feigns a querying stare.

"Mr. Manning, I said the other pocket—now!"

A wad of tissue paper drops onto the sergeant's extended hand. Branch unwinds the bundle, exposing the ceramic dove as he turns to the minister.

"Reverend, you were warned *not* to give the prisoner anything!"

"The Lord made me do it!"

The minister points a finger heavenward, then hesitates, squinting an eye at Kinsley.

"What?" asks Kinsley.

"My child, don't you belong to our congregation, First Baptist Church?" asks the minister. "Sure, you're Jimmy, Jimmy Kinsley. I've seen your picture on the *New Member* bulletin board."

The minister extends his hand. The two shake as an incredulous sergeant glares.

"Can Mr. Manning keep the items? This would be the Christian thing to do," says the minister.

"Sarge," says an embarrassed Kinsley, "I know the regulations, but so what? I can put this stuff in my trousers. After I've strapped him in, I'll give them back to him. No one will notice. I'll be sure to take em back when . . . uh . . . *after* . . . "

"Well, I suppose we can make an exception with this contraband since this man of the cloth made the request. But for Christ's sake, Jimmy, uh, pardon me, Reverend, *don't* tell anyone."

The sarge hands the items to Kinsley, who finishes strapping the prisoner in steel.

Chains rattling, Jerome trudges down the hall, held by Kinsley and the sergeant.

"Fear not my son," says the minister, trailing behind.

"Ya know, I never did get your name," says Jerome, turning his head back.

"They call me Peter."

* * *

Peter, still disguised as the Black minister, stands alone at the rear of the Viewing Room.

The last of the witnesses, members of the Citizens for Justice Committee enter. Filing past to their seats, they chatter about their chairman, Oscar Wilson. He was unexpectedly absent from his Citizen of the Year Award Ceremony this evening. His continued absence adds to their alarm.

The room has padded folding chairs, carpet, and freshly painted green walls including a black drape covering the Execution Chamber windows. There even stands a table full of bottled water. The two dozen witnesses sit in anticipation as the rattle of the air conditioner distracts the quiet. Peter's reminded of a theatre venue, the audience waiting for the start of Act One, as curtains shield the performance's setting from view. On stage in the Execution Chamber, Kinsely and the sergeant strap the star of tonight's performance into his chair.

A sweat of dread beads on Peter's forehead as his mind retreats to a hot afternoon ninety-two years ago when two hundred howling citizens stood in the dust, gorging their eyes on his half-naked body dangling from a rope. He muses how antiseptic and polite legal murder has evolved.

A correctional officer bursts into the viewing room. Appearing to recognize a well-dressed man with graying hair, he weaves through the spectators. After whispering into the man's ear, the officer leaves. The gray-haired man stands.

"Members of the committee. I have distressing news. I've just learned that the Barkersville police have found the body of our beloved chairman, Oscar Wilson. He lies dead in his office.

"It appears he died by his own hand."

* * *

Exactly as flashed upon the screen by Peter's magical projector at the Citizens for Justice Committee meeting over three years ago, the execution proceeds.

After strapping Jerome into the execution chair, Kinsley pulls from his uniform's pocket the three items he had taken from the cell. On one of Jerome's fingers, he slides the ring. Into the same hand, he inserts the folded note. In Jerome's other hand, Kinsley places the dove. The curtains of the execution chamber part. Jerome looks through the window into a sea of hate.

In the first row of chairs sits Timmy's father, Kevin, twisting in a hateful pose.

"I'm sorry," mouths Jerome to Kevin as he squeezes the note.

Straining to see Mary, Jerome sighs with relief to find her absent, as they both had agreed.

Jerome sees the Viewing Room's clock, 10:58 p.m. In the remaining two minutes, all his preparation for this final episode abandon him in a burst of panic. As he gasps, preparing to cry and curse fate, he looks into the Viewing Room, locking eyes on the Black minister named Peter. Their spirits converge, immersed in a protective calm.

"Are there any last words before sentence is imposed, Mr. Manning?" asks the warden after reading the death sentence.

Jerome, eyes still fixed on Peter, makes a final request for forgiveness of his crime, then breaks eye contact, gazing upward.

"Auntie Helen, Alice, I'm comin for a long visit."

The clock marks the eleventh hour. Cyanide pellets splash into a tank of acid. Death's aroma fills the chamber.

Feeling a hand on his shoulder, Jerome finds himself standing beside the minister there in the Execution Chamber. Jerome stares at his body writhing in the chair, but strangely, he feels no pain or fear, only a sense of peace in which he loses himself for the rest of his life.

"Be not afraid, my child, I am with you."

A white continuum engulfs Jerome. Standing beside Peter, he stares at a massive wooden gate. To one side of it wait two Black women and a young white boy: Auntie Helen, Alice, and Timmy.

Chapter 66

The Suicide Letter

*T*o whom it may concern:

I have been in great distress lately over Michael's death. I see no point in going on without him. I have decided to stop my pain the only way I know.

Before I leave this life, I must unburden my conscience and make two confessions:

First, I've been running a fencing operation from this room dealing in stolen jewelry. I've sold this merchandise in my store after making alterations to each piece. All proceeds have gone solely to help pay for my grandson's cystic fibrosis medical treatments.

Secondly, and with extreme remorse, I have participated with Judge Daring in influencing the outcome of Jerome Manning's murder trial. The judge and I conspired to ensure Jerome was convicted of first-degree murder and sentenced to death. I did this to protect my illegal jewelry operation. Jerome knew about my fencing scheme as he once sold me a stolen ring. His Honor's motivation was to ensure his re-election by showing the public he was tough on criminals, especially naturally violent Blacks.

Judge me as you see fit, but it will in no way be worse than I've judged myself.

Oscar Wilson
November 16, 1991

* * *

Impassive as reading a dinner menu, Judge Daring sets the typed confession on his desk. He leans back in his leather chair, arms folded across his chest, staring at the Barkersville Chief of Police, Jerry Stillwell, sitting on the opposite side of the mahogany desk. The chief twists and squirms. Pimples of sweat pockmark his face as though he is the co-conspirator accused in the letter. Time scored by the room's grandfather clock ticks pass.

"Judge Daring, the only other person who's seen that letter is the detective who found it last night in Wilson's desk drawer," says the chief.

Marching from his desk, hands clenched behind his back, the judge stops in front of the bay window overlooking the manicured plants in his gardens. In silence he glares outside, the veins in his neck protruding, bold as fire hoses.

The chief crouches in his chair. His eyes fawn like a puppy watching its master.

"Rest assured, Your Honor, he'll remain silent."

The judge returns to his seat and reads the confession again, flinging the note on the table.

"Stillwell, you were saying you're hesitant about declaring his death a suicide?"

"Yes, Sir. Several things bother me."

"Such as?"

"Well, take the shot to the heart. I've never seen a suicide like that. Yeah, cleaner than your brains splattered on a wall, but what if your aim is off? A headshot's a sure thing," says the chief. "Another concern is the room's alley door. Though the door was locked, anyone could have locked the knob from the inside then left. But the steel bar wasn't lowered, the deadbolts not thrown.

This could only be done from the inside. Employees say only Wilson had access to this door which he used for deliveries. He'd always immediately replace the bar.

"The suicide firearm's another issue. The pistol's serial numbers were filed off. The clip was full, minus the suicide round. No additional .45 ammo was found anywhere. But in a desk drawer, we discovered a new Lugar, including a full box of ammo. Wilson had registered the Luger, but not the .45."

"Sounds like the .45 was a throw-away," says the judge. "So what?"

"Yeah, but why fill the clip if you're going to shoot yourself? In case you missed?

"Which makes this whole thing about Wilson's suicide a little messy. Someone could have interrupted a suicide in progress, deciding to just 'help' it along. There's also the possibility someone could've coerced Wilson into writing that letter at gunpoint, killed him, then tried to fake a suicide."

"Well, if his death was murder," says the judge as a thought glows on his face, "I assume you have some suspects."

"Word on the street is there's an indigent Black male, Nathan Smith, who's been making threatening remarks about Wilson. Smith's unwed mother, Alice, and Manning were lovers."

"I remember all that from the trial," says the judge.

"The mother killed herself when she learned Manning was going to be executed. Mr. Smith found her body the next morning. He threatened to kill Wilson because he was the chair of the Citizens for Justice Committee lobbying for Manning's death sentence—Motive. Neighbors clearly heard the threat. So far we've discovered nothing that would place Smith at the scene, but we're looking for evidence, and him."

"Humph," grunts the judge, flashing a raptor's gaze at the chief. "I wonder if someone saw this Smith fellow running from Oscar's store that night."

The chief shifts in his chair, glancing at his watch.

"Am I keeping you from something, Jerry?"

"Uh, I've promised to take my wife to a late lunch this afternoon."

"Well, it's pretty clear what you need to do."

"Thank you, Your Honor, for understanding," says the chief, rising from his chair then stops in mid-air as his face furrows in a frown.

"Where the hell do you think you're going?"

"Well, uh, I was just going home, like you said, but Sir, there's somethin else I . . . "

Stillwell drops back in his seat.

"What I meant by 'what you need to do' is find Smith," says the judge. "Hold him for questioning."

"But we can only hold im for twenty-four hours without sufficient evidence. You know that."

The judge stabs both elbows on the table. This fuckin Stillwell can be irritating as a root canal without novocaine.

"What I know is you've disturbed my Sunday afternoon. You dare enter my home carrying this mendacious letter obviously written under duress by my dear friend Oscar."

The judge grabs a silver bell from the table, ringing for the maid.

"Chief, thank you for the courtesy of your visit."

"You want something, Sir?" asks the maid, opening the double doors to the office.

"Yes, Cynthia. Mr. Stillwell was just leaving. Please show him out."

"Yes Sir," says Cynthia. "Mr. Stillwell . . . "

"Uh, Ma'am, His Honor and I aren't quite finished," says the chief, wiping his forehead with a handkerchief, "are we, Sir?"

Her hand on the knob, Cynthia waits by the door.

"It seems I was premature, Cynthia. You may leave. Please close the door."

As the clatter of varnished wood striking the jamb fades, a drum roll of fingers thumps from the chief's side of the table.

"Uh, Your Honor, I was gonna mention something else, but I . . . Sir, my reason for coming here this afternoon was more than a courtesy call about Wilson's death."

"No shit. I thought as much since you didn't bring flowers," says the judge with crossed arms.

Hand trembling, the chief continues to mop his face.

"About our conversation this afternoon, and the letter. Sir, I'd never . . . "

"Use that fuckin letter against me? Blackmail? You're damn right you won't!" says the judge, picking up the bell.

"Judge Daring, please let me explain. Everything started when I bought some earrings from Wilson at a really good price. I'd heard rumors about his fencing operation. Knew these were probably stolen as they closely matched a pair reported in a home burglary."

Dropping the bell, His Honor's eyes glow with delight.

"Go on," says Daring, suspecting this rotten morsel is just the tip of a buried garbage dump.

"Well, they weren't for my wife. You see, I had this lady friend. We broke up. She's pissed. Knows everything about the earrings. She's said she's threatening to go to the mayor and the newspaper . . . "

"And shovel shit in the fan! So, besides a divorce and possibly being arrested for receiving stolen property, the City Council would most assuredly rescind your Chief of Police appointment."

Judge Daring pauses.

"However, since I'm on very cordial terms with the mayor and the *Gazette* owner, I could ask them to keep all this quiet; a little risky. Oh, I almost forgot, if you are arrested and brought to trial,

I'd be the presiding judge. Hmm, interesting . . . "

The chief descends deeper into his seat.

"So, in return for a promise to save your horny ass you offer this!" says the judge, waving the letter. "I'll have to give this careful consideration."

The old clock's monotonous cadence continues. By now, the chief cowers so low in his seat that the only thing visible is a handkerchief dabbing the top of his head.

"Alright, this is what you're going to do, *Jerry*. Find Smith. Detain im for questioning. Get the whole department involved. Get written statements from witnesses who overheard his threats. Before his twenty-four hours are up, someone will come forward swearing he or she saw Smith running from Wilson's store at the time of death. Then, you'll arrest Smith, charging him with Wilson's murder."

The chief rises. Distress twists his face.

"You seem a little reluctant, Chief. Let me play Rembrandt and paint you a picture," says the judge. "Nathan's Black, homeless. Besides making death threats, I'll bet he has a criminal record."

The chief nods yes.

"By an eyewitness placing him at the scene, a Barkersville jury will find him guilty of murder surely as spaghetti has meatballs. You get the glory of arresting the murderer of our beloved former mayor, cementing your standing with the City Council no matter what your bitch of a girlfriend says. I get another notch on my gavel for protecting the public from a dangerous criminal. But no one sees this!" says the judge, tossing the letter into a desk drawer, and then rings the bell.

"You and the missus have a pleasant afternoon, Jerry."

Chapter 67

Office of the Property Clerk

Six days have passed since Jerome's execution.

Mary walks through the office doorway marked IMCC Property Clerk, stopping at the waist-high, metal-clad counter. On the floor, she sets her cloth handbag over which she folds her wool jacket. On the counter, she places her red Christmas gloves over which she folds her morning edition of the *Barkersville Gazette*, blazing the headline:

"Black Man Detained in Wilson's Death"

Mary taps the desk bell.

"With ya in a minute!" says a man's gruff voice through an opened door while the institutional green walls cast the words back and forth as if playing catch.

Kneeling, Mary stuffs her gloves in her handbag.

From the ceiling dangles a heater. Its fan spins emitting a buzzing noise annoying as a swarm of flies but stirring less air. On the counter stands a two-foot-high plastic Santa Claus, a gun strapped around its waist. His hand rests on the holster. A plaque on its pedestal reads:

You Better Be Good!

From the opposite side of the counter, plodding boots interrupt the scene.

"Who's there?" asks the guard, searching the room for the visitor.

Mary stands, seeing an overweight, burly, and balding correctional officer unconsciously fondling his sidearm. Pinned over his shirt pocket is a name tag: Sgt. Larry Blankenship.

"Oh, just you!" he grunts, recognizing Mary. "I suppose you're here for Manning's shit."

Mary is accustomed to these salutations. Her frequent visitations with Jerome have not endeared her to the white prison staff.

Noticing the newspaper, Blankenship focuses on the front page. For the past five days, the suicide of Oscar Wilson has been Barkersville's sole topic of conversation. Mary is sick of hearing the news which has been the main course in the prison's cafeteria. Grabbing the newspaper, Blankenship points to the headline.

"I knew it weren't no suicide! That Black son-of-a-bitch's got somethin to do with it!"

Unfolding the newspaper, he recites the featured article like a fourth grader reading from his favorite comic book during show-and-tell:

"Authorities have detained for questioning an indigent Black youth, Nathan Smith, in the death of former Barkersville Mayor Oscar Wilson, owner of Wilson's Jewelry.

Yesterday, police said an eyewitness whose identity is confidential, saw Smith running from the jewelry store down an alley last Saturday night at approximately 6:00 p.m., close to the coroner's estimated time of death. A reliable law enforcement source told the *Gazette* he wonders why this witness waited five days after Wilson's death before coming forward. This source also wonders how this eyewitness could positively identify Smith at night, in the rain, as Smith ran away in a dark alley with his back to the witness.

As reported earlier this week, police found Wilson's body slumped over his desk with a .45 caliber handgun clutched in his right hand and a gunshot wound to his chest. Authorities as of press time have not officially ruled Wilson's death a suicide. Smith can be detained for twenty-four hours (until 6:00 a.m. tomorrow) at which time he must be released or charged with a crime."

"Ya gotta admit," says Blankenship, shaking the newspaper at Mary, "that Wilson fella killin himself don't sound right. Especially on the same night he's supposed to get that Citizen of the Year award for seeing that Black bastard Manning gets what he deserved!"

Grinning a tobacco-stained smile, he squints at Mary over crossed arms.

"Pardon my disrespect for the dead, but mark my words, they'll nail Smith's ass to Wilson's coffin. And since you love these murdering Blacks so much, you gonna come for his shit too?"

Blankenship slams the paper on the counter.

Mary breaks eye contact, then shoves the paper into her handbag. She will save this *Gazette's* edition. The newspaper features an article on Manning's execution which surprisingly includes several defaming excerpts from her interview with the reporter concerning certain individuals' "mishandling" of Jerome's case.

Blankenship, too, has read these excerpts. He scans the room, listening for any footsteps of a passerby in the hall.

"Ya might be careful," he says, confident they're alone, "about what ya say about folks around here. We wouldn't wanna see a celebrity like you in the obituary column."

The prickling of Mary's scalp, no matter how often she tries to ignore the reaction, is a warning to take these statements seriously.

"Are you threatening me, Officer Blankenship?"

"Just some motherly advice," he says, adding, "I'll get your boyfriend's shit."

Turning his back, he walks to a gray metal file cabinet. He pulls open a drawer marked M-P.

Yanking out a sheet of pink paper, he returns with the document flapping at his side.

"You Mrs. Mary Louise Cook?"

"Yes," answers Mary, rolling her eyes.

"Gimme some ID."

After Mary shows Blankenship her driver's license, he slaps the form down.

"Somthin's irregular, Cook. See here? He's marked a box sayin you're his next of kin."

Blankenship stares at Mary, his head cocked as though inspecting a fly in a punch bowl.

"You sure don't look like no next of kin, unless you one of em light-skinned ones."

"This's just a little error," says Mary, spinning the form around. "He checked the wrong box. I'm just a friend. But the form specifically says right here that *I* am authorized to receive his belongings."

"Well, I don't know, forms is forms. Don't want none of these valuables gettin in the wrong hands now, do we?" he says, laughing. "Well, I suppose we can make an exception. Just don't let it happen again."

Kneeling, he removes a small, black, zippered bag, which he smashes on the counter with all the might the tattooed correctional officer's IMCC-boxing-championship arms can muster.

Mary stumbles back, startled by the violent display.

"Better be real gentle-e-el with this. Might be breakable," he says.

From atop a stack of loose papers, Blankenship removes a coffee cup inscribed with:

Get the Shotgun. That'll Learn 'Em!

He grabs a yellow form.

"Sign here on the receipt."

Mary scribbles her name.

"Ya know, I've swept shit off the bathroom floor worth more than this."

Aiming flaming eyes at the sergeant, Mary takes the bag, noting its lightness. The gun-toting administrator grins as Mary walks into the green, tiled hall, her echoing footsteps fading in the emptiness of the corridor.

Bundled in jacket and gloves, Mary trudges through the glass doors of the reception room into the infant December afternoon. Though the day is an unusually warm 62 degrees, her spirits are not. Stopping at the edge of the concrete walk, she stares across the bleak parking lot she's used dozens of times visiting Jerome. Though Mary never ventured there before, this time she crosses the black expanse to a gravel walk which coils up a hill. A sign reads:

"PHANTOM RIDGE—ONE MILE"

* * *

Meantime at IMCC, Peter still in the Black minister's disguise he used in his last visit with Jerome, ambles down a hall. Peter has learned this deception is more readily accepted by the Black inmates whose numbers are overrepresented on Death Row. Accordingly, he has made the reverend's visits a weekly pilgrimage.

"Reverend Peter!" shouts a uniformed officer as he rushes forward, skidding to a stop.

"Jimmy. What's the hurry?"

"Boy, am I glad to see you!" says Officer Kinsley between labored breaths. "Mrs. Cook left the property clerk's office takin Manning's personal effects. I've got some more of his belongings but just missed her. Any chance you seein her today?"

"Coincidentally, I am," says Peter, then points to a small cardboard box clutched in Jim's hand. "Is that what you got in there?"

Jim nods yes.

"Those belongings, are they the same ones you let im take into the execution room?"

"Yes, Reverend. The ring, the ceramic dove, and that crumbled note."

"But weren't you supposed to give em to the property clerk?"

"Yeah, technically," says Jim, handing Peter the box, "but that asshole Blankenship's got a habit of confiscatin stuff. He would've snatched this ring sure as a starving dog a bone."

Jim self-consciously stares at his boots, then lifts his gaze to the minister.

"Reverend, I got to know Jerome. Got to like im, too. Sorry I acted so hard-nosed when we came in for the execution, but I had to play the part in front of the Sarg."

"My child, what you've done for Jerome's been a true act of Christian kindness, somethin I don't see much of inside'a these walls. God bless you."

Box in hand, Peter leaves, disappearing around a corner.

* * *

The next instant, Peter in his white disguise sits on the park bench next to Scott at Phantom Ridge. At their last meeting, the elm was fully attired in green. Now the tree stands naked against the winter sky. Twisting the cardboard container in his hand, Peter glances down at the prison.

"Mary will be here soon. What is on your mind, Son?" asks Scott.

"Dad," says Peter, drumming the armrest, "I'm nervous about meeting her. Why can't I just tape a short letter about the history of these items to the box, then leave everything in her apartment?"

"Well, that *is* one approach. But that letter would be as compassionate as installation instructions for a faucet," says Scott, slapping his son's thigh. "But if that is what you want . . . Oh, speaking of notes, what about that one in your shirt pocket?"

Peter looks down at his lapel.

"Oh, yeah, that's the second one Oscar wrote the night he was shot," says Peter, grinning. "I'll bet those two notes plus his suicide letter were more than he wrote his entire term as mayor."

Peter hands the note to Scott:

Peter:

I want you to do everything in your power to protect Nathan from any accusation that he participated in my death.

"I know what he wrote," says Scott. "But how are you going to honor your promise to fulfill this request?"

"I've already started. First, the night Oscar died, I returned to the Buying Room before the police. I found and took the ring and the dove. That was the easy part but the next won't be. That begins when Mary gets here and like I said, I'm nervous."

Peter takes a long breath.

"You know, Dad, I . . . I . . . love her as much now as I did when we last met."

"Mary was courageous asking you to erase all memory of your time together. You were just as courageous agreeing."

"Talking to her," says Peter, remorse tightening his chest, "will . . . it'll be like talking to a shadow, a dark void of something that once was a living, breathing part of my soul, but now that's dead. I don't know if I can do this."

"Son, heartaches litter a benefactor's path. You made the right choice when you raked all recollection of that relationship from Mary's thoughts, a relationship which would have ultimately caused you both great sorrow. Your choice was a testament to your love. That love will guide you now."

"You know, in some ways this is gonna be harder than watching Jerome's execution. At least that had a blessed closure: Sanctuary. Without Mary, there's only an aching hole inside of me."

"Instead of a painful void, use the fond memories you have of her to fill the emptiness."

Approaching footsteps on gravel crackle through the conversation.

"And remember," says Scott, "I am always near should you need me."

Hugging his son, Scott vanishes as Peter dons his cloak of invisibility and waits.

* * *

The secluded oak bench greets Mary's arrival at the summit.

Brushing away decayed debris, she sits. Mary churns on the bench, trying to erase images of her empty home which now after Kevin's divorce consists of a one-room, communal bath apartment. Beside her, Mary places her purse, then removes the black bag which patiently waits to offer the meager treasure inside.

Mary empties the bag in her lap. Receipt in hand, she checks the contents: a circular keyring holding three keys and three photographs in an unidentified leather wallet containing four dollars.

Twisting the keys in her hand, Mary wonders what locks they had freed. Perhaps one opened Alice's apartment door. Another might have unlocked the daycare center where Jerome had met Alice. Maybe the one resembling an old skeleton key was for Auntie Helen's house. Mary sighs. The keys disappear back into the bag.

Opening the wallet, Mary inspects the three pictures. Two are of Black women. One is aged, and robust, displaying twinkling eyes above an infectious grin. Must be Auntie Helen. The other is young with an attractive face sculptured in determination—Alice. The last picture freezes the image of a smiling family: Jerome, Alice, and Nathan, hugging each other so tightly one could not tell where one person ends and the next begins.

Removing the third photo, Mary presses the portrait between her hands, tears blurring the image of the only testament of this once-happy family. Who mourns for them? Why was happiness such a reluctant visitor? They had their joyous times, but like a cat playing with its prey, this joy was only a cruel temptation of fate. Two in the picture are dead, and a third is jailed, awaiting a murder warrant.

I prayed none of this would happen. I'll frame and set this picture next to Timmy's beside my bed.

Sliding the photograph in the wallet, she closes her eyes, squeezing it against her chest.

"Hate to disturb you, Ma'am, but may I rest on the bench?"

Chapter 68

A Cardboard Box

Surprised by the unexpected intrusion, Mary drops the wallet. It bounces off her lap, falling to the ground open, exposing the family picture. In front of her stands a middle-aged Caucasian man dressed in a dark business suit. Steady as rain off a thatched roof, perspiration drips from his wavy, brown hair. He carries a heavy load consisting of a large briefcase, a metal luggage container, plus a four-foot-long cylindrical canister.

Mary stares at the man. *Where the hell did he come from? Other than a few trees, there's nothing around to block my view. Must've been deeper in thought than I realized.*

"Sorry if I startled you, Ma'am," says the stranger, setting the luggage next to the bench.

He retrieves the wallet, inspecting its photo through inquisitive eyes.

"My, what a happy family. Friends of yours?"

Mary yanks the photo from his hand. Her annoyance overrides any fear she has of the intruder in this remote area. Her intuition says he poses no threat.

"I've come a long way, and I'm a little tired from lugging all this paraphernalia," says the gentleman, mopping his brow with a handkerchief. "Again, may I sit down and rest?"

Mary grunts yes.

"Thank you."

Though Mary is willing to share the bench, she is not willing to slide from the middle.

The stranger squeezes himself into the narrow void between her and the armrest. Minutes of silence pass when he, hoping to start a conversation, points to the black bag on Mary's lap.

"I see you've been to the property clerk's office. Is that Jerome's?"

"How'd you know that?" she asks, twisting her head.

"I'm a regular here at IMCC," says the stranger as a glimmer of success lights his face. "Know all the guys. I've even visited Jerome. That picture is the only one of him with Alice and Nathan. There's just one person who'd have that photo. You must be Mary. Happy to make your acquaintance."

He presents his hand, but Mary ignores the gesture.

"Who the hell are you, and what are you doing here?" she asks.

"Peter, resting my feet."

"Peter, huh?" *Funny, Jerome never mentioned a "Peter" to me.*

"I suppose you're wondering what all this stuff's for. I'm a movie producer specializing in educational featurettes." He explains the metal case holds the portable projector while the tubular container secures the movie screen. "In the briefcase are my scripts, including a special prop."

In the cramped confines, Peter's trousers are wedged against Mary. Unknown to her but clear as a telephone call, the connection allows her thoughts to speak in Peter's mind:

This guy must be cryin for an audience to come way up here. Thank God the nearest electrical plug is a mile away.

Then, almost against her will, Mary's lips betray her.

"What kind of special prop?"

Peter opens the brown case revealing a black, circular door chime, the size of a large serving plate, mounted on a two-foot square white panel.

"What's that for?"

"Audience participation. My card," says Peter, closing the briefcase.

Mary reads the printed promotion consisting of gold letters on a luminous, blue background:

PETER'S PRODUCTIONS
Movies guaranteed to excite, entertain, and educate.
Documentaries our specialty:
Historical, Contemporary, Ordained
Phone 777–1212 (A 501(c)(3) Enterprise)

"Tonight, I'm master of ceremonies for the semi-annual Correctional Officers Conference at the prison, though they don't yet know it."

Mary flips the card on the bench. This guy's really getting on my nerves. Attending the officers' meeting? Bullshit! I know those bastards. They'll never let an outsider in.

"I plan to pound some dents in their macho armor," he says, retrieving and placing the card on her lap. "Considering your experience with them, you might enjoy the entertainment. Care to accompany me?"

"Gee, I'd love to, but I've gotta get home and dust the Venetian blinds."

She prepares to leave when her curiosity delays her departure.

"Peter, why are you *really* here?"

"In answer to your prayers . . . about them," he says, pointing at the photo on Mary's lap.

Mary grabs the picture as apprehension tightens her chest. How does he know about any of "my prayers?"

"I've followed your efforts on Jerome's behalf," he says, touching her hand. "You went through hell. Care to share your experience? Would be a shame if I made this trip for nothing; I'm here to help."

From Peter's hand flows a warmth of trust soothing Mary's anxious spirit. Maybe confessing to a nonjudgmental stranger is the answer to my prayers. Maybe the time's come to empty this bottle of poison I've kept locked up inside. And for some strange reason, I feel he can be trusted.

"Peter," she says, summoning all her courage while squeezing his hand, "I've tried to accept what's happened: Timmy and Jerome's death, the divorce, being ostracized by the community."

She stares down at the photo as emotion floods from her lips:

"You know, I cheered when I heard about Oscar's suicide. Him . . . his damn committee . . . Why'd I let him intimidate me into voting for Jerome's death? If I hadn't, Jerome might still be alive. I'd do anything to make up for that! How I've hated myself.

"But just like I do for my dear Timmy, I pray some happiness waits for him, Alice, myself, and . . . you'll laugh at this . . . even Oscar. Sometimes the prayers help, sometimes . . . "

Head sagging in her hands, tears seep through her fingers, washing the family photograph in a bath of sorrow. Since the night of Timmy's death, this is Mary's first healing cry.

* * *

This is the first physical bond between the two since Peter numbed Mary's memory of him. The desire to never release her is as forceful as a drowning man's craving for air. He remembers telling Scott: "Without Mary, there's only an aching hole inside of me." Then as he clings to her hand, an epiphany flashes brighter than sunrise's first light. Though it may not be returned, my love for her can fill the void. Love isn't caged by time or chained in a chasm so dark its light is lost forever. Love is infinite, manifesting itself in our empathy for others, repaid or not.

* * *

Embarrassed, Mary releases her hand, molding herself into a lie of composure.

"So, if you *are* here to help, bring back my Timmy. Bring back Jerome . . . Alice."

"I . . . I'm not allowed."

Mary never expected an answer to this rhetorical question. But "not allowed?" Peter talks like he *could* bring them back. She trembles, fearful of the hidden powers she senses this stranger controls. But she also senses his powers are benevolent. There is a humility about this Peter, humility only acquired through great suffering. She has seen this before in the timeworn eyes of Black Baptist ministers.

"Peter, are you some sort of preacher?"

"Sometimes the spirit does carry me away, but I'm not a preacher. These feet haven't crossed a holy threshold in many years. But preacher or not, Mary, there's one thing I do know. One day you'll find the blessings hiding in your adversity."

"Blessings?"

"Yes, Mary, wondrous blessings, joy! You don't realize how much your visits of love meant to Jerome—the joy of compassion. You have wandered through the desert of doubt, the swamp of shame, emerging stronger—the joy of self-acceptance. Your courage as well as hope have inspired others—the joy of admiration. Adversity has bestowed these gifts. And more are to come."

"Adversity's gifts, huh? I prefer Christmas. An know what present I want? Him," she says, picking up the picture and pointing to Nathan. "The last thing Jerome asked of me was to find Nathan, help him. I agreed because Jerome was more worried about Nathan than about his own death."

"Mary, about Nathan, I don't have good news. The powers-to-be in Barkersville will try everything to prove he murdered Oscar."

"I was afraid of that. I know Nathan made threatening remarks about Wilson. But lots of people make threats and that's the end of it."

"Not that long ago," says Peter, "even a perceived threat by a Black against any white was fatal. Condemning Nathan is also about public face-saving. Oscar Wilson was a highly respected member of the white community, the cream of the crop. If his reputation's stained by a suicide or other unsavory deeds, their bleached dike of dominance springs a leak threatening to drown their unearned privilege. People like Judge Daring, and the chief of police, are scared to death. With a Black scapegoat to plug the leak, they maintain the status quo."

"Is there any real proof against him?" asks Mary.

"There's his threats, criminal record. There's also this so-called 'witness' who swears seeing im running from Wilson's store. All this when added to the weight of prejudice will dump the scales against him. You grew up in Barkersville, Mary. Tell me I'm wrong. Only a miracle can save him, a miracle named Mary Cook."

"Me?"

"Mary, I'm gonna tell you about a chain of extraordinary events concerning Nathan. But I must warn you to *never* pass this on to another soul. Not a priest, not the police, not even Nathan.

"I give this warning for your and his protection. Authorities would stop at nothing to find out how you got such information. And what could you say? You heard about it from a movie producer you met at Phantom Ridge?"

What would I say? Truth is, this guy's sitting right next to me, but I'm finding all this hard to believe myself.

"Peter," she says, words pinching in the lump in her throat, "why shouldn't I just get up . . . just leave right now?"

"Because you've agreed to Jerome's request to help Nathan, and the only way you can do that is to hear what I've got to say."

Though concerned such knowledge might place her in jeopardy, Mary's intuition remains trusting of this Peter. She agrees to hear this "extraordinary" chain of events.

"Very well," says Peter, relating the events perpetrated by Nathan in Wilson's Buying Room, ending in Oscar's death. Peter tells how Nathan found the suicide letter. After rearranging the scene to reflect a self-inflicted death, he fled without finding the ring or the dove. Police never found them either, but they did find the suicide letter and gave the letter to Judge Daring.

"How the hell do you know all this?" asks Mary.

"I have friends in low places."

Focused sharp as a cat at a gopher hole, Mary's gaze claws at Peter, blaming him for this maze of doubt.

"Peter, helping Jerome was one thing. He was a victim of circumstances. But based on what you've said about Nathan, he's different. He's a hardened criminal!"

"And how's Nathan so different?" asks Peter, reminding her how Nathan mirrors Jerome's troubled past. Both suffered poverty's pain. After losing their mothers at an early age, both succumbed to criminal influences leading each into actions that resulted in a man's death.

"Now, Nathan must battle a corrupt legal system. He needs a protector, a miracle worker. He needs *you,* Mary.

"You confessed your joy about Oscar's death. Remember, I said Nathan had a change of heart in the Buying Room, then lowered his gun. Would you've had that restraint? As for being a victim of circumstance, *all* Black people suffer from the circumstance of their complexion."

"Well, uh, I'm not saying Nathan or any other Black person hasn't been treated unfairly," says Mary. "What I *am* saying is a person's color, Black or white, doesn't entitle them to a get-out-of-jail-free card. We all have to hold ourselves accountable for our behavior."

"Spoken like a true racist."

"Racist! You asshole!" says Mary, her hand coiled in a fist.

"How can you say that after all I've done for Jerome? Because of helping him, I've been alienated by everybody in town, treated like an outcast!"

"You can always leave," says Peter, as a grin bends his face, "and start over in another town. Your whiteness entitles you to that get-out-of-jail-free card. But if you're Black, you're a prisoner of prejudice wherever you go."

Mary slumps on the bench, her string of thoughts tied in a knot.

"So, what to do Mary? Nathan's either freed from jail or he ends up *dead* like Jerome, a rerun of the Citizens Committee meeting. You get to play God again!"

"I don't want to play God!"

"*Everyone* plays God! You're the god of your universe, manipulating the world, and the people around you, as much as any deity. The *only* question is, are you a god of mercy or vengeance?"

"Peter, I feel sorry for Nathan, I really do. I promised Jerome I'd help, but let's say I *do* get an attorney to represent Nathan. How in the hell I'll pay him, I don't know. Let's assume a miracle does happen: he's freed. Then what? We both know he'll probably continue his criminal activities. God forbid, someone else could die. So, what do I do?"

"You *live* your promise to Jerome! But if you free Nathan from jail, that's just the beginning of your promise. Only an unending tide of love by *you* will lift him from the sewer.

"Mary, you said you'd do anything to atone for your actions at the committee meeting; here's your chance. You said Jerome was more afraid of Nathan's fate than he was of his own. Save Nathan, and in a way, you save Jerome."

An image of Jerome, phone pressed to his ear while sitting behind a security window in the IMCC visitor's room, flashes in Mary's mind.

"I know you want assurance," says Peter, "that by helping

Nathan you're *breaking* the chain of violence, not adding a link. Please, take my hand. Close your eyes."

Mary agrees. Holding his palm in hers, images of the Citizens for Justice Committee Meeting thrash through her mind like pages of a book flung open in a gale. That night's forbidden circumstances—the haunting movies of Jerome, the episode of the Black Button including Peter's display of his benefactor's supernatural abilities—overwhelm her thoughts as all the occult events Peter had erased from everyone's mind come into full view.

Mary realizes Peter exists beyond this mortal realm. Whatever abilities he might possess originate from some Higher Authority. She suspects through these supernatural abilities as he holds her hand, he can listen to her thoughts, and sense her emotions. Opening her eyes, Mary's disconcerted gaze retreats to the distant woods. But amid this turmoil, Peter's presence consoles her.

"Mary, I want you to understand why I removed much of the committee meeting's events from everyone's mind. The important thing about the meeting wasn't the mystical events which occurred, but its troubled outcome. I've restored full knowledge of the meeting to only two people: you and Oscar Wilson. I have done so because you two play important roles in events initiated by the meeting. This knowledge helps in your roles. The other committee members were just participants who would've had no major influence in the meeting's outcome. Kinda like extras in a movie whereas you and Oscar were the stars."

"I know what important role Wilson played, the executioner!" says Mary.

"Don't pass judgment on Oscar yet. Mary, just like I tried at the Citizens for Justice meeting, I've come today to provide some sense of serenity, closure to the violence which's occurred," says Peter, releasing her hand. "Remember I said I'm here in answer to your prayers? Well, I'm also here in answer to another's—Oscar Wilson."

"Him? I . . . I . . . refuse to believe it!"

"Believe it," says Peter, telling Mary how he accompanied Oscar on the night of Oscar's demise. "As his death neared, he wanted to atone for his past sins. As for the suicide letter in his desk, Oscar had typed it weeks before while in a deep depressed mood, but changed his mind. He kept the letter, made a copy, and due to its controversial contents, he locked the copy in a secret vault in his home. In the vault, he also placed a Fort Knox of cash."

Oscar's obsessive efforts concerning the letter do not surprise Mary. But I doubt atonement was his motive. Empowered by the God Almighty buck, the old Scrooge probably planned to blackmail the judge after rising from the dead! And the cash? Well, maybe he thought he could take it with him.

"Oh, something else," says Peter. "In his final moments, Oscar wrote Jerome a note which I delivered along with two other items to Jerome in his cell just before his execution."

"Note? Items?" Mary rifles through the bag of Jerome's belongings, consisting only of the keys and a leather wallet. "There's no note. Are these the two items?" she says, opening the bag for Peter's inspection.

Peter remains silent.

Knives of doubt stab Mary. What if I do try and help Nathan? Why should he accept my efforts? After all, at best I'm just another white bleeding heart. Why should my efforts to save him have better results than I did helping Jerome? What's to raise me to the rank of a miracle worker? Then, she points to the pile of luggage at the foot of the bench.

"I assume the Black Button is in one of those?"

Peter sets the large briefcase on his lap, unlatches a silver clasp, and removes the black device.

"Does that thing still work like you said at the Citizens meeting? You know, alter fate to punish someone for their evil deeds?"

Peter nods yes.

"Can you please hand the Black Button to me?"

Peter sets the instrument in Mary's lap. Staring, she recalls the Black Button's formidable powers.

"Let me see," she says. "How's it go? First, I state the accused's name, right?"

Another nod of Peter's head.

"Nathan Smith. Then I declare the accused's crime. The unpardonable sin of his Black birth."

"What fate shall the accused suffer for his crime?" says Peter. "Choose carefully. Your fate's handcuffed to his. Once declared, that fate is unalterable, even by another push of this button."

"Nathan's fate shall be a lifetime of service to humanity," she says, wondering if she chose wisely as she turns to Peter.

He says not a word.

Closing her eyes, Mary utters a prayer. Clouds choke the horizon. Then, struck by a bolt of courage, she presses the button. A chorus of thunder proclaims destiny's realignment. Mary opens her eyes, her face aglow with joy reflecting the light of a future which just hours ago cowered in the shadows of fear.

"What happens next?" she asks.

"*We* find Nathan."

From the moment she began helping Jerome, Mary felt alone. Upon hearing "we," she senses the solitude lifting. At last, a friendly soul who could help ease the loneliness of divorce, the anguish of Timmy's death, and the isolation of the Barkersville community.

Peter's crease of a grin unexpectedly wilts to concern. He shoves his watch in Mary's face.

"Just *look* at the hour," he says. "I've gotta go. Remember, the correctional officers meeting?"

"Oh, yeah, that's right. You're the surprise master of ceremonies, just like the Citizens for Justice meeting. You know, Peter, this benefactor thing, it's kinda like being Cinderella's fairy godmother. Good luck with the mice."

As the warmth of the Black Button tingles in her hands, Mary hands the mystic mechanism to Peter, which he slides into the case.

"Oh, I almost forgot," he says, kneeling to reopen the satchel.

Fumbling through a mess of forms, Kleenex, and candy wrappers, he removes the small cardboard box he received today from Officer Kinsley. Peter sets the container on Mary's lap.

"What's this?"

"A little present. It holds some things the correctional officer at the execution found on Jerome," he says, then takes his business card which has been waiting on the bench in anticipation. "On the back of this card is a sketch showing the location as well as the combination of the secret vault in Oscar's home. The contents of this compartment—the suicide letter and the cash—will provide for all of Nathan's needs. These two items are something I, uh . . . *we* want only you to have," says Peter, slipping the card into a fold of the box.

"*We*? We who?" asks Mary.

"Me and a friend of Nathan's."

Ignoring Mary's pleas for a name, Peter collects his luggage.

"Peter, please, don't leave. Not yet."

"Mary I *must*. You've got my card. Call me for anything," he says, taking her hand. "Don't worry, we'll be in touch. We have great deeds to perform."

* * *

Releasing Mary, Peter stands in a nervous tremble. By allowing her to remember certain past events, he elevates the possibility of restoring recollections of their past relationship. Though they will perform "great deeds" together, he will not materialize in his old familiar forms, white or Black. For to do so would risk reigniting the old blaze of their love, a blaze she had asked to be extinguished, a blaze which would consume a mortal. But some future images soften his torment. He foresees them working together, even if not lovers, as equal partners aiding Nathan and other casualties of prejudice, consoled by the knowledge Mary will eventually find love in another's arms. Maybe consoled is not exactly the right word, but the absence of her longing for his presence might help abate his amorous temptations.

Peter must depart *now*. To delay any longer stretches the vessel containing his desire. After all, he is only the essence of an eternal being, a spirit endowed with supernatural abilities—no match for Mary's charms. Leaving via a mortal walk is much too slow, so after a final glance at the earthly beauty of Mary, Peter vanishes. He teleports himself to the correctional officers' meeting hall.

* * *

As Peter evaporates, Mary leaps up, her eyes scouring the grounds, but he has vanished.

"Peter? Peter!!"

Slowly, her anxious heart calms, soothed by the knowledge that this benefactor named Peter also protects her. She wonders what "great deeds" await and when they will meet again.

Her attention returns to the box, wondering what secrets lie inside. Opening this pauper's package, she finds three gifts: two wrapped in tissue, the third, a folded piece of sweat-stained paper.

Mary removes the first item. Unwrapping the tissue she gasps, remembering how this object, a ring, had inspired many of her and Jerome's conversations. The ring is white gold, embossed with two crosses, one on either side of a large diamond, the same ring Peter had described. She places it back.

Next, she removes the tissue paper wrapped in a pink ribbon protecting the second gift. Again, Jerome's voice rings in her memory as she holds a small, white ornament—a ceramic dove. On the base is inscribed: *With Love: Nathan and Jerome.* She places the dove next to the ring.

Last, she uncovers the third treasure, the folded note. Carefully, she opens the paper, discovering a smeared though neatly hand-printed message. Her vision distorted by tears, she reads the note, sobbing as the words fold around her heart, melting into her soul:

Dear Jerome:

Time is short. I must be brief. Remember this ring? I return it to you with sorrow for the pain it represents. The dove I include as a reminder of Alice and Nathan's love. Oh, how I wish I could undo the harm I have caused you. But one harm I can undo is Nathan. He'll be fine. Mary will see to that. I deeply regret the horrible injustice you've suffered at my hand. Do not pain yourself if you never forgive me. Maybe in time, I can forgive myself.

May God Bless you.

Oscar

JEFF SPIRES was born and still resides in the San Francisco Bay Area. He is retired from a thirty-five-year career in civil engineering construction. His volunteer work with inmates in the California Correctional Center prison in Susanville instilled an awareness of the hardships and inequities endured by those living on the fringe of our society.

Jeff and Tricia combine their charitable efforts in projects assisting underprivileged communities.

ABOOKS

ALIVE Book Publishing and ALIVE Publishing Group
are imprints of Advanced Publishing LLC,
3200 A Danville Blvd., Suite 204, Alamo, California 94507

Telephone: 925.837.7303
alivebookpublishing.com